continued . . .

Berkley Sensation Titles by Kylie Brant

WAKING NIGHTMARE
WAKING EVIL
WAKING THE DEAD
DEADLY INTENT
DEADLY DREAMS

DEADLY DREAMS

THE MINDHUNTERS

KYLIE BRANT

BERKLEY SENSATION, NEW YORK

THE BERKLEY PUBLISHING GROUP
Published by the Penguin Group
Penguin Group (USA) Inc.
375 Hudson Street, New York, New York 10014, USA
Penguin Group (Canada), 90 Eglinton Avenue East, Suite 700, Toronto, Ontario M4P 2Y3, Canada
(a division of Pearson Penguin Canada Inc.)
Penguin Books Ltd., 80 Strand, London WC2R 0RL, England
Penguin Group Ireland, 25 St. Stephen's Green, Dublin 2, Ireland (a division of Penguin Books Ltd.)
Penguin Group (Australia), 250 Camberwell Road, Camberwell, Victoria 3124, Australia
(a division of Pearson Australia Group Pty. Ltd.)
Penguin Books India Pvt. Ltd., 11 Community Centre, Panchsheel Park, New Delhi—110 017, India
Penguin Group (NZ), 67 Apollo Drive, Rosedale, North Shore 0632, New Zealand
(a division of Pearson New Zealand Ltd.)
Penguin Books (South Africa) (Pty.) Ltd., 24 Sturdee Avenue, Rosebank, Johannesburg 2196,
South Africa

Penguin Books Ltd., Registered Offices: 80 Strand, London WC2R 0RL, England

This is a work of fiction. Names, characters, places, and incidents either are the product of the author's imagination or are used fictitiously, and any resemblance to actual persons, living or dead, business establishments, events, or locales is entirely coincidental. The publisher does not have any control over and does not assume any responsibility for author or third-party websites or their content.

DEADLY DREAMS

A Berkley Sensation Book / published by arrangement with the author

PRINTING HISTORY
Berkley Sensation mass-market edition / April 2011

Copyright © 2011 by Kim Bahnsen.
Excerpt from *Deadly Sins* by Kylie Brant copyright © by Kim Bahnsen.
Cover art: "Woman and Reflection" by T. Kruesselmann/Getty Images; "Man in Flames" by Andy & Michelle Kerry/Trevillion.
Cover design by Rita Frangie.
Interior text design by Tiffany Estreicher.

ISBN: 978-0-425-24068-7

BERKLEY® SENSATION
Berkley Sensation Books are published by The Berkley Publishing Group,
a division of Penguin Group (USA) Inc.,
375 Hudson Street, New York, New York 10014.
BERKLEY® SENSATION and the "B" design are trademarks of Penguin Group (USA) Inc.

PRINTED IN THE UNITED STATES OF AMERICA

10 9 8 7 6 5 4 3 2 1

For my new baby granddaughter, Kinley Nicole,
who already holds the key to my heart.

Acknowledgments

When it comes to imaginative ways to off people ☺, I'm never short on creativity but lack the factual expertise when it comes to the pesky details. I'm always grateful to those who fill in the gaps in my knowledge to help me stage my scenes realistically. A big thank-you goes out to Joe Collins, Paramedic/Firefighter, who assisted with all things fire related and helped ensure my villain didn't burn down entire cities enacting his evil acts. Your infinite patience with my endless questions is much appreciated!

Thank-yous are owed to Jennifer Gaston, Marketing Manager, and Matthew Scott, Director of Data Services, LWG Consulting, for answers regarding data recovery and analysis of videotapes and recordings; to Piper Rome and Sgt. Gary Vineyard, DEA Dallas Task Force, Rtd., for providing the necessary expertise when it came to questions about firearms. The details regarding Internal Affairs investigations were generously provided by Sergeant Michael Hervey of the Charlotte-Mecklinburg Police Department. And Elizabeth A. Peacock, MD, Bexar County Medical Examiner Office, San Antonio, Texas, weighed in with insight regarding pathology and the medical examiner's domain—I appreciate all your help! As always, any errors were mine alone.

And finally, thank you to Ali, Ryan, and Kat for the brainstorming session at Boltini's. My heroine never would have made it out alive without you guys!

Chapter 1

The figure did a macabre dance as flames leapt to engulf it. Screams knifed through the night shadows, hideous and agonizing. The smell of gasoline lingered strong and heavy in the air, mingling with the stomach-turning stench of seared flesh and hair. Garbled pleas for mercy interspersed the screams.

But there would be no mercy from the watcher.

Nude, he stood just close enough to feel the searing heat on his bare skin. The flames beckoned madly, enticing him to join them. Just a step closer, they seemed to hiss. Feel it. Share it. Make us one.

He withstood the furnace-like blast as long as he could before moving farther away, his gaze transfixed by the writhing human torch. Fire was endlessly fascinating. Unstopped, it would gild the body, melt skin, and singe bone until it was sated. By that time, the figure would be little more than charred fragments of teeth and bone. Flames purified, cleansed the act of evil until only the motivation mattered.

And no one had better motivation than him.

He flung out his arms like a preacher inciting the heavens, his form silhouetted against the brilliant glow. Justice had been a long time coming. And it couldn't be evaded any longer.

Marisa Chandler fought through the weight of sleep in a desperate bid for consciousness. Rolling from the bed, she immediately dropped to the floor, her limbs unresponsive.

But the jolt yanked her firmly from dream to waking, and for that alone she was grateful.

A bit painfully, she pushed herself to sit upright, leaning against the side of the bed. Sweat slicked her body, as if the flames in her nightmares had emitted real heat.

It had felt real. They always did.

She took a moment to will away the shudders that still racked her body. It hadn't been the same nightmare that had plagued her for four long months. She could give thanks for that, even as she fought to shrug off her fear of what the vision might portend.

Resting her head against the mattress, she closed her eyes. Dreams like this one didn't mean anything. Not anymore.

The recognition brought both relief and despair.

The peal of the doorbell shrilled through her thoughts. Risa opened her eyes. Thought about ignoring it. But there was faint light edging the shades over the window, heralding dawn's approach. Her mother would have just gotten off her cleaning shift a few hours ago. She deserved the sleep.

The bell rang again insistently. Heaving herself to her feet, she padded barefoot to the door, checked the judas hole. The image of the stranger on the front porch was tiny, but she didn't need a larger image to identify him as a plainclothes cop. Faintly intrigued, she pulled the door open, leaving the screen door latched in case she was wrong.

Her instincts hadn't been exactly foolproof recently.

"Marisa Chandler?"

She took her time answering, scanning first the detective shield he held up for her perusal, then, more slowly, him. Caucasian, six feet, about one eighty, all of it muscle. Black hair and eyes. Hard jaw, uncompromising chin. Only visible identifying mark was the small crescent-shaped scar above one eyebrow. And despite his lack of expression, impatience was all but bouncing off him.

"Yes."

"Detective Nate McGuire, Philadelphia Police Department." He slipped his shield inside his jacket. "I'm on my way to a possible crime scene. My captain passed along a request from the chief inspector of the detective bureau that I extend you an invite to ride along. In an unofficial capacity, of course."

A chill broke out over her skin, chasing away the remnants of heat that still lingered from the nightmare. "Why would he do that?"

McGuire lifted a dark brow. "I figured you'd know."

She shoved her heavy mass of hair from her face and shook her head. Risa hadn't looked up any old friends from the force since coming home four months ago. Had avoided news like the plague. That hadn't been difficult given her mother's penchant for watching only game shows and inspirational broadcasting.

"Apparently your employer, Adam Raiker, spoke to Chief Inspector Wessels about it." His midnight gaze did a fast once-over, clearly wondering what it was about the woman in faded yoga pants and an ancient Penn State T-shirt that would catch the attention of the head of the detectives. "So I was told to stop and ask if you're interested. I'm asking."

She swallowed, just managed to avoid shrinking away from the door. "No."

He nodded, clearly not disappointed. "Sorry to wake you." Turning, he began down the stairs, leaving her to stare after him, fingers clutching the doorjamb.

Raiker. Damn him, her boss wouldn't leave her in peace. Wouldn't accept what she'd already accepted herself. Guilt, well earned, had rendered her useless. To him. To his forensics consulting company. And certainly to this detective.

The small house didn't have a driveway or garage. McGuire was halfway to the street where he'd left his ride, a discreet black Crown Vic. He moved like an athlete, his stride quick and effortless. She had the impression she'd already been forgotten as he mentally shifted gears to his first priority, his response to the call out.

"What's the crime?" For a moment she was frozen, hardly believing the question had come from her. This part of her life was over. Had been for months.

But still she waited, breath held, until he hesitated, half turned to call over his shoulder, "Possible homicide. A burned corpse was found about fifteen minutes ago."

The air clogged in her lungs. Blood stopped chugging through her veins. Organs froze in suspended animation. The figure in the dream danced in her mind again, the engulfing flames spearing skyward.

But those dreams had become meaningless. Hadn't they?

Oxygen returned in a rush. "Wait!"

McGuire had reached the car now. And he made no attempt to mask his irritation. "For what?"

"Give me five minutes."

His response followed her as she turned away to dash toward the bathroom. "You've already used three." So she paused only to brush her teeth, drag a comb through her hair, and shove her bare feet into sneakers. Then she headed out again, snatching her coat and purse in one practiced move as she passed the closet. Risa took a moment to lock the door behind her before jogging down the steps toward his vehicle, already regretting her decision.

She didn't do this anymore. *Couldn't* do it anymore.

Which didn't explain why her legs kept moving in the direction of the car.

She'd barely slid inside the vehicle before he was pulling away from the curb. Shooting the detective a quick look, she pulled the door shut and reached for the seat belt. "What's the location?"

"Body was found in a wooded area in the northern part of the city," he said in a clipped tone.

"So you're from the Northeast Detective Division? Or the homicide unit?" She busied herself buttoning her navy jacket. It had occurred to her that the day was likely to be long and chilly. The temps had been unseasonably cool for May.

"Homicide."

It was what he didn't say that caught her attention. "If you're homicide, the call must have sounded fairly certain that there was foul play involved. Or else the crime bears some resemblance to one you're already working. Which is it?"

Dawn was spilling soft pastels across the horizon, but the interior of the car was still shadowy. Even so, she would have to be blind to miss the mutinous jut to his jaw. "What's your story, anyway?"

His attitude managed to slice through her self-doubt and land her squarely in familiar territory. She was well acquainted with suspicious cops. They would be the one element of her job she wouldn't miss if she left it for good. *When* she left it.

"I assume Inspector Wessels told you whatever he wanted you to know."

The sound he made was suspiciously close to a snort. "The chief doesn't talk to me. And Captain Morales wasn't in the mood for details when we spoke."

She was sidetracked by his words. "Captain Morales? Eduardo Morales?"

"Yeah. Why?"

Surprised delight filled her. "When'd he get his bars? I hadn't heard about his promotion." If she'd gotten in touch with friends since she'd been back, maybe she'd have caught up on department gossip. But first she'd been focused on recovery and rehab for the physical wounds and then . . . The thought skittered across her mind before she had a chance to slam that mental door shut.

Then she'd been licking her emotional wounds.

"How do you know Morales?" He did a quick right on red in an effort, she suspected, to avoid waiting for the light.

"I was eight years on the force here before joining Raiker Forensics five years ago. Worked out of the Major Crimes Unit—Robbery and Burglary." Amazing that the words would be accompanied by a tug of nostalgia. "Morales and I were tapped for special duty on a Violent Offenders task force for several months. He's a good cop. How long have you worked with him?"

"Just a couple months." And it was clear that he was nowhere close yet to deciding if he shared her opinion of the captain. He shot her another sidelong glance. "You don't look like a cop."

"Chances are if I'd been knocking at your door at the crack of dawn, you wouldn't roll out of bed looking much like one either." She gave him a bland smile. "Unless you sleep with your shield pinned to your . . . chest."

Amazingly, his teeth flashed, although he didn't shift his attention away from his driving. "So you were on the job. But not homicide. Makes me wonder why Wessels wants you tagging along for this."

"My experience has broadened since leaving the force." And now it was her turn to go silent and brooding. Nothing could be gained from this outing, unless it was ammunition for her ongoing argument with Raiker. She was done with this work. The only question was why her boss remained unconvinced.

Risa recognized the area of town McGuire drove to as one that used to be the haven of young drug users who wanted a remote place to get high. But it was deserted now, save for the police presence. The crime scene unit van was parked next to an unmarked car, and there were four other black-and-whites nearby. They got out of the car and made their way through a heavily wooded area before entering a clearing. It looked like the scene was secured and taped off, but those details were noted with a distant part of her brain.

Her focus was fixed on the blackened corpse lying inside the police tape.

A CSU tech was snapping photographs, and another man was kneeling next to the body, fiddling with a machine she couldn't make out from here. But those observations registered only dimly. It was the victim who consumed her attention.

Because her palms had gone suddenly, inexplicably damp, she wiped them on her pants. And wished once more that she were anywhere but here.

"Which one of you took the call?" McGuire stopped outside the tape and scanned the half-dozen uniforms in the vicinity.

"That'd be us." Two men stepped forward, both of them casting Risa a questioning gaze. One was tall and beefy, a good six inches taller than McGuire. The speaker was several inches shy of Risa's five-ten height. With his thick neck, skinny limbs, and sturdy torso, he bore an unfortunate resemblance to SpongeBob, of cartoon fame. "Officer's Tready and Lutz." A jerk of his thumb indicated his partner as the former.

"Detective Nate McGuire. Homicide."

The flash of Nate's shield seemed to only partially pacify the man. He was still eyeing Risa quizzically.

"So run it down for me." McGuire's tone held enough of an edge that it captured Lutz's total focus.

"The lady who found it—Heather Bixby's her name—was out walking her dog. Wasn't sure what it was, but the body was still smoking when she came upon it. She called nine-one-one. Tready took her statement. She's waiting over in the car there."

"Walking her dog in this area? Alone, while it was still dark?" Doubt dripped from McGuire's tone as he shot a look at the car the officer had indicated. Risa seconded his disbelief. Philadelphia had dozens of parks, many of them updated with miles of paved trails. There was one within walking distance of here. While this spot, if anything, had grown seedier since her time on the force. The trees and bushes were overgrown, and it didn't appear as if public dollars were going to be spent anytime soon on creating recreation paths for joggers.

Lutz lifted his shoulders. "That's what she claimed, and she's sticking with the story. Making noises about needing to get to work, so if you want to talk to her, might need to make it quick."

"Did you see anything else? Anyone else in the area?"

This time it was Tready who answered. His low rumbling voice matched his craggy features. "No one. But the usual freaks who hang out here would have taken off first sign of a uniform."

Nate nodded and dug in his pocket for a card. Handed it to Lutz. "Take the other officers and canvass the nearest neighbors. Write it up and send it to me at the homicide unit." He headed in the direction of the witness, who was sitting on the edge of the backseat in one of the squad cars, feet on the ground, with a huge brindle mastiff planted squarely between them.

Risa hesitated. No matter how much she regretted coming, she was stuck for the moment. And following the detective took her farther away from the blackened figured in the scorched grass. The distance would be welcome. She trailed after McGuire, who was already speaking to the witness.

"Missus," she was correcting him, one hand on the dog's

neck. "Like I told them officers, I brought Buster out for a run. I just live over on Kellogg."

If Risa remembered correctly, Kellogg was a street of tired row houses, in a neighborhood still clinging to a fraying aura of respectability. Of course, that had been five years ago. Things changed fast in urban centers, and north Philly had long been one of the roughest areas of the city.

"You live there alone?"

Impatience settled on the woman's face. "I've been through this once already. I live with my husband. He drives a semi. I work a split shift at Stacy's Diner, on Seventeenth and Spruce, and I'm way late. Hal—that's my boss—is going to be a total prick about it, too. So if you could write me something, maybe on police letterhead, telling him I was helping you, it would go a long way."

"We can work something out. So you were heading to work earlier?"

Letting out a stream of breath, Bixby leaned forward to give the dog an affectionate pat. "I came to run Buster like I do every morning. My shift starts at eight, so we left the house at five or so."

"And you always come here?"

The woman's hesitation was infinitesimal. "In winter we stick to the sidewalks. But yeah, when it's nice we come here sometimes."

"Reason I ask, it's not the best area." McGuire seemed impervious to the morning chill in the air, although it had Marisa turning up the collar of her spring coat. "This is a known spot for drugs."

The woman lifted a shoulder. "Users, not dealers. And not this time of day, anyway. Doesn't matter. No one bothers me when I have Buster with me." She gave the animal a vigorous ear rub, which had it closing its eyes in canine ecstasy.

The woman was lying. McGuire had to realize it. But his voice was easy when he asked, "Did you see anyone else around this morning?" When she shook her head vigorously, he pressed, "Even in the distance? Someone running off, maybe?"

"No, it was just me and Buster. He was straining at the leash, dragging me toward . . . that." Marisa resisted the impulse to turn her head in the direction the woman pointed. The longer she could put off looking at the victim, the longer she could dodge recalling elements from the dream. "I got close enough to realize it was something dead. Burned. Didn't know if it was human but I called nine-one-one anyway." Her heavily made up eyes gleamed avidly. "It is, though, isn't it? Human. You all wouldn't be so interested otherwise."

The detective reached in his pocket and withdrew a business card to give to her. "If your boss gives you any trouble, let me know and I'll call him." He accurately read the doubt flickering on the woman's face. "The cell is department issued. It'll show up on his ID screen."

Shrugging, she slipped it into her pocket. "So I can leave?"

"Has a tech taken a sample of the dog's hair yet?"

McGuire slid Risa a narrowed look. Clearly she was supposed to be seen and not heard on this outing. When the woman shook her head, the detective said only, "Wait here. I'll send someone over right away."

Bixby's voice was plaintive as Nate walked away. "But why? I really gotta get to work."

Following a hunch she didn't question, Risa stayed behind. "It's in case they find hair on the scene. They need a sample from your dog, so they can eliminate it in the identification process."

"I didn't let Buster get close enough for there to be any of his hair on that . . . thing." If Bixby didn't seemed resigned to waiting, the dog did. It flopped down on its belly, drooling copiously.

Risa shoved her hands in the pockets of her coat and gave the woman a knowing smile. "So what time were you supposed to meet him?"

"Who?" Heather frowned.

"The guy you were planning to meet this morning. What time did you have scheduled?"

She had the woman's attention now. "I don't know what you're talking about. I said I didn't see anyone. You heard me tell that to the detective, right?"

"But you were lying. Or least not telling the whole story." Risa squatted down on her haunches and offered the dog her hand to sniff. "If you left the house at five, you would have had to get up shortly after four. Because first you showered, dressed, put on makeup before taking the dog out to a place you had to know would be a bit messy." She nodded at the woman's attire. Her sneakers were muddy, as was the hem of her tight jeans. "You're not a runner, at least not today. You aren't dressed for it."

"Jesus, I got ready for work first, okay?" Bixby folded her arms over her ample chest.

"You said." Risa nodded. "Dressed and ready to go three hours before your shift. Stacy's Diner is only a few miles from here. Walking the dog for thirty minutes still has you back home at five thirty, two and a half hours before your shift begins. Plenty of time to sleep in for another hour or two and wait for daylight. So I'll ask you again, who were you meeting here?"

The woman smirked. "Can tell you're no cop. Your detective skills suck. And I know when a person is just fishing. So go to hell."

Buster was much friendlier than his owner. He gave her hand a lick and Risa stroked his massive head. "No problem. What time does your husband go to work? Maybe I'll have better luck fishing with him." She didn't relish the flicker of panic on the woman's face, but she'd also never been fond of being lied to.

"There's no reason to bother Frank. He drives all night and needs some rest before going on the road again."

Rising, she contemplated the other woman. "Then don't make me."

Moistening her lips, Heather said, "He never even showed up. We were supposed to meet but he was running late. I called him when I found . . . that. He said call nine-one-one but he turned around and went home."

Instincts she'd thought lost and buried were humming now. "Because he didn't want to be around when police showed up."

"It's not like that." But she could tell from Bixby's expression it was *exactly* like that. "He's still on parole. Just a misunderstanding," she hastened to explain. "He used some of the company's money for a couple weeks, and even though he put it back later, when the head of accounting figured it out, they nailed him on it. Bastards cost him two years in prison."

Risa didn't point out that two years was practically a gift for embezzlement charges. "His name."

Heather's mouth set in mutinous lines. "That's all I'm going to say. I don't want to jam him up. He wasn't even here and doesn't know anything about this."

"Your husband is Frank Bixby, right? On Kellogg Street?" Risa turned away. "Thanks for your time."

"Wait!"

When Risa faced her again, the woman was staring at her with open dislike. "You're a real bitch, aren't you?"

"You have no idea."

After several moments obviously spent waging an internal war with herself, Bixby finally said, "His name is Sam Crowley. But I swear, if you make trouble for him, I'll hunt you down and kick your ass." She smiled thinly. "I can be a bitch, too."

"I don't doubt it."

It had been far easier, Risa thought grimly, as she approached the crime scene, to play Bixby than it was to force herself closer to the charred remains in the grass. With every step closer her heart increased its tempo until it was beating a rapid tattoo she feared could be heard by the officers at the perimeter.

Was that nearby tree familiar, with its branches growing in an X shape, studded with leafy buds? Perspiration dampened her brow. Her palms. What about that building beyond the trees to the west, with its boarded-up windows and tarpaper roof?

"Hey, lady, you can't go in there." The hand on her elbow sliced through the sticky haze of memory and had her jumping in surprise. The officer released her when she shot him a look, but stood his ground. "Crime tape is up for a reason. You need to stay back."

She was tempted, more than she should have been, to do just that. To wait quietly for the detective at his car. To forget the dreams that seemed far too entangled with the body inside the tape.

The dreams that had been blessedly absent for four long months.

Instead, she scanned the area for McGuire and pointed. "I'm with him. You saw us come together, didn't you?"

The officer, with a fresh youthful face that pegged him as barely out of the academy, looked uneasy. "Well, yeah. But I thought . . ."

Mystified, Risa waited for him to go on. "You thought . . ."

The kid—and he really was little more than that—actually shuffled his feet. "Ah . . . look! The detective is waving you over." The relief on his face was almost comical. "Guess it's his call if he wants you to go inside."

Still confused, she gave a little shake of her head before bending down to snag shoe covers from the opened box at her feet. Donning them, she grabbed a pair of latex gloves from another opened box and ducked beneath the tape. She was halfway to where McGuire stood speaking to a slender blond man standing next to the remains—

—*charred bones, melted flesh*—

—when comprehension belatedly struck.

The officer had thought her presence here was due to a personal relationship with McGuire, rather than a professional one. Under normal circumstances, the realization would have had her grinning. But her chest was tight. Her throat closed. The nearer she drew to the body, the more conscious effort it took to keep oxygen moving through her lungs. To resist the urge to sprint, far and fast, in the opposite direction.

". . . use an accelerant?" McGuire was saying.

"Like I was saying . . ." The man broke off as Marisa approached. "Well, hello-o, beautiful."

Ignoring his words, she focused instead on the gas chromatograph the man was using. "What'd the VTA indicate?"

"Jett Brandau."

Because it seemed churlish to refuse the hand the man thrust out, she took it for a moment. "Marisa Chandler." When she would have pulled away, he made a point of squeezing her fingers for a moment longer before releasing them.

"Arson investigator?"

He sent a quick glance to Nate before responding. "That's right. For the PPD."

She nodded. As the fourth-largest police department in the country, the force was plenty large enough to employ their own arson investigators who were also trained police officers. "And the VTA results?"

Brandau patted the side of the Vapor Trace Analyzer's heating element. "Did three samples of the air over and around the body. Each yielded a substantial bump in temperature."

"Meaning a flammable residue is present in the area," she murmured, intrigued despite herself. It made sense. Setting someone on fire—if that's what had happened here—was more difficult than it sounded. Fire required fuel. The fabric of the victim's clothing would provide some, but with the wide range of fibers used, it couldn't be relied upon to burn evenly. If total conflagration were the intent, an accelerant would guarantee it.

"Let me know when you're done getting the samples you need off the body so I can let the ME in. Then you can take comparison samples in the area as we finish searching each grid."

"Will do." Though his answer was directed at the detective, the investigator's attention was on Risa. His smile was probably supposed to be boyish, but to her jaundiced eye it looked more than a little smarmy. "You're welcome to stay and help."

"I'll pass."

Her response didn't seem to faze him. He set down the VTA on one corner of the concrete pad before approaching the body with an evidence kit. "Hey, where's Cass?" The comment was directed at Nate and brought, to Risa's mind, a definite reaction.

McGuire's lips tightened momentarily before he turned away. "She's running late."

"Reason I ask, I thought maybe the lovely Miss Chandler was her replacement." Brandau deftly managed flirting with his other duties. He was already kneeling beside the body and opening his kit before looking up at her again. "It is miss, isn't it? As in unmarried? Or really, really unhappily married?"

"No, it's dis. As in disinterested."

"Ouch." But there was no offense in the man's tone as he carefully cut off a sample of charred fabric from the corpse and dropped it in a glass container. "On the other hand, I miss Cass."

"I'll wave Chin over since you seem so desperate for companionship." Nate turned and gestured toward a slight Asian woman leaning against the medical examiner's van who headed toward them with surprisingly long strides.

"No." The panic on the man's face was mirrored in his frantic movements as he sped up his collection process. "Seriously, no. I'm going as fast as I can here."

"Concentrate," McGuire advised blandly.

"You try to concentrate when you've got a pint-sized she-devil standing over you . . . Hey, Liz." His movements were almost a blur of motion as he quickened his pace even further.

The ME stared down at him with her hands on her hips, eyes narrowed. "How long are you going to be, Brandau? We've only got about a dozen hours of daylight. I'd like to start my examination before nightfall, so if you can just give me an approximate timeline . . ."

"A few minutes. Ten at the most."

The diminutive woman cast a quick look at Risa then at Nate. "Where's Cass?"

"Running late."

"Uh-huh."

Mystified, Risa was getting the distinct impression there was something in the air regarding the absent Cass, but it was apparent no one was going to enlighten her about it.

"I appreciate you coming yourself, Liz."

Nate's words spiked Risa's interest. Normally an assistant from the ME's office was sent to collect the bodies. The appearance of the ME herself was unusual. Not for the first time, Risa considered that this homicide might be one in a series.

He went on. "When Jett's done here, you can start your examination. Pinning down time of death would be very helpful to us, so the sooner . . ."

The medical examiner shot him a look that would have scorched metal. "You want me to pronounce time of death before I even get back to the lab with this? No problem, I'm a magician. I also pull elephants out of my ass in my free time. Which trick do you want to see first?"

"I don't have to eat sarcasm to recognize the flavor, Chin. I was just saying."

"You know I don't deal in assumptions. After I get the remains back to the morgue and do a proper exam, you'll be the first to know."

"But they're still warm, right, Jett?"

"Air around the corpse is about one hundred thirty-six degrees. Liz is going to have to use a shovel to transfer them to the gurney. You find the ID yet?"

"I just got here, remember?"

From the easy banter between them, it was clear they'd worked together before. Risa was the outsider here. And that was fine with her. She was still regretting the impulse that had made her accept McGuire's invitation to begin with.

And fighting an equally strong impulse to gaze at the steaming remains on the cracked cement pad beside her.

Back in her rookie days, she'd responded to her share of house fires or fiery car accidents. It was impossible to forget the sickeningly sweet, metallic smell of burned flesh. She would have recognized it even had she not known the circumstances surrounding the call out today.

The pitted concrete square on which the body lay had once been covered and meant to hold a couple picnic tables. But roof and tables had disappeared long ago, leaving only skeletal wooden posts and rafters. The rafters were completely scorched, and fragments from them littered the cement pad. The pavement had kept the fire from spreading into the neighboring trees and brush. Risa wondered if the choice had been intentional.

She forced herself to gaze at the burned figure clinically. This close, there was no mistaking it for anything other than human. Its limbs were drawn up in a hideous fetal position, wrists and ankles close together.

Intrigued despite herself, she sank to crouch beside it. "Were the wrists and ankles bound?"

The ME threw her a quick glance. "You mean because of the positioning? I won't know for sure until I get back to the morgue. But the limbs will shrivel on a burn victim, and they'll draw up toward the body."

"Pretty damn hard to set someone on fire if they aren't bound," Nate observed.

She thought of the agonized dance of the victim in her

dream. From its movements, at least the legs had seemed to be unfettered. But those visions might have nothing to do with this homicide. Especially if this death were related to other similar ones.

"Even if his limbs were completely secured, he could still roll, trying to put out the fire." She nodded toward the area in question. "There's no evidence of that. Which makes me wonder—"

The detective followed the direction of her gaze, and her thoughts. "If he were kept in place by a rope thrown over those rafters."

"We'll know more after the body cools down and I can examine all sides."

Risa nodded at the ME's words. Had the person been burned while lying down, it would be reasonable to expect the burns to be uneven. It wasn't unusual for such victims to look relatively normal on the side pressed against the ground, where the flames had been unable to wreak their damage.

But the figure in the dream hadn't been prone.

She looked at the detective. "How many others like this have you found?"

At first she thought he wasn't going to respond. Instead he watched as the ME strode rapidly toward the city van, snapping out orders to her assistants. But finally he responded, "This makes the third, although it's too soon to tell if it's connected to the others."

"What linked the first two?"

He shot her a grim smile as he rose. "The first victims were found in remote areas. A combination of gasoline and diesel fuel was used as an accelerant. Both had their hands bound with duct tape but not their feet. They weren't gagged." His frown sounded in his voice. "That's hard for me to figure. It's easier to control the victims if they're completely secured. Gagging them would ensure their cries wouldn't summon help."

"But neither would be as satisfying." Her voice was soft, but from the sharpness of his gaze, she knew he'd heard her. "The remote locations give a guarantee of privacy. And even if someone comes . . . by that time it will be much too late to save them."

"You think he needs that? Their screams? But that still doesn't explain why he wouldn't bind their feet."

"Maybe he needs that, too." The death dance, she thought sickly, her eyes on the corpse once again. The frenzied movements of panic and agony. She'd felt the watcher's ecstasy as he surveyed the spectacle. The near-orgasmic exultation from seeing what'd he'd wrought. "It might be part of his signature."

Something shifted in the detective's expression, leaving it impassive. "Signature. You're a profiler, then?"

She rose, scanning the area. "All of Raiker's investigators are trained in profiling, too." Memory of the dream skated along the hem of her mind, and she sought to gather it in, to examine the details more closely.

That had been the last thing she'd been thinking of when she'd wakened from it this morning. Although she had art supplies in her bedroom closet, she'd gotten out of the habit of keeping an easel in her room with fresh drawing pencils and paper to sketch the visual elements.

The dreams had been gone for months. She hadn't missed them.

And although Risa was far from accepting this one as anything more than a subconscious mind bump, it was second nature to try and wring any useful information from it that she could.

If it were the victim's death alone that had so satisfied the watcher, a gun or knife could have been used with far less effort. Her shoulder throbbed, as if in agreement. No, his pleasure had been linked to the particular type of death he'd arranged. The flames had driven him delirious with delight, and he'd stayed as close to them as he'd dared.

Like there was an affinity there. Not just a murderer, but also one who chose fire deliberately because it satisfied a need inside him.

"It has to be death by fire," she said finally. "And he needs to watch." To *experience* it, deriving a sort of vicarious thrill from its kiss of heat on his naked flesh. One of the crime scene investigators was photographing the area. Another was sketching it. Two others appeared to be waiting for direction from McGuire. "What'd the crime scene techs turn up in the other two deaths?"

"No wallets, but IDs were left nearby." When she turned to him, brows raised, he said, "Yeah, just far enough away to be sure they weren't destroyed in the flames. Whoever the son of a bitch is, he wants to make it easy on us."

His jaw was clenched, and Risa suddenly realized there was more going on here than a killer choosing arbitrary targets.

"So you've established a pattern in the victimology?"

Nate's face was a grim mask. "Pretty hard to miss. If this one follows the same pattern, we'll discover the victim is either currently on the job or he used to be on the force."

Chapter 2

Nate raised his brows at Risa's shocked silence. "So if you have any ideas, I'm all ears. I figure Wessels is grabbing at any straws he can and that's why you're here. I don't put a whole lot of stock in profilers—"

"I've got more experience than—"

"But you used to be a cop," he went on grimly. "Maybe a more than decent one, if the chief is requesting you. So if your instincts haven't been destroyed by all this profiling crap, maybe you have something to offer. I don't mind admitting that so far we've got jack shit."

He seemed to have a knack for igniting her temper and disarming it in the next moment. It'd be difficult to recall the last time she heard a cop confess to a lack of direction in a case. So in the end, she ignored the slam embedded in the invitation. "You do like off-the-cuff assumptions, don't you?" He'd made a similar demand of the ME, with a discernible lack of result. "Fine. You're likely looking for a male. They make up eighty percent of arsonists, and those odds jump significantly when you figure in the statistics for serial homicide. Since the victims don't seem to be chosen at random, the offender may be motivated by revenge."

Justice had been a long time coming. The snippet from the dream flashed across her mind. Ignoring it, she continued. "The manner of death will be specific to his signature, rather than his MO. The use of fire means something to him emotionally, something connected to his past experiences."

He made a dismissive gesture with his hand. "I got most of that from Jett. He also says the vast majority of arson is targeted at property."

She gave a small smile. "That's right. You aren't looking for an arsonist per se, which is lucky because profiling arsonists can be an iffy proposition. I'm willing to bet this guy has a lot of instances of fire setting in his background, however. And if the link between the victims hold, you aren't necessarily looking for a typical serial offender either."

He nodded in the direction of the burned corpse. "All appearances to the contrary."

"If this victim also turns out to be on the force, it's likely the killer is retaliating for some perceived offense. Maybe the individuals are chosen specifically, or perhaps their selection is merely symbolic. At any rate, you'll have already started looking for intersections in their case files."

He slanted a look at her before nodding. "Haven't found anything that pans out yet. First victim, Roland Parker, was a detective sergeant who retired out of the northeast division last year. Second was Detective Sherman Tull, central division. Parker's widow wasn't sure whether he knew the second victim or not. Tull was divorced a decade ago, so we're still tracking down his ex. Talking to his friends. We do know the two men were never assigned to the same division as detectives or the same district as officers."

"Maybe a task force they both served on," she suggested. She hadn't known any of the other detectives on the task force where she'd met Morales.

He shook his head. "Not that I've discovered so far."

"But they were both detectives, rather than uniforms," she mused. That in itself was a link. Much more than coincidence, especially if it held true with this latest victim. It suggested the killer knew the men. It would be difficult for the average citizen to make plainclothes detectives as cops.

"Detective."

They both turned at the CSU tech's call. "You're going to want to see this." They both walked over to where the man squatted, near the thicket of overgrown bushes that separated the clearing from the denser growth of trees a few yards away.

She and McGuire flanked the man as they crouched on either side of him. Based on what Nate had told her about the first two bodies, she'd fully expected to be summoned over to look at a driver's license.

Instead, the tech was pointing at a police badge lying in the uncut spring grass.

Or—upon closer scrutiny she immediately revised her conclusion—a fake badge. The dull silver plastic sort that was sold in dime stores for kids.

"Looks like the others."

The tech nodded. "Just let me get some pictures and measurements and I'll bag it."

Catching her eye on him, Nate shrugged as they rose. "Besides their IDs, a toy badge like that was the only other thing found at the scene."

Risa restrained an urge to send a hard elbow jab to his gut. Like every other cop she'd ever known, he'd held something back when he'd filled her in on the case. Probably more than one thing. But it still burned. And reminded her of the petty annoyances she'd avoid if she didn't return to her job with Raiker Forensics, which had paired her with hard-headed cops that could have been McGuire's clones.

Resolutely, she pushed aside the stab of desolation at the thought. His reticence shouldn't bother her. It wasn't like she was going to work this case with him. She still didn't understand the impulse that had brought her to the scene, but it had been just that. An impulse. Not a return of her natural instincts for an investigation. Not the insatiable curiosity that had once had her following every lead to its end in search of the smallest shred of truth.

That part of her life was over.

And as soon as McGuire finished here and returned her to her mother's house, her part in this case would be finished, too. The realization brought a flicker of relief.

"You might want to run a Sam Crowley and have him

brought in for questioning." Surely it was small and petty to feel a thread of satisfaction at his surprised look.

"Why?" But he was pulling a notebook from the pocket of his navy muted-plaid suit jacket and unhooking the pen clipped to it. "Is he someone you ran into on the job? Does he have a history of this sort of thing?"

"No, he's the man Heather Bixby was coming to meet this morning."

In the act of writing down the name, his gaze bounced to hers. "She told you that?"

"When I pressed her." Because they were freezing, she tucked her hands in her coat pockets. She couldn't resist the opportunity to needle him a bit. "You really thought a woman would fix herself up like that to walk the dog?"

His eyes narrowed. "I said there was something odd about her coming to a place like this when it was still dark."

"Not that odd, as it turns out." She hunched her shoulders a bit, wishing she'd taken the time to change her clothes. The thin yoga pants weren't much of a barrier to the chilly breeze. "I think you'll discover they had a tryst planned, which I hate to think of occurring in front of the dog, but there you go. Crowley shouldn't be hard to find. He's got a sheet."

McGuire flipped the notebook shut and slipped it back into his pocket. "Let's hope his record includes assault and playing with matches," he said, in dark humor. "Make my life a helluva lot easier."

"I don't think it'll be that simple. But he may have seen someone in the vicinity. If this guy is as enthralled with fire as I suspect he is, he'd want to hang around and watch as long as he dared."

The watery moon glowing through the crossed branches of the nearest tree. His nude body silhouetted against the bright flames, arms outstretched.

"I'll have him brought in."

The ME and her assistants were transferring the remains to a stripped-down gurney. Deliberately, she moved away, leaving the CSU techs and the ME to their jobs. Having delivered the information she'd gotten from Bixby, she was overcome with a desire to be gone. And after today she'd have nothing more to do with this case. Certainly, Raiker wasn't going to get his way this time round. The man might be some kind of wizard when it came to knowing his people, but he'd miscalculated if he thought throwing her into another case would rid her of misgivings about returning to the work.

It went deeper than that. The hell of it was, Raiker, more than anyone else, should understand.

McGuire had joined the CSU techs and was directing the search. One of the men was rephotographing the area where the body had lain. Risa drifted farther from the activity, into a grid the detective had searched before moving on. Something about the tree drew her. It had figured in the dream last night, although the details were fuzzy. Its two largest branches had grown into an X, and it stood directly to the east of the cement pad. The closest vegetation to the fire, it was still far enough away to have escaped unscathed. She wondered if that were by chance or planning.

Although she hesitated to draw conclusions unsubstantiated by facts, she had a feeling that the offender left very little to chance.

Leaning against the tree's massive trunk, she stared at the blackened cement pad that had held the human carnage. The vantage point placed her directly beneath the juncture where the tree's branches bisected, like a sentinel with crossed fingers. A mental snippet from the dream flashed across her mind. Of the way moonlight had paved a watery glow through the fork of those branches . . . a diffused spotlight for the horror being played out in the night shadows.

But the moon hadn't been out last night, had it? She frowned a bit, trying to recall. When she'd gone to bed after midnight, the sky had been a dark smear that had blocked out both stars and moon. The cloudiness continued today, when sun would have bumped up the temperature a few welcome degrees.

An all too familiar chill trickled down her spine. Spread icy fingers over her skin. Slowly, she tilted her head back to squint upward at that fork in the branches.

———

"Tillman. Mitchell. Over here."

Crouched on his haunches, Nate waited for the two techs

to amble over to him. He pointed to the rim of white he'd spied peeking between blades of tall grass. "Looks like ID."

Quinn Tillman bent over and set down a plastic evidence marker before straightening to aim the digital camera. "That it does. Which is both good and bad news."

"Bastard's definitely targeting cops," muttered Hank Mitchell. He pulled the pad out of his coat pocket he'd been using to sketch the overall scene and placement of evidence. He quickly added to the sketch, pinpointing the ID's location from the spot where the body had been found.

When the two men were finished, Nate carefully picked up the ID by taking a corner in his gloved fingers. It was Philadelphia Police Department issued, a close duplicate to the one he had in his own wallet. "Patrick Christiansen." The name meant nothing to him, but with nearly seven thousand policemen in the city, that wasn't unusual.

The circumstances of these deaths were.

He looked questioningly at each of the men, but they both shook their heads. So they didn't recognize the name either. Tillman produced a plastic baggie and Nate dropped the ID inside. While the man sealed and labeled it, Mitchell shoved the pad back in his coat pocket. It was rare to see the big man's ebony face without its perpetual smile. His visage was grim. "So what do we have? A torch with a hard-on against cops? One who blames his sucky pathetic life on anyone with a badge?"

"You'll have to ask my companion. Apparently profiling perps is her deal."

"Detective McGuire isn't a believer."

Nate jerked around. He hadn't realized she'd come up behind him. Some detective that made him. But the woman was quiet as a cat.

She shrugged, as if his attitude was no big deal. And it probably wasn't to her. She'd made no bones about her reluctance to be here. He still couldn't figure out what had made her change her mind and come along.

"Anyone think to bring a portable ladder?"

"Why, you got an urge to climb some trees?"

Her expression remained unsmiling. "I'd like a closer look at one, anyway." She pointed at the one several yards to the right of the concrete pad. "You're done with that area, right?"

Glancing back toward the two CSU techs, he saw that they both looked as mystified as he felt. "Yeah, we finished that grid," he responded finally.

"I've got a twelve-foot Quikstep sitting outside the police tape," Tillman offered, pointing at the briefcase-sized foldable ladder unit.

"Thanks."

As she headed toward it, Nate just shrugged at the two men's questioning looks. The workings of the female mind were enough of a mystery when he knew the female in question. He'd been around Marisa Chandler for less than an hour, and he didn't know anything about her. Except that she'd once been a Philadelphia police detective.

And that the slim-fitting pants didn't do a thing to disguise her mile-long legs.

A belated thought occurred. "Don't touch anything," he called out as she passed by carrying the portable briefcase holding the ladder.

She slanted a glance his way. "I've been around a crime scene or two."

Which didn't tell him a damn thing except that temper made her eyes more gold than hazel.

The observation made him edgy. "Let's get back to the search." The other techs had continued walking their grids, bagging and labeling every beer can and wrapper in the vicinity. Evidence markers dotted the area, but unless a piece of litter yielded a usable print, the only real finds so far had been the police-issued ID and toy badge.

And that, too, would be similar to the other two cases.

Mitchell looked beyond him, cocked a brow. "What is it she's doing up there?"

Frowning, Nate turned to spy the woman at the top of the ladder. She'd leaned it precariously against one large branch of the tree several yards to the right of the cement pad. "What the hell?" he muttered, just as she turned and waved an arm at him.

"McGuire!"

Tillman tilted his head, plainly transfixed. "Not a bad

view from this end either," he said meaningfully. "She's got legs that don't quit. And there's nothing wrong with her"—he broke off when Nate's attention snapped back to him, before amending—"eyes. Looks like she's found something."

But Nate was already striding in her direction. All the while wondering what the hell the woman was up to. He stopped several feet short of the trunk, staring upward. And noted, reluctantly, that Tillman had been right on both counts. Long endless legs were topped with what appeared to be a singularly spectacular ass.

The recognition was more than a little unwelcome. He folded his arms over his chest. "You stuck?"

"Move to your left another six inches. Can you see this?"

He did as she requested and squinted up to where she was pointing. From this vantage point he could see a dark shape, but a large knot on one of the crossed branches made it difficult to identify the item. "What is it?"

"Looks like a camcorder. An older model that takes VHS tapes. And if the red light is any indication, it's set to record."

Nate watched silently as Mitchell repositioned the ladder and clambered up it to begin dusting the device for prints. "If it was placed there by the perp, he picked a good hiding place." He cut his eyes toward Risa. "How'd you happen to see it?"

She moved her shoulders but didn't look at him. Her attention seemed glued on the tech. "Just happened to be standing in the right position when I looked up, I guess."

"So you saw it before you asked for a ladder?"

He didn't think it was his imagination that she went still at the question. But her hesitation was barely discernible before she answered. "I thought I saw something up there. I wanted a closer look. I didn't touch anything."

"I know." He'd been watching to make sure of that. At least that's what he preferred to think his focus had been on when he'd watched her on that ladder. He traced the direction of the camera's lens to the cement pad that had held the body. It looked to be in perfect placement to catch the scene at the pad. "So what are you thinking? Did he record the scene to replay and relive it later or is he getting his rush watching us work?"

"I take it you didn't find a camera at the other scenes."

"No." But that fact was niggling at him now. Had they missed something? Had the UNSUB actually gotten away with filming the entire thing and sneaking back later to retrieve the device? He didn't want to think so. Didn't want to believe that he could have overlooked a camera not once, but twice.

"The answer is both." She finally looked at him and must have seen the confusion in his expression. "You asked if he wanted to relive the scene or record you working. Both would give him a rush. But I guess you'll know for sure when your lab discovers how much tape you have there."

He gave a nod. If he remembered correctly, the VHS tapes could be set to record for as little as two hours or as many as eight, depending on what speed was used. Discovering how long the tape had been set to run would give them even more information, however. It might help pinpoint time of death.

A car door slammed in the distance, and with a quick glance Nate determined that Cass had arrived. Finally. Tamping down an accompanying flare of frustration, he said, "Maybe he outsmarted himself this time."

The slight smile on her face had him blinking. It transformed her features, replacing the carefully blank expression with a vibrancy that was punch-in-the-gut sexy. The observation was as out of character as it was alarming.

"You won't find any trace of him on that tape. Or his prints on the camera."

It was annoying how closely she'd read his thoughts. He just hoped she hadn't keyed in to all of them. "Could be you're giving him too much credit."

The smile was gone now. And it was a bit of a relief to be faced with her impassive mask again. "After three deaths targeting cops, maybe you need to start giving him *more* credit."

"This vic was connected to the other two, then?" Cass pulled to a stop beside them. He took a quick visual inventory. The bruise she'd sported around one eye for the last week had been carefully disguised with makeup. Since it was harder to see today, he assumed it was fading. And there were no new ones, at least not where they showed.

"I'll fill you in," he said as evenly as he could manage. "We were just walking the grid." He waited until they were out of earshot of anyone else before he demanded, "Where the hell have you been?"

"Don't start with me," she muttered. Her gaze, like his, was carefully trained on the ground, searching for trace evidence. "Donny showed up as I was on my way out the door. It took a while to get rid of him."

"Jesus." The word was released on an explosion of breath. "You could have gotten rid of him by calling for a unit. You took out a restraining order last week, right?" Her silence had his instincts rising. "Right?"

"I didn't see the need. I can handle him."

Anything he could have said to refute that—and there was plenty—was put aside for now. It wasn't the place or the time. And pointing out the obvious, that Cass was a bum magnet who replayed the same mistakes in her personal life over and over like a movie reel on permanent rewind, would fall on deaf ears. It always had.

"The job's looking at you." He kept his expression carefully impersonal. From a distance everyone would believe he was catching his partner up on the case. "My guy in Internal Affairs tipped me off. Your relationship with Donald Larson means you're colluding with a known felon. An ex-con. And it's putting your shield in jeopardy. So if you don't give a damn about what he does to you personally, maybe you'll care what he's doing to you professionally." A quick look at her face showed she'd paled beneath the makeup. And her eyes were worried. "Lose that guy, fast, or you may not remain on this investigation with me. You may not be on the force at all."

Risa wished she could shut off the adrenaline humming inside her as easily as the CSU tech had flipped the switch on the camera she'd found. She didn't want this. She didn't welcome a return of instincts, long dormant, that were now alert and quivering. Was panicked by the curiosity revving to life.

And she especially didn't want to admit that Raiker might be right. That she couldn't walk away from this work. The thought brought simultaneous stabs of exhilaration and panic. She'd once thought she was destined for this sort of career. It gave her dreams meaning and made them something more than a curse.

But recent events had taught her she could no longer trust the dreams that had guided her instincts in her cases. And where did that leave her, other than just as confused as she'd been for the last four months?

"If you're not busy, you can hold the ladder while I inspect the rafters."

Brandau's voice jolted her from her thoughts. And she wasn't unhappy at the diversion. She followed him over to the cement pad and watched dubiously as he rested the portable ladder against a scorched wooden beam. "You may get up there and discover there's more damage to that beam than it looks like down here."

Jett shot her a smile, the charm in which was wasted on her. "In that case I'll expect you to catch me in your arms. Or at least to break my fall." Carefully maneuvering the VTA machine, he headed up the ladder.

"That's what I'm afraid of," she muttered. But she held the ladder firmly. It wasn't like she had anything else to do. She'd welcomed the errant Cass's arrival because it had meant an end of McGuire's interrogation about how she'd come to look in the tree for the camera. She thought she'd covered well enough. Because there was no way in hell that she could have told him the truth.

The only person she'd ever shared it with was Raiker. And him only because it was impossible to do otherwise. The man was like a human lie detector.

Brandau lifted the instrument, turned it on, and started taking readings. After several minutes he headed down the ladder. "Well, that's not surprising."

"No trace of accelerants up there?"

He shook his head. "No need for it, really. His intent wasn't to burn the thing down. Just to consume the victim." He set the machine down and bent over a kit before ascending the ladder again. She grasped it to steady it as he climbed.

"Were you called to the other scenes, too?"

"Not the first one." He unscrewed the lid of the glass jar

he'd taken from the kit and began taking scrapings of the charred timber.

"But you'd know which accelerant was used at the first, even if you weren't there."

"That's right. It was a mixture of diesel fuel and gasoline. Unless I've lost my touch—and that's highly doubtful—it was used this time around, too. Gasoline burns off too quickly to be relied on. The diesel fuel makes it burn longer."

"Because he isn't relying on whatever is handy," she murmured. "He goes into the kill prepared."

He glanced down at her as he screwed the lid shut on the glass container holding the scrapings. "That's right. Has it down to a tee, if you ask me. Our guy has had some practice, even though we've struck out with ViCAP."

The words elicited a renewed burst of interest. The FBI's Violent Criminal Apprehension Program database allowed law enforcement to submit details of a crime to compare with similar ones around the country. "You didn't get any hits?"

"Oh, we got plenty. Nate could tell you the exact number. But none were close matches for what we've seen with these crimes, taking into account the type of accelerant, material used to secure the victims, the manner in which they were bound . . . Here, take this, will you?" He broke off to hand her the jar with the sample he'd taken.

She reached for it. The factors he'd mentioned could all be part of the offender's MO, which could change over time as he perfected the kills. But his signature wouldn't change. "Were any of the other victims from the results cops?"

"No. But Nate still figures he might have practiced first, so he hasn't given up on ViCAP." Brandau handed her another glass jar with more scrapings in it. "Maybe this time around we'll get more details to feed into the search."

Something inside her was relieved by the exchange. It sounded like the case was being managed competently. There was no reason to believe she could bring something to this case that McGuire couldn't. Especially since the dreams that had always been at the root of her "uncanny instincts" had been absent for months.

Until last night.

"Well, well, looks like you were right again."

Nonplussed by the remark coming so close on the heels of her thoughts, she sent a startled glance upward. And saw Brandau holding up tweezers with something that looked like blackened hair in its grip.

But in the next moment she recognized it for what it was. "A strand of rope?"

His expression was grim as he dropped it into another jar and labeled it. "There's a few more up here. The bastard kept the victim in place with a rope thrown over these rafters, most likely." His assessment was an almost eerie affirmation of her and Nate's guess earlier today.

And a macabre reminder of the burning specter in her dream last night.

Chapter 3

Risa unlocked the small house she'd bought for her mother three years ago. It was past six. Hannah Blanchette would have already headed out to catch a bus to her job, cleaning office buildings after hours. So catching sight of the figure sitting on the brightly floral secondhand couch had her stopping short in the doorway, her hand going automatically to a weapon that wasn't there.

One she would have been unable to fire even if it'd been present.

Her eyes slid shut for a moment in frustration. "Adam."

The lack of welcome in her voice had no discernible effect on her employer. "Marisa. Your mother left about twenty minutes ago. She assured me it was all right to wait for you."

"I'll bet she did." Hannah was fascinated by Adam Raiker, while maintaining a healthy wariness of the man. It might have been his appearance, which Risa had to admit was ferocious. A black eye patch covered one laser blue eye and a hideous scar ran across his throat. More scars covered the backs of his hands, one of which clutched the knob of the cane he was never without. He looked like a man who had entered the gates of hell and made it out, barely alive.

If even half what she'd heard was true, the description fit.

"You've been gone all day," she said. Didn't leave a note, so she wasn't sure where you were."

"Shopping," she lied, and watched with satisfaction as his eye narrowed in annoyance. "I hate to miss those spring sales."

His gaze swept her. "No bags."

"With my height everything has to be altered." Because she'd never been one to enjoy being manipulated, she continued the pretense. "Once it's done they'll be delivered to me. Pretty good deal." She shrugged out of her coat and hung it up in the postage stamp front closet.

When she turned back, he seemed to have relaxed against the couch. She wasn't fooled. Raiker never relaxed, and his brilliant mind was always operating on multiple levels simultaneously. "Nice try. But there's not a woman alive who'd go shopping dressed like that." He nodded to her attire. "I can only think of one thing that would have you rolling out of bed and leaving the house without changing." His pause was full of meaning. "A case."

Risa dropped the farce. It was useless with him anyway. She also didn't bother hiding her irritation. "I'd be more impressed with your powers of deduction if I didn't know damn well that you were behind the invitation from Detective McGuire today." She set her purse on the hallway table with a bit more force than needed. "Had a little chat with the chief inspector of the detective bureau, I understand."

His shrug was negligible. "Actually, I spoke with the commissioner. I assume he made a suggestion to the chief inspector." He waited, but when she said nothing, he added, with a familiar note of impatience, "Well? So you were invited to look over the case file on the torched cops?"

"Not exactly. I rode along to a response to the newest victim."

Adam's impatience faded to be replaced by a gleam of interest. "Another policeman?"

She nodded, trying, and failing, to ignore the pitch of excitement that was always present at the onset of a new case. "I don't even know why I went. I can't help them. I can't help *you*. How many times have I told you that?"

His smile was feral. "I don't know. I wasn't listening."

Risa hissed in a breath, an all too familiar sense of frustration filling her. It was maddening to be faced with a man who refused to take no for an answer. Who constantly thought he knew better than she what was in her best interests.

And heartbreaking when his dogged persistence inevitably had doubt rearing.

And that was perhaps the most difficult emotion to deal with. She knew what the spectacular failure in her last case meant. Her career was over. Her usefulness on an investigation at an end. And sometimes she could almost hate the man for trying to make her think differently. For making her *hope*.

"So a third cop is dead, burned alive if the same MO was followed." He looked to her for confirmation, found it in her nod. "The department is going to pull out all the stops. A task force was being formed even before this latest casualty. An UNSUB targeting cops is going to bring a high-profile effort after him. No expenses spared."

"So hiring a consultant from the firm of the legendary Adam Raiker would be welcomed by the brass," she guessed caustically.

"I wouldn't know." His answer stopped her dead. "I never suggested it. What I did suggest is that the commissioner might be interested in using the voluntary services of one of my employees while she's in the vicinity on leave. A former employee of the department with enough commendations in her file to be something of a legend herself within the PPD."

Sick fear twisted through her at the thought, even though she'd figured out how it must have gone down. "I can't."

"You did. Today." His expression was fierce. "Last month . . . hell, last week you would never have gone to that scene."

"Last month I hadn't just had a dream about a similar crime," she said flatly. Raiker knew all about her nocturnal visions. She'd been upfront about them when he'd first contacted her about working for him. Had been shocked when he'd eventually offered her a job anyway.

He'd stilled at her statement. "The dreams are back."

A frisson of ice splintered through her. The words sounded stark. Inescapable. "One dream. One time."

"Well." He eased his form more comfortably against the ancient couch. "That had to have been . . . a surprise."

A short laugh escaped her, although humor was the last emotion she was feeling at the moment. *A surprise*. Masterful understatement. And so Raiker. "You could say that. As a matter of fact, you predicted the nightmares would fade and that eventually the dreams would come back. I didn't believe you."

"You didn't want to believe me."

Risa looked away. The welter of emotion from this morning returned. The sick dread for what the dream indicated. Filtered by a shuddering relief that the normal had returned. Or what had always been normal for her.

And layered by the paralyzing self-doubt that had been her constant companion since that dark cellar in Minneapolis.

"It might not mean anything." She desperately wanted to believe that. To distract them both she headed toward the kitchen. "I'm getting a water. Do you want one?"

"No."

Risa took her time, taking a bottle of water from the fridge and twisting off the cap to take a long swallow. It wasn't necessarily avoidance. She'd been out on the scene with McGuire all day, with nothing but a soft drink from the selection one of the officers had brought back after the canvass.

But as one minute turned into two, and then three, she knew evasion was at play. That recognition had her heading back into the living room. She'd had to face some hard truths about herself in the last few months. Cowardice hadn't been one of them, despite what her employer might think.

She dropped into a chair across from Raiker's seat and observed that the man looked curiously out of place in Hannah Blanchette's modest home. There was a veneer of gloss to Adam Raiker, a sophistication that owed little to the expensive suits. It almost hid the shimmer of danger that emanated from the man.

"The dream could have been a fluke," she said finally, in the face of her boss's silence. "And even if it's not, we already know that they can't be trusted."

"Then don't," he said tersely, his gaze intent. "I didn't hire you because you go to sleep and dream of murder. I hired you because you're a damn fine investigator with some of the

best instincts I've ever seen. Accepting a role on this case
will give you a chance to learn to trust them again."

Bitterness surged. "I think Minneapolis proved my instincts are flawed." She had lived with the knowledge, with
the guilt, for the last four months.

"That case proved you're not infallible." His flat tone would
have sounded cold to someone who didn't know him. "None
of us are, and sometimes it takes a fucked-up case to make us
realize it." She looked at him then, saw the faintest flicker of
empathy in his expression. The sight had her throat knotting
up. "Once we live through something like that . . . we're not
the same. We aren't meant to come out of it unchanged. The
question is, are you going to let it merely change you or evis-
cerate you?"

She couldn't reply. Wouldn't have known what to say if
she was able. But Raiker was better at commentary than conversation. Already he had his cell phone out, texting a message
that would doubtless have his driver returning for him. He'd
pulled the necessary strings, applied the necessary pressure.
Now the ball was in her court. She could return, in an unofficial capacity, to the work that had once identified her.

Or she could continue to hide and dodge coming to a
decision about her future.

The familiar longing and self-doubt warred inside her,
emotions crashing and colliding in an inner battle that left
her feeling bruised and weary. But Raiker couldn't help her
with that. No one could.

Risa eyed him. "What are you doing in Philadelphia anyway?" This was his second visit. Usually he contented himself with short, terse phone calls. He had a reason for coming
here. Raiker had a reason for everything he did. "Shouldn't
you be concentrating on finding the guy trying his damnedest
to kill you?"

"*Failing* to kill me. The verb is rather important." His
shrug was negligent. The navy pin-striped suit would have
made another man look like a banker. It merely gilded that
faintly lethal air that surrounded the man, like a wolf disguis-
ing itself in sheep's clothing. "He's imaginative. I'll give him
that."

She blew out a breath. "You mean tenacious. Blowing up

your penthouse was what? The fourth attempt on your life in the last few months?"

His grin faded as quickly as it had appeared. And the look in his eye reminded her that this was a very dangerous man in his own right. "He miscalculated again. I'm still alive. But he's got my attention."

And that alone should have the would-be assassin quaking. If it was only one. "Did you ever consider this might not be the work of a single man? Tampa, LA, Chicago, DC . . . How is he, or they, discovering your itinerary anyway?"

"Risa." The gentleness of his tone didn't hide its finality. "Paulie and I are on it."

She folded her arms over her chest and met his stony stare. Intellectually she knew he was right. Not only would his own formidable talents be turned toward finding the assassin, a number of police departments would be involved as well. But emotionally . . . that was another issue. "Do I have to call Paulie for the details?" Her bluff was empty and they both knew it. Paulie Samuels was Adam's right arm at headquarters, and despite his breezy, friendly demeanor to all, he was fiercely devoted to Raiker. If they were playing this one close to the vest, she'd get no more out of Samuels than from Adam.

Shifting tactics, she said simply, "We're worried. All of us." Enough so that she checked in with one of Raiker's other operatives weekly, just to compare notes on their boss's well-being. Because Kellan Burke had a history with the man longer than anyone else's—with the exception of Samuels—he was invariably the one they all turned to for information.

He was as out of the loop as the rest of them. Whatever Raiker had uncovered about these attempts on his life hadn't been shared with Burke.

"Don't be. It's been tried before." He fingered the scar that bisected his throat. "We'll track him down, and when we do, we'll get some answers. Until then you have enough on your plate." With the help of his cane, he got to his feet. Even with the prop, few would make the mistake of considering the man disabled. Not with the edge that showed beneath the polish, the shrewdness apparent in his eye.

"You've got plenty to keep you occupied. Three torched

cops, remember?" He surprised her by heading to the kitchen. In the next moment she realized he was planning to leave by the back door. Which meant he'd be cutting across two yards to meet his car on the other side of the block.

He was varying his routines. The realization had her breathing a bit more easily. So despite his nonchalant words, he was taking the threats seriously. She supposed having an incendiary device shot through the window of his home to blow it up—fortunately without him in residence—had made a believer out of him.

He paused in the doorway, looked back at her. "You're wasting your time worrying. I look forward to facing whomever, whatever is intent on destroying me. You concern yourself with facing your own demons."

The door closed behind him, and she was left to stare at it, his words ringing in her ears. Raiker's penchant for having the last word wasn't his most infuriating trait.

Being right was.

"Jonas. Over here." Johnny waved the last of their group to arrive over to the corner booth where the rest of them waited. Casting a suspicious eye around the gloomy interior of the bar, he was satisfied there was no one within earshot. The spot had changed ownership several times in the nearly twenty years they'd been using it, but efforts at updating had been halfhearted. The clientele was sparse and desperate, usually satisfied to huddle over their beers on cracked stools at the bar. Since the place didn't run to waitstaff, they didn't have to worry about anyone showing up to take or deliver orders.

Not that he'd turn down a drink right about now. But he'd wait until he was home. From the looks of his companions, it wasn't liquor they needed, it was leadership. No matter what Sean and Hans had liked to believe, Johnny had always been the true leader of the group.

"Is it true what Juan said?" Jonas slid into the booth. "They found Giovanni this morning, fried like the others?"

Johnny sent a look at Juan, who wouldn't meet his eyes. "Is that what he said? Because I fucking told him to set up a meet and we'd discuss the topic once we were all together."

"You're not the only one that hears things." Juan wiped at the sweat beaded on his broad forehead. The years had cost him his first wife and house, then his hair. From what he knew of the man, Johnny figured he missed the hair the most. "I got a buddy in the seventh district. A couple coworkers caught the call and ran the canvass. Someone's lighting up cops, think the details don't get around?"

"This is getting out of hand." Jack looked like ten years had settled on him over the last few weeks. "Three dead cops, there's certain to be a task force, right? How long's it gonna take to connect the victims? And then link them to us?"

"I knew it'd come to this."

Johnny jerked around to glare at Jonas. He'd never fully trusted the prick. Always whining about right and wrong and consequences. Fuck consequences. A real man shaped his life to suit himself. He didn't wait for whatever crumbs life left him. "The last thing we need right now is for you to go weak on this, Jonas," he said meaningfully. "You've gotten rich along with the rest of us over the years. You wanna clear your conscience, see a fucking priest. We hang together, same as always, and cover our asses. A task force might keep the rest of us alive, ever think of that? Every cop in the city is going to be looking for this fuck."

"And if they find him before we do, and he talks, we're in prison, which might as well be dead," Jonas shot back. "Or do you think it's coincidence the three dead cops happen to be members of our John Squad?"

"Keep your damn voice down." But a quick look reassured Johnny that they'd garnered no attention from the bar. Other than from the beefy bartender who kept shooting them sour looks. He knew better than to hassle them about taking up space without ordering, though. Johnny had made sure of that long ago. "No, it's not coincidence. Likely one of our business associates got greedy and decided to quit profit sharing. Once Hans and I find out which one it is, we'll convince him of the errors of his ways." And maybe give the bastard a taste of his own medicine while they were at it.

"Johnny and I have this thing in hand." Hans had the type of soothing grandfatherly voice that calmed any crisis. Johnny watched it work its magic on Jack and Juan. Jonas still had a stick up his ass, but that was nothing new. "We're following up on our various partners. We'll find whoever's responsible. In the meantime, just sit tight and don't panic. We've been careful to avoid any connections over the years."

"Don't you get it?" Jonas's palm slapped the scarred table top with enough force to draw the attention of the hulking bartender. "The torch has made the connection. Whoever is doing this knows the members of the squad. How'd he get that information, huh? We were always careful to split up the business areas. Different suppliers, different parts of towns. How could any one of them put us all together?"

A damn good question. But then Jonas always had been a smart one. He actually had more smarts than guts, and that's exactly what worried Johnny.

"We don't know that he has," Hans pointed out matter-of-factly. "All we know is that he put Giovanni, Jon-O, and Johann together."

"Jesus." Jonas looked away, disgusted.

Hans leaned forward. "Listen, we've all got contacts on the street. We need to start tapping them for any scuttle on this thing. If one of our business partners is involved, there's no way word isn't going to be out somewhere about that. So I want you to lean on your informants. Hard. Just like every other cop in the city is going to be doing, right? Let Johnny or me know if you get something worth pursuing." The other two were listening to him, and Johnny figured that was a good thing. Jonas was always the crybaby, but he didn't have the balls to make trouble. Thank God for that anyway.

"We're not standing still on this," Hans was saying. "But this is no time to get stupid. The money's still coming in, right? We're all still getting rich, and there's no way in hell any of it's traced to us. So stay smart and careful. Keep your weapon close. Giovanni, Jon-O, and Johann were seasoned cops, and someone still managed to get the jump on them. So don't trust anyone, even if you know 'em." He smiled grimly. "Maybe especially if you know 'em."

"What about the task force?" Jack's anxious look swept all of them. "Any word who'll head it up? The brass wouldn't bring the feds in on this, would they?"

"Only if they want it fucked up." Everyone snickered at Johnny's remark except for Jonas. "Way I hear it, a homicide detective by the name of McGuire has been on the cases. No way of knowing who'll be in charge if a task force is formed."

"So we sit tight." Juan was bobbing his head, looking to Hans for more reassurance. "I got a kid at Columbia. I can't afford to have anything fuck this up. We lean on our informants, yeah, but I say we also try to get any details we can about the investigation. I almost hope there is a task force, since they leak info like sieves."

Johnny actually smiled at the possibility. "That's a thought. Because if a suspect surfaces in the case, Hans and I would sure like to talk to him." And if they did, he wouldn't live to be arrested. He certainly wouldn't live to cut a deal with the DA.

Since there was little reason to linger, the group broke up shortly after. Juan and Jack walked out together but Jonas left alone. Johnny's gaze followed him. "Who brought him into the squad anyway?" His gaze shifted to Hans. "Was he one of yours?"

The older man shook his head. He still had a full head of wavy gray hair, of which he was ridiculously vain. "He was one of Sean's boys, wasn't he?"

"Must've been." They'd all been recruited over twenty years ago by either Sean or Hans. "Never did like him."

"You never liked him because he's good-looking and women dropped their panties for him. Still do." Hans tried to get the bartender's attention. After throwing them glowering looks for the duration, he was now studiously avoiding looking their way.

"Reason enough. But he nags like an old lady. I'm telling you, he's a weak link."

Hans looked at him, a frown settling on his creased face. "Will you give it up? He's nervy. Who the hell isn't? With Giovanni buying it, I'm gonna sleep with the light on myself." He waited expectantly, but Johnny wasn't in the laughing mood.

"Jonas had a point. You and me have focused on one of our various partners being behind this, but you know what a stretch that is. These hits take a coordinated effort, and there's no coordination behind our different suppliers."

"What're you saying?"

Johnny hesitated. It was one thing to think it, another to say it aloud. But he trusted this man, as much as he trusted anyone. And he needed to hear Hans's reaction to his idea. "Maybe we're overlooking the obvious. Seems to me the only ones who know who all's in the John Squad are its members."

He'd have felt better if Hans had blown off his idea. Talked him down, tried to point out how it couldn't be betrayal. Couldn't be one of them. Instead the man pursed his lips. Gave a slow nod.

"It'd be stupid not to at least consider the idea. When's the last time you talked to Sean or Johnson?"

Johnny lifted a shoulder. "Talked to Sean last year, I think. Haven't talked to Johnson since he retired and moved away." Both the men had retired to sunnier locales, one to Florida and the other to California, two and three years ago respectively.

"Let's check in." Finally the bartender deigned to leave the bar and approach them with two bottles of beer. He delivered them with plenty of attitude, but he'd remembered their brands, which meant Johnny wasn't going to be required to do any ass kicking before he left here. They went silent until he'd sauntered back to the bar. "They should be careful, too, until this bastard is found. And maybe one of them will have an idea on this guy's identity. And whether we should be looking close to home or farther out."

"Then again, Sean might be the reason for these murders. He made a helluva lot of enemies in his time on the job."

"Made a lot of friends, too." Hans took a drink and then regarded Johnny over the top of his bottle. "Some of them in high places. Can't hurt, especially if one of them ends up having ties to someone on the task force." Neither of them questioned whether a task force would be formed. Three dead cops, even if one of them had been retired, were going to bring a helluva scrutiny to the case. Which could be both a blessing and a curse. "Be nice to have a friendly ear close to the investigation. Might get lucky."

Johnny took a drink and nodded. "The way things are going, we're gonna need all the luck we can get."

It was after midnight when Nate let himself into the house. He stood inside the door for a moment, working the tight muscles in his neck. Fatigue was edging in, but he knew from experience he needed to unwind before even trying to sleep, regardless of the hour. He toed off his shoes and shrugged out of his suit jacket, making a mental note to retrieve the tie he'd jammed into its pocket before he'd made the drive across town.

After the din in the conference room for the last several hours, the silence of his home seemed blessed. With single-minded focus, he headed toward the kitchen. The thought of relaxing with his feet up and a cold beer had been all that had gotten him through the political jockeying that had eaten up the last few hours at headquarters.

He hung his suit jacket over the back of a chair. The shoulder harness and weapon had been locked in the gun safe in his trunk before he came into the house. The dim light of the open fridge split the darkness when he pulled the door open and reached inside, mentally cataloging the games he still had DVR'd. The 76ers were winding down their season. And although it hadn't exactly been a resounding success, he was a fan through thick and thin.

Things had been on the thin side lately.

Twisting the cap off his beer, he took a drink and then padded toward the family room that held his big screen. Halfway there, something caught his eye and he paused, senses heightened.

The last bedroom's door was shut. It was never closed. Not at night. But there was a telltale glow seeping beneath the door. He approached it silently. Easing it open, he was unsurprised to see the figure that should have been under the covers sleeping, sitting up staring fixedly at the lava lamp someone had put on the bedside table.

"Pretty late for Spider-Man to be awake."

Tucker didn't turn. Didn't respond. He wouldn't. The constant forming and reforming of the hot wax in the lamp never failed to transfix him.

Nate padded into the room, sat down on the side of the bed next to his nephew. "You have school tomorrow, bud. What's Mrs. Mallory going to say if you fall asleep in class again?"

"Sleep is food for the brain."

The tone and pitch of his voice was eerily similar to that of his special education teacher. Nate hid a grin. The kid was an excellent mimic. "That's right. And you don't want to nap through recess again. That's no fun. C'mon." This was where it got tricky. Tuck didn't do well transitioning from one task to another. Especially when one of those tasks involved sleeping. "We don't want to wake your mom."

"Momma has to go out now."

Nate's smile abruptly dissipated, although Tucker's rendition of Kristin's voice was just as dead-on as his teacher's. "Your mom isn't here?"

"You watch the pretty light until Uncle Nate gets home." He still hadn't shifted his gaze from the pink and blue light surrounding the bubbling wax. And Nate felt an all too familiar surge of emotion. Dread. Anger. Frustration.

Helplessness.

Without another word he rose, went out the door and down the hallway to the next bedroom. But he already knew he wouldn't find Kristin in her room, even though her car had been in the garage.

Earlier thoughts of relaxation had vanished. His hands closed into fists, and it took far more effort than it should have to squelch his first impulse. To track his sister down by checking all her old haunts. Her former "friends" who had always been more than happy to accompany her on whatever self-destructive path she was bent on. One of which must have picked her up to take her . . . wherever she'd run off to.

He forced himself to concentrate on what was important. The boy in the next room. For the last few years Nate had done what he could to protect him. Even from his mother.

Especially from his mother.

It wasn't easy to shift his focus away from Kristin's possible slide off the wagon. Away from whatever liquor she might even now be pouring down her throat. She wasn't his priority anymore. Tucker was.

He rejoined his nephew in his bedroom. The boy hadn't moved. He probably hadn't in the hours since he'd been left alone. "You know what makes that light even prettier?" Dropping onto the bed on all fours, Nate crawled to the far side of the twin bed and propped himself on his side, head resting on one end of the pillow. "If you lie down and watch it. The shapes look completely different from this position. Don't take your eyes off it, though," he continued. No chance of that. Tucker would stare at the thing until exhaustion overtook him. "Just keep looking at it while you slide down into bed. When you lie your head on the pillow like this—still looking at it, just like this . . . wow." He manufactured an awed tone. "Looks just like Spidey's web from here."

He continued to speak in a soft litany, one that garnered no verbal response from Tucker. But after several long minutes, the boy began to move, just a little at a time, until he was peering at the light, head cocked at a right angle.

"Easier to look at it from the pillow. Won't get a crick in your neck that way." It took a lot more talking, but the boy eventually slid inch by infinitesimal inch to a prone position. His head on the edge of the pillow. His gaze still on the hot wax in the colored light, twisting and swirling into new shapes from one second to the next.

Not unlike, Nate thought, his sister, Kristin. Who'd tried, more times than he could count, to shape herself into someone who could hold a job. Stay sober and out of trouble. Care for her son.

"Doesn't look like a web."

The words were whispered, but they tugged a smile from Nate. Tuck could do that. Make him grin even when the world seemed desolate.

"Just keep watching," he said nearly as inaudibly. And hoped like hell that just getting the boy's head on the pillow would help nature take its course. He didn't even want to consider how few hours he had before he had to get back to the station house.

Or that in all likelihood he'd have to get Tucker off to school first.

"Spider-Man, Spider-Man. Does whatever a spider can."

Worries subsiding for the moment, Nate looped an arm around the boy's waist.

"Spider-Man, Spider-Man . . ." He joined in the singsong, knowing from experience that the repetition would lull the boy to sleep.

In the end, it worked its magic on them both.

Chapter 4

"Thank you for coming."

Risa stared at the man soberly. "Thought about saying no. But I've always had this innate subservience to the brass."

A wry smile cracked Eduardo Morales's face. "I don't remember you being so easily cowed. As a matter of fact, you always said that interagency task force we worked had more brass than the Penn State marching band."

Leaning forward to give him a hug, she said simply, "You look good, Eddie. How's Renee? And the little one?" Searching her memory in vain, she tried, and failed, to come up with the child's name. "He must be what? Eight now?"

"Almost. And he has two little brothers he spends most of his time leading into trouble."

There was a sort of surreal air to the moment. Seven years and each of them had continued their careers. But unlike her, Morales had managed to continue a personal life, as well. According to her ex, that had never been her forte.

"That's wonderful," she said sincerely. Just because a normal home, a normal family life, seemed out of her grasp, didn't mean she couldn't appreciate what it meant for others. "Tell Renee I said hi."

The sound of the door opening behind her had her turning. She recognized Chief Inspector Wessels as one of the two men entering, although he looked as though he'd gained fifteen years and forty pounds in her absence. She didn't know the man with him, although it wasn't difficult to guess his identity from the uniform and polished brass. A deputy commissioner. Maybe even the commissioner of police himself. Whichever he was, he was unfamiliar.

The mystery was soon solved. "Commissioner of Police Douglas Lawton." At Eddie's introduction Risa took the man's outstretched hand. "And you'll remember Inspector Wessels. Marisa Chandler."

They all found seats. When they sat, they were nearly elbow to elbow in the cramped space. "I assume Captain Morales already briefed you about our request." Lawton lost no time getting to the point. "Although I'm not personally acquainted with your record, I am with that of your employer, Adam Raiker." His narrowed gaze passed over her, not missing a detail. "And with his agency, which has made quite a name for itself since its inception. He assures me that you will be invaluable on this case. Inspector Wessels and the captain recall your work for the department, and they concur. That's good enough for me."

Somehow Marisa thought that Raiker had held more sway with the man than had his employees. The thought came without rancor. There were few in law enforcement circles that weren't familiar with Adam's legendary rise in the bureau, or with his last near-fatal case. But it would be the reputation of the agency he'd built since leaving the FBI that led to this man's stamp of approval.

"You understand I'm still on sick leave," she offered. Her nerves were jittering wildly. Doubt ping-ponging inside her. But after Raiker's final words to her yesterday, it had been impossible to turn down Morales's request when he'd called last night to invite her to this meet.

"Through with physical therapy, your boss said. No permanent muscle damage." Lawton's smile creased his face but managed to look only perfunctory. "Glad to hear that. Your former coworkers can't say enough about your uncanny instincts. We'll take any edge we can get on this case. In an unofficial capacity, of course."

"Of course," she murmured, and avoided, barely, the impulse to wipe her damp palms down the front of her crisp black pants. Unofficial, she thought wildly. Without pressure. Without unrealistic expectations.

If only it could be disconnected from the haunting specter of Ryder Kremer's death.

The commissioner continued. "We spent last night compiling a task force of the best talent our department has to offer. Detective McGuire will be reporting to Captain Morales, who in turn will keep us informed every step of the way." He rose, signaling that the meeting was at an end. "We appreciate any assistance you can offer."

"Yes, sir." What else could she say at that point? Risa thought, a little wildly. The three men seemed to take it for granted that her presence here was tacit acquiescence to join the task force.

And wasn't it? If she'd hoped to convince Morales she had nothing to offer, the time to do so would have been on the phone last night. By agreeing to the meet, she'd taken the first step toward following Raiker's advice. She was facing her demons.

God help her.

Eduardo's expression was grim when his superiors had gone. "How much did McGuire tell you yesterday?"

"Someone is targeting cops. Plainclothes detectives, which is even more suspect." Because she thought better on her feet, Risa rose and shoved her hands into the pockets of her black suit jacket as she paced. "No connections have been found between the first two suspects." She threw him a look. "Unless a link has been discovered with yesterday's . . ."

Morales shook his head. "Not yet." With a quick glance to the clock on the wall, he rose, as well. "Briefing should begin in a few minutes. It'll be the first full report some of the task force members have heard. I'll let you get the full rundown from McGuire. We'll talk later."

Nodding, she preceded the captain out the office door, her estimation of McGuire kicking up a notch. Getting himself named lead detective of the task force was no small feat. When she had a moment maybe she'd quiz Eddie about the detective's experience. She recalled her impression yesterday that McGuire seemed unsure about his new captain. She wondered if Eduardo held McGuire in higher esteem than McGuire seemed to him.

The conference room was filled with detectives and uniforms both. Most still stood around the coffeepot at the back of the room or in small clusters, talking in hushed voices. She saw Jett Brandau in the back of the room with Cass, the woman who'd arrived late to the scene yesterday. Risa took a seat near the front of the room and heard Morales ask the harried young man bringing in more coffee, "Where's McGuire?"

"Sorry, Captain," the auburn-haired man responded over his shoulder as he tried to get to the back table with both the pots he carried intact. "I haven't seen him."

"I'm here." Nate strode into the front of the room, looking as if he'd gotten very little sleep. Certainly he hadn't shaved that morning. Given Morales's jaundiced expression, the captain was none too pleased with his tardiness or with his appearance.

But McGuire seemed all business as he handed out case files to everyone in the room. If he was surprised to see her there, he didn't show it. His gaze lingered on her for just an instant before he addressed the group at large. "If everyone will take their seats, we'll get started." There was a scuffling of feet and scraping of chairs while he waited.

"Roland Parker. Sherman Tull. Pat Christiansen." The sound of those names, his terse tone, quieted the room as nothing else could. "Three of ours. All targeted by what's likely to be the same unknown subject. At this point all we know is that our UNSUB is selecting detectives, active and retired, from the Philadelphia Police Department. They were approached when they were out alone, and it's possible they recognized their killer."

A murmur swept through the group. Risa's interest sharpened. She knew only what she'd discovered while on the scene yesterday. McGuire had dropped her off at home before returning to the station house once they were done with the scene. Any information that had been uncovered since that time would be as new to her as it was to the rest of the task force. As would any details the detective had neglected to mention.

"If we're correct that the attacker was a stranger to the victims, they likely didn't perceive him, or her, as a threat. I can't think of any other way someone would get the drop on three different competent members of the department."

"Any chance these are dump sites? Secondary scenes?" a voice called out from the back of the room.

"ME's not done with the most recent body. But there was nothing to indicate that for the first two victims. Each was burned alive at the crime scene."

A chill skated up Risa's arms at the blunt pronouncement. And the room went suddenly silent.

"The offender is deliberately targeting plainclothes cops and making it easy for us to identify the victims. He wants us to know what he's done and to whom. We may be dealing with someone with a vendetta against detectives in general, or someone with a personal reason to single these men out." For an instant Nate's gaze met Risa's. "We don't believe he'll stop at three, so we're going to try and find him before there's a fourth. The top sheet inside your folders is your assignments. Shroot, Finnigan, and Alberts—you'll be following up on the victims' case files trying to discover a connection there. We haven't found anything so far on the first two victims, but you'll add Christiansen to the mix and see if anything pops.

"Edwards, you and Tomey will look for links in their personal lives. Go way back. Schools they attended, neighborhoods they grew up in, families, friends, church . . . find us an intersection."

"There may not even be an intersection," one of the men muttered, flipping through the folder. "Any crazy can get our names off the department website. Or by calling the station houses."

"Except that Parker was retired," Nate reminded him. "Eighteen months ago. Maybe the murders are random, but I think it's more likely there's some sort of connection. We just need to find it. Brandau and Recker will take Christiansen's family and neighbors, and cross-reference with those of the first two victims. Hoy and Mendall trace his steps his final day. I want to know everywhere he went. Everyone he talked to. Get the security tapes from any place he might have passed by." He took a quick look at his watch. "That's enough for now. My cell number is in the folder. Call if you get anything. Otherwise we'll meet back here tomorrow morning."

Chairs scraped as the detectives began to rise. They sank into their seats again as Captain Morales went to Nate's side to speak for the first time. "This case is top priority." The room went as still as a tomb. "Everyone on the force wants to get this guy. We've no shortage of manpower, and we'll have more volunteers than we can use, which is great. But that also means everyone we work with is going to want to know about the progress of the case. They'll be quizzing you about it." He looked from one face to another. "I shouldn't have to remind you, but confidentiality is an issue on any task force, and this one is no different. Let's keep the details in this group. If I find out that anyone's talking—to anyone—that will be grounds for immediate dismissal from the investigation." Risa noted that a few of the detectives exchanged glances, but none said a word as they filed out of the room.

She also observed Cass shooting a final look at McGuire before exiting with Brandau at her side. She took a moment to wonder if there was something personal going on between the two before dismissing the thought. The man's personal life was nothing to her. And it certainly had nothing to do with the case.

When the room was empty save for Morales, McGuire, and Risa, the captain spoke again. "Nate, you'll be paired with Risa for the duration of the case." He seemed to watch the detective's face closely. "Will that be a problem?"

It came to her in a flash that the assignments had been determined by the captain, although he'd allowed McGuire to run the briefing. Which explained why the man wasn't working with his regular partner. She, too, observed Nate for a reaction to the assignment. But his expression remained impassive. "No, sir."

"She'll have access to all details pertinent to the case," Eduardo went on. A smile flickered at the corner of his mouth as he looked at Risa. "Let's hope you still have those famous instincts of yours."

The words started her heart hammering in her chest. *No pressure. No expectations.*

Yeah, right. "I hope I can be of some help," she managed inanely, and searched for something, anything, to change the subject. "What about the tape?" She looked at both men in turn. "I'm sure IT isn't done with it yet, but did anyone come back for it last night?"

Nate shook his head. "We put a dummy camera in the place of the one he left. I've had some undercover officers posted there around the clock since we left the scene. There have been a few people in the area, none of whom approached the tree. But they questioned and ID'd all of them."

"He'd be expecting a police presence at what's still a crime scene," Risa mused. "He may wait a while before returning." The UNSUB could afford to be patient, up to a point. There was no rain in the forecast this week. All he risked was a dead battery on the camera. And it had been well hidden in that fork between the branches. Chances of it being discovered were small. Most would never have noticed it.

Most wouldn't have dreamed of the scene.

"We'll keep someone posted there for the duration." The corner of his mouth pulled up briefly. "We can only hope it gets solved that easily." Taking a sheet from the folder on the table in front of him, he continued, "Results of the latents test were back this morning. No prints on the ID, toy badge, camera, or the tape. They'd been wiped clean."

"IT will make a dub of the tape for us before going to work on the original," the captain put in. "I'll let you know when that's ready."

Nate nodded. "In the meantime, I finally tracked down Sam Crowley, the guy the witness was meeting when she happened on the body yesterday morning. No doubt she'd given him a heads-up that she'd named him, because he did a good job of making himself scarce last night. But we grabbed him when he was going to work this morning. He's in the interview room right now."

Morales pursed his lips. "He's the ex-con, right? Anything in his background that rings a bell?"

"He did a two-year stretch for embezzlement. Before that he had a couple arrests for simple assault and leaving the scene of an accident."

"Might've seen something on his way to meet Bixby," Risa put in.

Morales jerked his head toward the door. "Go find out." They got as far as the door before his voice stopped them. "Nate, swing by Darrell's desk and pick up a visitor's badge for Risa until we get her a temp ID."

She followed the detective out of the room and through the maze of cubicles and desks to the front of the district house. Darrell turned out to be the red-haired man who'd brought coffee to the conference room. He barely came up to Risa's chin, was whipcord lean, and from her few seconds of observation, was never still.

"Excuse me, ma'am," he was saying as they approached his glassed-in cubicle, turning away from the woman, waiting impatiently for his help, to answer the phone. Risa knew from her time on the force that the glass would be bulletproof. If the woman were waiting for a copy of an accident or police report, it would be slid to her through the small horizontal opening where the glass met the counter. The precautions had never seemed overly cautious to her. There were a lot of crazies in the world, and a full moon seemed to draw every one of them to the police station.

"Philadelphia Police Department, Seventh District, will you hold please?" He stabbed his finger at a button and answered yet another call. Then he twirled toward them on his wheeled office chair and beamed. "Nate, I took a message for you while you were in conference. From your not-so-secret admirer." He opened up the door to the cubicle to hand him a note. "Your person of interest is in interview one. And you'll want this for your guest."

Nonplussed, Risa took the visitor badge he handed her. It had a photo ID on it, although she hadn't posed for one. With one glance she noted that an old department photo had been affixed to it. Distractedly she observed that her unsmiling persona from seven years ago looked almost impossibly young.

The rest of her focus was on Nate's admirer. He'd given the note one quick glance before shoving it into his pocket.

But she didn't think it was her imagination that a slight flush of color was spreading beneath the stubble on his jaw.

After shooting them both a blinding smile, Darrell was back in his glassed cubicle, wheeling to the phone to answer it. "How may I direct your call?"

"Thanks, Darrell." Nate's mouth quirked at Risa's expression as she fell into step beside him. "Radar, we call him around here. Like that character from the old *M.A.S.H.* reruns? Has a knack for knowing what we want before we do sometimes."

"That must come in handy."

They went down a corridor with doors on each side. Nate placed his hand on the knob of the first door on the right, hesitated. "I'll take the lead on this."

Hardly earth shattering. "All right."

"With the runaround Crowley gave us when we were trying to pick him up, I don't expect him to fall all over himself being helpful. But if I'm not getting anywhere and you see an opening, a different direction that might work, feel free to jump in. We'll play off each other."

He'd managed to surprise her, but there was no time for a response. Nate was pushing the door open into the room. She followed him inside.

Sam Crowley had crimped brown hair, a square jaw, and the pumped-up body so many ex-cons exited prison with. His hands were laced tightly on the table in front of him, but nerves showed in the way his knee bounced under the table. And the door had barely opened before he started talking.

"Hey, do I need a lawyer? I can't get this guy to say one way or another." He jerked his head at the uniformed officer standing in the corner of the room. At Nate's nod, the officer went out the door.

"I don't know, Sam, do you?" Nate's voice was mild enough as he and Risa sat across from the man at the table. "I imagine you've got one on speed dial after your last run-in with the law, right?"

Crowley's lips tightened. "Can't ever let a guy get clear of it, can you? One mistake, and I'm paying for it the rest of my life. Does that seem fair? I'm cooperating here. Came in on my own free will, and all that."

That claim took some imagination, given the fact he'd been dodging them for the better part of twelve hours, but apparently Nate was willing to let it pass. "We appreciate your cooperation. Good citizens like you make our job easier."

The man looked at him suspiciously, but Nate's expression was impassive. "Yeah. Well. Honestly, I got nothing to tell you. I was on my way to meet a friend of mine. You talked to her. Heather Bixby? And she called to say don't come, things are a mess here and all that, so I turned around and went home. Like I say, I don't need any more trouble with the law. My parole officer tells me to think through situations, avoid them if they're going to get me jammed up, right?" He looked at them carefully, as if to assess their appreciation of his decision making.

"And what was the nature of your visit to Wakeshead Park yesterday morning?"

Clearly prepared for Nate's next question, he gave a grin that encompassed both of them. One that was clearly meant to disarm. "Me and Heather, we got a thing going. Just hooking up. No harm, no foul."

"Her husband might disagree with that."

The smile abruptly vanished from Crowley's face. His weight shifted. "Last I heard, getting a little on the side wasn't a matter for the cops."

"Ordinarily it isn't. But when an affair is used to hide a crime," Nate's voice hardened, "then it concerns us. A lot."

Risa watched the other man closely. A faint sheen of perspiration glistened on his brow. His Adam's apple bobbed as he swallowed convulsively. "Whatever happened in that park, I had nothing to do with it. I hadn't even gotten there yet."

Nate turned to her, a sardonic twist to his mouth. "And there's the cover."

Taking his cue, she nodded. "Start something up with a new woman in the area and then just happen to suggest that particular park as a rendezvous point. Gives him a perfect opportunity to scout the area, figure exactly how he's going to pull it off. Then just set up a meet for the morning after he offs that cop—"

"I didn't kill any cop!"

"—and he has a ready-made alibi." Her gaze cut to Crowley then. "Except you don't. Bixby never even saw you yesterday morning before she called and told you to stay away. And she certainly can't attest to your whereabouts the night before, during the time the murder was committed. So I hope you have another lady lined up for that time frame. Say two nights ago between nine and four A.M.? Because otherwise, we're looking at you for the murder, and we're looking hard."

The man swiped at the moisture beading above his upper lip. "How stupid would I have to be to take Heather to a place I was planning to commit murder?"

Risa looked at Nate. "I'm guessing that chair he's sitting in has known any number of stupid occupants."

Nate nodded, his eyes flinty. "I can't even begin to count them."

"Well, if I were going to commit murder"—Sam lurched forward in his seat—"I'd be smart enough to arrange for someone to vouch for my whereabouts, wouldn't I? I was home alone. Watched TV until ten or so before going to bed. I get up early when I'm meeting Heather."

"And what time was that?"

He lifted a bulky shoulder. "I was running late. Didn't wake up until five, and I was supposed to see her in a half hour. I barely got into the park before she was calling and telling me there were cops all over the place."

"Because she knows that would make you uncomfortable?"

Crowley aimed a derisive stare at Risa. "Uncomfortable. Yeah. The terms of my parole are pretty clear. I have to steer clear of trouble, and that's what I did. I went home and went back to bed. Figured I could catch another couple hours before work."

She nodded. "I can see that. No use getting caught up for several hours answering questions, right?"

"Questions I wouldn't have had the answers to. I didn't see anything. Didn't get close enough. Didn't see anyone at all going in or on my way out."

Her senses heightened. They always did when a suspect offered information that they hadn't gotten around to asking yet. "Did that seem odd to you?"

"What?"

"That you didn't see anyone around. That park is a known hangout for druggies. Lots of users, buyers, and sellers. I'd think you'd have run into some of them."

He shook his head emphatically.

"But you've seen them there before?"

Hesitating, he considered the question for a moment before deciding it was harmless. "There are always losers around there, I guess. I don't pay much attention to them."

"But you paid enough attention to notice none of them were in the area two mornings ago."

Crowley's eyes darted to Nate. "Like I said, I was running late. I was barely inside the park before Heather called and I left."

In an aside, Risa told Nate, "It goes to figure he might not see anyone if he didn't get deep enough inside it." She shifted her attention to the other man. "Heather was in the northeast corner. What entrance did you use?"

"Uh . . . the southwest."

"So you would have passed that World War statue. How far would you say you traveled beyond it before you got her call?"

"Not far. Seventy yards or so."

She rested her forearms on the table and leaned against them. "Here's the thing, Sam. That statue is situated nearly in the center of the park. If you were seventy yards past it, you were a helluva lot farther inside the area than you claimed earlier." She let the moment stretch. Then another. "You want to rethink your story?"

"Jesus." He shoved back from the table. "Statues, how many feet past . . . What the hell difference does it make? I'm trying to say here that I didn't see anything."

"A guy tells one lie, he's liable to tell a lot more. That makes us think you're holding out on us. Maybe about seeing the killer."

He was sweating profusely now. Flicking a glance at Nate, he clearly saw no mercy in his expression. "I didn't. I swear it."

"But you saw someone."

"Jesus. Jesus." He wiped his face on the sleeve of his shirt. "He's going to kill me."

"Who?" Nate pressed relentlessly. "Who did you see? Who did you talk to?"

"He's got nothing to do with the other. That killing."

"His name."

"Juicy." With the word, all the fight seemed to stream out of him. "I only know him by that name, I swear. I stopped to, uh, talk to him, and the next thing Heather called and I left."

"You bought drugs from him?"

He didn't answer. Using drugs was an automatic parole violation and could land him back in prison. But it explained his lies and his reluctance to come clean about his trip into the park.

"Here's the thing." Nate hooked an elbow over the back of his chair. "You can tell us now, or we track down Juicy and ask him the same question. He's not going to be likely to hold back, seeing as how you gave him up to us, told us he's a dealer. And he will know that." He paused a moment to let the import of that statement sink in. "I'll make sure of it. Right now I don't care whether you're using or not, but if I have to go to all that work to find him to ask the same question I'm asking you, I'm going to care. And when I do, your parole officer gets a call."

"A little pot. That's all, I swear."

Risa surveyed the man in silence. He was an idiot if he thought he could successfully pass the drug screenings if he was using. But that wasn't their concern. His supplier just might be.

After several more minutes of questioning, it became apparent that Crowley had nothing more to offer. Nate shoved a legal pad across the table to him. "Write it up. Everything from when you left your place to meet Heather until the time you got back home."

It was another twenty minutes before Nate was satisfied with the man's statement. He and Risa left the interview room, and he gave a nod to the officer waiting outside the door. "Kick him loose."

She easily kept pace with the detective as they headed

down the hallway. "Admitting to the drug use explains his unwillingness to talk to us. I doubt he can shed any light on the identity of the killer, though."

"But the mysterious Juicy might."

"Exactly." She slanted him a glance. The stubble of beard lent him a vaguely lethal air that had been missing yesterday. "I wouldn't be surprised if he has an arrest record and that Vice is very familiar with that name. Shouldn't be hard to find, if so."

"You read my mind."

Chapter 5

Nate felt in his suit pockets. He hated the sight of other people chewing gum and suspected he looked just as ridiculous when he had a piece in his mouth. But swapping cigarettes for gum had helped him kick the nicotine habit when Tucker had come to live with him a couple years ago. Now he just needed to find something to replace the gum habit he'd picked up in its stead.

His search was in vain. Instead his fingers came in contact with the crumpled paper he'd shoved in there earlier. Tatiana. He felt a quick surge of embarrassment. He hadn't heard from her in over a month. He'd thought—he'd *hoped*—she'd given up. But apparently she fed off disinterest.

They entered the squad room and he spotted a wastebasket next to one of the desks. He pulled the paper from his pocket, meaning to three-point it into the trash. Was shocked to have it snatched out of his hand.

"'Nate the Great?'" Risa read off the note. Her mouth quirked as she turned slightly to prevent his grab for the paper. "One of your conquests, detective?"

"She's sixty if she's a day, and has a strange fixation on me. I don't encourage it."

Risa flicked a nail at the message. "So inviting you over for borscht and kotlety isn't an ethnic euphemism for sex?"

Dammit, he could feel his ears heating. "I was throwing that away."

"No problem." She tossed it neatly in the wastebasket from an admirable distance, then cupped a hand to her ear. "Is that the sound of a heart shattering I hear?"

"You're hilarious," he informed her, lengthening his strides. She kept up with him easily. She was nearly as tall as he was. And her legs . . . well, he'd noticed how long they were yesterday. Before he'd realized she had a sense of humor.

The fact that he was the butt of it tempered his appreciation of that quality. "Keep your voice down. These guys don't need much encouragement."

She smirked. "Ah, department humor. I miss it."

"Stick around. A few days here should cure that." He pushed open the door to his office, belatedly remembering to step aside for her to enter first. "You can take Cass's desk. She's set up temporarily near Brandau." And hopefully Jett would keep her mind on the job. It had required some fast-talking to convince the captain that Cass belonged on the case. He hadn't been exaggerating when he'd told her she was on very thin ice, professionally.

Rounding his desk, he powered up his laptop and accessed the departmental database. He tapped in Juicy's alias, and after a moment he added *drugs* as a keyword, hoping at least for an arrest report to get them started. A minute later he gave a long low whistle. "Jackpot."

"What? You found something already?" Slipping out of her suit jacket as she spoke, Risa hurried to look over his shoulder.

"Found a few somethings. Juicy is apparently a hot nickname among dirtballs." He shifted to allow her a better view. "But my bet is on this guy." He scrolled back up to the top of the screen.

"Possession with intent, assault with a deadly weapon, attempted murder . . . a varied career."

"For which it looks like he's only done time once. Three

years on the attempted murder charge. That doesn't make sense." He read more carefully, jotting down notes on a pad he took from his center desk drawer. One of the arresting officers was in a neighboring district. He took out his cell and called the number given on the report. Risa leaned forward and nudged his hand away from the keyboard so she could scroll through all the listings.

She had her dark blond hair pulled back today, but one long strand had worked free and curved along her jaw. In profile she looked almost delicate, which was a joke. Even in the short time he'd known her, he had a feeling that she was about as delicate as a pit bull.

"The third one's a possibility, too," she said, and turned to look at him. Her eyes were an odd amber color, wide and thickly fringed. And when the call went to Randolph's voice mail, he had to clear his throat before speaking.

"This is Detective Nate McGuire, Homicide. I'm heading the task force on the three dead detectives and one of your old arrests may be of interest to us." To divert his attention from the female standing too close to him, he scrolled back up the screen to check the name again. "Javon Emmons." He read off the arrest report number. "I'd appreciate it if you'd give me a call back at this number." He rattled off his cell and disconnected. Thankfully, Risa moved away, her arms folded across her chest, looking thoughtful. He made a second phone call on the photo she'd indicated, identified as Dwayne Jersey, and once again had to leave a message, this time for an Officer Pelton. After consulting the list on-screen once more, he made a third and final call concerning one William Fox.

"We could show Crowley an array of these photos and see if he IDs one of them."

"And we will. But I'd like to have a pretty good idea who he met there so if he thinks about lying to us again, I can nail him."

Before Risa could respond, the ancient department phone on Nate's desk rang. He reached out to snag the receiver. "McGuire." After listening for a moment, he bolted out of his chair. "On my way." He dropped the receiver in the cradle with a clatter. "That was the captain. IT just dropped off a dub of the tape we found at the scene."

———

Morales already had a wheeled cart with a TV/VCR combo sitting in his office when they got there. Nate took a moment to wonder where he'd dug up the system. From the thick coating of dust everywhere except on the freshly dusted screen, no doubt it'd been resurrected from the tombs of the basement.

"Karen Loomis. Detective Nate McGuire. Marisa Chandler." Morales made short work of the introductions as they crowded around the TV. "Ms. Loomis is from IT. She's going to explain what we've got here."

Loomis was a foot shorter than Nate and probably only twenty pounds lighter. Her dark brown hair was sticking up in odd spikes all over her head. After a moment he decided the style was deliberate. But she carried her weight lightly and sounded authoritative when she began speaking.

"What you've got is one very old tape." She tapped the panel covering the tape insert. "Well, not the copy we made, but your original. It's well worn and I'm guessing it might be a relic from the eighties. Mainly because that's the decade the camera heralds from. But given the wear on the tape, it was either used over and over or it's aged, as well. Or both." She punched the buttons to turn on the TV and the VCR. If the unit came with a remote, it was obviously missing.

There were a few moments of blank screen before the recording came into view. Nate saw immediately what she meant. The picture crackled with static before settling into view. And the scene had his throat drying out.

"Ah, Jesus," he whispered, when he saw the flames shooting skyward. They were imprinted on the inky blackness of the surroundings. A macabre beacon against the night sky, gilding the dark figure at their core.

"Is there sound?" Morales demanded.

Loomis turned up the volume. The crackle of the flames was heard. In the distance was a barking dog. But nothing else.

It took a moment for Nate to find his voice. "The other victims weren't gagged. Liz didn't mention finding anything to suggest this victim was either. Chances are he was dead by the time the tape was turned on."

"Which begs the question of why the tape was started at that time." The captain was frowning fiercely at the television screen. "Either he wants to film the entire scene to relive later or he wants to catch the crime scene being discovered and worked. Each way means he's coming back for the tape."

"Maybe he'd already filled one tape," Risa suggested. It was the first time she'd spoken. Nate glanced at her. Her face was bloodless. Her eyes fixed on the screen.

"Possible," Loomis answered cheerfully. "And no way for us to know for sure. What we can be certain of is that this particular tape was set to record for eight hours. Which means, of course, that you get a lower-quality recording. And you've only got about six hours of recorded material here. The first hint of a live person in the area comes sometime around dawn." She fast-forwarded the tape until she found the bit she was looking for.

An unseen woman's voice sounded. "Buster. Buster, stop it. Damn, would you just . . ." An excited barking was heard. "Yeah, I see it. What is that? It looks . . . ohmyGod, ohmy-God . . ." They all listened in silence as a still unseen Heather Bixby called 911, described what she'd found.

Afterward they watched as the woman moved onto the screen, pulled by the large mastiff, and got much closer to the smoking body than she'd led them to believe. Her next call, as expected, was to Crowley.

"Baby, you're not going to believe this. There's been nasty doings in the park last night." She stopped. Listened. Gave a bray of laughter. "No, not that kind of nasty. You have a one-track mind. Yes, you do! Oh, shit." She fumbled with the phone as she tried to pull the straining dog away from the pad of cement. When her voice came again, she had moved out of the picture. "I'm telling you, someone burnt something here last night and I think it was alive. Maybe even human." After a moment a pout sounded in her voice. "I'm not exaggerating. Whatever it was is still smoking. I called the cops. Why? Because I had to. I'm telling you, this . . . thing . . . it might have been a person. You shouldn't come. You know what your parole officer told you about avoiding trouble."

There was a great deal more that Nate could have gone without hearing. Apparently Crowley berated her for calling prior to their hooking up, instead of after. And then there was a long-winded conversation about the details of the acts they were going to have to forgo because of the call she'd made summoning the cops. Details that included a great deal of imagination and an ingenious flexibility that had him frowning consideringly.

She hung up only moments before other voices were heard. The uniforms had arrived on the scene.

Loomis fast-forwarded again. "You appear shortly here, detective. And you, Chandler. But this is what I wanted to show you." When she stopped the tape again, Risa was leading Nate in the direction of the tree. Several minutes passed before the picture tilted, righted itself, then went abruptly black.

"Ke-e-ep watching," Loomis murmured, her eyes glued to the set. There were bursts of static as the picture scrambled, then cleared to show a different scene.

Nate moved closer to the set, his shoulder bumping Risa's as she moved at the same time. He squinted, trying to make out the image. It looked like a group of people gathered around a table. Not for a meal. There were no dishes in sight, although there were plenty of beer bottles. Part of the video was cut off, as if whoever had filmed the movie hadn't centered it.

Three men were in view, although one could be seen only from the back and one in profile. And given the length of the sideburns sported by the men, it had clearly been shot decades earlier. The conversation was a jumble of voices for the most part, with an occasional outburst of laughter.

An unseen man was heard. "How the hell are you gonna make sure of that, Johnny?"

The man shown in profile responded, his voice ringing out over the others. "How am I going to make sure? I'll tell you how. 'Cuz if he doesn't, I'm going to cut off his long black dong, chop it into little pieces, and force-feed it to that nigger-loving bitch of his." He turned his head and looked across the room in the direction of the camera. "You hear that, Lamont?"

Raucous laughter sounded. A jolt of recognition struck him, but he couldn't put his finger on the feeling of familiarity. "That man." He reached out and tapped the face on the TV screen. "Not the loud mouth. Second to his right." He frowned, searching his memory. It wasn't someone he knew, at least not directly. Swearing silently, he tried to recall the context in which he'd seen the man. Someone he'd arrested? Not likely. He'd probably been a kid when this thing was filmed. An old newspaper clipping?

The realization slammed into him with the force of a fist.

He looked at Morales. "It's the first victim. Roland Parker."

The captain looked from him to the screen, then back again. "What? Are you sure?" They leaned nearer to the TV. "Can you back that up, Karen? Right to the spot where they all start laughing? Yeah, there. Stop." They stared in silence for a moment. "Maybe. Maybe," Morales muttered. "How can you be certain?"

"I can't be positive. But I attended Parker's memorial service. No viewing, of course, so his wife had pictures everywhere. Lots of them were older. I'd swear it was him." He looked at the IT tech. "Is it possible to get a picture from this tape? Like a close-up?"

She nodded. "It won't be the clearest, since blowing it up will blur some of the clarity. And the tape isn't in that great of shape to begin with. But yeah, we can pause it, take a picture, and you can show the photo to the widow for an ID."

Risa spoke. "Or compare it to the man's older department ID photos."

"Yeah. Yeah." Nate was concentrating fiercely on the screen. He had to approach this cautiously but certainty was growing inside him. It was Parker, he was almost sure of it. And if he was right, they'd found their first link on this case. "Get us a still of the speaker, too, will you?"

"We'll do our best. What happened is the footage from the crime scene was shot over this older tape," Karen said after they watched the tape until it ran out. "And I already know what you're going to ask." She sent a sly look to Nate. "The answer is no."

"Can you remove what was filmed over it two nights ago . . ." he began.

"Negative. Once these old tapes have been recorded over, the original material is erased. It's not like a computer where you can trash items but they still exist somewhere on the hard drive. This material is *gone*. I can't tell you how many stories I've heard about kids taping over their parents wedding video, or some ex-jock's football highlights lost forever because his wife taped her soaps over it. There is no retrieval system for something that ceases to exist, and that's the case for the material you're talking about."

"What about the sound on the remainder of the tape?" Nate refused to feel disappointment. They might not have the rest of that film, but they had a snippet of it. And it might be enough to provide them with their first real leads in this case. "Can it be enhanced so we could hear more of the conversation?"

"Now that's a possibility." Karen hooked her thumbs in her waistband, which only served to draw attention to her girth. "Again, it's going to depend a lot on the wear and tear the tape has already undergone, but I think we can do better than this, yeah. Maybe, *maybe* mind you, we can do well enough to give you a sample for a voice match on a speaker or two. Don't know if that will do you much good or not."

"You never know," Nate murmured, staring blindly at the TV as his mind raced. "Better to have it, just in case."

Long after Karen had gone back to IT, the three of them watched and rewatched the tape. If there was something to see on the footage shot prior to Heather Bixby happening upon the crime scene, none of them found it.

"Careful bastard." Nate rubbed his eyes with the heels of his palms. They felt like they were filled with grit. "He was damn cautious about staying out of the camera's view."

"That makes me think he set this tape up before he left." Risa's voice was expressionless. And her face had regained the color that had leeched out of it when they'd first begun viewing. "Or maybe that's when he changed tapes. At any rate, you're right, he would be careful about not exposing himself that way."

"Let's go over the end of the tape again, the part that shows those men," Morales said. His suit was rumpled and his eyes red rimmed. Nate could only imagine that he looked the same, or worse. "I'll call Loomis and tell her to focus on where that neon sign reflects on the window in the door." They'd stared at that portion of the tape until their eyes bled, but could only make out what they'd agreed was a *z* and a *p*. "Until and unless IT can figure out how many voices are heard in that segment, we can't know the number of men sitting around that table." His voice went hard. "And we can't discount the fact that any one of them could be the suspect we're after."

Chapter 6

It felt more than a little anticlimactic to Risa to be standing in her mother's living room staring out the window at barely six thirty P.M. She'd imagined they'd be working the case until late. She'd welcomed the possibility. Long hours meant exhaustion, which sometimes led to a deep dreamless sleep.

She hoped so. She couldn't afford to avoid sleep in an effort to evade dreams that came without her consent, sneaking into her subconscious like a thief in the mist.

Broodingly, she stared at the near-empty street. She'd committed to this case for better or worse. And God help her, things couldn't get much worse than they had over the last few months. It was as if she'd become stuck in place, while time passed her by. If she didn't want to become a still life, she had to move forward. And if that thought still had the power to strike fear in her heart, at least she was moving toward something.

That would have to suffice for now.

She watched a dented-up navy compact drive slowly by, only to be forced to turn around at the cul-de-sac at the end of the street. The house she'd bought her mother was modest but it was in a safe neighborhood, and Hannah felt comfortable here. The others she'd shown her had been pronounced "too grand," although they were anything but. Life had long since stripped Hannah Blanchette of pretensions.

Just like a series of poor choices in male companions had robbed her of illusions.

Shaking off the mantle of melancholy that threatened to overtake her, Risa strode to her bedroom. She thought Eduardo had been as surprised as she at Nate's awkward explanation that he had to get home because of "family matters." It had appeared as if he knew little more about the man's personal life than she did. Nate had promised to call her if he were able to make it back to the station house later, but she'd known even as he'd made the promise that no call would be forthcoming. And once the captain had left, there had been nothing keeping her downtown.

Stripping off her clothes, she changed into a pair of shorts and a tee. The house next door had been unoccupied since last winter, when Hannah's neighbor and friend who'd lived there had died. But it had a basketball hoop, and she'd spent many an hour rehabbing her shoulder by taking shot after shot at the ancient rim. She grabbed the worn ball from her closet and headed out the door.

Thirty minutes later, her shirt was drenched with perspiration, her muscles weeping from exertion, but her head was clear. Her mood more cheerful. There was nothing as happily mindless as the grueling drill of three-point practice, midrange shots, grab the rebound, lay-up, and repeat. She lost track of time. Lost track of thoughts. Just focused on muscle, movement, and response. Over and over again.

Finally weary, she bent over, resting her hands on her knees, lungs heaving, and a wave of contentment settling over her. Exercise had always been able to bring her peace.

And with it, escape.

Applause sounding nearby had her rearing straight, jerking around in the direction of the noise. A short, stout man, grinning hugely, stood between the cracked driveway and the house. "That was amazing. Absolutely incredible. Like . . ." His eyes rolled upward as he seemed to search for description. "Like watching Xena the Warrior Princess practice for battle. Knife, sword, hand-to-hand, bow and . . ."

Risa dribbled the ball rhythmically with her left hand while she surveyed him. "It's basketball," she reminded him, and wondered if there was a nearby mental facility he might have wandered away from. He looked like an eighties porn star, with the heavy gold chains and rings and his shirt opened halfway down the front, showing a thicket of curly chest hair. The vest he sported was meant to be fashionable. Probably. But it was too tight for his portly frame and instead managed to make him look like a sausage breaking free of its casing. "No weapons in sight." Although she'd once broken a guy's nose by slamming a basketball to his face, she'd matured since then. And learned far more effective ways to take down a man who was intent on changing her very emphatic no to a yes.

"Chandler the Handler, right? Watching you just now, I knew it had to be you. Penn State hasn't had a player since who could match you with the basketball."

She winced a little at the old nickname. "That was a long time ago." Turning, she released a hook shot. Jogged over to scoop up the rebound. "Another lifetime."

"I remember going to the Penn State–Ohio game." His dreamy tone was the sort some men reserved for their cars. "Usually I just watched on TV, but I was taking film classes and it was my turn to videotape the game. That Mokey Hollis from Ohio. Tall hillbilly-looking gal with shoulders like a linebacker? She'd been fouling you hard the whole game, and they weren't calling anything. Hooked you around the throat when you were going for a lay-up and laid you flat. Ref couldn't find his whistle. The home crowd was screaming for blood. You couldn't get off the floor. Remember that?"

The memory wasn't an especially fond one. "I remember."

"The coach wanted to take you out of the game but you refused. You went on to score a double-double. Eighteen rebounds and twenty-nine points. Your record still stands."

Observing him more closely, she could feel tension returning to her muscles. Switching the ball to her right hand, she bounced it slowly. No fan she'd ever met had a memory like that, at least when it came to women's basketball. But it would be easy enough to dig through old stats. Watch old footage to get enough details to strike up a conversation.

But for what possible reason?

"Who are you?" she asked bluntly.

He looked surprised. Then, oddly, hurt. A moment later he shrugged and thrust out his hand. "Jerry Muller. Northeast High? We graduated the same year. Well, actually I was a year ahead but was a few credits short. Ended up graduating with your class. That's probably why you don't remember me."

She crossed to give his hand a shake. "That must be it." That and the fact she'd graduated in a class of over eight hundred.

He smoothed back his thinning brown hair. "I didn't even know you still lived in Philadelphia. Kind of lost track of you after your knee injury your senior year at Penn State."

Jerry Muller seemed to have kept pretty close tabs on her for someone whose existence she'd been ignorant of until ten minutes ago.

"I don't." Although she'd been born and raised in the city, nothing about Philly had ever felt like home to her. She pointed at her mother's house. "My mom still lives here."

He looked poleaxed. She wondered if he were really that good an actor. Normal people didn't have her innate suspicion of strangers. But then, she hadn't been *normal* since she was five.

"Your mother is Hannah? Hannah . . ." He seemed to be waiting for her to supply the last name. When she didn't, he came up with it on his own. "Hannah Blanchette." He jerked a thumb at the house next to the drive. "This is my mom's house. Eleanor Dobson?"

Her defenses lowered a fraction. She'd met the woman only once, but her mother was still heartbroken over her friend's death. "I'm sorry about your loss."

"Yeah." His face fell a little as his gaze lingered on the house. "I only had time to stay long enough in February to make the funeral arrangements. I had a film in production and had to get back. This is the first chance I've had to return. Just got in last night. I need to get the house cleaned out so I can put it on the market, but . . . it's harder than I expected. Going through her things, I mean."

"I can imagine." She could, too well. There had been two occasions in the past when she'd feared she'd be doing the same for Hannah. Twice when her latest scumbag husband had nearly beaten the woman to death. After the last time, she'd made sure the man would never harm her mother again. Having her eventually die of old age would be a blessing, after the death she'd barely been delivered from.

But this man wouldn't understand that. Few would.

"I've been using the hoop occasionally." She gestured toward the battered rim. "Didn't realize anyone would be around. I won't bother you again."

His smile was back. He waved away her response. "No problem. I just wanted to see who was out here. Never expected it to be you, though." He shook his head. "Chandler the Handler, Big Ten Player of the Year, in my driveway. Wow."

Embarrassed, she began making her escape. "Thanks for the use of the hoop. Maybe I'll see you again before you leave."

His face lit up like a kid's at Christmas. "That'd be great. I'd like that."

As she turned to walk swiftly to her mother's house, it occurred to her that snippets of her past had a way of ambushing her when she least expected it. Basketball was all that had saved her at one time. But she doubted she could go anywhere else in the state and be recognized as a former NCAA all-star athlete.

As memories went, that one seemed harmless, if distant. And she wondered as she walked back into the house when that part of her life had begun to seem so very far away.

––––––––

"I'm sorry, Nate. Tucker isn't here."

A splinter of ice-cold fear pierced his heart. Nate stared hard at Debbie Lipsky's freckled face and prayed he'd misheard her. "Not here?"

"Kristin came for him about an hour ago." She looked

uncertain. Debbie had been babysitting Tuck for three years. She knew some of the backstory about his mother. "She usually does pick him up, and you didn't mention that you'd be back for him." Her voice faltered. "Should I have called you first?"

His throat felt tight. It took effort to force an even tone. "No, that's all right. Sounds like Kristin and I just got our wires crossed. How was his day?"

But he wasn't really focused on the journal the woman showed him. She kept careful daily notes on all the children in her care. His mind was on her earlier words.

So Kristin was back. She hadn't been home this morning. Hadn't been answering her cell. No surprise there. He'd gotten Tucker up earlier than usual in order to get him to the babysitter on time. In turn, Debbie saw that he got to school each morning. He hadn't seen this sort of behavior from his sister in over a year.

But he'd seen plenty of it before that.

He left after assuring Debbie once again that she'd done nothing wrong. And then drove home with a baseball-sized ball of lead sitting in his chest. He'd been to hell and back with Kristin, but those times were behind them.

He had the thought and tried the entire trip home to convince himself that it was true.

But the wave of relief that hit him when he pulled into his drive and saw Kristin's slightly dilapidated red Mazda in the open garage called him a liar. She must have been dropped off at home, then taken it to pick up Tuck. The fact barely registered. His muscles tensed at the thought of another confrontation with his sister. Kristin's journey on and off the wagon had been a long and arduous one. And trust was harder to rebuild each time it was broken.

They both had cause to know that.

He parked in the drive and, hearing Tucker in the backyard, headed in that direction. The gate in the six-foot fence he'd erected around the perimeter took a moment to open. He'd made sure the lock was Tucker proof. Sometimes it gave him a bit of trouble, too.

The picture that met his eyes when he walked through the gate had some of the tension easing from him. Utter normalcy. At least on the surface. Tuck was swinging, his face tipped skyward, a beatific smile on his face. Kristin had her arms folded across her chest as she watched him. It was chilly enough for a jacket. The child had a hoodie zipped up but Nate's sister was wearing jeans and a tee. Her long hair, as dark as his own, hung loose to her shoulders.

Experience had taught him to play the scene low-key. "Hey." He strolled up to his younger sibling.

"Hi." Her glance slid by him.

"I just left Debbie's. I didn't know you were picking Tucker up."

"I pick him up every afternoon." The words were couched in defensiveness.

He could feel his muscles tighten again. "You do." He gave a slow nod. "Thing is, you usually drop him off in the morning, too. You didn't, so I didn't know what to expect this afternoon."

Her lips tightened. "Let it go, Nate. Just this once, let it go."

He blew out a breath, wished for a beer. "Know what time I got home last night? Close to midnight."

She looked at him then, her eyes wide and worried. "Midnight? I thought . . ." Biting her lip, her words trailed off.

"How long was he alone?" It took a great deal of care to make sure there was no censure in his tone.

"I figured you'd be home anytime. I never dreamed . . . Was he asleep?"

His gaze held hers. "What do you think?"

Kristin hugged herself tighter and returned to watching her son. "I would have asked if you'd been here."

"He can't be left alone, Kris. No five-year-old can, but Tucker especially. He needs constant supervision."

"Do you think I don't get that?" When the boy frowned and looked in their direction, Kristin smiled and waved at him. Then she lowered her voice. "I needed a break. Sometimes I just need time for myself. If that makes me weak, if that makes me *unfit*, then there you go."

It was like feeling his way in a minefield. He was never certain which words would result in detonation. "Understood. He can be a handful at times. But there's a list of trustworthy babysitters next to the phone. You could have called one . . ."

She laughed, an ugly, bitter sound that was so at odds with her youthful looks. "Not from Tucker. At least not only from him. I needed a break from *you*."

He shoved his hands into the pockets of his suit coat. Was reminded when the jacket pulled open that he hadn't taken off the shoulder harness and weapon to lock them in the trunk as he normally did. He narrowed his eyes against the glare of the sinking sun and said nothing for a few minutes. Because it was never wise to arm Kristin with more ammunition to use against him, he wouldn't let her know how deeply her words wounded.

"Well," he managed finally. "You're not exactly the first woman to tell me that. Although the last one used a bit more finesse." His attempt at humor fell flat.

Her jaw was quivering. And he felt his usual flare of panic at the thought of a female's ensuing tears. "I've been checking in to classes at the local community college."

Staggered, he could only stare at her. "What? When?"

She lifted a shoulder, rubbed fiercely at one eye. "Think I want to work at KFC for the rest of my life? I thought I had a good chance at a couple scholarships they offer. Actually thought that for once in my life, something would go my way. I was wrong. I didn't get either of them."

It took a moment to gather his fragmented thoughts. He had no idea she'd even considered returning to college. "Honey, if you want to enroll for classes, I can help with tuition . . ."

"I don't *want* your help!" Her tone was no less ferocious for being quiet. "Don't you understand how tired I am of Saint Nate riding to the rescue? Of depending on you for *everything*? You cast a damn large shadow, big brother, and I've lived in it all my life. I'm sick of it. Sick to death of being the fucked-up mess of a sister that the perfect all-star, hero big brother has to rescue."

His own temper bubbled to the surface. "Watch your mouth around him." He wasn't going to get drawn into the familiar argument. It never failed to tug on dual emotions of anger and guilt. And he was *trying*, for chrissakes. Shouldn't he get credit for that?

"That's right." Her mouth pulled down wryly. She shoved the tips of her fingers into the pockets of her jeans. "You're the responsible one. You're the only one with Tucker's best interests at heart."

"Well, I'm not the one that walked out and left a disabled five-year-old alone at night," he snapped. He cursed himself as soon as the words left his tongue. As soon as he saw the bleak expression in his sister's eyes.

"You ought to be thanking me. Last night just gave you more material for your lawyer's case file. You are going to tell him about that, right? Use it to try and take my son away from me for good?"

His throat was tight. "That's not what I want." What he wanted was to believe Kristin was off alcohol forever. That she was ready to make the kind of decisions that meant she could be trusted with Tuck's welfare. That Nate and she could shake free of the slights of their childhoods and have a real relationship.

But if he'd learned one thing, it was that you didn't always get what you wanted.

She walked by him. He heard her a moment later fumbling with the lock on the gate. But he didn't go to help. She'd made it pretty clear what she thought of his assistance.

Bleakly, he watched his nephew swing higher and higher, and wondered why the most complex, intricate case at work always seemed simple in comparison to his family dynamics.

A hand clapped him on the shoulder, and he jerked around, already going for his weapon. Seeing Hans behind him, Johnny relaxed, but only a little. "Motherfucking Christ. That's a good way to get yourself killed."

The older man had the balls to laugh. "Shit, you're jumpy. If this place makes you so nervous, let's go inside."

They were in the alley next to their usual bar. Johnny didn't want to be seen inside again so soon. He knew paranoia had him by the short hairs, but shit, the situation called for a little paranoia.

And what he had to tell Hans couldn't be overheard by anyone.

"You came alone, right?" He peered past Hans into the street in front of the tavern. The others were spooked enough. They didn't need to hear this. Especially Jonas.

"Christ." Hans eyed him carefully, the humor fading from his expression. "What's going on? I've never seen anything get you this worked up before."

"Worked up?" He gave a short laugh, dug in his pocket for a pack of cigarettes. He'd been chain-smoking waiting here for Hans to show up. "Yeah. You might get worked up, too, after you hear what I have to say. You told me to check in with Sean, right? And you were going to call Johnson. You ever do that? Get in touch with him?"

Hans accepted the cigarette Johnny offered and the light. Drawing in deeply, he exhaled a long stream of smoke. "Tried. The cell number I had for him was disconnected. Haven't had time to track down his new one yet."

"Don't bother. He doesn't have a new number." Johnny broke off to light his own cigarette. Noted with a tinge of disbelief that his hand was shaking. Just a little. "He's dead."

"What?" Hans's jaw dropped. "You're shittin' me."

Shaking his head, Johnny told him the rest. "Car accident eight months ago. Went off a bridge on a gravel road in the next county. His widow has no idea why he was even there. And get this." He used the cigarette to point for emphasis. "The newspaper reports it as a 'fiery car crash.' If the accident didn't kill him, the fire afterward sure as hell did."

"Fire." Hans stared at him through a drift of smoke. Then he shook his head. "Okay. That happens. Cars go up after a bad wreck. Took a couple of those calls myself, back in my rookie days."

"Yeah, I would have thought the same thing if I hadn't tried calling Sean first. Same deal." Just the memory had ice water washing through his veins. "Cell number belonged to someone else. Couldn't find a new one for him, so I went to the Internet, right? Think I'll use white pages and start tracking him down. His name pops right up on the search page." Because he needed the nicotine, he took a long drag before continuing. "In the obituaries."

"Fuck me," Hans whispered. Johnny had the man's attention now.

"Want to know how he died? Want to guess?" Johnny gave him a caustic grin. "House fire. Killed him and his wife five months ago."

Hans was silent. Taking quick puffs off the cigarette. Barely exhaling before he drew on it again. Then finally, "You're sure about this."

"Damn straight. Read all the online news reports I could find about each incident."

Dropping the cigarette butt, the other man ground it beneath the toe of his shoe, his movements slow and methodical. For the first time he looked old to Johnny. Every one of his nearly sixty years, and then some. "Because people have the same name. See that all the time where someone is being dunned because someone else with that name has bad credit. Or a record. Or . . ."

"Jesus H. Christ, you think I'm an idiot?" For a minute Johnny had his doubts about whether Hans was. "Pull up their obits yourself, if you don't believe me. They both list their service to the city of Philadelphia. It's them. And I don't care what the official report reads for each, it was murder."

"Christ Jesus." Hans wiped his brow, and Johnny knew he wasn't imagining the real fear in the man's eyes. "That means whoever is torching members of the John Squad has gotten five of us so far. Picking us off like ducks in that stupid carnival game."

"Not anymore." A little calmer now, Johnny dropped the stub of his cigarette and let it burn out on the ground. He lit another, then said, "I'll tell you one thing, I'm not waiting around with my dick in my hand for the guy to choose me next, you know?"

"I see a few scenarios. You mentioned a couple the other night. One is that our business partners somehow got organized—" Hans waved away any objection Johnny might make. "Somehow . . . and put this all together. Decided to take us all out, keep a larger piece of the pie themselves. They don't consider the protection we've provided them every time one of them does something stupid and lands in lockup. They think short-term, and go cowboy. Problem with that idea is these dirtballs spend more time shooting each other than they do talking and comparing notes. They'd be more likely to knock the next guy off, take over his territory, and get all of *that* pie. I also don't see it being their suppliers who got involved. Makes no difference to them one way or another."

He held his hand out in silent demand. Johnny lit another cigarette for him. "Maybe we're giving them too much credit. It could just be one of them that put it together. He goes to the others, says, 'Hey, I'll take care of those cops for you and I'll take two-thirds of their share. More for each of you.'"

"Maybe. Maybe." Hans was concentrating fiercely. "But why not just take us out? Shit, follow us to a call and do a drive-by shooting as we get out of the car. Isn't going to raise any more hell than lighting up cops one at a time."

"See that's what I'm saying." This is why he'd called Hans in the first place. The man could reason things through. He didn't let fear color his thinking. "Why the human torches? Offing cops is going to bring a shitload of attention to bear anyway, but doing it like this? He's trying to prove something. Can't be one of those dickwads from the street. Doing it this way takes too much finesse."

"Yeah." Hans brought the cigarette to his lips. Blew out a cloud and waved it away from Johnny. "Finesse. We can't discount them, since they have the most to gain. But maybe we're making this too complicated. We're assuming none of us ever talked about our deals. With anyone. Not to a wife. A son. A partner."

Johnny stopped breathing for a moment. Such was the sacredness of the silence invoked by the group, the thought had never occurred. "Fastest way to end up in cuffs." Or dead. Because if he ever heard of one of the members talking, he'd personally put a bullet in him.

The older man gave him a humorless smile. "So maybe whoever hears about it bides his time. Works out the details for a way to take over the entire sweet deal for himself. And this is how he chooses to do it. For whatever reason."

"Okay, I can see if one of us talked to someone." Even if the thought of that sort of betrayal had his chest going tight. "But to have given up all our names?"

"Just throwing out possibilities."

"And ignoring the obvious," Johnny retorted. "That it's one of us."

"Fuck that." Hans pointed the cigarette at him. "*Fuck* that. I've trusted these guys for over two decades. And now I have to wonder which one is targeting us? To what, take over the whole operation? That's too much exposure. One of us would never risk it."

"Maybe it's not about the money. Maybe it's conscience. Hell, maybe one of them got religion." But one of them had had religion all along, he recalled. Hadn't stopped Jonas from taking the money, though, had it? Somehow money always trumped God, when it came right down to it. "You can do what you want, but I'm taking a closer look at some of the squad. Maybe I'll hear something about one of them having a gambling problem. Or their kid has cancer." His imagination deserted him at that point. Because even those scenarios couldn't have made him turn on the group. "Hell, maybe one has IA up their ass, and they gave us up to save themselves."

Hans made a rude sound. "Oh, now IA is killing cops?" He smiled then, his usual good humor returning. "Besides, you're the only one I know of under an active IA investigation."

"What, that excessive use of force bullshit? Just a punk trying to weasel out of an attempted murder rap."

"So you didn't kick him in the balls once you cuffed him?"

"Well, yeah," he drawled, recalling the moment with pleasure. "Think I want the little asshole reproducing?" They laughed, a little longer and louder than was warranted. Two men in desperate need of some relief.

After a minute, Hans asked, "I hear that McGuire got himself appointed lead on the task force."

Johnny grunted. He'd heard the same thing. "I've never met any of them on it. You?"

"One of them. He isn't giving up much yet but I'll keep working on him. We need to keep tabs on how close they're getting. He did say they haven't connected the victims yet."

"*Yet.*"

"We take what we can get, Johnny boy. Maybe we should meet up again in a few days. Compare notes."

"Good idea." They could confer before calling the others together. Decide what to tell them. What to keep quiet.

They walked toward the street. A drunk lurched around the corner, nearly plowed into them. Johnny gave him a shove and the man fell to his knees, cursing him in a slurred voice.

"Tell you one thing," Hans said. "With this idea of yours that it's one of us? Next time you call, I won't be meeting you alone in a dark alley."

The screams were hideous. They reverberated through her skull, bouncing and echoing, one after the other. Risa burrowed deeper into the covers, trying to muffle the cries. The nearby tree swayed in rhythm with the cries, its twisted branches reaching out as if to extend assistance.

The heat from the flames seared her skin. The smell from burned flesh filled her nostrils. Her lungs.

And through it all, the nude figure danced before the flames in a frenetic exultation at what he'd wrought.

Her eyes opened, the breath sawing in and out of her chest. And the relief of discovering it was just a dream almost overtook the dread of knowing they were back. Really back. Her breath shuddered out of her lungs at the realization. It hadn't been a one-time thing. This had been a near duplicate of the one she'd had the night before last.

She sat up, used the sheet to wipe the perspiration from her face. There had been nothing new in this rendition. Except for the fact that she'd been closer. Not just a passive watcher, but near enough to smell. Hear. Feel.

Pushing her damp hair away from her face, she discovered her hand shaking. Goose bumps broke out on skin that was still overly warm to the touch. She crossed her arms to rub at the raised flesh. And forced herself to concentrate. To examine each minute detail and try to draw information from it.

Coming to a sudden decision, she surged from the bed, found her legs unsteady. Flipping on the lamp on her bedside table, she tugged open the lone drawer.

The tablet and pencil had sat unused the entire time she'd been here. There was a time when she'd thought—hoped—

they'd go unused forever. And the possibility had elicited twin spires of hope and despair.

Shoving aside the thought, she drew out the drawing pad. Flipped it open. Better not to think. Better to dwell on the individual elements of the dream. They lost power that way, extracted from the whole. They'd absorb her for a time. Until the sketch was complete, a vivid reminder of what her unconscious had wrought.

It had been this way for nearly three decades. Since the first time she'd pointed to a newscast showing a murder suspect and announced to Hannah and whoever the boyfriend had been at the time that that was the bad man from her recent nightmare.

Her head began to throb, a common enough souvenir from the dreams. She worked through the headache, anxious to have the task done. When she was on a case, she treated each sketch as part of her personal investigative file. After the drawing was complete she'd jot down notes, impressions.

Like the figure was definitely male. In good shape. More than that she couldn't be certain. At least not until the next time the vision recurred.

She knew from experience it wouldn't be long. And if they were going to torture her sleep, they may as well be put to good use.

That idea is what had driven her to join the academy in the first place. That desperate need to make the psychic episodes useful. If she was never going to be normal, if she was going to spend her life a freak, the dreams damn well would count for something.

Chapter 7

Risa had meant to get an early start that morning. It wasn't as if she'd gotten much sleep the night before. Her mouth pulled up humorlessly as she waved at Darrell behind the bulletproof glass and quickened her step toward the conference room.

But she hadn't counted on her mother being awake. Hannah hadn't even been to bed yet, although the bus had probably had her home by two A.M. "Too much to do and not enough time to do it in," she'd told Risa. But it had given them a few minutes to sit down and visit. Their paths hadn't crossed much in the last couple days. As a result, Risa had been later than she'd wanted in calling for a cab. Then it had taken longer than expected at the car rental agency. She couldn't depend on taxis to get to and from the station daily.

Slipping into the conference room, she found it full. Nate was talking and Morales was standing silently in the front of the room. Rather than call attention to herself, she leaned a shoulder against the wall just inside the door and listened.

". . . be pursuing the identities of the men on the tape, see if that connects to our case. We've also got a lead on another person who was in the park the morning Christiansen was discovered. I'll be following up."

"What about the autopsy report?"

The voice calling from the back sounded familiar. With a glance, Risa determined it was Brandau.

"Nothing yet. Hopefully today. Let's start with report outs on yesterday's assignments. Brandau and Recker, what do you got?"

"Not much." Cass did the talking this time. "We visited Parker's widow and showed her pictures of Detective Christiansen. She'd never seen him before. Although she obviously couldn't say whether Roland knew him, she could tell us he'd never been to the house and she didn't recognize his name." She stopped reading her notes to look at Nate. "Except from the newspapers, of course." Without waiting for his nod, she went on. "We're still trying to track down the ex-wife of Sherman Tull. Got a lead on her from the neighbor across the street from his house. Apparently the women were friends. She claims the ex never made it back for the funeral." She shrugged. "Anyway we have an address to start with on her."

"You canvassed the neighbors? Showed pictures of the three men?"

"Just Parker's and Tull's. No one recognized them. We'll hit Christiansen's neighborhood today."

Nate's gaze moved on. "Shroot, what about you and your team?"

"Combing through the case files is going to take a while." Shroot was the tall, lanky detective with ginger-colored hair, Risa observed. His voice had a distinctive southern drawl, causing her to wonder how he'd ended up in the City of Brotherly Love. "We've found a couple things to tug on. Tull and Christiansen were once called to testify on a case against a con artist running scams on the elderly. Parker busted a B and E guy, one Tommy Naigle, about ten years ago, and seven years later Christiansen and his partner brought him in for the same charge. Near as we can tell, Naigle is still serving his stretch but we'll follow up."

"Do that. There's a lot of material to dig through. All these men had long careers with the department. That's a lot of arrests, a lot of potential perps harboring grudges."

"Edwards."

Risa studied Nate as he moved on to the next pair of detectives. He'd managed to shave that morning. If she had to choose, she preferred the look he'd sported yesterday. The stubble had added a touch of the uncivilized. The unfamiliar. Today he was solidly back in command. The same controlled, if slightly impatient, detective who'd shown up on her mother's doorstep a couple mornings ago.

"Nothing in their schools, for sure. We checked their records. Tull and Christiansen graduated from the same police academy, but years apart. None of them pulled an instructor stint in the academy, either. Didn't want to go at Christiansen's widow, with the funeral coming up. But his obit lists the United Methodist on Arch Street. Each of the ceremonies has been held in different churches."

"Hoy, what'd you and Mendall find?"

But mention of the upcoming funeral distracted Risa for a moment. The ceremony would have a massive department turnout. As such, it presented an almost irresistible scene for the suspect.

Her attention turned belatedly to the detective speaking. A pair was walking up to Nate. The speaker held two DVDs in his hand. "This may be something that will help. Mind if we use the TV?" They continued to the unit in the corner of the room as the one continued talking. "So Christiansen's wife said he was running to the convenience store to get milk, right? Surveillance tapes had him inside the store. Got a few other customers in there, too, but no one in the parking lot. But here, I'll show you."

Several minutes passed as the two of them fiddled with the TV and DVD player. Finally the original speaker stabbed a finger at the screen. "Plenty of activity out front of the parking lot, right?" An older man walking a Boston terrier that bore a startling resemblance to his owner. A shaggy-haired skateboarder. A guy with his arm around a woman, both of them in hoodies, and in the midst of what looked like a disagreement. A figure in a Windbreaker, hood pulled up over his head passed. "So a minute goes by." He began the recorder again. "Two minutes." The time stamp from the original tape was displayed at the bottom of the screen. "Now look." The DVD was paused again. "See that?"

Risa pushed away from the wall, straining to see. Nate was partially blocking her view by the position he'd taken up before the screen. "The shadow? Does it move?"

The detective started the recorder again. "It surely does. Right there."

"I'll be damned." A murmur rippled through the room. And although Risa hadn't seen the shadow they'd spoken of, she saw the back car door of a late model Malibu ease open. Close again. A moment before a customer exited the store and headed to a short-boxed pickup truck.

"For the record, Christiansen was driving a 2010 navy Chevy Malibu that night. License plate matches the vehicle we see in the lot." Nate gave the two detectives a grim smile. "Good work. You checked the traffic cameras on his route there and back?"

"We did," the shorter, rounder of the two detectives put in. "Funny thing, he took a different route from the convenience store. One that didn't pass any nearby streets with those cameras on them."

"And one that didn't lead home," Nate put in. "Okay, let's center on the convenience store and fan outward. Get a map of all the traffic cameras in that area, and plot out which ways he could have taken to surpass all of them and get to that park. Maybe the car passed some other camera that caught a glimpse of it. An ATM camera or one mounted at a store."

"Has Christiansen's car been found yet?" It was Cass's question.

"No." The Captain spoke for the first time. "We've got his and Parker's vehicle descriptions flagged and nothing has shown up yet. The unknown subject might have disposed of them in the Delaware River. Or he may have abandoned them in a part of town where he could be assured no report would ever be filed."

Risa had had the same thought. Why take the chance of possibly being seen running a car into the river when there were a number of areas of the city where one could just leave it and walk away? The vehicle would be stripped, stolen, or land in a chop shop in a matter of hours. Any of the scenarios would destroy whatever trace evidence the UNSUB might have left behind.

Nate wrapped up the briefing by running through the assignments. It left her wondering what he had planned for them to work on today. She had a few ideas, but she still didn't feel like she knew him well enough to predict how he'd react to her suggesting them. Tiptoeing around fragile law enforcement egos had to be one her least favorite aspects of her job.

She waited for the detectives to shuffle out of the room. A couple of them gave her a quizzical look, as if wondering what her role there was. With her visitor ID, they'd know she wasn't on the force. And McGuire had made no effort to introduce her to the group and explain her place on the team. Maybe that was for the best. She wasn't sure he was comfortable with her presence on the task force himself, although he'd never given any indication that he resented her.

Of course, knowing of her personal relationship with his captain, he'd be careful to make nice, lest he jeopardize his standing as lead investigator on the task force.

She made her way over to where he was conversing with Morales. The captain shifted to make room for her to join them. "I assume you'll be talking to the ME today," he was saying.

"I haven't gotten a call from Liz, but I figure I've given her enough time to come up with some answers. I plan to drop by the morgue this morning on my way to see Christiansen's widow."

Eduardo nodded. "That's a good idea. You can be damn sure his wife will have plenty of questions."

"Then let's hope I get a few answers for her."

Risa fell into step beside him as they left the room. "So it sounds like you've got an agenda worked out for today."

He took a package of gum from his pocket and held it up questioningly. When she shook her head, he took a piece out and replaced the package. "Couple things so far. You have something in mind?"

They entered the squad room and the noise level rose accordingly. She swerved in the direction of his office. "I'd like to follow up on those guys that popped on the search yesterday."

"I did a little more digging on that last night."

But she was focused on his early words. It took effort to keep her voice mild. "Last night?"

"Yeah, I came back to work around seven thirty." Seeing her expression, he raised a hand placatingly. "I know I said I'd call you, but you neglected to leave your cell number with me."

And he'd neglected to ask for it, she thought wryly. Her bad. If she wanted to be kept in the loop on this investigation, she was clearly going to have to make all the overtures. She put her palm out.

He looked at it. Then at her. "You decided you wanted gum after all?"

"Give me your cell phone. I'll log in the number."

They'd come to his office. Without waiting for him, she opened the door and walked inside.

"I'll do it. What is it?" He took the cell from his pocket. She took it from his hand.

"Don't want to take the chance of you punching it in wrong," she said blandly.

"I didn't deliberately exclude you."

"Yeah, yeah." She dropped in a chair and quickly added her number to his contacts. Then she took out her phone and did the same for his number. Handing his back to him, she said, "There. Now there won't be any excuse next time."

His eyes gleamed. "I keep late hours but I don't expect you to live the case. You'll have to let me know when you've had enough. Given your unofficial capacity and all."

She cocked a brow at the arrogance in the words. She had a feeling they were the first truly unguarded ones he'd spoken to her. "My capacity on this case won't be an issue." At least not for him. The issues it was causing *her*, while she slept, would continue whether she was key to the investigation or not. Experience had taught her that.

But her involvement would make them increase in frequency. In intensity. The acknowledgment had her throat drying. The only thing that had ever made the dreams worthwhile was using them to bring about justice. For years she'd taken solace from that.

She just wasn't certain that was true any longer.

Risa shifted her knees out of the way so he could pass en

route to his desk. "So catch me up. What'd you accomplish last night? Did you hear anything from the arresting officers regarding ID on the Juicy trio?"

He cracked a smile at that. She stared, surprised. It softened his features and made him more approachable. And devastatingly attractive. Who would have guessed that Nate McGuire harbored a lone masculine dimple? Or that it could provoke such a maddeningly female response in her?

"Catchy. Sounds like a musical group." He sat down and rifled through a stack of papers on his desk until he found the three depicting the hits he'd found yesterday. "Nothing from any of the arresting officers yet. But I took these pics by Crowley's address last night. You can imagine his enthusiasm when he saw me again." His expression said the man's lack of welcome bothered him not at all. "He ID'd this guy as the one he scored the weed from, Dwayne Jersey." He turned around the photo in question so she could see it. "And the way he was talking, I got the impression he knows him a whole lot better than he let on to us yesterday. I also found out that one of the three, Fox, is a guest of the state and will be for another six years."

Her expression must not have looked pacified, because his eyes gleamed. "Then I combed through the ViCAP files I got back until my eyes bled. Still wishing you'd spent the night here?"

She ignored the question. "Once we make a swing by the morgue, maybe we'll have enough to resubmit a request to ViCAP."

"I need something that will narrow down the search." He thumped his index finger against the thick file folder on his desk. "You can take a look at these if you want. A pair of fresh eyes can't hurt. I only got a couple dozen hits the first time I submitted a request, so when I resubmitted I cast a wider net."

Risa nodded. In the interest of thoroughness, she always made the first ViCAP request fairly broad. In the beginning of a serial case, one never knew which details of the crimes would change. Which ones were part of the offender's signature and which were merely enacted as part of his MO. "I'd like to go over them." Sometimes something would jump out at her, some fairly innocuous detail that matched an element from the dream. Something that might be hard to explain to her colleagues but which would have her focusing on a certain subject more thoroughly. "I'd like a copy of the case file, too. Include the ViCAP requests in it, crime scene photos, and updated briefings as they come in. I often work on the profile at night from home. Those details will change as we acquire more information on the subject."

He was already shaking his head. "I'll have a copy made, but it stays here. And when you leave at night, it'll be locked in that file cabinet there." He jerked his head in the direction of a battered metal government-issue piece sitting in the corner of the room. "The brass were clear on the need for keeping this investigation under wraps."

Risa eyed him. His tone had been final, that hard jaw of his angled. Clearly he was used to not having his orders questioned. But she was a little out of practice at making nice on a case.

"That's fine." She kept her words mild as she took out her cell again. "I understand that you don't have the authority to clear it." Maybe that last verbal jab was a bit much, but there was something about his unshakeable air of command that had her wanting to jar it. Just a little. She quickly looked for a contact she'd recently added and rang the number. It was a moment before the call was answered.

"Eduardo." Because she was looking, she saw the way Nate's dark eyes heated and narrowed. "I'd like a copy of the case file, photos, updates from the briefings . . ." She stopped when the man immediately agreed to have one started for her. "I'm planning to work on the profile at night from home. Is that a problem? Thanks."

There was a muscle ticking in his jaw. Probably came from being clenched so tightly. But he said nothing as he took the ViCAP folder and shoved it into his desk drawer and locked it.

The phone on his desk buzzed. Still without looking at her, he answered it, listened briefly, before saying, "Thanks for the heads-up."

After a moment it became clear that he wasn't going to share the details of the call with her. Risa's mouth quirked. So there was temper beneath that professional surface. She'd suspected as much. And if she had the stray urge to discover what else lurked there, she'd firmly push it aside. She didn't mix her personal and professional lives. Her one attempt at marriage had shown her what a recipe for disaster that was.

When the knock sounded at the door, Nate seemed to be expecting it. He rose, rounded the desk, and opened it.

"McGuire?" The man on the other side would have looked perfectly at home on the streets, with his baggy jeans, torn black T-shirt, and shaggy hair. A couple days' growth of beard shadowed his jaw. But as Nate stepped aside to allow him to enter, Risa caught sight of the PPD detective's shield clipped to the pocket of his shirt.

"Detective Randolph. I appreciate the face-to-face."

The name had Risa straightening in her chair. She'd seen it on an arrest report just yesterday. They exchanged a handshake. Nate gestured toward her. "Marisa Chandler, outside consultant on this case."

Randolph's gaze sharpened. "Consultant? What exactly do you do?"

Risa offered him a bland smile. "I consult."

"I left you a message yesterday about a Javon Emmons." Nate's words had the detective's attention returning to him. "We're trying to run down a possible witness who goes by the name of Juicy. Sold someone a little pot in the park where we found the last victim."

The man nodded. "Christiansen."

"Did you know him?"

Randolph shoved his hair back, revealing a diamond stud winking from his earlobe. Although his hair was still dark, the stubble on his jaw was sprinkled liberally with gray. "Naw. Didn't know any of the vics, but there's not a guy on the force that doesn't want the bastard responsible put away for this. Everyone keeps up on the details. That's why I came here instead of calling. Anything I can do to help, you got it."

"We appreciate that."

"So, Emmons." Randolph handed Nate a file folder he carried. "Here's a brief rundown on what I know of him. Where was that park you mentioned, northeast side? He'd have been well outside his area. He operates mainly in the 'hood surrounding Temple University." He gave a dour grin. "Runs an 'enterprise' that encompasses about ten square miles, give or take."

"You put him away for a few years."

The other detective snorted. "Damn few. Some dirtball encroaches on his territory, right? Emmons ties him up, has his goons dip the poor bastard in a vat of acid, as a warning to anyone else with the same idea."

Risa's stomach gave a quick vicious lurch. "Nice."

"Yeah, he's a charmer. How the guy doesn't die isn't the miracle, though. I had Emmons solid for the crime and he walks on appeal." Obviously the memory still rankled.

"Tough break. What happened?"

"Some of the physical evidence went missing from the evidence room and couldn't be used at the next trial." He shrugged. "He's supplied by the Rodriquez family, and they have very deep pockets. I imagine their influence is far reaching, although why they'd give a shit about someone like him, I don't know. He's just a cog in the wheel."

Risa and Nate exchanged a glance. "How big a cog?" she wanted to know.

Randolph lifted a shoulder again. "Too big to bother with selling a little pot to your wit, I'd think. He'd send a runner. You sure you got the right guy?"

"No." Nate smiled wryly and held up the folder the man had given him. "But this might help us figure out who the right guy is."

Randolph half turned to leave. "Well, if your wit was looking to score, there's no shortage of scumbags willing to deal it to him. I run into plenty of high school kids selling dope. The guy you're looking for might not even have a record yet."

"Thanks again for your help."

The other detective nodded. "Like I said, we all want to see you catch who's responsible. You need some eyes on the street, just give me the word."

Risa waited until the door closed behind the man before looking at Nate. "If there's another Juicy out there with no record yet, it'll make the search a bit more interesting. But Crowley identified the other guy, right? Dwayne Jersey."

Nate was already reaching for his cell phone. "I'll give Pelton another call." A few minutes later, he turned on the speaker-phone. "Officer Pelton, this is Lieutenant Detective Nate McGuire calling from the . . ."

"McGuire, I was just going to return your call." There was an almost continuous sound of phones ringing in the back-ground. "Got your message when I got in this morning. I want to do whatever I can to help you catch the bastard kill-ing cops. Just ran down the most recent information I could find on Dwayne Jersey."

"I appreciate that."

"Ah . . ." There was the slight sound of shuffling papers. "You've got his basic info on the arrest sheet you pulled. Hasn't been in trouble with the law recently, at least nothing he's been caught at. Been in trouble of a different sort, though. Word is he had his ass handed to him the other night for hit-ting on the wrong woman at Lil Tony's nightclub."

"What'd you find on him the time you arrested him?"

"Couple pounds of marijuana, a few pills. He didn't go away for it. Did a stint in county lockup because he couldn't pay the fine. I checked with his probation officer and he's not exactly a model of clean living, but he hasn't flunked a drug test yet."

Nate's gaze met hers as he said, "He's been identified as someone who sold some pot in the park where the last victim was found."

"Damn. Christiansen, right? Everyone's talking about the murders. And Jersey might be your guy. The way I hear it, he doesn't deal much with the heavier stuff, but he does move a ton of weed. Unless that last arrest worked a miracle of reha-bilitation."

"Where do we find him?" murmured Risa. Nate narrowed his eyes at her and turned partially away.

"Do you have a current address? I want to verify his whereabouts for a couple mornings ago."

"Sure, I got it right here." Nate scrambled for a scrap of paper on his desk and a pen to write down the address the man recited to him. "But if you're talking about a couple days ago, it wasn't Jersey in that park selling dope."

"How do you know?" Risa and Nate uttered the words simultaneously.

"He's still in the hospital. Has been since Saturday night. Well, early Sunday morning, I guess. That fight at Lil Tony's? Jersey got the crap beat out of him. Way I hear it, he's already had two operations and still has a couple more coming. Guy can't even walk right now."

Risa rose, suddenly impatient for the call to end.

Nate obviously felt the same. "I appreciate the information. It helps."

"Hey, we're all looking to help you any way possible. Let me know if you need something else."

Nate hung up, his face thoughtful. "Crowley lied."

"Obviously." She grabbed her jacket, although the weatherman had promised a return to seasonable temperatures. But given his record, she saw no reason to trust him. What other occupation got to retain their jobs when they were right only half the time? "The question is, why did he lie? Was he just trying to give you a face to go with the name?" She immediately corrected herself. "But that's stupid. He had to know we'd find out."

"But if Jersey hadn't been alibied for the time in question, it would have been Crowley's word against the dealer. We'd have gotten nothing anyway."

"And the real Juicy would never be questioned; hence, he'd never know that Crowley had given him up," Risa concluded. She cocked a brow. "So are you driving or am I?"

That put a hurry in his step. "I am. It's a department-issued car."

"I've driven them before." She waited until he'd locked the door behind them before striding toward the front door.

"Not with me you haven't."

She smiled to herself as she wended her way through the desks and cubicles. "Something tells me you don't trust me, detective."

He grunted. "Don't take it personally. I don't trust anyone."

———

From the quick Google search Risa ran on her phone on the way to see Crowley, Lesser's Plumbing Supply Business was a mom and pop company that had been in operation for fifty years. And given the seamed faces of the gray-haired couple that met them at the scarred service counter, mom and pop were still actively running the store.

"Yes, Samuel Crowley works here." The man's bushy eyebrows drew together. "Why, what's he done?" In an aside he said to the woman, "I told you it was a mistake to hire him, Martha. But oh, no, you said, give him a chance. I knew in my gut that . . ."

"Mr. Crowley hasn't done anything, sir," Risa put in smoothly. The red embroidered name on his crisp blue shirt read BOB. "He's actually helping us in an ongoing investigation."

Her explanation didn't seem to pacify the man's suspicions appreciably. "Person gets mixed up with the police, it's usually because they were where they shouldn't be in the first place."

"Oh, stop it, Bob." Martha's voice was surprisingly strong for someone who looked so frail. They might not be eighty yet, but they were both knocking at its door. "You were part of an investigation a couple years back when our store got broken into. Does that make you a crook?"

"It makes me a victim." The man glared at his wife from behind thick black-framed glasses. "That's a completely different thing. Unless . . ." His attention switched back to the two of them. "Was Sam the victim of a crime?"

"We're not at liberty to discuss it," Risa said gravely. "But if Mr. Crowley chooses to share the details with you, that's up to him." Which left the man clear to feed his employers whatever story he wanted to concoct for them, while skirting the need for Nate and her to tell the couple anything.

The bell over the door rang then, heralding a customer. The man opened his mouth again but Martha shushed him. "You tend to business." Her faded blue eyes shifted to Risa and Nate. "Come with me. I'll take you to Sam."

They followed her down a cramped hallway lined with bulging cardboard boxes to a door with a smoked pane of glass in it. Opening it, she announced, "Sam, you've got visitors." Despite her admonition to her husband, a bit of Bob's suspicion gleamed in her eyes as she aimed a hard stare at the man. "We'll talk later."

But Risa didn't think the promise Martha left them with was the reason for Crowley's sickly pale expression.

"What are you trying to do?" he hissed as the door closed behind Martha. "Make me lose the only shitty job I can find?" His words were no less heated for being whispered. "What'd you tell them? They watch me like a pair of old buzzards anyway."

"I figure that's on you," Nate said unsympathetically. "Couple takes a chance on hiring an ex-con, can't blame them for being mistrusting."

"What do you want?" Crowley's tone might have sounded belligerent if a flash of fear in his eyes didn't accompany it. "I told you everything I knew last night. Did you find Juicy? Ask him about our meet?"

"Not yet." Nate folded his arms and propped his hips against a rickety table piled with file folders. "Wanted to double-check with you before questioning him. Be sure we have the right guy."

"What's to double-check?" Crowley's confidence was returning. Carefully he smoothed a hand over his crimped brown hair, his gaze flicking to Risa for a moment. "I already identified him from the photos. The rest is your job."

"You know what else is our job, Sam?" Her voice was conversational. "Knowing when a jerk-off like you is lying to us. That comes from experience, and unfortunately we have *lots* of it."

Tension settled in the man's thick shoulders. "Listen, is he lying about meeting me there? Because that goes to figure. He's not about to tell the truth if he thinks it's going to get him arrested. And he probably didn't see anything anyway. I got there before he did. Waited a couple minutes for him."

"The details keep changing but you know what stays the same? It's all bullshit." Nate slapped his palm hard against the table he was leaning on. The towers of file folders started to sway. Sam's eyes went wide and he lunged from his desk.

"Dammit, you know how long it took me to organize those?" He ran to the table in time to catch the pile that made a slow topple toward the floor. "Could use some help here!"

"Yeah, see I feel the same way." Nate shot a look at Risa. "How about you?"

She gave a nod, watched Crowley juggle folders in a doomed attempt to save them from hitting the floor. "Yeah, we could use some help, too." Papers spilled as one folder after another slipped from his grasp to hit the floor.

"Fuck!" Crowley kicked one of the folders in frustration. "You guys are nothing but trouble."

"Trouble has a habit of following you around, doesn't it, Crowley?" Nate's tone was hard. "'Course you bring most of it on yourself." He took two photos from his suit jacket pocket and tossed them on the man's desk. "You need another look at these?"

The man barely glanced at them. "I already . . ."

"The guy you ID'd last night has been in the hospital since Sunday. So he sure as hell wasn't meeting you in the park on Monday. You've been jerking me around since I caught up with you."

"The fancy word for 'jerking us around' is obstruction," Risa informed him. "That's what we're going to charge you with, right before we cuff you and march you out the door in front of your former employers. With that and your own admission of buying marijuana, we have enough to send you back to Somerset. And I can guarantee it will be for longer than two years this time."

Giving up on retrieving the folders, Crowley rose, inched back toward his desk. He was sweating now. Beads of perspiration dotted his upper lip, his brow. "Okay, so none of the pics were the Juicy I met with. I figured you'd think I was lying if I said that, so I pointed at one of them." He tried a weak smile, couldn't quite pull it off.

Risa surveyed him consideringly. "You must really be afraid of him."

"I told you, I . . ."

She turned to Nate. "Let's give him one more chance. I'm betting Juicy's number is on his cell phone. We can have him set up a meet, scoop this guy up, and end this thing once and for all."

Crowley dropped heavily into his desk chair, looking ill. "You have no idea what he's capable of. And he didn't have anything to do with what happened in the park. He was only there because I was going to be there anyway so that's where

I arranged to meet him. Honest." He looked from one of them to the other, his eyes wild. "This has nothing to do with him."

"Convince us," Risa advised him.

Crowley licked his lips. "This job . . . it doesn't even pay the rent. I'm supposed to feel lucky someone will let me do their books after my last job, right? But I needed money, and I know this guy . . ."

"Javon Emmons?"

He looked blank at Nate's words. "Who?"

Leaning forward, Nate tapped one of the photos.

"Oh. I just know him by Juicy. We go back a way, back to my college days. If you wanted to score a little, Juicy was the go-to guy, right? We met up a couple times after I got out of Somerset, and maybe I said how it was tough to get a job, you know, with a record. He said maybe he'd have some work for me."

Surprise flickered. Somehow Risa hadn't been expecting this. "You're selling drugs?"

He actually looked shocked. "What? No! God, nothing like that. I'm doing his books."

"His books," Nate repeated carefully.

Crowley lifted a shoulder. "He's a businessman, right? Every business is a balance of profit and expense. I get the feeling he's moved up the ladder some since I knew him from Temple. Dealers work for him now. Part of my job is to figure out what he owes to who so he can pay them."

Risa rubbed her brow. They'd stumbled on something much further reaching than another possible witness to question. "Do you have a copy of his books?"

"Well, not now." He looked anxious. "We were making the exchange the other day in the park. I'd finished them up and given them back to him. I won't talk to him again for a couple weeks. I keep trying to get him to let me put everything on a spreadsheet, and then we could e-mail it back and forth. But he doesn't trust computers. He's afraid someone could hack into his account and get hold of his financial information."

Crowley buried his face in his hands. His voice muffled, he said, "If he finds out I've told you this much, I'm dead. I heard this story about him dropping a guy in a trough of acid." He raised his head then, looked hopeful. "Probably just an exaggeration, right?"

"No, I'm pretty sure that's true." Even as Crowley went ashen, Nate went on. "So were you telling the truth about him getting to the park after you?"

The man hesitated for a moment. "I don't know when he got there," he admitted finally. "I just turned around and there he was. He's creepy that way. If he doesn't want you to, you won't see him."

"Okay." Nate straightened and gave Crowley a small smile. "Thanks for your help. When we talk to him, we'll keep your name out of it. Make it sound like someone else spotted the both of you there."

Crowley chewed his lip. "You sure? 'Cuz maybe it'd sound better if I called him and said how you talked to me and would be coming by. Like I'm warning him."

"Let's let him think that I haven't gotten around to you yet and that you're next on my list." Nate moved toward the door. "We'll be in touch if we need anything else."

Mystified, Risa preceded him out the door and back down the narrow hallway. She sent a blinding smile to the still suspicious-looking Bob and said, "Thank you so much for allowing us a bit of Sam's time. He's been a great help."

Nate waited until they were on the sidewalk before murmuring, "Laying it on a bit thick, weren't you?"

"Not as thick as you were with Crowley at the end." She slanted a look at him. "What are you planning?"

"I'll put out the order for Juicy to be brought in for questioning, but I'm guessing we're not going to get anywhere with him as a possible witness," he admitted, as they started in the direction of where he'd parked the car farther down the street. "The rest of it? Crowley doing his books? I'm turning that over to Morales. Likely he'll contact the captain in Vice. If they can get hold of Emmons' financials, they might be able to build a case on him, maybe even go after his supplier."

"Hopefully this case will stick." She stopped as they reached the car. Annoyance briefly flared. Battled with dark humor.

Someone had dumped a very full litter box on the hood of the dark Crown Vic. Scratched into the driver's door were the words *COPS SUCK*.

Nate looked up and down the street, but the sidewalks were unusually deserted. Blowing out a breath, he surveyed the damage. "Well, shit."

Risa nodded. "Literally."

Chapter 8

"If I were done, I'd have called you, McGuire. Did I call you? I don't believe I did." Liz Chin had to tilt her head up a long way to meet his gaze, but she wasn't fazed by something as unimportant as stature. Her hands were on her hips, her tone sharp. Of course, it was always sharp, usually sarcastic, so Nate couldn't tell if she was truly pissed off or just giving him her usual hard time.

"It's been two days. I've been plenty patient."

She sent him one last glare before relenting. "I expected you yesterday." Her gaze settled on Risa then. "You still around?"

"Obviously."

Nate winced, braced himself for the explosion. But amazingly Liz remained calm. "You're hired as an independent consultant, I hear."

He shot her a narrowed look and she held up a placating hand. "Don't get your boxers in a bunch. I listen, I don't talk. And that outfit she works for isn't exactly low profile." She turned around and started to stride away. He knew her well enough to realize they were supposed to follow.

"The Mindhunters, right?" she threw over her shoulder as

she walked at a surprisingly quick pace. "I heard one of Adam Raiker's scientists speak at a conference I was at a couple years ago. Alfred Jones. Smart guy. And everyone's heard of Raiker."

Nate resisted the urge to hunch his shoulders. No way in hell would he admit he'd never heard of the man or his company until he'd researched both after having one of Raiker's consultants thrust on him. And yeah, it was hard not to be impressed by the man's resume. Or the details of his last case for the bureau.

He'd been captured by the serial child killer he'd trailed to the Louisiana swamps. Been held and tortured for three days before escaping and killing the man. Such was the stuff of legends. But it was the more recent news about Risa's boss that had captured his attention. Four attempts on his life in as many months should have kept him too busy to intervene in a police investigation in Philadelphia. And it was the details behind *those* actions that interested him most about the man.

"What's he like?" The question, directed at Risa, was tossed over Liz's shoulder.

"Who, Jonesy?"

"Jonesy. Yeah, that fits. No, I mean Raiker. I'd like to meet him sometime."

"He's . . . indescribable."

"Not surprising, with his history. Here's your guy. I'm just finishing up on him." Liz opened up the door to one of the morgue's main rooms. It was lined with a half-dozen workstations, each consisting of a large sink, a scale, and a small counter with a surgical light. The exam tables would be rolled out of one of the walk-in refrigerators where the bodies were stored.

What remained of Pat Christiansen lay on the gurney at the first workstation. A quick glance assured Nate that none of the man's organs were sitting on the scale, or worse, mid-dissection on the counter.

"Relax, Nervous Nellie, I've sewn him up already." Liz poked an elbow at Risa. "He hates this place. The first time he came here—"

"I don't think we need to go into that story," he objected.

"—he tossed his cookies in that sink over there." Liz pointed a gloved finger at the third workstation. "And then he blames his weak stomach on the smell. Smelled a lot worse when he left, let me tell you."

"In my defense, I was twenty-two and just out of the academy," he started.

The women shared a grin that would strike fear into the heart of any thinking male. "I know. Guys, right?" Risa said, and the two of them laughed.

He examined the ceiling. "Like it wasn't enough I had to clean five pounds of shit off the hood of my car an hour ago. I have to listen to it here, too."

"What?"

"From one of his many admirers," Risa explained, and the ME laughed again.

Nate eyed them unkindly. In all his years of working with Liz, he'd never heard her laugh. Rarely saw her smile. He should have known both would be as cutting as her speech. "You're as mean as she is," he informed Risa. "And it's a well-known fact that she uses her tongue as a scalpel in here." Although Liz and Cass were friendly enough, he didn't recall Liz ever taking to a newcomer so quickly.

On the other hand, when Risa was laughing at him, it was a helluva lot easier to forget how attractive she was. That wasn't all bad.

"Your patient?" he reminded the ME. "You're done with the autopsy, you said?"

Finally Liz moved toward the exam table. "I'll have a preliminary draft of the report to you by the end of the day. Cause of death is smoke inhalation, but I don't have to tell you he suffered before death."

"How long?" Nate asked softly, his gaze riveted on the remains of the man.

"At least an hour. Maybe a little longer. Let me show you one difference I found from the last two victims." He and Risa moved silently to the end of the table. "I cut the remnants of the clothing off. Some, of course, melted into the flesh. But look here." She pointed to where the man's feet should be. What was there was unrecognizable to Nate. Two shriveled blackened stumps.

"What am I looking at?"

"Had a helluva time cutting the shoes away. Couldn't

separate the leather from the skin," Liz explained. "Like the first two, this one had his arms duct taped behind him. The others were burned more or less uniformly. This time I suspect he started the fire at the victim's feet." She gestured toward the other end of the table. "His head wasn't burned as severely as were the others either. You'll notice there's more tufts of hair remaining."

"Varying his MO."

"But not his signature," murmured Risa. She didn't appear to share his squeamishness. She was staring at the body consideringly. Nate gave a mental shrug. There was a reason people said women were the stronger sex. "Maybe he's trying to make it last longer."

"Prolong the torture?" Because he didn't know what else to do with them, he jammed his hands in his suit pockets. "That'd be in keeping with a sadist."

She sent him an approving glance. "Someone has more psych background than he's let on."

Her words warmed something inside him, which was stupid. He'd given up being stupid about women when he was seventeen and caught his girlfriend of ten months in the backseat with Joey Gelner. That Joey was his best friend had been the secondary insult.

It'd been *Nate's* car.

He'd developed, more than one woman had told him, a singularly unromantic view of relationships in the time since.

"I pay attention." He shifted his gaze to Liz. "Enough to wonder if there was a difference found in the lungs. Did he succeed in keeping the victim alive longer?"

The ME patted her heart and addressed Risa. "He makes me so proud." To Nate she said, "I can tell how much smoke the victim inhaled and I can estimate from that how long he lived. But if your offender managed to reduce the amount of smoke, or slow the burning process, I'm not going to necessarily be able to tell that. Just the cumulative amount. I did find something else that might interest you, though."

Rounding the table, she walked swiftly to the opposite end. "Help me turn him over." Gingerly he reached out to do as directed. But only because Risa was helping and he didn't want the women to start in on him again. "See this?"

He got closer to peer at whatever Liz was pointing to on the skull. "What?"

"Nothing. No evidence of blunt force trauma. But I did find traces of $(C_2H_5)_2O$ in the lungs. Ether," she explained before they could ask.

"Makes sense," Risa mused. "He changes the approach to fit the situation. He took Parker when he was out for a jog. And we still don't know exactly how and where he got Tull. But since blunt-force trauma was found on both those victims, we can guess that he used some sort of surprise or blitz attack for them. For Christiansen, we think the offender got inside his car."

"And so far it's looking like the driver managed to avoid every traffic camera in the area after that," he put in.

"So the UNSUB was directing Christiansen on what route to take," surmised Risa. "Held a gun to his head maybe. Or made him believe he'd left a buddy back at the detective's house, that his wife was in danger."

"He wouldn't have used the ether until they were at their destination. But why bother by then?"

Liz interrupted their ponderings. "This Starsky and Hutch thing you've got going on? Very educational. But I've got another—ha, ha—lucky stiff waiting to go under the knife, so maybe you kids could take it outside. Go on." She shooed them when Nate opened his mouth. "I gave you the highlights. The rest will be in my written report, which you'll get when it's ready. Now get out."

"As always, I appreciate the hospitality," Nate said with mock politeness. But he knew Liz well enough to start moving to the door before she threatened him with the bone saw.

Risa continued speaking as she followed him out. "The methods of attacks could point to the offender being slighter, weaker than the men he was assaulting. Or it could simply point to expediency. Goes to figure if you're attempting to take out a cop, even a retired one, that you'd expect them to be tough to take down. Makes sense to go in prepared to enact the abduction as quickly as possible to avoid being seen."

Their steps echoed hollowly as they made their way down the long hallway to the front desk. "Three weeks between Parker and Tull. Not quite two between Tull and Christiansen." When Risa didn't respond, he slid her a glance, found her frowning slightly. "I expect you to tell me that means he's escalating."

"Not necessarily," she said with an air of distraction.

If that hadn't surprised him enough, once outside she moved around the hood of the car without stopping to comment again on the message scratched on the car. Something was definitely going on in the woman's mind. Once they'd both gotten in the vehicle, he said, "Not necessarily?"

She looked up from fastening her seat belt. "Ordinarily I might assume the pattern meant escalation. It's the victims he's chosen that makes me wonder. Like we mentioned, cops aren't exactly easy prey. They're usually more observant than civilians, more aware of their surroundings. They've had plenty of self-defense training. And there's a chance they'll be armed, even off duty. Not to mention that once the murders start, word is going to spread among the force, making everyone doubly cautious."

"Meaning we can expect him to vary his approach."

"Yes. It also means if there's a next one, the timeframe might have more to do with how much he was able to stalk them prior to starting the crimes." She stared meaningfully at the keys, which he'd put in the ignition but had failed to turn. "If you want me to drive, the offer still stands."

"Not a chance." He started the car, began backing out of the parking space in the lot. "You didn't help with cleanup this morning. You've forfeited any chance of taking the wheel."

"Life is a series of trade-offs."

The expression on her face said she wasn't unhappy about the one she'd made. "Okay, he stalks them. Learns their routines."

"He does, yes. Maybe simultaneously. He also bides his time. That opportunity with Christiansen couldn't have been planned. All he could do was watch him. He couldn't know the man would go out on that precise night. He followed him, saw his chance, and made a move."

He narrowed his eyes in thought. "If the offender was following Christiansen, he had to have left a car nearby. Somewhere easy to slip in and out of." He made a mental note to look at the area surrounding the convenience store more closely to search for likely spots. If the offender left a car, he had to come back for one. Either way, if there were security cameras anywhere in the vicinity, maybe they'd caught the guy on tape. Slim as the possibility was, he'd make sure it was followed up on.

He came to a halt at a stoplight. Saw a punk elbow his buddy on the sidewalk and point. Then cup himself and thrust his hips forward shouting, "Yo, cop, suck this!"

It occurred to him that some of his coworkers would have even more pithy comments to make. "I'm requisitioning a new vehicle as soon as I get back to the station house," he muttered. The light turned green then, and he pulled away before giving in to the urge to draw his weapon.

"Good luck with that. The dented piece of tin I had to drive when I was on the force remains the stuff of legend."

She was right. Requisitions were notoriously stingy, and requests for vehicles were the slowest to process, with the highest incidence of rejection. But he was blessed with imagination and stubbornness. He'd finagle something.

"You realize he's already picked his next victim?"

Her voice was so quiet he had to strain to hear it. "A moment ago you said 'if.' Now you're assuming there will be a next victim."

She stared straight ahead into the thick congestion of the normal midday Philly traffic. "These guys were specifically targeted. Someone's going after cops, yeah, but not just any detectives. The UNSUB selects these particular guys, he stalks them, he makes his move. And I'm guessing the whole thing is tied up in a messy little pile of revenge for him. So when that need for revenge is satisfied, ostensibly he'd be done."

"But you don't think he's finished yet." It wasn't a question. The ball of dread that seemed permanently lodged in his chest intensified.

He felt her eyes on him. Met her gaze.

"I hope I'm wrong. But I have the feeling he's just getting started."

The man the media had unimaginatively dubbed Cop Killer had indeed picked out his next victims. He wasn't fussy about the order in which they died, except for the one he was saving for last. He'd been focused on this for years and had planned out every last detail. But a man had to be flexible. Ready to adapt to the unexpected.

Marisa Chandler was unexpected.

He'd been prepared for cops. Was delighted by the task force. He liked the idea of a whole army of cops running around trying to figure out where he'd hit next. He was smarter than all of them. He was proving that.

Chandler didn't worry him. Not yet. But it bothered him that no one seemed to know what her role was. None of his contacts had come up with anything.

It was always the unknown that tripped people up. Chandler wasn't going to be allowed to trip him up.

She'd been a cop; he'd found out that much. Supposedly a good one. Then she'd left. Got herself hurt last winter in Minneapolis, although the details on the Internet had been sketchy. There'd been a few photos of her and a story that had been short on answers.

So he'd get them himself. It'd be easy enough to wait for her to leave work. Follow her home. Maybe get a feel for how big a threat she might be.

The answer to that particular question would determine if he allowed her to live.

————

Bonnie Christiansen wore the slightly shell-shocked expression Nate had seen on the faces of those who life had suddenly hit too hard. When he introduced Risa and himself, her smile was perfunctory but her eyes held the vacant look of someone who probably wasn't going to remember details of this time a few years down the road.

What she would recall was the vicious way her husband had been taken from her, altering her life forever.

"We're sorry to disturb you at this time," Risa was saying gently. "We don't want to intrude."

"Have you . . . Is there news about Patrick?" They were seated in a small family room that seemed dominated by the empty leather recliner in the corner. A slight indentation was permanently worn into the seat. Nate didn't have to be told that the chair had been her husband's.

"The autopsy has been completed. You should receive word today about the body being released. Tomorrow morning at the latest."

"Good. That's good." Her words were vague. She reminded him of a small bird, with her short cap of smooth hair and skittish manner. Her hands on her lap fluttered as if she didn't know what to do with them. Finally she clasped them tightly together. "I've been talking to Pastor Warren about the service. And our children have been helping choose pictures. We'll need pictures. We can't . . . Patrick isn't . . ." Her voice choked as she repeated, "We'll need pictures."

"That'll be nice." Risa reached over and covered the woman's hands with one of her own. "Surrounding yourself with memories always helps."

"Thirty-one years together, we had plenty of memories." Her attempt at a smile trembled at the edges. "Some good, some bad, like most marriages, I guess. But it's all about the good outweighing the bad. In the end, that's what matters."

"Mrs. Christiansen, would you mind looking at a couple photos for me? See if you recognize the people in them?"

At her nod, Nate took the pictures of the other two dead detectives and handed them to her.

"I've seen them. Both of them," she murmured.

He and Risa exchanged a glance. "You have?"

"In the newspaper." She seemed to release the words on a little sigh as she handed them back. "They were the other detectives that died, weren't they?"

"That's right. But I was wondering if you recognized them from a time before that. If maybe they'd been to the house. If you saw Patrick speak to them somewhere?"

She frowned, as if trying to focus, then shook her head. "Not that I recall. Of course if he spoke to them at a police function, I wouldn't remember. Those things are so huge, so many people . . . Patrick loved crowds, but I'm more of a homebody. After a few years I started making excuses to send him alone."

"I don't like to go to them myself," he offered, and she sent him a grateful look.

"We developed our own interests. Couples do," she added defensively, as if they'd judge her marriage and find it wanting.

"Maybe that's the secret to a lasting marriage," Risa told her, and a bit of tension eased from the woman's frame. "Mine crashed and burned after three years, so I'm hardly in a position to know."

Shock jolted through him, and it took effort to keep it from his expression. He hadn't realized Risa Chandler had been married. There was no reason he should know, probably. But he couldn't help wondering what kind of man had successfully peeled away the many layers to get to the real woman beneath the smart humor and sharp mind.

And there was no excuse for wondering what it would take to discover that woman for himself.

"It happens." Bonnie was nodding sympathetically. "And the incidence of divorce is even higher for cops, I hear."

"Well, that explains it then. We were both on the force. Young and stupid." She stopped, as if reconsidering. "At least I was young and he was stupid."

The two women laughed a little and Nate blinked. The vague, shell-shocked woman who had greeted them at the door had undergone something of a transformation in the last few minutes, and he knew he had Risa to thank for putting her at ease. For drawing her out of her grief, at least briefly. Even if it didn't help her open up a bit more to them, it was worth it just to give the woman a couple minutes reprieve from her sorrow.

"What sort of outside interests did Patrick have?" Risa asked.

"Oh, guy things. He used to be quite an outdoorsman, loved fishing when we first got married. He'd steal away on weekends sometimes to go to the river. A few times he went on a bigger trip." She screwed up her brow, searching her memory. "He went to Canada once, I recall. But mostly to Lake Erie and Raystown. He'd fished other lakes but those were the ones he liked best."

"Pennsylvania has a lot of good fishing," Nate put in.

The woman nodded uncertainly. "I guess. I was never much for the outdoors. He did less and less of it after he took that second job. He didn't have as much free time, I guess."

But Nate's interest was caught. Keeping his tone mild, he asked, "He had a second job?"

One of Bonnie's hands began to flutter again. "Oh, I know it used to be frowned on by the department, but Patrick said everyone did it. And he only worked the odd night or a few hours on the weekend, filling in for a friend. Security guard at some warehouse, he said." She looked nervous. "Is this going to get him in trouble with the pension board?"

"No," Risa assured her. "There's no reason they need to know about it."

The woman relaxed again. "That's about it, I guess. I had my quilting and the church choir. After working all day, I mostly like to stay in and relax. But I know men need their time, too. That's why I never said a word about his monthly card group. Some women try to keep their husbands on too short a leash, but I always thought as long as you can trust them, you need to give them a little space to run." She looked at Risa then, her narrow face alight in dismay. "When I said some women, I wasn't talking about you, dear."

"I know. Although as it turned out, I'd have needed to forgo the leash and use a choke collar."

They shared another laugh but Nate's mind was racing. Hobbies. Edwards and Tomey were focusing on finding intersections in the victims. He made a mental note to tell them to check out the men's leisure activities. The link they were looking for might lie in the victim's outside interests.

"Where did he meet his card buddies? Were they neighbors? Old friends?"

Bonnie's hand went to her throat and she frowned. "No-o. I just assumed they were on the force. Can't recall if Patrick ever did say or if that was in my mind."

"Did he ever play cards with his group here?"

She shook her head. "No, they always met in a bar they were fond of. Don't ask me the name. And since he didn't come home too late or wasted, I never put up a fuss."

"But you know the names of the men he played with?" Risa put in.

"Oh, he'd mention a few of them from time to time. Let's see." Her eyes slid closed for a moment. "There was a Juan, I remember that name. And Jonas, he mentioned him a few times. Mostly I remember him speaking of a Johnny. If I'm not mistaken, Johnny went fishing with him on one of his lake trips about ten years ago." She smiled faintly. "The only reason I remember that is because it was the trip Patrick caught that huge trout. We have a picture of him with it somewhere around here. He knew a picture was all he was going to get, because there won't be any stuffed fish mounted and hanging anywhere in *my* house."

Nate smiled easily. "Understandable. Do you happen to have that picture handy? I'm not much of a fisherman, but I'd sure like to see it."

The mention of pictures had her face losing its animation as memory intruded. She swallowed hard. "I'm not sure. It sat right there on that table"—she pointed at an end table next to the recliner—"for years and years. I don't recall when it was put away or whether Patrick did it or I did." Her eyes filled with tears and she blinked them away rapidly. "At any rate I can look. Tell the kids to be on the watch for it as they go through the photos."

"I appreciate that." He caught the slight gesture Risa was making and rose. "Thank you for your time, Mrs. Christiansen. I want you to know the department is putting a lot of man hours into finding the person who did this."

"I heard there was a task force." She stood, too, and her gaze was searching. "How long, do you think? I mean, I realize you can't predict, but . . ."

"We've got a lot of people on this investigation. I'll personally let you know as soon as we have a suspect. And keep us abreast of the memorial arrangements. I'm certain a lot of officers are going to want to pay their respects."

She didn't seem capable of speech then, but she gave a jerky nod and saw them to the door.

As they walked down the drive, he noted that the tiny lawn was just as immaculately kept as the neat white ranch-style home had been.

Risa spoke first. "Okay, total coincidence, right?"

"The fact that she mentioned a Johnny?" They reached the car parked at the curb and both paused at the driver's door. "And there's a Johnny on the final segment of tape left at the crime scene?"

There was a flare of excitement in those odd-colored amber eyes. "Of course it might cease to be coincidence if that tape was left there for a reason."

It wasn't difficult to follow her line of thought because he was thinking the same thing. "You mean if we were meant to find it."

She nodded, moved to round the car to her door. "Makes me really interested to see if anyone else is pictured in Christiansen's fish photo."

———

Jonas knelt before the statue of the Virgin Mary, kissed the rosary beads, and bowed his head. Weeks like these, when he worked second shift, allowed him to go to daily mass. But he took comfort in the time he had to pray in the solitude of his own home, as well.

He had more to pray for than ever.

The guilt that had eaten at him for over twenty years was a constant weight that lived inside him. A writhing fanged beast, it would lie dormant for days or even weeks at a time. And then spring forth in all its fury, teeth and claws flaying him alive from the inside.

It was the penance he deserved for living in a state of mortal sin.

He wept freely, the rosary clutched so tightly in his hands that it cut into his flesh. He didn't pray for forgiveness. Jonas knew it was much too late for that. He didn't pray for guidance. He'd never had the courage to follow through on the instructions he'd received from the confessional all those years ago.

He wasn't sure he'd ever find that courage.

His eyes squeezed together tightly, and his shoulders shook with emotion.

The Holy Mother looked kindly down at him, her arms spread in a gesture of compassion. A compassion he knew he didn't deserve.

In the end, all he could do was pray for the strength to follow through on the plan he'd set in motion. It might not make things right. But it'd end things.

Once and for all.

Chapter 9

Risa tacked the department photos of Parker, Tull, and Christiansen above her desk and studied them. She needed to cull all their personal details from the briefing reports and interviews to compile a victim grid on each. *Know the victim, know the crime.* It was one of Raiker's most oft repeated mantras.

She powered up her laptop and opened the investigative file she'd started, adding that reminder and another to have Nate direct her to the first two crime scenes. Her grids wouldn't be complete without a visit to the scenes. She had to place herself at the location of their deaths. See the things they'd last seen. Imagine what they'd felt. What they'd heard.

Knowing the victims meant walking through their last hours and placing herself in their shoes. So that's just what she'd do.

And if immersing herself in the familiar details of the job helped keep the old doubts and insecurities at bay for hours at a time, then that was a very welcome bonus.

She scanned the documents from the file on her portable scanner to load them on her computer. All of Raiker's investigators were cross-trained, and he made sure all of them were profiling experts. But the organizational methods they used differed. Her colleague Abbie Phillips preferred setting up a victim board where she pinned up tags of pertinent information and used colored string to delineate intersections between the victims' lives.

Risa was more comfortable with computers. Cutting and pasting the pertinent information into one grid, using different colors for each victim was her method of choice. Intermittently she backed her work up on a flash drive, which would be left here when she took the laptop home each night. The need for backing up their files had been beaten into her by Gavin Pounds, Raiker's cyber wizard, after her one and only computer crash two years ago.

The familiar task soothed her and left her mind free to turn over the information she and Nate had discovered today, as well as the details from the briefing she'd just left. As she worked she forgot to wonder what was keeping him. When she'd left, he was deep in conversation with one of the task force detectives.

When the door pushed open, she looked up, blinking distractedly. But instead of Nate, she found Eduardo in the doorway.

"Nate still in the conference room?"

"As far as I know." She eyed the manila envelope he was holding. "What do you have?"

"IT sent this over while we were in the briefing."

Adrenaline flared. "The stills from the video left at the last crime scene? Let's see them."

Although he came farther into the room, he didn't make a move to open the envelope. Instead, his eyes searched her face. "How are things coming? McGuire keeping you in the loop on the investigation?"

Inwardly she squirmed at the question. She'd never worked under Eduardo's command. Had left the force before he'd climbed to his current rank. And while she recognized the obligations of his job, she was uncomfortable juggling the friendship-brass aspects of it. "I've got no complaints."

He smiled wryly. "Wouldn't voice them if you did, you mean."

"It's been going all right, Eddie. McGuire's a decent guy.

Believe me, working for Raiker and hiring out to different law enforcement entities all the time, I've come in contact with far worse."

"Hardly high praise, but I guess I'll take it." Nate's voice sounded behind Morales and Risa's face heated. No use wondering if he'd overheard their conversation. His carefully impassive expression said it all.

As did the level stare he exchanged with his captain.

Eduardo made no attempt to explain or apologize for checking up on him. And that, Risa thought, was another facet of his position. He merely held up the envelope. "Got these from IT. Haven't looked at them yet."

Nate walked into the office and began to shut the door.

"Hold that open for a sec, please?"

Darrell Cooper, the red-haired man who worked the front desk, stopped by the still open door with the wheeled cart he was pushing. "Just cleaning up the conference area. Will you guys use this coffee? Otherwise I'll take it to the staff room."

"Yeah, sure, we'll take it." Morales gestured for him to wheel it into the room. Then he looked at Nate. "I'm guessing you're going to be here awhile."

He nodded, tossed the younger man an easy grin. "Thanks, Darrell. Your coffee is becoming famous around here."

"Don't say that too loudly." Cooper's expression was mischievous. "Flo's on duty."

The words brought a slight frown to Morales's face. "You should have been off a couple hours ago, then."

"I stayed awhile longer so she could go to her son's track meet."

"Nice, but don't let people take advantage of you," Nate advised, heading to the cart to pour himself a cup. "Seems like you pull extra hours more often than not."

He shrugged, smiled. "They have families, I don't. And I can use the cash. The ladies these days have high standards."

As he backed out of the door, they heard him greet a passing detective. "Barnes, I sent some flowers in your name to your girlfriend. Florist will be sending you the bill."

"What? I didn't order any flowers."

"I know. You should have."

Morales reached out to swing the door closed, an abashed

grin on his face. "Don't tell Flo, but it's not only coffee he's better at. Reminded me of Renee's birthday last month, too. She would have killed me if I'd forgotten."

Risa raised a brow. "You did forget."

"Only until Darrell reminded me. As far as she knows, I remembered. And that's all that counts."

"Ah, the complexities of the male brain," she mocked, as she joined them to refill her cup. "A miracle of nature."

"Tell it to Renee." Eduardo hooked a chair leg with his foot and dragged it over. He looked at Nate. "Captain Steiner in Vice is very interested in that information you called in with on Javon Emmons. He's going to have Crowley picked up, see what sort of other details they can get from him. If they use him to set up a sting, how reliable will he be?"

"Depends on what's in it for him," Risa answered bluntly before Nate could fashion an answer. "He's scared to death of Emmons, and helping build a case against him is going to dry up a nice little revenue stream Crowley's got coming in."

"It might take a combination of cash, protection, and immunity to get him to cooperate." Nate leaned his hips on the front of his desk, facing the two of them, and sipped from his steaming cup. "They'll want to make it clear he goes down for his activities if he doesn't help them get Emmons. He'll cooperate. He's pretty motivated by self-interest."

Morales nodded, set his cup on the edge of the cart, and opened the envelope. "Then he's exactly like ninety-nine percent of the people we get coming through here. Let's see what IT came up with." Risa and Nate moved to flank the captain, and he fanned out the top three of the five-by-seven photos.

Risa leaned down to study them more closely. As the IT tech had warned, the pictures were grainy, with some of the resolution lost. Two of the pictures depicted the speaker on the video. Johnny. One was of the man Nate thought was Roland Parker.

"Need to get this photo over to Parker's widow for a positive ID."

Nate glanced at his watch. "I'll run it by there on my way to work tomorrow morning. While I'm there, I'll ask her about any hobbies her husband had."

"And anyone he might have known by the name of Johnny."

Seeing Morales's quizzical look, Nate quickly filled him in on the information they'd received from Bonnie Christiansen. When he'd finished, the captain looked thoughtful. "Interesting. I wouldn't pin too much hope on the two Johnny's being one and the same, though."

Risa exchanged a quick glance with Nate. "We can presume the offender may be one of the men sitting at that table or the person recording their meeting. If it's one of the men at the table, the tape was likely supposed to do exactly what we first supposed. Record the crime for the offender to relive later. But if it was left deliberately, the likelihood increases that the offender is the person recording, or someone close to that person. It would help to get a rundown on the location of that scene."

Morales shuffled the photos until they were looking at a close-up of the corner of the room's window. There was definitely a street scene outside it, although it was fuzzy. They all surveyed it silently for a moment.

"Well . . ." Risa said doubtfully, cocking her head a bit. "Those two letters still look like a *z* and a *p*."

Nate stabbed a finger at another partial letter. "That could be *b*. Or maybe an *l*."

"Or the tall part of an *h*, *f*, or *t*," she retorted. "At least this one looks like an *e*." She stopped. Squinted. "Possibly a *c* in that font."

"Yeah." Morales seemed more than happy to hand the packet of photos over. "Have fun pinpointing the location."

"Of a business that existed sometime in the last twenty to thirty years?" Nate's tone was wry. "No problem."

The captain stood. "Oh, and the message from IT was that they're still working on the sound and voice enhancements. I'll let you know when those come through."

"Thanks." Nate rounded the corner of his desk to sit after Morales exited the room. "We've got old telephone books in the reference room."

The information filled her with resignation. The task of combing through three decades of phone books didn't exactly rank high on her list of plum assignments, but someone needed to do it. "I'll put together a list of letter combinations to look for."

He nodded. "Good. Leave it with me and I'll start Shroot on it tomorrow."

Brightening at the suggestion, she said with more enthusiasm, "Good idea."

His eyes glinted. "Glad it met with your approval."

She knew without asking that he was referring to the partial conversation he'd heard when he entered the room. Turning to face him more fully, she leaned back in her chair. "If you've got something to say, Detective, go ahead. Don't be a girl about it. Put it out there."

The temper she'd tried to stoke was visible but still held in check. "Nothing to say." The dangerous gleam in his eye gave lie to the words. "I knew the score going into this. I'm a team player, and I know what it takes to run a task force. So when the brass pulled you in without a full explanation of what exactly you were expected to contribute, I swallowed it. When I was instructed to make sure you were fully apprised of every detail on the investigation, I didn't question it. You and Morales have a history. I get that. But I didn't appreciate walking in on your grade report on me or my performance in the case." His teeth bared in a grim pretense of a smile. "I also know there's not a damn thing I can do about that either, so I guess I'll be swallowing that, too. I expect it'll become an acquired taste."

She studied him silently for a moment. Risa was all too familiar with the ego massage necessary in instances like these. She'd just never developed a liking for it. The fact that the topic had arisen wasn't surprising.

Discovering that she cared, more than a little, about his feelings did.

"This is what I do." Her sweeping gesture included her desk, his office. "Usually Raiker's agency is hired to send in an investigator to assist law enforcement with high-profile cases." She lifted a shoulder. "It came about a little differently this time, but regardless, I have a conversation like this, almost verbatim, in seventy-five percent of the cases I'm involved in. Lead detective isn't happy about me being invited in, and I spend more time than I'd like tiptoeing around sensitive toes to avoid treading on them. Sometimes I have to fight for details the cops want to hide. Other times I have to elbow my way into the inner circle of the investigation. I'll tell you the same thing I tell all of them.

"You are running this investigation. I consider us partners. Full partners. But ultimately I answer to the administration, those responsible for me being here." She nodded toward the door Morales had closed behind him. "He's doing his job. But I don't need anyone else to run interference for me. If I had a problem with the way you were handling my position on the investigation, I'd tell you about it."

He regarded her for a moment from those midnight dark eyes. They gave away nothing. The spark of temper she'd seen in them earlier was gone. Or perhaps only hidden.

When the silence stretched, annoyance settled in. She swung her chair back to face her desk. "Was it the adjectives that bothered you? Because I might be able to come up with better than 'decent' next time. But there's no way in hell I'm going with 'Nate the Great.'"

She heard the crumple of paper a moment before it hit her in the back of the head. Bit her lip to keep from smiling. "Aiming for the trash can, McGuire? Remind me to help you with your hook shot."

"Actually working on my fastball." And the tone in his voice reassured her that they were back to what passed for normal between them. "And that was definitely within the strike zone."

It was nearly ten when Risa locked the rental at the curb and headed for the house. Hannah had left more than just the security light on, and that was unusual for her. She was frugal to a fault, and if she could figure out a way to douse the constant gleam from the security light, she'd have done so in the interest of knocking a few cents off her utility bill.

But she'd left a lamp on inside, along with the TV. Risa quickened her step. Her mother being that careless was just as unlikely as her not having gone to work this evening.

But there she was when Risa opened the door, her face arranged in a strained if welcoming smile. "Honey. I didn't know when to expect you. Do you work this late every night?"

"Sometimes. Mom, what's wrong? Why didn't you go to work tonight?"

The older woman skirted her gaze as she smoothed her crisp navy uniform pants. "Oh . . . I didn't feel just right. A little tired, I guess. I called in sick."

Risa stopped in her tracks, scanning her mother's form with growing concern. Hannah Blanchette did not call in sick because she didn't feel "just right." She'd gone to work the evening before she'd landed in the hospital with pneumonia three years ago. The only other time in Risa's memory that she'd missed work was when her scumbag husband had punctured her lung, ruptured her spleen, and left her to die on the kitchen floor.

"I'm feeling better, now." She sent her daughter a reassuring smile. "Probably should have gone in. I laid down for a while but started to go stir-crazy, so I got up and began a little cleaning. Thought with you still out it'd be a good time to tidy up in your room."

"Mom." The word sounded on a note of exasperation. "You don't have to clean up after me." She was almost certain there'd been nothing in the room to clean. Hannah's penchant for tidiness had rubbed off on her daughter.

"Well, I guess I can do a little light dusting in my own house when I want to," the woman said mildly. She smoothed her hair in a manner she had, checking for loose tendrils that had dared to work loose from the tight bun she wore. As usual there were none. Her appearance was as pin neat as the home she kept.

"I saw that you'd started drawing again." Hannah picked up the remote to turn the volume on the TV down. "I took a look, hope you don't mind. You were always so talented." Her brows drew together in worry. "I just wish you didn't draw such terrible sights. If you drew flowers and animals, you'd sleep better. I just know it."

Risa's throat was tight. She couldn't have forced out a response if she'd had to. Her gait was jerky as she went to the closet, hung up the jacket that hadn't been necessary that day. Set her purse on the table next to the TV.

"I always thought that's what caused your bad dreams,

those horrible pictures you sketched." Her mother's attention was diverted by the evangelist on TV, thundering about the evils of today's world. She increased the volume a notch.

"I draw what I dream. Not vice versa." As soon as she spoke the words, Risa wished them back. Hannah had never understood. Not because she hadn't tried, but because it was beyond her. Although Risa had never doubted her mother's love, she'd also realized early on that the woman was limited. Her perspective of the world held none of the shades of gray that Risa's did.

"A God-given talent like that, you should put it to use," Hannah tempered the words with a wan smile. "I know I never said so before, but I've always wanted you to draw me a picture that I could frame and hang on the wall right here. Something pretty and nice. Something I can look at, when you're not here, and think of you."

The sentiment coming from a woman usually lacking in it touched Risa. Neither her artistic talent nor her athletic ability had ever drawn much in the way of notice from her mother. "I'll work on something for you," she promised, although she had no idea how. Art had long been nothing but a tool for her. A way to document the torturous dreams that left her drenched with dread. She hadn't picked up a pencil to sketch anything other than the nightmares that plagued her in longer than she could remember.

"That nice young man next door mowed my lawn today." Hannah was keeping up the conversational gambit. "You know Eleanor's son. He said the two of you talked the other day and that you'd gone to high school together. I'd known that but forgotten it somehow. He's in the film business, you know. He's directed lots of movies."

"I thought he said he was a producer," Risa said.

Hannah looked confused. "Isn't that the same thing? Anyway Eleanor was awfully proud of him and I can see why. Such a nice young man."

"I pay a lawn service to mow your lawn."

At the reminder, her mother replied distractedly, "Well, I'll cancel them tomorrow. Save you some money." Her gaze darted away, couldn't seem to find a place to land.

Risa contemplated the other woman. "What's really wrong?"

Trepidation was pooling in her stomach as she sat down on the old couch beside her mother. Maybe she'd gotten bad news from the doctor, although Risa couldn't recall the last time the woman had visited one. Or lost her job. Or . . .

"I got this in the mail today." There was a crinkle of paper as Hannah carefully drew a letter out of the pocket of her plaid and navy uniform top. "It was addressed to me in care of the cleaning service I work for. They sent it on. I'll admit it shook me up a bit. Silly, I know. But it's like having the past jump out at me when I least expected it. Gave me a bit of a jolt."

Risa took the envelope from her mother. Took out the letter and unfolded it, scanning the scrawled writing quickly.

Heat, a white-hot tide of it, surged inside her. Raymond Blanchette, that son of a bitch, had always had more balls than brains. But she didn't recall him ever having a memory problem before.

And she'd made it very clear the last time she'd spoken to him what would happen if he ever came near her mother again. Ever tried to contact her.

Apparently he needed a reminder.

"Reading that . . . I could almost hear him saying the words. Promises like he used to make me. How things would be different if only I'd give him another chance. He always was a real sweet talker." Hannah wouldn't meet her daughter's eyes. Her fingers plucked nervously at her pant leg.

Comprehension belatedly pricked through fury. She had no idea what her mother felt for the man. As far as she knew, they hadn't seen each other in eight years. But Hannah had refused to press charges against him the last time he'd put her in the hospital. Had forgiven him a multitude of times prior to that for a whole raft of sins.

Risa chose her words carefully. "Maybe I should speak to him." She'd thought she'd come on forcefully enough the last time to put the fear of God in him, but time and circumstances might have dimmed his recollection of the scene.

She'd take great enjoyment in jogging his memory.

"No, I 'spect I need to do this myself."

It was only when Hannah reached over to pat her hand that Risa realized it was balled into a fist. "Don't worry. I'm not the same woman I was back then." She waited for Risa's eyes to meet hers before smiling slightly. "I know you didn't understand what kept me going back after some of the times he and I had. I didn't understand myself, until after I was out of it. After you moved me here and Eleanor and I became friends."

It took a moment for Marisa to put it together. Eleanor Dobson, the deceased friend from next door, had once worked in a battered women's shelter. Apparently the women's friendship had been healing in more ways than one.

"What will you tell him?"

"Well, I haven't the words yet but I do have my answer. And knowing Raymond, it's best to keep it short. More would just encourage him, whatever else I wrote."

That was true enough. Risa rapidly sifted through options. Although Hannah refused to have anything to do with a cell phone, Risa had arranged for an unlisted landline number. And Raymond didn't have her address or he wouldn't have tried to contact her through work. Her checks were automatically deposited, so there was no reason for her mother to go to the office of the cleaning company for anything.

The realization relaxed her. "Okay. If you're sure you're up to it."

"Up to it," the older woman said with rare spirit. "Well, my goodness, Marisa Lyn, you're not the only tough broad in the family, I'll have you know."

Her mother's words surprised a laugh from her. They bumped shoulders companionably.

"I guess I had to get it from somewhere."

———

It was just four of them tonight. Jonas was on the job. Which was just as well, Johnny figured. The pansy ass would probably freak out at the news.

It had been Hans's idea to get together again. They needed to compare notes, he'd insisted. Had to keep on top of this thing. And the others deserved to know about Sean and Johnson.

So they sat there at the corner booth, each nursing a beer.

Johnny couldn't help wondering if anyone else had the same thought that was swirling around in his head.

Which one of them would be next to burn.

Juan and Jack sat across from him and he could almost smell their fear. He wanted to think he didn't have the same stench. Almost believed it.

"So this task force has some woman on it. Some sort of consultant." Jack looked at his companions over the top of his beer as he took a long swig. After he put the bottle down he continued. "Chandler's her name. Did a little digging around. Used to be on the force."

"Yeah, I heard that, too." Hans loosened a corner of the bottle's label with his thumbnail. "Works for a private outfit now. Adam Raiker runs it, if you've heard of him."

"Wasn't he the mole they found in the bureau? Sold secrets to the Israelis or something?"

Hans flicked a rolled-up piece of the label at Juan. "No, you dick. He was the fed's top profiler who brought down John LeCroix about eight years ago, that perv that killed twenty-seven kids."

The other man hunched over his beer. "Knew the name sounded familiar," he muttered.

"He's got his own firm now. With his rep, he can hire the best, so Chandler must have some chops if she's working for him."

Jack looked worried. "I don't like the sound of that," he muttered. "The task force is sniffing around Javon Emmons. McGuire wants to talk to him."

Johnny felt the spaghetti he'd downed tonight begin a slow burning rise in his chest. "Shit. How do you know that?"

"Because he told me, that's how." The man twisted the gay-looking earring he wore. He'd always claimed it was part of the street guise, but Johnny had never been too sure. "He called wanting some information on him, said something about him being a possible wit to Giovanni's murder."

"What?" Johnny was dumbfounded. "You think he might have been involved?"

"Hell no. He has no way of even knowing Giovanni. He's

always dealt with me. McGuire's on the wrong track, but he's got officers beating the streets looking for him. I told Emmons to lay low for a while."

Hans eyed him consideringly. "You're going to have to tell him go in and talk to McGuire at some point."

Jack shook his head stubbornly and took a long pull from his beer. "I don't see why. If Emmons wants to keep a low profile, believe me, he can stay lost for as long as he wants."

"But he can't," the older man explained patiently. "He's got business to conduct, and he'll be too cocky and stupid to stay put. So he'll get scooped up the next time he ventures out to conduct a deal, get caught with something incriminating probably, and then we have a bigger mess on our hands than him going in to answer a few questions. We have enough to deal with right now without having to worry about bailing out one of our dumb-ass business partners."

Jack clutched the bottle until his knuckles turned white. "Easy for you to say. It's not your ass on the line if he says the wrong thing."

"Bullshit," Johnny put in. Jesus, the guy was acting so fucking stupid he wanted to kill him himself. And Juan sitting over there was no better. Tearing his napkin into little balls as if that were going to help anything. "It's all our asses on the line. If one goes down, we're all in danger. What you need to do is coach your boy very carefully before he goes in. You can control him, right?"

Jack rubbed a hand over the graying stubble on his jaw nervously. "Yeah, of course."

"Then lay it on the line for him. Let him waltz in, then waltz out again. McGuire is going to know what Emmons is into, but it doesn't play into the investigation. At least not as far as I've heard." He shot a sideways look at Hans.

"Johnny's right. Better to let them talk to Emmons on our terms. You're the best judge of the guy. You're the one who's been handling him. If you don't think he can be trusted in there, you'll have to eliminate him."

Jack paused in the act of lifting the bottle to his lips. "Eliminate him?" He took a drink. Set the bottle down carefully. "That isn't necessary. I told you, he'll do what he's told."

Cocksucker was lying for all he was worth, Johnny thought. Jesus, what a clusterfuck. 'Course if the tables had been turned, and it was his associate going in for questioning, he might have a few bad moments himself. They weren't exactly in business with mental giants. And none of their associates had any particular love for cops.

"Maybe when you're having your little discussion with Emmons, you should find out where he was the night Giovanni, Jon-O, and Johann died."

"What?" Jack stared at him, then laughed. "You're paranoid. There's no way Emmons could pull something like this off."

"The way I hear it, he dropped some poor bastard in a vat of acid for trying to move in on his territory," Hans said dryly. "Lighting people up wouldn't be a stretch for him."

"I'm the only one of us he knows," Jack pointed out. "I'm the one he's paying off. Wouldn't I be the first one gone if it were Emmons?"

"He has a point. We need to be looking at Johann, Jon-O, and Giovanni's partners."

"Except Johann had been out of the business for a year," Juan interjected. "Retirement from the force means an end to the other business dealings. His associate would have no motive to off him now."

Grudgingly, Johnny acknowledged that the man wasn't as worthless as he'd seemed. But his next words had stopped him cold.

"Maybe we ought to give Sean a call. Run it all by him." The man sent an anxious gaze from Johnny to Hans and back. "He's a smart guy. Even being retired, he's still got plenty of contacts, right?"

"I don't think that's a good idea," Johnny said, as much to warn Hans to stay silent as in answer to the suggestion. He'd reconsidered sharing the discovery he'd made about Sean and Johnson with the rest of the group. Look at them. Jack was sweating like a middle schooler with his first hard-on, and Juan looked like he'd burst into tears at any minute. They didn't need more bad news. Fear made for bad decision-making.

They were all dealing with enough fear.

"Johnny's right." Relief filled him at Hans's words. "The fewer who know about this the better. Sean and Johnson have been out of it too long. There's nothing they can do. We have to take care of it ourselves. So." He slapped his palm lightly on the table and looked at each of them in turn. "What have you heard from your informants? Any scuttle on the street about this?"

Juan and Jack shook their heads. Regretfully, Johnny had to as well. "None of my people have got anything either. No gossip, no one claiming credit. Nothing."

Hans looked thoughtful. The condensation on the bottle had moistened the label enough that he could peel the rest of it away in one piece. "I didn't hear much either. And what I did get didn't check out. Unusual."

"If we're not hearing anything, then the task force can't be either, right?" Jack drained his beer and set it down on the table. Looked around like he needed another. "Don't know if that's good or bad."

"We have to stick together," Hans told them all. "More now than ever. Way I hear it, this guy grabbed Johann when he was out for a run. Giovanni was out on an errand. Somehow the guy got into his car."

Johnny jerked toward him. "How do you know that?"

Hans gave him a cool look and sipped from his beer. "I know people who know people. What I'm saying is, keep your weapon on you at all times. I mean, you get up in the middle of the night to take a piss, have your dick in one hand and your gun in the other."

"Easy for you," Juan muttered. "You don't got kids in the house."

"Nothing about this is easy," Hans countered. "But we do what we have to. Jack, you put the fear of Christ Jesus in Emmons and get him in for questioning. Fewer problems that way. And you guys all be as careful as a virgin in a whorehouse." He eyed them grimly. "I don't know about you, but I don't want to be readin' about any more of us in the paper."

Chapter 10

The UNSUB is almost assuredly motivated by revenge. The victims determined because of their occupations. He stalks them first, likely more than one at a time. The offender is probably following a random sequence. After the initial selection, the victims are chosen according to opportunity and taken to a deserted area that has already been scouted and prepared in advance.

The UNSUB is male, age undetermined. Leaving the victims' IDs nearby can be construed as an insult to the police force in general, a reminder of the offender's power and their vulnerability.

Risa stopped there, the cursor blinking questioningly. There was still too much undetermined. Not enough facts to stop with what was known without reaching into conjecture.

Her boss had never been a big fan of conjecture.

But if she were relying on her gut to fill in the holes between facts, she might guess that the IDs were a message. A taunt to the next victims, guaranteed to strike fear. I'm coming for you next.

She frowned. That possibility meant the victims knew each

other. Were connected in some way. And the one thing they had failed singularly at so far was finding a link between them.

And what about the kiddy police badges left at the scene? She made a note to ask Nate more about them. Some departments' public relations officers gave out something similar when visiting schools.

She shifted her position against the pillows she had propped against the wall at the end of her bed. The laptop lay on her outstretched legs. Not exactly a position guaranteed for long-term comfort.

The badges weren't left as insults. She'd bet on that. They meant something personal to the offender. She just couldn't quite get an angle on what.

Serial offenders typically fell within a given age range, but she wasn't willing to add it to the profile just yet. If she were right about these being revenge killings, the UNSUB may have served time after being put away by one of the victims. The prison stretch could put him outside the normal age boundaries.

And given him a whole a lot of time to plan his revenge.

She pressed Save and set the computer aside. She'd come full circle. Because they'd gotten very few hits on individuals who'd been arrested by more than one of the victims, and nothing had turned up on that end yet.

Her cell rang then and she reached for it, intent on answering before it could wake Hannah. She checked the caller ID before answering. "Adam."

"We're on your back porch. Let us in." The terse message, followed by a dial tone was typical Raiker.

What was atypical was having him drop by at—she checked the alarm clock as she swung her feet over the bed and stood. Eleven o'clock P.M.

Yanking on a pair of shorts to go with the oversized tee she wore to bed, Risa hurried to the back door, unlocked it, and swung it wide to allow Adam and his companion inside. "Paulie." Her smile was genuine. "How have you been?"

"Gimme a hug, kid." She was hauled against his stout body with one long arm while his pudgy hand clapped her on the back. Then he set her apart a bit and grinned at her. "You're looking good. You been sandbagging it? I didn't figure a little knife wound would keep you down. What was it, again? A little Boy Scout number, wasn't it?"

"Close," she responded dryly, shutting the door behind them. "A bowie with an eight-inch blade." The last time she'd seen him, he'd been hanging over the side of her hospital bed entertaining her with card tricks. "New tie?"

He was renowned for his neckwear, each of them depicting his love affair with gambling of all forms. This one was pale blue watered silk embellished with a sly-looking cat dressed as a riverboat gambler, holding a pawful of cards with a stack of flattened mice nearby to use as poker chips.

Smoothing the tie with one hand, he beamed. "Like it? Treated myself when I had a good weekend on the Riviera last month."

"If the gossip fest is over," Adam said dryly. Moving past them into the kitchen, he set his cane against the counter and began opening cupboards. "What do you have to drink in this place?"

Hannah frowned on alcohol use of any kind. Risa imagined it came from being on the receiving end of drunken violence meted out by Raymond. She followed Raiker around the counter and nimbly hoisted herself up on it to reach the highest cupboard over the sink.

Retrieving the bottle tucked behind dusty vases and warped Tupperware, she bent her knees and jumped to the floor again, presenting Adam with the bottle.

He studied the label, raised one dark brow. "No Scotch?"

She turned to take three juice glasses out of the cupboard next to the sink. "Did it look like I was well stocked up there?"

"Quit your bitching, Adam. At least it's Crown." Paulie beamed broadly and poured an overly generous splash in each glass. Adam reached out and took one of the glasses, tipped two-thirds of its contents into another, and nudged the glass with the remainder toward his colleague.

"You're driving."

Paulie looked woeful but picked up the glass to sip.

Risa took one of the glasses and leaned against the counter. "To what do I owe the unexpected company?"

Adam was adept at dodging direct answers. He did so now. "How's the case progressing?"

"Three days since the last victim was found. We've covered a lot of ground but haven't found a link between the three men yet, other than their occupations."

"It's there," Adam said surely. He took a healthy swallow of whiskey. "The connection might not be obvious so you'll have to look for something more nebulous. That case Ryne and Abbie worked last year, the serial rapist in Savannah? Offender was a temp nurse targeting women he came in contact with through his various jobs."

She recalled the case. She also recalled the link hadn't been discovered until after they'd caught the offender. But she wasn't going to waste an opportunity to bounce the details of the case off the most brilliant forensic mind in the country either.

Nearly twenty minutes later, her boss was regarding her with a slight smile. "Sounds like you've settled back into the job without much problem."

Tension shot through her muscles. She sipped from the glass, welcoming the liquor's scalding slide down her suddenly tight throat. "I'm not at the forefront of this. And it's early days yet."

"Any more dreams?"

"One." She used the tip of her nail to draw an imaginary line down the back of the glass. "Pretty much the same as the first."

"They're back. And they'll come whether you're involved in the work or not. They always did." The words were inexorable. Irrefutable.

And true.

Although it was difficult to meet that laser blue gaze, she forced herself to do so. "I'm dealing. Taking it a day at a time."

"That's all anyone can ask for. Isn't it, Adam?"

But Paulie's not so subtle remark was lost on their boss. His glass made a small sound as he set it against the counter. Then he reached into his suit jacket to withdraw something, which he extended toward her. "You'll need this."

Her slight gasp mingled with Paulie's exasperated, "Shit, Adam." She barely heard him. Her mind was frozen. Her eyes rooted on the gun he held out to her. The one she'd handed in, via a third party, along with the resignation he'd chosen to ignore.

"You know my rule. None of my operatives work unarmed. I got a permit issued in your name the day I spoke to the chief."

She made no move toward it. Couldn't have forced herself to if she wanted. She hadn't touched her weapon since—

The earthen walls were cold. Dank. The makeshift lighting flickered. On one moment. Dissolving into absolute darkness the next. A boy's thin, desperate whisper. "Risa, don't leave me!"

She tried to swallow. Felt like she was drowning.

Adam set the weapon on the counter next to her. She could feel its nearness, as if it radiated a human heat.

"I can't even pick it up," she managed.

His good eye glinted. "You'll have to, won't you? At least to put it away." Downing the rest of the liquor, he set the glass on the counter in a gesture of finality. "I'll be in touch."

She didn't answer. Didn't respond to Paulie's last commiserating look before he followed his boss from the kitchen. Out the back door.

Her attention was rooted on the weapon. The black Beretta 90 nine millimeter was nestled snugly in its leather shoulder harness. It was just a gun. The emotions attached to the sight of it had nothing to it with the weapon.

And everything to do with the memory of the greatest failure in her life.

"You push too hard."

They were the first words Paulie had spoken since they'd left Risa. He'd been silent as they made their way across two narrow yards to the car left on the other side of the block. Adam hated having to rely more heavily on the cane to support his leg across the uneven ground. Despised even more being forced to dodge and hide from the assassin who'd targeted him.

So his voice revealed all his frustration when he answered shortly, "I know my people."

He waited for Paulie to disengage the high-security alarm

before easing into the front seat of the car. Pulling the door shut, he waited. The man wasn't done. And until he was, the subject wouldn't be closed. They enjoyed something more than an employer-employee relationship. They'd been friends well before he'd stolen the man away from the forensic accounting department at the bureau. Their fates had been entwined since one life-altering decision eight years ago.

Adam still didn't know if he should feel grateful to the man for the path he'd chosen that day. He only knew they were on the path together.

"She's not ready. That's clear. You have a bad habit of not hearing what people are saying to you if it's not what you want to hear."

"It's what they don't say that I listen to. And she won't ever be ready unless she's pushed."

Paulie shook his head as he started the car. "She's strong. She'll get there on her own."

"Not until she drops the load of guilt she's hauling around with her. It'll factor into every decision. Color every response. I know my people," he repeated, settling back into the luxurious leather of the town car. Before hiring someone on, he familiarized himself with every facet of their background. Observed them in their line of work. Many people looked fit on paper, but psychologically were a poor match for the demands of his company. It wasn't enough to know their lives inside and out. He made sure he walked around inside their minds before offering them a job. He didn't think he'd made a mistake in hiring yet.

And he didn't want to be wrong about Marisa Chandler.

"She's not you." Paulie had an uncanny and damned annoying habit of reading his mind at times. "People deal with trauma in their own way. You can't dictate the road posts to their recovery."

"She's strong. And I'm not dictating," he countered. "I'm just handing her a map." He pulled out his cell and checked for the one message that would keep them in Philadelphia another night. When he didn't find it, he muttered a curse.

Paulie nosed the car down the street and checked in his mirror to be sure the vehicle with their security detail followed. "Our guy didn't take the bait?"

"It was a stupid plan," muttered Adam. And one he'd only succumbed to under pressure.

"It was worth a shot," the other man corrected. In conjunction with four different city police departments, and the bureau that seemed only too eager to jump into the mix, Adam's would-be assassin had been identified. Tyler Jennings had been raised in Philadelphia and should have felt comfortable making a move here.

He *should* have fallen for the look alike masquerading at the Ritz, while Adam and Paulie stayed at a much more modest nearby hotel. The fact that he hadn't, when they had proof that he'd followed Adam to the city was troubling.

"He's smart," he said grudgingly. The man would have to be to have evaded law enforcement in four cities so far.

"And tenacious. He won't give up." Paulie slanted a glance at him. "His name still doesn't ring a bell?"

Adam shook his head. "I don't know him. Hadn't even heard of him until we made the ID a couple days ago." There was no reason he should have. He'd put away his share of men just like Jennings over the years, and there were always more to take their place. Men without scruples who sold their services to the highest bidder.

He didn't care about Jennings. The man was just a tool. Adam wanted whoever had hired him.

"I still think this is tied somehow to the Mulder kidnapping you worked with Kellan and Macy last winter in Colorado."

Because this was familiar territory, Adam leaned his head against the headrest and closed his eye. "There's no proof of that."

"It was during that time that we started getting hacking attempts into our financials," Paulie said doggedly. They were driving down a street edged in neon. To his credit, he gave barely a glance at a sign giving directions to a casino.

"Which the new fire wall you constructed took care of."

"Well, of course." He shrugged without modesty. "But the attempts on your life started almost immediately after that case. Makes me wonder if Castillo might have been telling the truth about LeCroix's son being alive. About him maybe wanting revenge for you killing his father."

"Enrique Castillo is a miserable self-serving child-trafficker. He blames me for his life sentence. Anything he'd say is suspect. And John LeCroix was hardly the last man I've been in contact with who wants me dead." Although to be sure, the man had come a damn sight closer to succeeding than most.

Broodingly, he fingered the scar on his throat. He almost preferred LeCroix's methods. At least he could fight back against an enemy he could see. He had a feeling he was going to run out of patience with this current game long before Jennings did.

––––––––

Nate glanced up as Risa pushed into the office, then stared. "You look . . . tired," he amended when her eyes slitted. "Late night last night?"

"I stayed up awhile working on the profile," she said brusquely.

He had enough experience with female moods to gauge hers at a notch past dangerous. And enough wisdom to keep his mouth shut, accordingly.

She set her computer case on her desk and unzipped the side pocket to withdraw the file folder. Turning, she tossed it on his desk. "Keep in mind it's an evolving document. It'll change as we have more details on the case."

"I'm familiar with profiles." His tone was mild. He was becoming something of an expert of treading with caution. Living with Kristin recently was like serving as tiger bait. He never knew when one false move would have her pouncing.

The hell of it was, Tucker was starting to pick up on the undercurrents, and his behavior had taken a turn for the worse. Bedtime last night had surpassed battle status and taken on the elements of a full-fledged war. By the end of the night Kristin and her son were both in tears, and the old cravings had returned full force. Nate would have smoked a rolled-up newspaper if he could have figured a way to get nicotine in it first.

"There's coffee." He felt a need to point it out and hoped it'd have the same effect on her it'd had on him when he came in.

"Ah. Bless Darrell." She got up and headed to the pot he'd

filched from the staff room. He opened his mouth to warn her. Shut it again.

She poured a cup and carried it back to her desk before taking a healthy swallow. Her sputtering cough had him grinning. "It's Darrell's day off. Flo made this."

She aimed a hard stared his way. "You might have told me that sooner."

"I might have." He hid his grin by tucking his head down and unrolling the map on his desk. "But you didn't take as big a taste as I did and misery loves company."

Risa grimaced and took another sip, more cautiously this time. "Well, if nothing else, it should clear the fog out of my head this morning."

"And then some."

"I took a look at the LUDs last night."

He raised his brows. "I have a team combing through the phone records already. No calls to duplicate numbers have been placed or received."

"Couldn't sleep, remember?" Despite the words, her tone was slightly less caustic than it'd been earlier. Caffeine was a good jumpstart. And Flo's coffee was high octane. "Did your guys mention that all three victims received a call from a public phone in the last month?"

He lifted a shoulder, unimpressed. "Informants use public phones all the time. They didn't come from the same number." Couldn't have, or the detectives would have caught it.

"No." She put her coffee down and took out a thick green binder. He recognized it as the one she was keeping her case file in. "But they did all come in on the same date. All within a half hour of each other, in fact."

Letting the edges of the map roll back, he looked instead at the page in the binder she was indicating. "Okay, this one went out to Roland Parker and the number is identified as being located inside Hanley's Market on the sixteen hundred block of Post. But fifteen minutes later someone placed a call from this number"—she riffled a few pages before finding her spot—"which is identified as a phone booth on the corner of Collins and One Ninetieth, to Patrick Christiansen." She waited, but whatever she was getting at escaped him. "Collins and One Ninetieth is three blocks away from Parker's home address."

He studied her. "You think Parker placed the call."

"Twelve minutes later Tull received a call from a public phone located inside Joe's Tavern." She hitched her hip on the corner of his desk to stab the page emphatically. "Everyone uses informants, yeah, I get that, although mine all seemed to have cells even before I did. But this isn't coincidence. It can't be. I don't know what it means, but it's a link."

He flipped the pages again to look at the numbers, dates, and times she'd highlighted. The calls had only occurred once in the last thirty days, as she'd noted. "I need to go back further," he muttered. "See if this is a onetime thing or if it occurs regularly. If it shows up in other months . . ." Looking up, he gave her grin. "Good catch, Chandler."

The smile she graced him with hit him like a fast left jab to the solar plexus. Jesus, her smile should be outlawed. With effort, he hauled a bit more oxygen into his lungs and cleared his throat. The slim hip and thigh perched perilously close to his arm were encased in navy today. There was nothing remotely sexy about the no-nonsense suit she wore, although he couldn't say the same about the red top beneath it. It hinted at cleavage and the curves that might lurk beneath the tailoring.

He jerked his gaze back to stare blindly at the pages in front of him.

"What's with the map?"

Welcoming the change of subject, he unrolled it again. "Got a blow-up of the area around the convenience store where we think Christiansen was snatched. This line"—he traced the yellow highlighting—"is one possible route that would have skirted any traffic cameras on the way to the Wakeshead Park. The pink highlighting shows another path. The only other routes take him miles and miles out of his way, which would have slowed him down considerably."

"Not to mention upping his risk."

"Exactly. With the estimated time of death, we can be reasonably certain one of these two routes were chosen. I have Hoy and Mendall going door-to-door on both routes, checking for any businesses along the way that might have security cameras pointing toward the street. ATMs. Anything that may have caught the vehicle as it went by."

"And the phone books?"

"Shroot caught that assignment." Something inside him lightened at the memory. "He . . . uh . . . expressed his undying gratitude in advance."

"I'll bet."

To his relief she gathered up her binder and removed her shapely ass from his work space. He made a mental note to have that corner of the desk bronzed. "I swung by Nora Parker's house, Roland's widow, on the way to work. She ID'd him as the man in the still IT got us from that old video segment."

She turned and gave him a sharp look. "And the other?"

Somehow he'd known that question had been coming. "She didn't recognize the other one in the video. The one they called Johnny. I also ran the names by her that Bonnie Christiansen recalled as being part of her husband's card club. Struck out there, too."

"Roland didn't happen to belong to a card club, did he?"

"She said no. She also said he didn't have a second job." He hesitated, feeling a stab of guilt for what he was about to say. "I think she's lying."

Risa reached for her coffee again. In college he'd faced all-American linebackers intent on mowing him down on the field, but she appeared to be made of far stronger stuff than he was. One swallow had been more than enough for him.

"About . . ."

"The extra job." He watched her sip, felt slightly better about himself when she winced a little as she swallowed. "She didn't want to talk about it. But the tells were there. I'm having the captain make a case to the brass for a warrant on the three victims' financials. With Christiansen's widow acknowledging that he worked somewhere, although she was vague with the details, we should be able to present an argument that the intersection for the three victims might lie in something they were working off the job, rather than on it." He didn't envy Morales his task of selling it to the administration, but with the bars came the responsibility.

"I don't suppose you had time to go through the ViCAP reports while you weren't sleeping last night," he said, joking.

To his shock, she nodded. "I did. Didn't see anything that jumped out at me, though."

"Wow, you really didn't sleep." His attention drifted back to the unrolled map once again. "Got a full day's work in before most people woke up."

"I'd like to go to the first two crime scenes. Get a feel for them."

"You've got all the pictures."

"I want to see them," she said stubbornly. "You don't have to go along. I know my way around Philly."

He sat back, vaguely annoyed. "I do have to go. You won't get past the officer stationed at them otherwise." Pushing back from his desk, he shrugged into his beige suit jacket. "Okay. Afterward we'll hit the area surrounding the convenience store, look for a spot the offender could have stashed his car."

"Sounds like a lot of driving," she observed.

He nodded unenthusiastically. Philadelphia recently had been named the tenth-worst congested city in the nation in terms of traffic. Opening up a desk drawer, he took out a new supply of gum and pain reliever for the headache that was sure to result.

"If we're going to be on the road that much"—she set her cup down and picked up her purse—"you can stop somewhere for better coffee."

The warehouse Nate parked in front of was at the end of a street, flanked by the Schuylkill River on one side and a couple empty lots on the other. An occasional truck rumbled down the road toward them, but all turned off before reaching midway down the block.

Risa slammed the car door behind her and tilted her head up at the building. Windows had been covered with plywood and painted a dark brown. There had once been huge matching doors on the front of the structure, large enough to swing inside and allow semis to unload. But what was left of the doors hung useless on their hinges now, yellow police tape crisscrossing the gaping opening.

A fresh-faced uniformed officer posted at the door straightened at their arrival. When Nate badged him, he relaxed visibly. "How's it going?"

"Been quiet here, detective. This street doesn't see a lot of traffic."

Nate bent to pick up a couple hard hats left inside the doorway, handed one to Risa. "We're going to look around."

"Yes, sir."

Donning the hard hat, Risa gingerly stepped inside the shadowy building. Her eyes were drawn immediately to the center of the space, where a large blackened circle stained the dirt floor.

"The offender went to a little trouble finding this place." Nate's voice was impassive. "We think he used that hoist chain to keep the victim upright before the fire was started."

Risa looked at the massive rusted chain and hook hanging down from one metal beam overhead. A chill broke out over her skin. The chain was blackened but the beam appeared untouched.

Turning back toward the double doors, she frowned. "Doesn't make sense. There's no fuel to keep the fire spreading . . . oh-h."

"Yeah, before he left he must have sprayed more of the gasoline mixture toward the front doors. Probably broke in the back door and exited the same way." He nodded toward the doorway in the rear, which had a yellow X of tape crossing it.

Silent now, she moved into the center of the blackened area. There would have been no one to hear the victim's screams. Even if the warehouses farther up the street employed watchmen, little sound would have escaped the brick and mortar building. Glass was a noise conductor, but the windows had been replaced with wood long ago. The structure's distance from the other buildings gave it an air of seclusion. There would have been no hope of rescue.

She moved across the area to peer out the back entrance. A rutted path—alley would be too generous—was worn into the weedy ground outside the structure. The land did a gradual roll into the river, about half a block away. "He pulled up here, all the way to the door. Left the vehicle out back. Who's going to see it? Walked Parker through this door. Shut it behind him." And with that door swinging shut, the victim's hope for help had vanished.

Turning, she was surprised to find Nate on her heels. She nearly ran into him. "Where did you find the ID? And the badge?"

"His ID was just inside the back entrance. The badge was over there." He gestured to the opposite shadowy corner. "No trace evidence, other than the body and the fuel residue the lab identified on it. The offender took the fuel container with him."

"After he left a fuel path for the fire to follow to the entrance. He needed for the body to be found," she mused aloud. "A place like this, the fire could have burned itself out. No telling how long before the body was discovered. He wants immediate attention. Why does he need it? Thumbing his nose at the force in general? Doesn't feel right." Turning on her heel, she surveyed the blackened circle again. And the heavy hoist chain and hook. "He needs the attention but not necessarily from us. He wants to generate unease. Fear."

Nate frowned. "From who?"

"From his future victims."

———

There was less to see at the next scene. It wasn't as well chosen as the first or third spots had been. The offender had secured Tull to a tree to keep him upright. The spreading fire had torched that tree and those around it.

Risa scanned the charred remains of the wooded area. It looked like a forest fire had raged a crooked path through the space, leaving devastation in its wake.

"Once the trees torched, I understand the fire could be seen for miles. It probably drew the quickest response of the three."

"And he left the badge and ID over there, right?" She pointed toward the clearing several hundred yards away. Nate made a sound of agreement. "Took a chance that they wouldn't be found, that far away from the victim. But he wanted to be sure they didn't get destroyed in the fire. That wouldn't have suited his purpose at all."

Nate's cell rang. While he answered it, she moved closer to the clearing, turning to get a different angle. Neither scene was familiar to her. She hadn't dreamt of any but the third one. It was useless to wonder why. There had never been any rhyme or reason to the visions. What they showed or what remained hidden. Little about them was clear at first. If the same one repeated, sometimes more was revealed with each recurrence. Sometimes not.

Much remained open to interpretation. Some showed scenes from the past, others dealt with future events. They couldn't be summoned by force of will, and the details from the scene couldn't be sharpened. They were tortuous in every way. Hideous visions of agony that haunted her sleeping hours. Nebulous intangibles that spoke more to emotion than logic.

But she'd spent her career trying to make sense of them. Trying, finally, to put them to use. Because otherwise they existed only to torment.

"Change of plans."

She jerked a little at Nate's words. Looked up to see him striding toward her. "We'll have to put off our next stops until later. Shroot came up with some possibilities for the location where that tape segment might have been shot."

As he headed back toward the center of town, Risa had his phone and was talking to the detective. "Z's Place? Spell that, please." She jotted it down with the rest of the possibilities on the notepad she'd pulled from her purse. "Ah. Zee's Place. Address?" She scribbled down his answer. "What year phone book is that in? Is it in the current one? When did it stop appearing?"

The man had found three places in all, one that was currently in existence and two that had apparently gone out of business in the mid to late eighties. "Nice job," she said when he'd finished relaying the information. "Keep looking."

His response had her laughing in sympathy. "I'm sure Detective McGuire will figure out some way to make it up to you."

Nate shot her a narrowed look as she handed back his phone. "Your detective is ready to stab pencils through his eyes. Have a little empathy."

"I could always make it up to him by having you take his place."

"On the other hand, I'm sure he feels good about the assistance he's lending to the investigation." Her sympathy didn't run quite far enough to sharing the thankless job. "Intrinsic reinforcement is really the most meaningful reward." She spied a Starbucks up ahead. "Aside from good coffee, that is."

When he drove past the store, she shot him a look. His profile was expressionless.

"Bu-u-t . . . I guess I can get along without it." She went back to studying the notes she'd jotted down.

"You know what we might need here?"

"Coffee?"

"Some sort of city historian or a book on commerce in the city. If the place in that picture hasn't existed for a couple decades, there has to be a record of it somewhere. Doesn't the historical society keep a history of neighborhoods?"

"Probably. Or what about city tax rolls?" she suggested. "Problem is, we've got possible names of businesses *across the street* from the one we're interested in." The letters of the neon sign reflected in the window had to have come from that direction. "So first we have to match the name to that business. Once we find it, we have to see if someone remembers the surrounding area well enough to identify the place across from it."

"You make it sound like a piece of cake."

She decided sarcasm wasn't a good tone for him. "Maybe we'll get lucky and the place is still in business. Or that it's a settled neighborhood with people who like to talk about the good ol' days. Hey, maybe we can track down a beat cop that used to work the area." Traffic was a logjam. Risa had the thought that she could probably jump out of the car, jog back to Starbucks, order, and catch up to the vehicle before it had progressed more than a few blocks. Problem was, she needed the energy a good jolt of caffeine would provide before she could summon the energy.

"Better chance of finding a longtime resident of the neighborhood than tracking down the officer walking a particular neighborhood beat twenty years ago," he muttered. At the first opportunity, he turned off onto a side street, saying by way of explanation, "It's longer this way in miles, but we'll get there quicker by avoiding the traffic."

"A long shortcut." She gave a nod. "Makes perfect sense to me." As it would to any Philly native who'd spent an alarming fraction of their life in commute.

Settling more comfortably into the seat, she closed her eyes. The day promised to be a long one, and it would seem even longer with no sleep.

She'd already resigned herself to one with no coffee.

Chapter 11

The sudden deafening lyrics of Lady Gaga had Risa jolting up and forward, smartly rapping her knee against the underside of the dash. Rubbing the injured area, she sent Nate a glower. "A simple 'we're here' wouldn't suffice?"

He grinned, turned down the radio. "I thought you'd like to wake up with a song in your heart."

"If I did, I'd pick an artist I actually like." She gathered up the notes she'd taken while on the phone with Shroot as Nate jockeyed for a parking place.

"What's not to like?" To her shock, he sang the refrain from "Poker Face" in an amazingly bad baritone.

His clowning was disarming. It was a completely different side of the taciturn detective. "I can't believe you even know that song."

"Why? I like poker." Slinging an arm over the seat, he performed a parallel parking job that would have dazzled a seasoned driving instructor.

"You mean you like twentysomething artists singing about poker while half naked and hanging upside down from a trapeze." The musician's antics and costumes were a source of bemusement to Risa.

"Hey, musicians suffer for their art. I'm there to suffer with them."

Because it would only encourage him, she hid her smile by starting to open the door. Then pulled it shut again when the blare of a taxi's horn and a shouted curse warned her that the door was in danger of being taken off.

The vehicle whizzed by them, Jiffy Kab's finest offering her a one-fingered salute. "Maybe you should get out on my side," Nate suggested.

There was no dignified way to scramble across the vehicle's front seat, so Risa opted for speed over grace. And wanted to smack the man holding the door for his undivided attention to her progress.

Once she hit the sidewalk, she contented herself with an accidentally on-purpose elbow jab to the gut. "Oh, sorry," she lied.

"Uh-huh." He slammed the door and locked it with the remote access fob. "Just for that I'm going to have to tell you that you snore."

She studied the address on the notepad, looked up to compare it to the street they were on. "No. I don't."

"Why do women all say that?" he asked reasonably as they fell into step together. Almost immediately he had to step aside to allow an elderly lady and her two yapping Pekinese to go by. Catching up with Risa again, he continued seamlessly, "It's not like you'd know you were snoring if you're sleeping."

"Without casting aspersions on your vast experience with unconscious women . . . I wasn't asleep."

His answering snort said it all.

"I was dozing," she emphasized. "Partially aware at all times." There wasn't a chance on earth that she'd fall asleep in the presence of anyone else. The dreams appeared at random intervals and could be difficult to explain to others. Her ex had known only that she had occasional nightmares, which she could usually attribute to bad take-out. She'd never told Mac Langel about the dreams that haunted her. Doing so had never even occurred to her. Risa was sure that said something rather sad about her three-year marriage. But if her own mother hadn't understood them, how could she have expected Mac to?

Adam Raiker was the only person on earth she'd entrusted the truth to. And him only because there were no secrets left unburied in the grueling series of employment interviews for Raiker Forensics. She'd fully expected her admission to eliminate her from the running. Been more than a little shocked when it hadn't. And gratified that he hadn't treated the news as proof that her worst fears were true: that the visions made her a freak of nature.

"Zeke's Food Plaza?" She stood in front of the storefront he led her to and looked at it dubiously before casting a considering look at the businesses across from it. Both sides of the busy street were bordered with strip malls. Tucked into the one across from them was a nail parlor, a dog-grooming salon, and a fabric shop. The enormity of their task struck her again.

Zeke's was surprisingly busy, and it took a few minutes before the harried-looking checker looked their way. "Help you?"

Nate flashed his shield. "Looking for some information on the neighborhood. How long have you worked here?"

"Dunno." The woman scratched one pockmarked cheek. "Eighteen months?"

"Is there anyone who's been here longer? Is the owner around?"

In lieu of an answer, she merely bent the stem of the store microphone at her checking station and said, "Zeke. You got people who want to see you on station two." Obviously thinking she'd done her duty, she began checking out the customer waiting in her aisle.

"Send them back to the meat counter." The order blared on a speaker across the store. The clerk jerked a thumb toward the rear of the place to indicate the location, and they headed across the store.

Nate unwrapped a stick of gum and placed it in his mouth. He offered her the pack and she shook her head. It was hard for her to imagine a place like this as it must have been decades ago. There had certainly been no strip malls in evidence in the scene from the video.

Zeke, however, would have been in his prime at the time it was shot. Easily pushing seventy, his eyebrows boasted more hair than did his head, and his expression was set in dour lines. He looked like a man who expected the worst out of life and whose expectations were consistently met. They had to wait for a woman to dither over the merits of lamb or beef for her dinner party before he wiped his hands on his stained apron and ambled their way. "You looking for me?" His faint accent pegged him as a displaced New Yorker.

Nate briefly explained their purpose while he waited with barely concealed impatience.

"Been here since '89. Before that the place was another food mart, but it was mostly produce. I bought the place next door and expanded to this paradise you see before you today."

"I'm sure there have been a lot of changes over the years," Risa said conversationally.

The man made a rude sound, sent a quick glance at the two other customers that had come up to the counter and were waiting. "Changes ain't usually for the good, know what I mean? Strip malls sprouting up all around me. If I hadn't owned this place free and clear, they'd have put me right out of business when the developers started sniffing around with their fancy ideas. Wanted to buy me out, but I told them, 'Nope, I'm staying put. Why don't you find some other neighborhood to ruin?' Instead they've got me penned in with scrapbooking stores and tattoo parlors."

"I'll bet a lot of businesses sold out when the developers made them an offer," Nate observed pleasantly. "You remember the name of the ones across the street when you started here?"

"Sure, there was Juno's, a great little steakhouse. And a mom and pop dry-goods store. What the hell was it?" His eyes rolled upward, as if consulting the heavens. "Dacy's, that was it. Had a Sinclair gas station over there on the corner." He jabbed an index finger to indicate the direction.

At the mention of the steakhouse, Risa felt a spark of interest. "I noticed your sign out front. Is it original?"

"Naw." The man did a visual check on the waiting customers again. "My nephew talked me into replacing it a few years back. Nothing wrong with the old one, if you ask me."

"Was the original sign neon, by any chance?"

The suggestion garnered Zeke's full attention. "Neon?" He glared at Risa. "Does this look like the kind of place that advertises in neon? You know what neon signage says?" Obviously the topic got him worked up. "It's says cheap. Fly by night. Neon says booze and women. You don't put neon on a family grocery store. My old sign was hand painted. Liked it a lot better than the one up now, to tell you the truth. 'Scuse me." He stomped away to bless the waiting customers with his sunny disposition.

"What do you want to guess that his nephew got a similar earful when they were discussing new signs for the business?" she said as they strolled toward the front of the store. She stopped by the checker again on the way by. "You don't sell hot coffee by any chance, do you?"

The woman never lost a beat in the items she was scanning. "Got cans and bags in aisle five."

Risa sighed and followed Nate out the door. The day wasn't starting out very promising. At the risk of mirroring Zeke's attitude, she had a feeling it'd get worse before it improved.

Several hours later she was ready to wrestle McGuire's cell phone away from him and toss it into oncoming traffic. He regularly used it to check in with the detectives on the task force, and with the station house. Shroot occasionally called with updates whenever he found another business name that might fit the letters they'd given him. As a result, even though they'd made five stops so far, their list had actually grown longer.

Nate reached over and took the notepad out of her hand, studying the addresses. "Let's try this one next."

She looked at the one he'd tapped and frowned. "That's nowhere close to here. I thought we were working in enlarging circles to avoid crisscrossing all over the city."

He'd already backed out of the lot they'd been parked in and was waiting for a break in traffic so he could turn onto the street. "If I don't miss my guess, that address puts us in the vicinity of the one Randolph gave us for Juicy. Since he hasn't seen fit to grace us with his presence yet, I thought I'd stop by and extend a personal invitation."

"None of the men you've put on it have been able to locate him," she pointed out. It didn't much matter to her one way or another. The stops they'd been making had taken on a mind-numbing sameness. "What makes you think you'll have better luck?"

"Probably won't," he admitted, making a quick turn onto the street when he saw his chance. "But like I say, his address is close to that name on the list. We can kill two birds with one stone. I have orders from Morales to go easy on him if and when he does surface."

"Because of Vice's plans for him?"

Glancing in the rearview mirror, he did a deft lane switch. "They're definitely interested in what Crowley might be able to give them on him, yeah. I don't envy them trying to hold Crowley in check, though. The first sign of trouble and he's likely to shift loyalties."

Again he got off the more congested street and began taking side streets to his destination. She had a vague sense of where the next address was. Unless city renovation had recently made its mark, the area was crime ridden, with dilapidated project housing and tired tenements hemming weary storefront vendors. "Used to be a great gym in the area of this address," she recalled aloud. "A bit closer to Temple University, maybe. A bunch of us from the force used to work out there when I was a rookie."

"The Ironhouse Gym. Yeah, I knew that place. I had a membership for a while. Got tired of having my hubcaps missing every time I got back to my car, though."

Oddly, the remark made her nostalgic. "Yeah, we used to lay bets on whose car would get hit. I actually met my ex there." The memory didn't generate tender feelings, but the circumstances around the meet did. "Humiliated him on the court in front of his buddies."

"He was a cop, you said." His tone was carefully even. "Did you keep his name after the divorce?"

"Never took it." She watched the general appearance of the buildings flanking the streets erode with each block. "Didn't see the point." She sometimes wondered if she'd known intuitively it wouldn't last and had wanted to save herself the headache of switching back. The thought was vaguely depressing. She might have entered the marriage for all the wrong reasons, but she liked to think she'd gone into it with some level of commitment.

"What's his name?" His tone was entirely too casual as he slowed the car for the members of the pickup baseball game to scatter from the street. "Maybe I've run into him."

With well over six thousand police officers in the PPD ranks, it was doubtful, but she told him anyway. "Mac Langel."

His expression was shocked. "You were married to Mac Langel?"

"Relatively briefly. Watch that kid."

His attention switched back to the street, where a girl who couldn't have been more than four was darting out in front of him. "Mac Langel. Wow."

Pursuing the topic was a mistake. Intellectually, Risa knew it. But there was a load of disapproval layered over the disbelief in his voice. She blamed the poor choice she was about to make on hunger and lack of sleep. Not to mention, she never had gotten that coffee. "You know him?"

"A little."

After that reaction, she'd expected a bit more detail. "Sounded like more than a little."

He turned into a deeply rutted parking lot wedged against a Thai restaurant. "Enough to know you were way out of his league."

The unexpected compliment softened something inside her. Just when she thought she had him pegged, he could take her unaware. "Thanks. And just so you realize I caught it, nice dodge."

He hesitated long enough to put the vehicle in park. Turn off the ignition. Then he faced her. "Okay. He's an idiot. Got a chip on his shoulder and a constant need to prove himself. I don't like playing with him or against him on the court. I sure as hell wouldn't want to be partnered with him. You had a lucky escape."

Shrugging, she said only, "It was a long time ago. I was looking for . . . permanence, I guess." Something that had always been sorely lacking when she was growing up. "We seemed to have a lot in common." Oddly, she appreciated the rude sound he made at that. She'd come to realize that when it came to values, at least, she and Mac were continents apart. "What about you? Any former spouses you'd like me to rip on?"

One corner of his mouth quirked up. "Never been married. Had someone serious a few years ago. Then I had to take over guardianship of my nephew and she bolted."

A nephew. All sorts of layers were exposing themselves in Nate McGuire today. "Your nephew lives with you?"

"My sister's back now, too. It's complicated." He opened the car door and got out, leaving Risa to agree silently. She'd never had any siblings, but she could certainly attest that family was complicated.

The Thai restaurant didn't match the address they were looking for, but the liquor store next to it did. Its flickering neon sign promising WINE, BEER, SPIRITS wasn't a match for the one they sought, but she hadn't expected it would be. The last telephone listing for Zena's Place that Shroot had discovered was in the 1992 Yellow Pages.

What was even more disheartening was the fact there was no building at all directly across from it. An empty lot punctuated the street front like a gap-toothed grin, litter and rubbish piled in precarious heaps.

Without much hope, she followed Nate into the store and found him already speaking to the middle-aged eastern Indian clerk there. "We have been here nine years," he was telling Nate. "Bad neighborhood. Very bad. I have been robbed thirteen times. My third insurance company is threatening to drop me. Maybe I will move the business. But to where? Other places sell liquor, too."

Rather than aisles of product, he had his wares displayed from floor to ceiling behind the full-length counter. Obviously an attempt to prevent shoplifting.

"Was this place a liquor store when you bought it?" Nate asked him. A stooped, grizzled old man shuffled through the front door.

The owner shook his head. "A Laundromat. And the owner, he promised no trouble from the neighborhood. None, he said. Ha!" Without speaking to the newcomer, he went to the section that housed the vodka and unerringly plucked a bottle from the shelf. The older man withdrew an ancient wallet from his pants pocket and painstakingly counted out the appropriate amount while the storekeeper rang up the sale and placed the bottle in a sack.

"Was there a building in that lot across the street when you first opened up?" Risa asked.

"Nothing as long as I have been here." The owner and his customer made their exchange silently.

"What about the Laundromat's name?"

The storeowner was clearly losing interest in the conversation. "I do not remember."

"Suds 'N' Such," a quavering voice put in.

Risa and Nate turned to the old man. He was trying unsuccessfully to replace his wallet in his pocket. After several attempts he finally succeeded. Looking up, he found their gazes on him.

"Didn't last long, though."

"Do you remember Zena's Place being here?"

"Oh, yeah. Of course. Nice little lunch counter. Opened for dinner some nights, too." He hadn't bothered to put in his bottom partial plate. Or maybe he didn't own one. "She's been dead now . . ." He rubbed his grizzled chin reflectively. "Shoot. Since '91 or so."

"You've lived in the neighborhood a long time?" Risa thought he looked as if he could have been here when the buildings first sprang up. He wore a floor-length army green topcoat, hanging open, although the temperatures had turned much warmer in the last couple days. Baggy black pants with matching suspenders over a stained white T-shirt and boots completed his attire.

"Lived upstairs for nearly forty years. Back then this wasn't a bad place to raise a family. Lots of poor folk but nones that'd do you no harm if you left them alone. Not like now."

"Maybe you can tell us about what used to be in that empty lot across the street."

"That's been empty nearly fifteen years now," he said in response to Risa's question. "Was condemned long time before that. Thought the city never would get around to tearing that old place down. Were two buildings there at one time. A little shoe repair shop called Jimmy's and a two-story building. Looked sorta like the one still standing over there." He pointed a shaking finger to the boarded-up building on one side of the lot. "It was a nice little tavern by the name of Tory's." The words sounded wistful, as if he'd spent his share of time in it. "Tory and her boy lived in the apartment above."

"Can you describe the exterior?" It was a sure thing, Risa thought, that he'd be able to describe the inside.

The old man's shrug moved his whole body. "Nuthin' special. Just a door to go in and a big front window. The bar was on the left when you got in, next to a storeroom where they kept the beer. Bunch of tables and a real nice jukebox. Tory liked to keep the music up-to-date, but she'd keep on some oldies for those of us who asked special."

"What happened to it? Why was it condemned?" Nate asked.

"Fire gutted the place back in '86. Burnt the repair shop, too. Cavanaugh's there repaired and reopened for another dozen years or so. Tory and the boy weren't hurt but never did see them after that, neither."

A car went by outside, rap music blaring, the hind end bouncing on tricked-out hydraulics. A beer bottle went sailing out the window, landing squarely on the driver's side of the Crown Vic before the car full of teens took off, hooting and catcalling.

The old man watched the scene, his mouth working silently. Then, "Nope. It wasn't a bad place to raise a family. Not back then."

When they returned to the vehicle, Risa observed, "This car should qualify for battle pay."

"It's not going to get better treatment where we're headed next."

Juicy's address, she recalled. At the rate they were going, they'd be lucky to have a vehicle to get them back to the station house. "It works, what the old man told us."

"Tarrants."

She nodded. They'd gotten his name and address before letting him leave; he'd been visibly anxious to get back to his apartment. "The rest of the places Shroot found will have to be checked out to be sure . . . but a bar could easily have been the scene of that video clip featuring Johnny and Roland Parker." The table had looked to be large. Littered with beer bottles. And a neon *z* and *p* reflected in the front window.

"Not to mention the way it was destroyed."

Exactly what she was thinking. "Too many coincidences to be entirely comfortable with," she agreed pensively. And far too many threads in the investigation, none of which could be tied up nicely yet.

The area didn't improve in the seven blocks or so to Juicy's address. The curbs had cars lined up along them. Rather than searching for a spot, Nate reached beneath the seat for a portable LED dash light and put it on the dash, setting it to strobe, and double-parked. The group of youths on the stoop of the building in front of them stopped talking and stared as they got out of the vehicle.

"It's the po-po."

"Back to the cop shop, man, we ain't doing nuthin'."

"Yo, where'd you get your car door detailed? I want me some of that." Raucous laughter accompanied the words.

"We're looking for Javon Emmons," Nate said evenly. "Juicy. He live here?"

"Never heard of him."

"Juicy? You looking for Juicy?" One of the young men with his baseball cap twisted backward nudged his neighbor. "Juicy is that fine thing you got with ya. Can't get juicier than that. Mm-mm." He licked his lips suggestively.

"Unless you want your tongue ripped out and handed to you, you'll answer the question," Risa told him. "Or get out of the way so we can go in and look for ourselves."

"Ooh-hoo, you got dissed!" A chorus of jeers bombarded the speaker. But they moved aside for Nate and Risa to move up the middle of the steps and push open the door to the apartment building.

Nate flipped the light switch inside the darkened hallway, to no avail.

"Two eighteen is upstairs," he murmured, and they turned to the littered stairway to begin the climb.

"If Juicy is as high on the feeding chain as Randolph indicated, why's he living in a place like this?" she muttered. A man was curled up on the first landing, snoring softly. Risa decided he must be sleeping off the effects of something. The noise inside the building should make sleep impossible. The cries of babies, shouts of children, and a shrill argument melded together for a near-deafening din.

"It's his territory. He'll live in the center to exact his control over it. No absentee businessmen in his line of work."

Two eighteen was at the end of the hallway, to the left of the lone window. Nate knocked at the door. Once. Again, this time harder. "Javon Emmons," he called.

Someone was moving inside the apartment. After several minutes the door swung open and a young woman stood there, one hand on her hip and the other clutching the edge of the door. After one quick glance, she dismissed Risa and focused all her attention on Nate. "Why you yelling at my door?"

"We're looking for Juicy," he replied, and tilted his head to look inside the apartment. "Tell him we'd like to talk to him."

"Everyone looking for Juicy." She sighed, skating one hand over her waist, which was left bare between her low-riding shorts and short top. "He ain't here. You can look. That's what the rest of them do."

A quick scan of the rooms in the apartment ascertained that the woman was telling the truth. Nate handed her his card. "Give him this and ask him to come in to see me. I'd like to ask him a couple questions."

"Mm-hmm. People all the time wanting to ask Juicy questions." She ran the card through her long fire engine red nails and gave him a smile from lips slicked in the same color. "I'll tell him you was here."

Back outside Risa gave a silent sigh of relief to discover the car where they left it, looking untouched. The same guys sat out front and immediately started messing with them when they came outside.

"Hey, there was someone gonna steal your po-lice car and I run 'em off. I should get a reward."

"Shut it, that was you, man."

"You don't have to leave with him, sugar. You want to set your fine self down and let me show you 'nother use for your handcuffs."

Risa didn't bother to point out that she wasn't carrying cuffs and that the suggestion wasn't especially original. The young men found it hilarious, though, as she and Nate picked their way down the narrow path allowed through the bodies.

When they were on the sidewalk again, she turned to face them. "Any of you know anything about a bar that used to be in this neighborhood?" She recited the address. "It burned down around 1986. Called Tory's."

"Eighty-six?" The speaker wore a do-rag and a large tat on the right side of his throat. "Man, I wasn't born 'til ninety-one."

She slanted a look at Nate. "Geez, they're all fetuses." He'd tensed. A moment later she noticed why.

The stranger approaching them was at least a decade older than the ones on the stoop in years, far more in experience. It was in his eyes. In the flat, hard expression with which he regarded them. "You don't got business here." The stranger wore a thigh-length black leather jacket and low-brimmed hat and held sunglasses. She'd lay odds he was carrying.

"Now, how would you know that?" Nate asked, the slightest edge to his voice. "You have a name?"

"They looking for Juicy," one of the stoop sitters offered. "They already been inside and talked to Jasmine."

The man's head jerked toward the speaker. "Nidge you better shut it before I bust a cap in your ass." The crowd on the porch went silent again.

"Tell Juicy I want to talk to him. My card's inside."

"I don't take orders from you." The stranger spit on the sidewalk, narrowly missing Risa's shoe.

"No, I'll bet you take orders from Emmons, though." She smiled at him, mockery dripping from her words. "I'll bet you jump through every hoop he holds out." The tightening of his lips was evidence that her words had found their mark. "The longer he takes to come in, the more company you're going to be getting in this neighborhood. That can make it difficult for things around here to get back to normal." She shrugged. "If that's what Juicy wants, no problem."

They moved away toward the car. Got in. As they drove off, the unidentified man on the sidewalk was still staring after them. "No matter how high he is in the organization, it'll be Emmons making the decision about whether to come in or not."

"I'm guessing they're starting to think about what constant visits from the force will do to their ability to conduct business. At least we can hope so." She turned to cock a brow at him. "What's next?"

He was silent for a moment. Then, "How about we make the rounds in a radius around the convenience store and collect any security tapes we can find before heading back for the briefing?"

"Only if you promise to let me run into the convenience store for a hot sandwich and restroom break."

"I'll do better than that." He shot her a grin as he nosed the vehicle through a green light. "I'll buy you popcorn for when we go over the security tapes later."

Risa leaned her head against the seat rest and smiled. "I have a feeling that's the best offer I'm going to get all day."

———————

He'd waited for the old lady to leave the house. Drove behind her for a couple blocks and saw her sitting at the bus stop. Once she'd actually gotten on the bus, he circled around and parked in back of her block. Cut across the yards and headed for her back door.

It was just past dusk, but Chandler's car wasn't out front yet. He had time. Just enough for a peek inside the house, a quick look through her things. He hadn't decided yet if she posed any particular threat. Had almost dismissed her. She didn't seem like anything special. But he'd never been caught because he didn't overlook anything. So he'd be thorough.

The security system was better than decent but his skills were outstanding. He wasn't standing outside any longer than someone having difficulty with his key. Still he resolved to be quick inside, in case one of the neighbors got nosy.

The first bedroom was the old lady's. He swiftly went to the next. Found the tailored suits and bright tops in the closet and knew he had the right place. He looked around for a computer and realized disappointedly she'd probably have it with her.

There wasn't much else to see, but he went through her

drawers, checked her closet to be sure. Found nothing of interest, because *she* was of no interest. No threat. Not even worth the time wasted thinking about her.

He grinned, cocky now. His plans were set and neither she nor McGuire could prevent the inevitable. In an effort to be meticulous, he opened the drawer of the bedside table. Whistled soundlessly when he saw the holstered weapon there. It was impossible to resist taking it out. Drawing the gun from the holster and sighting it.

The Beretta was a bit too small in his hand but probably was a good fit for the woman. Checking, he discovered it was unloaded. Either he'd overlooked a magazine in his search, or she didn't have ammunition for it. Either way, it didn't worry him.

He replaced the weapon and started to head out of the room, brushing a pad of paper off the bedside table to the floor. He picked it up, searched for the pencil that had gone rolling. Everything had to be left exactly as it was found.

Idly, he flipped through the pad, and when he saw the sketches, he stopped to look more closely. Then felt the blood congeal in his veins.

The fire was so real he could hear its crackle and hiss, even in the black-and-white drawing. The trees hemmed the clearing, not so close that the fire would be in danger of spreading to them. He hadn't made that mistake twice. He turned the page, saw a sketch of the old oak with the crossed branches.

Everything inside him went still. He stopped breathing for a moment.

And there he was. A black silhouette against the flames, arms out-flung in exultation over what he'd accomplished.

The pad started shaking. It took a moment for him to realize his hand was trembling. She knew everything. Had seen everything.

Frantically, he flipped through the pictures, examining every page with desperate eyes. He wiped a hand over his face, fought for calm. The drawings were all of the same scene. Painstaking details of Christiansen's death. It was as if she'd been there, documenting how it went down.

But that wasn't possible.

It wasn't possible, he assured himself and worked his shoulders impatiently. The bitch wasn't there because nobody had been there. He'd made damn sure of that. If she had been, if she'd been close enough to see the detail for these sketches, she'd have seen *him*.

And if she'd seen him, he'd be in jail right now.

The logic of it calmed him as nothing else could. It was just a figure of a man. The details didn't identify him. Of course. She was working on the case. She'd seen pictures. Maybe even been to the scene. It'd take nothing but memory and a little talent to draw a visual of what must have transpired that night.

He'd almost believe that. He looked through the sketches again, his heart still racing. If it weren't for the figure she'd drawn. The familiar pose of it. And try as he might, he couldn't find a reasonable explanation for that portion of the sketch.

With quick, jerky motions he shoved the sketchpad under his sweatshirt. Strode toward the kitchen. He had to get it together. Too many years had been spent planning. Chandler wasn't going to interfere with that. There was nothing here to convince him to deviate from his schedule. Preparations were made. Everything was set.

But there was enough, more than enough, to convince him that once he'd dealt with more pressing issues, Chandler would have to die.

Chapter 12

The detective pushed the door shut behind him and locked it before dropping his keys on the wicker table nearby. He hated wicker. Even the name sounded wimpy, but Cheryl had insisted that decorating the house was her domain. If the house were her domain, he'd have figured the bedroom was his. But a year ago he'd found out she was using it with their accountant to go over more than their numbers.

It'd seemed only fair then that he'd kept the house. Or probably she just hadn't given a damn. She'd moved in with the boyfriend in the suburbs. When the divorce was final, he was going to load up all the shit she'd bought. Every last damn flowered curtain, vase of dried flowers, and for damn sure, all the wicker. He'd haul it to her new home and dump it on the front lawn for her fuck buddy to deal with.

He'd start over and fill the place with stuff a guy could feel comfortable in. The first thing he'd done after she'd walked out was smash the collection of antique teapots displayed on a unit in the family room where a TV should have gone.

The second thing he'd done was go out and buy the biggest-screen TV he could find.

He toed off his shoes and padded stocking footed to the

kitchen. Opened the fridge to grab a beer. Twisting off the cap, he tossed it to the counter and kept the refrigerator door open, peering inside as he drank, hoping the contents would change.

They didn't. The one thing he still missed about having Cheryl around was that she'd taken care of the grocery shopping. It looked like it'd be peanut butter again tonight.

He let the fridge swing shut with the intent of trying the cupboard when he heard a small sound. Instinct had him going for his weapon as he turned. He stopped in midmotion when he found a Sig P220 equipped with silencer shoved in his face.

"Jesus." In a split second, he evaluated his chances of completing the draw. Found them dismal.

"You think you're that fast? Want to see?"

The whispered voice was vaguely familiar. But the oversized hooded sweatshirt the guy was wearing shadowed his face. "What the fuck do you want?" But, God, he knew what the cocksucker wanted. His body knew anyway. His knees felt like Jell-O and his heart was pounding hard enough to tear through his chest. Sweat slicked his brow.

"Turn around."

Slowly, mind racing, he did as he was told.

"Hands behind your head."

His arms rose slowly. He wasn't going like the others. Knowing what was in store for him made the decision easy. He'd take his chances with the gun. Hell, he might take a bullet but he could still get a shot off.

And he'd rather go down in gunfire than be torched like the rest of the guys.

He felt the Sig pressed against his spine. Half expected a bullet to shatter it as he went for his weapon, turning at the same time. He hadn't completed the turn when something was shoved in his face. A nauseatingly sweet, pungent smell filled his nostrils. As he dropped to his knees, his weapon clattered out of his hand.

The first thought that made it through his groggy brain was that he had a helluva headache for not stopping at the bar tonight.

Then comprehension rushed in. His bowels went to ice water. He was in a cellar. At least the stone all around him seemed like one. But there was a mess of stars overhead. A slivered moon. It was probably no more than a crumbling foundation somewhere. Outside the city maybe.

Far from help.

Fear unlike any he'd ever known had Randolph lunging forward. Chains jangled. His hands were fastened above his head and secured to a spot in the stone behind him. And the smell that filled the air was terrifying.

Gasoline.

Panic did a fast sprint up his spine. "What do you want? I'll give you anything you want."

Except the words came out muffled. He shook his head, trying to dislodge whatever was surrounding his face.

"That's a smoke mask, Jack." The tone was conversational. "Hate to go to all this trouble and have you succumb to smoke inhalation too quickly. Seems rude not to stay alive long enough to appreciate all I've done here. How tough are you? Let's find out, shall we?"

A match scratched and flared in the darkness. Illuminated the face of the last man he expected to see here. Shocked disbelief filled him. "You? But why?"

"That's right." The match was tossed in a slow descent toward his feet. "It's me. And we'll have a lot of time to talk about why."

Frantically Randolph stomped out the match that landed near his foot. And the next one. Then the one after it. Soft laughter sounded. The entire matchbook was lit and made a slow arc toward his feet. He tried to stomp it, too, but the hem of his pants flared. "No!"

He tried to rub his other leg over the flame, only to watch aghast as the other pant leg caught fire, too. The first scorch seared his flesh. "Oh, God, please!"

"I didn't realize you were a praying man, Jack. I guess there's lots we don't know about each other. When the fire really gets going, I'm going to have to crawl up and out of here and watch from above. So first let me fill you in on a few of those details about me."

———

"Next time, I'm picking the movie." Risa yawned and watched without enthusiasm as Nate got up to put in yet another security tape they'd collected. "Yours don't seem to have a plot."

It was past one. They'd moved to the conference room where the briefings were held because the TV, VCR, and DVD player were already set up there. Both of them had long since gotten comfortable. They'd shed their jackets and Nate was minus his tie. Her feet were propped on another chair, and until a few moments ago, he'd been in a similar pose.

And, as promised, there was popcorn. Microwave, but she hadn't had enough to eat today to be especially choosy.

"Eleven and a half minutes passed from the time Christiansen pulled in to that convenience store lot and the security camera caught the back door of his car opening. In that time, the offender had to find a place to park, run to the convenience store lot, and break into the car."

"We've already watched the videos from the areas closest to the lot," she said around a yawn. He had to have left the car in a spot that he could access quickly without scouting beforehand. "He may have lucked into a parking place near no cameras."

Nate dropped the tape he was extracting and, muttering a curse, bent to pick it up. Because she wasn't dead, Risa tilted her head for a better view. The man was built. Broad shoulders tapered to a narrow waist and a tight behind. Topped off by his smoldering dark good looks and he was three for three in the tall, dark, and handsome category. She was only surprised she hadn't tripped over some of his admirers yet.

Her mouth quirked. Of course, there had been the older woman calling to offer borscht. Which may have been wrapped up in an ethnic culinary bow, but there was little doubt what she'd really been suggesting. Risa was certain most women were far more obvious in their interest.

He turned then to say something, caught her gaze on him. A purely masculine smirk settled on his face. "Made you look, huh. See anything you like?"

Oh, yeah. Nate McGuire was definitely used to female attention. "You've got a hole in the seam of your pants."

The smirk faded in dramatic fashion as he rose and

twisted around, one hand going to his butt. Then he glanced at her. "I do not."

It was her turn to smirk. "Made *you* look."

"That's what I like about you, Chandler. Your maturity."

"That's only because you don't know me well enough to be familiar with my myriad other charms." Punchy with weariness, she slouched farther down in her chair. "I'm a kick-ass chess player."

Looking unimpressed, he slid a different tape into the slot and picked up the remote before heading back to the table. "I'm more of a checkers guy, myself. Although I've been known to get beaten by my five-year-old nephew, most of the time it's because I let him win. Almost always," he corrected himself.

Unwillingly charmed, she considered him. It was late. She was low on caffeine, sleep, and food, in that order. But there was something appealing in the open affection with which he spoke of his nephew. Coupled with the dangerously desirable sleepy-eyed and stubbled look he was sporting now, and she was skating perilously close to attraction.

She wouldn't let it bother her. Tomorrow, when she was well rested and proactive enough to buy her own jug of coffee before heading in to work, she'd be back at the top of her game. Professionalism firmly in place. But right now, she let herself consider how long it'd been since she'd simply enjoyed the company of a good-looking man with whom she shared a common interest. Found the answer dismally difficult to summon.

There had been men since her divorce, but none that couldn't be forgotten the moment Raiker sent her to whatever location a case demanded. Las Vegas, Chicago, Tampa, New Orleans. Few males of her acquaintance were content to put up with the weeks-at-a-time absences demanded by her work. Fewer still had elicited any real regret when they'd moved on.

She had a feeling that leaving Nate McGuire behind could lead to a boatload of remorse. Which was only one of the many reasons there was no way she'd allow anything to start between them.

Risa was carrying all of the regrets she could handle already.

To distract herself from the familiar gloom just threatening to settle, she picked up the original thread of the conversation. "Took my police basketball team to the city championship three years running."

"Yeah?" That disclosure was met with more interest than the first. He resettled himself in his chair and started the tape. "Why do I have the feeling you think you're hot shit on the court?" His look was appraising. "You play college level?"

"Penn State."

"Bunch of pussies." He coupled the trash talk with a smile. "I quarterbacked for the Fighting Irish. We regularly kicked the Nittany Lions' ass."

"That's because the women's basketball team wasn't on the field."

That drew a laugh from him. Their attention to the black-and-white action—or lack thereof—on the screen was desultory. "I seem to recall them being good a while back. It was a couple years after I'd graduated. Was that . . ." His voice trailed off abruptly. Both of them straightened, their feet hitting the floor in unison as they leaned forward.

"That's the same guy, isn't it?" Risa asked, weariness banished by a flare of adrenaline. "Where's his girlfriend?"

The man on the screen looked a lot like the one that had been filmed in front of the convenience store that had been Patrick Christiansen's last stop. Same dark-colored hoodie, pulled up over his head, shielding his features from the camera. Except he was minus the girl he'd been having an argument with when he was filmed in front of the store. "Back it up."

Ignoring the remote, Nate made his way to the TV. He re-ran the tape. Paused it and started again. Risa got up to join him to get a closer look at the unfolding scene. The car pulled into the lot in front of the pawnshop and jolted to a stop, as if the driver was in a hurry. The guy in the hoodie got out, took something out of the backseat, and jammed it under his over-sized sweatshirt before straightening to slam the door behind him and head across the lot toward the east.

"That pawn shop is a block east of the convenience store," Nate murmured, his gaze fixed on the screen. "He must have been tailing Christiansen from a ways back. Saw his stop and picked the first the place he could leave the car."

The figure had moved well beyond the sight of the camera. He reached out to rewind the tape again.

"If this is our guy, he wasn't arguing with his girlfriend," she theorized. "But it makes a great cover. He sees a lone female, grabs her, and pretends to shower her with some unwanted attention. She tells him to get lost, we pick up that argument on the convenience store's external security tapes, but it looks like something else. He probably keeps up the guise just past the camera's range, drops it to run around the building, and comes back on all fours." He'd stayed well out of range of the convenience store's cameras, she recalled. Even with enhancement, all they'd gotten from that tape was the shadow initially shown slipping into the backseat of Christiansen's car. "Maybe later in the tape we'll see him come back for the vehicle."

If he heard her, he gave no indication. He rewound the tape several more times, seemed to focus on the car rather than the figure. Then she sat in silence as he ran it forward, pausing it occasionally. Eventually nearby bars and restaurants closed, leaving it the only car in the lot. The passing of time on the tape was evidenced by the gradual lightening of the sky. By the time the tape had run out, the time stamp on the screen said nine A.M. A clerk had pulled into the lot, given the car a glance, and headed into the store. At eleven A.M. the car still sat there.

At eleven thirty A.M. a tow truck backed into the lot and hooked up the vehicle. Hauled it away.

"Son of a bitch," Nate breathed, sounding as stunned as Risa felt. "Is it possible the offender's car ended up in the impound lot?"

"Maybe as the truck loads it, we'll get an angle that shows the vehicle's license plate number," she said hopefully. They were standing shoulder to shoulder now, inches from the screen. Nothing short of a natural catastrophe could have had her tearing her gaze away. As the scene unwound, she scarcely dared to breath.

When the plate came into view only the first half of the number was displayed. Nate was diving for his jacket, scrambling for the notebook he always carried in the pocket. She reached out to pause the tape until he was ready, then started it again so he could write the number down. It was impossible to tell the color of the car on the black-and-white tape. "It's a Ford, isn't it?" Car models weren't her forte.

He looked up. Stared at the screen again. "Ford Five Hundred. Two thousand seven or two thousand eight is my guess."

The information rang a bell. "Isn't that the same model . . ."

He finished her sentence for her. "The same model that Sherman Tull was driving when he disappeared." They stared at each other, disbelief warring with excitement. "Son of a bitch," Nate said again, his tone slightly awed. He slipped an arm around her waist for a hard hug. "We've been wondering what the offender did with the victims' cars. Could he really be that ballsy?"

The warmth his touch elicited sent an answering shower of sparks through her veins. It suited Risa to blame that on the excitement generated by a possible break in the case. "Does the partial plate match Tull's vehicle?"

Nate strode quickly back to the table, where he'd left the bulging case file he'd brought downstairs with him. It took several minutes for him to look for the necessary information. She remained where she was. It seemed safer that way.

Finally he looked up, his excitement visibly dimmed. "No. But if we go back to my office, I can access the database to determine who the vehicle belongs to."

She extracted the tape and helped him pile it along with the others into the large cardboard box he'd carried them in. Then they headed back to Nate's office. The initial adrenaline from the discovery had subsided, leaving Risa with an overwhelming sense of exhaustion. She needed sleep. And more than that, she needed distance. Spending long hours penned up with Nate McGuire was playing havoc with her normal good sense.

And good sense dictated never, ever getting personally involved while on a case.

While he accessed the information, she sat down, uncertain how much longer she could remain upright.

Finally Nate looked up from the computer screen, his expression pensive. "The state of Pennsylvania issued fifty-seven plates beginning with those three digits to owners of

2007 or 2008 Ford Five Hundreds. Half of them list Philadelphia or the immediate surrounding area as their address."

There was more. Something in his voice alerted her. "And?"

"There was a local report of stolen plates with the same three digits made just last week. The owner is seventy-two and rarely uses her vehicle. Keeps it in the parking garage for the apartment complex she lives in. She hasn't driven the car in over a month."

They looked at each other in mutual understanding. "Which would have given the UNSUB ample opportunity to switch the stolen plates to Sherman Tull's vehicle."

The fire was licking up a stone wall, engulfing the figure chained to it. The body gilded by the flames was almost silent as it writhed in inhuman agony, only muffled sounds that had to be screams escaping it. The watcher stood over the scene, elevated as if levitating, cavorting nude in a joyous dance as the figure burned.

The watcher bent and spun, releasing something into the air. Once and then again. Each article spun in a speeding arc to land in opposite directions in the tall weeds. Then the watcher resumed his dance, celebrating the death that was taking place below. A picture of triumph and sheer madness.

The moan that wakened her didn't belong to the victim. It was her own.

Risa sat up, sweating and shaking, her heart racing in her chest like a runner's after a record-setting sprint. It took long moments to regulate her breathing. To focus on the simple act of hauling oxygen in and out of deprived lungs.

It took far longer to calm her pulse.

She rubbed the perspiration from her face with a hand that that trembled as if with palsy. And made herself, through sheer force of will, consider the details revealed by the newest vision.

There was no rhyme or reason in the way the dreams played out. In one she might be a spectator, in yet another it would be as if she were in the victim's place suffering their pain.

It was those dreams that took the worst toll on her.

After all of them, she was left to decipher what they meant. How the events unfolded. When they might have happened. Who was involved.

It was the "who" that made it especially difficult to return her breathing to normal.

Because the man engulfed in flames was Detective Mark Randolph.

Sneaky little needles of doubt pierced her then, detracting from her conclusions. The dreams were rarely specific. Her interpretation of them could be erroneous. That had been all too evident in Minneapolis.

Drawing her knees up, she enfolded them with her arms, rocked a little. She'd been to all three scenes. This one was different, she was certain of it. Outside, but not the park where Christiansen had been found. Not the woods that had been torched with Parker.

Was the dream a depiction of the past or the future? If the past, it would have to be fairly recent. They'd just spoken to the man a couple of days ago. She and Nate had been at the station house until after midnight. No call had come in.

She looked at the alarm clock on her bedside table. Would Nate have contacted her if there had been another report? She'd like to think he would. Liked to think that their relationship had eased into something resembling mutual respect, at least, in the last day or so.

Her mind scuttled away from the memory of his enthusiastic celebratory hug. She wasn't ready to interpret *that*.

The scene might be a psychic interface with the future. A snippet of what was to come. There was no doubt in her mind regarding the identity of the victim. There had been no identifying the voice behind those garbled muffled screams. No visual, certainly, of the face being eaten by flames.

But there had been an up close look at one of the items the watcher had tossed. The police identification had been easily read. Illogical, because of the darkness. But logic had no place in the dreams. Their very existence defied it.

The ID had shown a familiar face. Borne a familiar name.

Either Mark Randolph had fallen prey to the man the media had dubbed Cop Killer. Or he was going to.

She looked at the cell phone on the table consideringly. Randolph's contact information would be in her copy of the case file. She could call him now, pretend an urgent need for information . . . on Juicy, maybe.

But she'd have to explain that call to Nate, if the detective mentioned it to him later. Not difficult to do under other circumstances. She was used to having to manufacture cover stories for her "instincts" about events she shouldn't know about. But it'd be easier to cover a phone call made to the detective on the way to work than one in the middle of the night.

And the depressing truth was, if the vision was from the recent past, Mark Randolph was already dead.

A familiar wave of frustration surged through her. Rarely did the dreams provide her with enough detail to prevent something from happening. Their only positive benefit was when they gave her information that helped track down an offender and prevent him from hurting anyone else.

It was the only thing that made them bearable. And for the past several months, she'd been questioning their effectiveness in even that area.

To distract herself from the self-doubt that circled, she looked for her sketchpad. Found it missing from the table. Her lips tightened. No doubt Hannah had moved it, or removed it from the room completely. Years ago she'd often whisked away Risa's supplies when she found drawings of the hideous events from her visions. She'd never made a secret of the fact that she found the images disturbing.

Risa had always wondered if she found her daughter equally so.

Sliding open the drawer, she stuck her hand inside to see if perhaps her mother had placed it there, out of the way. Instead of the drawing pad, her searching fingers found the familiar shape of her weapon.

She snatched her hand back as if it had been burned. It had taken her over an hour last night to screw up the courage to touch the weapon. And only the worry of Hannah getting up the next day and finding it on the counter could have convinced her to pick it up. Take it to her room.

The safest place for it, of course, had been the trunk of the rental. But there was no way she could have forced herself to carry it that far. She'd practically sprinted to her bedroom to deposit it into the drawer. It'd taken far longer to screw up her courage to hold it long enough to unload it.

Which was a ridiculous waste of courage, any way you looked at it.

Snapping on the lamp, she pulled the drawer out farther. Stared at the gun that had once felt so natural she felt naked without its weight.

It was an inanimate object. Surely not deserving of the weight of blame she cast on it. *She* had failed Ryder Kremer. She'd made a serious error in judgment. Relied too heavily on details of the visions that had seemed so very clear.

Releasing a long shuddering breath, she reached her hand out. Forced herself to rest it on the weapon. Resisted the powerful urge to snatch her hand back. To shove the drawer closed as if she could shut away the memories as easily.

Her fingers trembled wildly. And she couldn't take the weapon out. Couldn't grasp it if she tried.

But it was enough. With her free hand, she shut off the lamp. Left the room in darkness once again. She'd been fooling herself by thinking she could ease into an investigation the way a swimmer dipped a toe in dangerous waters. Either she tried to work with the dreams or she disregarded them. Either she was an investigator or she wasn't. She couldn't play half-court. It was all or nothing.

Just a few short days ago she'd been convinced it would be nothing. That she was done.

Now . . . the image of Randolph's ID flashed across her memory again.

If it were going to be all . . . Her breath caught at the mere thought. Her palm dampened where it lay against the Beretta.

Then she needed to prove to her boss, to herself, that she was all the way back. Healed emotionally as well as physically.

And she couldn't convince either of them as long as she still couldn't bear to strap on her weapon.

Chapter 13

The impound lot didn't open until nine, so once Nate got to work, he left a message on the office machine to call him back. By the time he'd finished doling out assignments to the task force detectives and updated Morales on what had been discovered on the tapes last night, he'd figured to find Risa waiting in his office upon his return.

When she wasn't, he glanced at the phone. Considered contacting her.

And then called himself the worst kind of sap.

She wouldn't welcome the inquiry, and she didn't exactly need to punch a clock. Her role in the investigation was unofficial and ambiguous.

Her place in his head was just as ambiguous. And largely unwelcome. He'd never had difficulty setting aside thoughts of a woman when he was on the job. That had been his greatest problem, he'd been told loudly and at great length. One in a list, as it'd turned out. There was no reason in the world that Marisa Chandler should prove the exception to that rule.

Moving his shoulders uneasily, he blamed it on their proximity. Long hours sharing a cramped car coupled with late nights could imitate a growing intimacy.

The problem with that excuse was that he'd shared similarly long hours with Cass Recker, and his feelings for her were about the same he had for Kristin. Big brotherly, with overtones of protectiveness that both women frequently took him to task for.

Nothing like what he felt whenever Risa was around. Not by a long shot. And that should scare the hell out of him. There was too much riding on this case to allow for distractions of any sort. His relationship with his sister took more effort than he could afford right now just to keep it on an outwardly even keel. She hadn't taken off again without telling him, but if she did, he'd have his nephew to care for while juggling the long hours required by the investigation.

Most men would consider that more than enough complication in their life to avoid the temptation of a woman, no matter how damn sexy she managed to look in those severely tailored suits of hers. Which, if he were making a suggestion, would be in bright bold colors rather than black, navy, and gray drab.

Not that he'd voice *that* suggestion out loud.

Resolutely, he turned his attention to jotting notes from yesterday's briefing and managed to avoid thinking of Risa at all.

It was nearly nine by the time she entered his office. Deliberately, he kept his head down at her arrival, until a large foam to-go cup was set on the desk in front of him. "See, I'm much more reasonable about morning coffee. I even share."

"I shared yesterday," he said, finally looking up. "You just didn't . . ." He stopped then. He had to because he was at serious risk of swallowing his tongue.

Be careful what you wish for. The old adage echoed mockingly in his head, which had gone otherwise blank. Because Risa wasn't wearing a dark-color suit today. Women probably had a fancy name for the shade of suit and blouse she wore. The only one that came to his mind was nude.

Just a few tones darker than her skin, it suggested the softness and texture of flesh. It was designed to make a man's palms itch to peel it away an inch at a time, to reveal the woman beneath. At least it would tempt a man who allowed himself to be distracted.

"I didn't what?"

Her question jerked his attention back. Clearing his throat, he looked away. Picked up the coffee, although he'd already drank two of Darrell's brew. "Nothing. I'm just waiting for the impound lot to get back to me. I left a message asking them to check the VIN of the car we saw get towed on the video last night."

She turned away and approached her desk, her movements jerky. For the first time he noticed the tension in her muscles, in her stance. And she was gulping from her coffee as if it were a lifeline.

He hadn't noticed it at first glance because his mind had been observing other things, but it was obvious now that she was armed. Shoulder holster, weak side. And he damned well would have noted if she'd carried before. He seemed to be hyperaware when it came to her.

Aware enough to recognized the woman was as jittery as he'd ever seen her. In which case, the coffee she'd stopped for didn't seem to be doing a whole lot of good.

Before he could broach the subject, she said, "I called Randolph this morning. Wanted to see if he had had any contact with Emmons since he spoke to us yesterday morning. But he didn't answer his cell."

"He'll probably call back." His response was made absently. He was still focused more on what she wasn't saying. And wondering what the hell had brought about such a change.

"Yeah. Probably." The words lacked conviction. "I've also got a call into the courthouse. A clerk agreed to do a search for 1986 tax and property records for Tory's. While I'm waiting, I thought I'd see if there were any online records of the fire that destroyed it."

"Already looked. There's nothing."

She nodded, sipped again. "Then I'll comb through the archives of the *Inquirer* and see what I can dig up. Surely the fire was deserving of a mention, even in that neighborhood."

Nate's desk phone jangled. He was still studying her speculatively when he answered it.

"A Mr. Emmons to see you, detective. He's been escorted to interview four."

He rose so swiftly he banged his knee on the desk as he dropped the phone back in its cradle simultaneously. Darrell's call had firmly yanked his mind back to business.

"Showtime." She'd risen when he had, looking quizzical. "Juicy finally decided he wanted to talk."

———————

The man in interview four looked to be about the same age as the stranger they'd encountered when leaving Juicy's apartment yesterday. There the resemblance stopped. Juicy had about a foot on the other man, was tall and lean, and sported two half sleeves of tattoos. His short hair was heavily gelled. The jeans and T-shirt he wore were similar to the attire sported by the group on the stoop.

Emmons was lounging on the chair at the table in a studiedly casual pose. He spoke as soon as they opened the door. "You McGuire?" At Nate's nod, he said, "I heard you was looking for me." He spared only a quick appraising glance for Risa before returning his attention to Nate.

"Thanks for coming in." When he and Risa were seated, he said, "I wanted to talk to you about your whereabouts on May seventeenth."

The other man studied him. "What you think I did?"

"I have a witness that places you and another man in Wakeshead Park that morning."

"Naw, I wasn't there. I don't like parks. And I don't like mornings." He included Risa in his grin. "I sleep all day. Like one of them vampires."

"The photos of you and your friend were picked from a photo array," Nate lied without compunction. He'd promised Crowley he'd avoid making Juicy think the other man had given him up. And then vowed to Morales he'd tread lightly so as to not screw up Vice's plans for the dealer. "The woman seemed pretty certain."

"There's all sorts of research out there now saying how eyewitness accounts can't be trusted. That's how my last conviction got overturned. Witnesses said one thing at the trial, 'nother at the appeal. Maybe you showed her only photos of me to pick from." He leaned back, hooked an arm over the back of the chair. "I'm a chameleon. The kinda guy looks one way one time, 'nother way the next. That's probably how your witness got it wrong. I wasn't there."

"The park was the scene of a homicide a few hours earlier," Risa interjected. The nerves he'd noticed earlier appeared under control. "We need to question everyone who was seen in the vicinity. Did you see anyone while you were there?"

"Sweet thing, I wasn't there." He slapped his palm lightly on the table in emphasis. "I'd like to help. Be a John Q. Citizen and all, but you don't want me to lie, do you?"

"No, but something tells me I won't be able to stop it, either."

His teeth flashed. "That wounds me deeply. I came here of my own free will to help out the trusted men in blue, and alls I get is mistrust?" His eyes watchful he asked, "How 'bout that other guy? The one supposed to be there with me? What he got to say?"

"He's been uncooperative."

At Nate's words, Juicy seemed to relax. "There you go, then. He probably wasn't there neither. People gets things wrong all the time. Your witness just must have been seeing things."

After several more minutes of getting nowhere, Nate gave up. The man wasn't going to come clean about his whereabouts, and there was no way to press the issue without telling him Crowley had given him up. Since that wasn't an option, there was nothing to do but to kick him loose.

"All right you can go."

Juicy remained sitting, looking from one of them to the other. "That's all you got? Seems like a waste to leave already after coming all the ways down here."

"You have something else to say?"

Although it was Nate's question, the other man addressed Risa with his answer. "Heard you was asking questions about Tory's, a bar used to be in my neighborhood."

"That's right. Did you know of it?"

"I remember it. I was just a kid but I ran the streets 'bout every night. Used to be a nice place. I remember Tory, too. She had a kid my age. Skinny little blond kid. Nose always running. But sometimes he'd slip out of the place if it was busy and no one was looking to make sure he was in bed. Then me and him would hang out. We was just kids."

"Do you know Tory's last name?" Risa asked.

He lifted a shoulder without interest. "Never cared. And never saw her or the kid again after the place burnt down. Played in the building a lot after that, though. Took the city forever to tear it down." He gave a grim smile and leaned forward. "Heard the building was haunted because someone got caught in that fire. Burned right along with the bar. Never got out of the upstairs apartment. If I died like that, I'd haunt a building, too."

Seeming to have said all he was going to, he got up and ambled to the door. Went through it. The officer on the other side of it fell into step beside him to escort him out.

"Interesting," Risa murmured.

"But hardly surprising." The chair scraped as Nate rose and stretched. "Guys like him deny everything. And I couldn't use the only leverage I had that might have gotten to the truth so the whole meeting was a bust."

She rose, fell into step beside him as they left the room and headed back to his office. "I think he told the truth about one thing."

When he cocked a brow at her, she continued, "He's a chameleon. Just like he said. He dropped the street vernacular when he was telling us about the fire, did you notice that?"

"And that tells us what, exactly?"

"It tells us that he's adept at fitting in wherever he needs to."

An hour later found them both on their cells. Nate finished first and waited impatiently for Risa to do the same. When she did, she had a page full of notes and an expression of satisfaction. "Okay, I'll still need to get more background from the newspapers archives, but the clerk in the property office gave me a place to start. Tory Marie Baltes had owed the business in question. She'd bought it five years earlier. Paid her taxes on time. No problem on file until the building burnt. Technically she still owned the structure. Insurance should have paid off, if the owner carried it. But it was listed as abandoned and eventually the city took it over."

"Is she the one who died in the fire?"

Risa lifted a shoulder. "Can't tell that from property tax records. But if what Juicy told us is true—a big if—I have a hard time believing the story wouldn't have been big news, at least for a day or two. I'll start checking the newspaper's archives."

"You can do it on the way to Bonnie Christiansen's house." He rose, shrugged into his jacket. "I just got off the phone with her. They've found the picture taken of her husband with his big fish. She says there's another man in the photo with him."

———

Nate and Risa stared at the picture in the cheap plastic frame. The glass was cracked. The fish Christiansen was holding was indeed impressive, if one cared about things like that. But it was the man standing in the background, half in and half out of the picture that captured his attention.

It depicted the same person speaking in that video segment in the tape found at Christiansen's crime scene. The one they'd called Johnny.

"The kids never did find it when they were putting the pictures together for the service," Bonnie was saying. "I ran across it when I was hunting down an extra pen to write thank yous with. Found it stuffed in one of the desk drawers." She nodded to a small desk tucked into the corner of the room. "I remember now, the picture had gotten knocked off the table and broke. I put it away meaning to get a new frame sometime and forgot all about it."

"Would you mind if we took it with us?" At the woman's alarmed look, Nate assured her, "You'll get it back. I'd see to that."

"I suppose that's okay," she said slowly. "If you're sure I'll get it back."

"You have our word," Risa said as they walked to the door. "And thank you again for calling us about this."

She waited until they were down the steps at least before clutching at Nate's arm urgently. "Okay, that's one coincidence erased. The Johnny in the video and Christansen's poker buddy are one and the same."

"What do you want to bet that the bar the group met in to play poker was Tory's? At least until it was destroyed by fire."

"If that's what they were really doing," she added. She pulled open the door and slid into the front seat of the vehicle. Her jacket gaped as she went in search of the ends of the seat belt, and he got a better view of the weapon she was carrying. He was reminded of the nerves she'd worn when she'd first arrived at the station house today. Nerves that had gradually subsided as the day progressed.

He waited until he was buckled in the vehicle and had started it. "What do you mean 'if'? You don't think they were playing poker together?"

"I don't think poker gets you killed," she said. "At least not the way I've always played it. Let's assume that Bonnie was right when she said the group was all cops. And let's take it a step further and assume they used to meet at Tory's. Who was Johnny referring to when he made the racist remark to someone named Lamont? A bartender maybe?"

"If we knew, and if we could track him, maybe he could give us the answers we need. In the meantime, I'm going to see what we can do about matching the photo of Johnny to personnel records for officers on the force."

"And hope that Johnny isn't a *former* officer."

He inclined his head. The idea might not lead anywhere, especially if Bonnie's memory turned out to be faulty. But the commonality of the man named Johnny was too good to pass up. First he'd been seen in the video taken at Tory's, in the same shot with a much younger Roland Parker. Then he'd appeared in a photo with the third victim, Patrick Christiansen. They'd been trying every way possible to find links between the victims.

The stranger called Johnny was the only real link they'd come across.

Nate was halfway across town when his cell rang again. He checked the ID screen. It was Eduardo Morales.

"Captain." Traffic had slowed to a near stop, snarling ahead for what appeared to be miles. And it didn't look like there was going to be a chance to turn onto a side street anytime soon. "What have you got?"

"I just took a courtesy call from the Montgomery County Sheriff. They had a call early this morning about a fire in a rural area over there."

Startled, it took a moment for Nate to answer. Each of the crime scenes had been solidly within the city limits. He even wondered if that were part of the offender's MO, to make it easier to ID the victims. Strike fear in the heart of others, as Risa had said.

"They find a connection to our case?" Out of the corner of his eye, he caught the sudden attention his words got from Risa.

"Said they found a police ID and a plastic badge, just like the three victims we found. The police commissioner has been on the phone making nice. By the time you get to the scene, hopefully he'll have convinced the sheriff to allow us to take precedence in the case. But step carefully. We're out of our territory, and technically you're the guest of Sheriff Williams for the duration."

"I understand. Any word on the identity of the victim?" A small movement caught his eye. Risa was as white as a sheet, the tension from the morning back in spades. He wondered at it, but the captain's next words drove the concern for her to the back of his mind.

"I think you've met him. ID reads Detective Mark Randolph."

———

Nate cast one last look at Risa. Found her expression unchanged. She'd been silent and still since he'd talked to her about Morales's phone call. Been monosyllabic the entire ride to Montgomery County. She'd been acting strangely all day. But his frequent inquiries about what was on her mind had been rebuffed.

He'd had plenty of experience dealing with a female's moods. Hell of it was, he just hadn't thought Risa was the mercurial type that would need handling. He could allow himself to be a tad disappointed about discovering differently. Until they got to the scene and his focus settled solely on the case.

Montgomery County was a frequent commute for people who worked in Philly. The area was an oasis of suburbia, just far enough from the big bad city to be rid of its disadvantages, but close enough to reap its benefits, too. It still had a rural feel, with plenty of rolling hills and wooded areas in between the towns and housing developments dotting the county.

The crime scene was easy to find. Five sheriff's cars were parked along the side of the road, blocking the entrance to what appeared to be an old farmstead. The rutted drive looked overgrown, but there was evidence of plenty of recent traffic through the young saplings and tall weeds that punctuated the area. With the windbreak of towering firs blocking the front, and the lightly wooded area along the twisting drive, the activity farther up the property was hidden from sight.

Nate got out of the car and headed toward the nearest deputy, who had straightened at his approach. "Lieutenant Detective Nate McGuire, Homicide, Philadelphia PD." He felt, rather than saw Risa at his side. "Risa Chandler, special task force consultant. Sounds like you've got one of our guys in there."

"Deputy Kyle Berding. Sheriff Haffey said to be expecting you." His look encompassed Risa. "You'll have to walk in. They've got the scene contained. I'll radio him that you're on your way."

Thanking him, Nate headed toward the trail that had at one time been a driveway. The place was too wooded to have been a working farm. Likely it'd been acreage, although from the looks of the overgrowth still visible where the recent traffic hadn't mowed it over, it'd likely been abandoned some time ago.

"So what do you think? A structure fire this time? Maybe used an old house or barn that was on its last legs anyway?"

"No. There was no structure."

"You sound certain."

She stepped over a recently downed small tree in the center of the drive. "He avoids structures, doesn't he?" she said finally. "Other than the warehouse, which was a good pick, in its way. Empty, steel beams, brick exterior, no windows. He likes to be outside because he likes to watch. To stay as close as he can, as long as he can. You set a building on fire, and you're likely to be consumed along with the victim. Fire burns a lot hotter with that much fuel."

"If he's got some of the arsonist psychology going on, the bigger the fire the better."

"He's more than that." When she stumbled, gave a hiss of frustration, he reached out to grab her elbow. "The fire means something to him emotionally, but he's most concerned with his victim's suffering. And he wants to see that. Has to. It makes sense he consistently chooses a spot that allows him to stay close enough to experience his victim's pain. That's what gives him joy."

They'd come to the top of the drive. The clearing ahead was alive with activity. Two fire trucks were still on scene, and three more sheriff vehicles were parked in a semicircle at the perimeter. There were far more people in the area than Nate was comfortable with on a crime scene, but as Morales had gone to great pains to remind him, it wasn't his scene. He was the visitor here.

Sheriff Tom Haffey was a good two inches taller than Nate's six foot height, and outweighed him by at least eighty pounds, most of it muscle. His face was flushed in a permanently ruddy complexion, and his pale blue eyes were shrewd as he considered Nate and Risa.

"Irony here is our fire department burned the old farmstead and out buildings down in a practice drill just last fall." He shaded his eyes in order to better watch the progress of his people. "Property owners were supposed to fill in the cellar this summer to make sure trespassers didn't fall into it and break their neck."

"When did the call come in?" Nate asked.

"The fire department were alerted about four A.M. Someone reported smoke coming from this direction as they were heading into the city to work. Wasn't much of a fire by the time we arrived. First we figured some kids threw a bunch of trash down in the cellar and started themselves a bonfire that was burning itself out. It wasn't until after the firefighters put it out the rest of the way and it cooled down enough to start poking around down there that we realized we had a homicide on our hands." His nod was courteous. "Heard about the string of murders you're handling. But didn't link this to your cases until we found the police ID. I called your chief immediately."

"Did you happen to find a plastic badge?" The sheriff shifted his attention to Risa as she spoke. "The sort they sell in toy stores?"

"We did. My investigators are finished with the area. I'll show you."

They followed the big man to a spot twenty feet from the front corner of the foundation. The plastic evidence marker indicated the area. After a moment Risa straightened and turned to scan the area, before walking toward the north side of the cellar.

Nate stared after her in surprise. The sheriff glanced at him and shrugged. "Follow her." They trailed in her wake until she halted by yet another evidence marker. Nate measured the distance from the cellar with his gaze, trying to visualize the scene.

There were stone steps leading down to the cellar from the back. At one time they had probably been covered with double wooden doors that had to be pulled open from the outside. The stairs were cracked but still usable. He no longer wondered why the killer had wandered so far outside the city.

This spot had everything he wanted. Isolation and a wide outdoor expanse that allowed him to do what Risa said he most needed. To watch.

"Is there another way to access this property?" she asked the sheriff.

"Funny you should ask." He pointed toward the southwest. "See where the property starts to get more wooded? There's a farm drive in there. Leads to a gravel road beyond those trees. There are signs that a vehicle passed through there recently."

"The other victims were forced upright by a rope to a tree limb or rafter," Nate observed.

"Looks like there was a large metal ring recently drilled

into the stone wall," Haffey observed. "The victim's arms were attached to it with a chain. One of the sickest damned things I've seen on the job, and that's with nearly thirty years of experience. You got any leads at all?"

"The investigation is progressing." Nate chose his answer carefully. Since the local law enforcement were cooperating fully, they'd expect and deserve some professional courtesy. But he was still mindful of Morales's warning about leaks the first day the task force had been formed. "We're getting a better idea of why it's happening. Obviously haven't progressed yet on the victim selection. But some leads are opening up on that end, too."

"Wish you luck," the sheriff said heavily, his gaze back on the blackened form in the cellar. "I can't think what anyone could ever do that would be bad enough to end them this way, though."

Because the brass had smoothed the way for a city assistant ME to handle the transport, Nate and Risa left shortly after. A brief conversation with Morales on the way back to the city assured him that the victim would be delivered to the morgue where Liz worked. It was easier for the sake of consistency on the case to work with the same facility. He was hoping Liz would jockey to do the autopsy herself. The healthy respect he had for her was fueled at least as much by her professional talents as for her wicked tongue.

Risa waited until they'd jolted down the drive again and turned back onto the road. "Are we heading to Randolph's house?"

He gave a grim nod. "The captain dispatched a team when we headed to the scene. We know he worked until eleven last night. A couple coworkers invited him to stop for a beer but he said he was going home. Now we need to figure out if he ever made it."

"He took Randolph in his house." Cass's expression was sober. "The neighbor across the street got home at the same approximate time. Noticed the detective's garage door going up about the time he was pulling in to his."

"Did he happen to see a car leave here again?" Nate

asked. They were standing in the empty garage. There was nothing to see except for a lone evidence marker near the door.

Cass shook her head. "He went right to bed, he said. We've canvassed the rest of the neighbors. Nobody else saw anything." Seeing the direction of Nate's gaze, she pointed at the evidence marker. "We did find a three-quarter-inch screw on the floor there. No telling how long it was there."

"Using the oil stains on the garage floor as a point of reference, that might be the approximate area the rear license plate would be," Risa murmured. He gave her a look. She'd still been quiet on the way over, but her color was back. And given what they'd seen on that video last night, he tended to agree with her.

"The UNSUB likes using cars from the victims to conduct the crimes," he said for Cass's benefit. "Let's start running reports for stolen plates on similar makes and models." He raised his brows and she consulted the notepad she held.

"Two thousand five Chrysler Pacifica, burgundy." She read off the plates and vehicle identification number for Randolph's vehicle.

"Check for stolen plates from others with that make and model. He'll copy the VIN from them, too. And if you find one, talk to the owner yourself. See if we can get an idea where the UNSUB does his shopping."

He followed Cass back into the house via the garage entrance. "We think the UNSUB was waiting for him in the house. There's no evidence of forced entry, so either he had a key or he's got some background with security systems."

"We need to adjust the parameters for a ViCAP request," Risa murmured behind him. "At least add in the kidnapping component."

"Fine, but he hasn't used the same method twice to snatch these guys that we know of," Nate responded.

"And we need to factor in a possible criminal background," she continued. "Someone familiar enough with stolen vehicles that he's adept at changing VIN numbers. Circumventing security. He had to do that at least one other time that we know of. Christiansen's car was equipped with an alarm."

He stopped in the kitchen to allow Trimball time to finish

the picture he was shooting. Then they progressed to the kitchen. "A nine millimeter was found lying there." Cass indicated the spot where an evidence marker sat. "A check confirmed that it was a department-issued weapon identified as having been issued to Randolph. It hadn't been fired."

So the man had drawn it but hadn't had an opportunity to get a shot off? Nate scanned the area thoughtfully. "How long had Randolph been on the force?"

Cass consulted her notebook again. "Nineteen eighty-four."

Which meant if the victims turned out to be tied together by the mysterious Johnny, it was possible Randolph was in Tory's the night that video was shot.

"We've got another commonality besides the fact that the men are detectives," Risa murmured from his side. Glancing at her, he knew they were on the same wavelength. "They're a similar age, aren't they? Within a decade anyway. So far all of them were on the force by 1986 or sooner."

"Roland Parker was the oldest of the four." Nate shifted to the side to allow the crime scene techs room to pass. "He'd made it to retirement. Passed it. I think it's time to pay another visit to his widow and press a bit harder on the outside job she claims he didn't have."

Chapter 14

"This is the quickest way to have the job looking at us."
Juan slipped into the booth, his expression uneasy. "I'm on
duty. I can't stay away long. What's so important we have to
meet in the middle of the day?"

"There's been another victim." Johnny watched the others'
expressions closely. They looked at each other. Then across
the table at him and Hans.

"Jesus. Jack? Jesus." Juan dropped his head, hauled a deep
shuddering breath in. Released it on a sob.

Jonas crossed himself. "Retribution," he said in such a
low voice that Johnny had to strain to hear. "To every sinner
comes a time to atone. It's atonement day."

"Christ, shut the fuck up, both of you." Johnny looked at
Hans for help, but the older man was unusually silent. "If he
got at Jack, this guy can get to any of us." Maybe even him.
A bolt a fear twisted through him. Jack was used to undercover work. Living day to day with the possibility of being
made for a cop. His instincts were so ready that he'd once
drawn down on Johnny for surprising him in the can. Who
the hell was out there?

"You're ignoring the obvious. You have all along." Jonas leaned forward, his face grim. He looked like shit, Johnny noted. Gaunt. Without that slick polish the women all seemed to go for. "You're forgetting Lamont."

"Lamont?" Johnny didn't pretend not to recall the name. "He's dead. He's been dead for nearly twenty-five years. The one thing I am not worried about in this whole clusterfuck is Lamont."

"He had people," Jonas explained urgently. His eyes were a little wild. Maybe the guy was finally losing it. Johnny had never trusted those religious types. Liked money just fine, same as the rest of them. He just had to wrap it up with talk of right and wrong and atonement to rain on everybody else's fucking parade. "He had family, right? Brothers, sisters maybe. And what about Tory's kid? The boy? He idolized Lamont. The guy saved him from Tory every time she was coming off a high and meaner than a swamp rat. The kid saw him burn."

"Bullshit." Johnny looked at the other two for support. Found none. "Bullshit," he said louder. "I don't remember no kid."

"Little blond boy." Hans nodded. "Used to run the streets sometimes at night after Tory was too wasted to know he was gone. Yeah, Lamont was good to the kid. I saw them together sometimes."

"This isn't good. This isn't good." Juan was mumbling almost incoherently.

"So there was a kid. Big deal. We need to be focused on the here and now. Juicy was Jack's associate, right? I say we scoop him up and put the screws to that motherfucker. He probably iced Jack to keep the profits all to himself."

"It doesn't fly." Hans was finally speaking but he wasn't saying anything Johnny wanted to hear. "You're ignorin' what's right in front of your face. If it were the partners, why the hell would they go after Sean and Johnson? Those two were no longer in it. It makes no sense."

"He got Johnson and Sean?" Juan bolted upward, pushed on Jonas to move him from the booth. "You should have told us that, Johnny. You had no call to keep that between the two of you."

Jonas's lips looked cracked and dried, and his grin was

horrible to see. "You can't avoid it. None of us can avoid judgment day. It's inevitable."

"I'm getting the hell out of here." Juan was babbling now. Jonas showed no signs of moving so he began crawling over the table to exit the booth. "Going in and taking vacation. Or sick leave. Whatever. Then I'm taking my kids and getting the hell out of the city."

Shit. The only thing missing from the scene was a giant flushing sound because Johnny could see everything he'd ever worked for being sucked away. Jonas and Juan were so crazed right now that if they did ever happen to get questioned in connection with the murders, they'd have immediate diarrhea of the mouth and take everyone down with them.

"Maybe that's good, Juan." He looked at Hans for confirmation. But the older man was frowning and contemplating the scarred tabletop. "A little time away sure as hell isn't going to hurt anything. Take a couple weeks off to visit relatives and maybe when you come back it will be all over."

The idea had enough merit that he was wishing he had some leave accumulated. But Johnny didn't believe in saving vacation and sick leave for a rainy day. If he didn't feel like going in that day, he damn well stayed home. He couldn't scrape together more than forty-eight hours if he tried. And with the damned Internal Affairs assholes breathing down his neck, he had to be a model employee until the excessive-use investigation was deemed a bunch of shit and closed.

Juan nodded, backed up, and settled back in his seat, visibly calmer. Even a bit abashed now that he had a plan. "Yeah, I will. I have my kids to think about, you know?" He looked at Jonas. "You should go, too. You look like you need the break."

Jonas just kept smiling that weird-ass smile. "There's no avoiding the demon when the demon lives in us all."

Johnny lunged across the table and grabbed the other man by the tie. Twisted it around his fist. "Shut the fuck up. Jesus, are you crazy? You want someone reporting you to Psych, is that it? Then you'd have an excuse to blab to your heart's content, wouldn't you? You're just waiting for a chance to spill your guts."

"That's enough." There was a hum of temper in his ears. It

drowned out the voice at his side. But the hand biting into his arm was more difficult to ignore. He cast a sullen look at Hans, loosened his hold on Jonas. Sank back down into his seat.

"Jonas, go home and get some rest. You look like shit." Hans's words were spoken in a kindly tone. "Juan, take some time with your kids. We'll keep you posted on things here."

The relief on the man's broad face was obvious. "Thanks, Hans. I don't want to be running out on the group, but there's no sense in us waiting around like sitting ducks, right?"

Hans and Johnny waited until the other two had gone. Neither of them moved.

"Jonas is full of shit. This isn't the work of no kid." It didn't add up. He hadn't seen Tory since they'd burned her place down. She'd gotten the hint and taken off, the kid with her. "Tell you what, I'm going to do a little research on Tory Baltes. Maybe the crazy bitch got some wild hair to pay us back after all these years."

"Makes as much sense as anything else in this mess," Hans muttered. He looked Johnny right in the eye. "If I were you, I'd be extra careful. The way I remember things, when her place was torched, you were the one who lit the match."

———

"You've got no call coming around asking questions about Ro. Acting like he was some sort of criminal." Nora Parker sniffed indignantly and dabbed at her damp eyes with a tissue. Both of her chins quivered, and mascara was smeared in streaks beneath her eyes. Risa had never been able to figure out women who didn't use waterproof mascara. Did they like looking like raccoons?

"We're not accusing your husband of anything, ma'am." Her tone was respectful but firm. "Something has to link the victims together. We think it might be an outside job they all held." Not that there was anyone to verify that for Sherman Tull. His ex still hadn't been located. But it was a question they'd be putting to Randolph's estranged wife when she was questioned, as well.

"I . . ." The woman twisted the Kleenex between pudgy hands. "I just can't help you. Roland never talked about another job. But he was gone a lot, at odd hours when he wasn't on the late shift. Sometimes I know he was with friends. Just out with the guys. But others . . ." She raised tear-drenched eyes, the lids crusted with blue shadow. "I thought maybe he had a woman on the side. He always denied it. But a part of me wondered." Nate's cell rang then, and he got up and moved away to answer it.

"What about when he retired?"

The other woman drew another tissue from the box and blew noisily. "What about it?"

"Surely he was home more. You retired at the same time?"

Nora nodded uncertainly. Risa gave her a reassuring smile. "So you know how he passed the hours. Who he spent them with. Easier to keep track of each other when you're both home full-time."

"He'd turned into a homebody. We both did." Nora nodded determinedly. "We were making plans of maybe a vacation to take. A cruise, we were thinking. Right before he . . ."

And once again they'd circled away from the topic of the outside job.

Nate came back, slipping the cell in his pocket. "Ms. Parker, that phone call was from my captain. There are some questions about your and Roland's finances."

Nora's eyes grew wide. "Questions? From who? Our finances are our own business. I don't see what they have to do with you."

"You recently bought beachfront property in Florida. After you buried your husband."

It took effort for Risa to keep from reacting. The information was news to her. The warrant for the victims' financials must have come through, and Eduardo would have taken a look at them.

The tears were flowing in earnest now, and Nora's large bosom was heaving. "Ro had insurance," she sobbed. More tissues were sacrificed to her tears. "And I can't bear to be in the house without him. There are just too many memories."

"Our information shows that the price of the property you bought was over a million dollars." Nate's tone was hard. "Your husband didn't carry that much insurance."

The tears stopped as suddenly as if someone had turned

off a faucet. "How dare you come here and interrogate me! Why haven't you caught his killer yet? It's all over the news. Another detective has been killed. Go do your jobs and stop the murderer before someone else dies."

"That's what we're trying to do," Risa said evenly. "But our job is just made harder when people aren't honest with us. Like you. Now."

"He didn't do anything wrong," Nora insisted, and dabbed at her tear ravaged makeup. "I didn't want to talk about it because he said the department didn't like it when officers moonlighted. It didn't take that much of his time. An evening a week maybe. Sometimes a while on the weekends."

"What was the second job, Nora?"

"Protection, he said." She raised her gaze to look at them hopefully. "I figured maybe he filled in on the security detail sometimes for a celebrity or local politician."

"Because the money was good?"

The woman blew her nose noisily before answering Risa's question. "I never knew how good because Roland always took care of it. I never saw bankbooks or anything until after he died, and I found the one to that overseas bank." Her eyes filled again. "He always said it was our retirement nest egg."

———

There was a charge in the air at the briefing that afternoon. Mark Randolph's death, coming just days after Christiansen's, lent the meeting a sense of urgency.

"The offender may have a criminal history," Risa told the silent group when it was her turn to speak. "We know he's adept at changing VINs and circumventing security. We'll resubmit the ViCAP with those details, see if we can find any intersections with kidnappings." They'd already struck out a couple times on the manner in which he killed his victims. Which made her think his criminal background perhaps included car theft and burglary, but not homicide.

These homicides had been planned. They were special. Revenge a long time in the making.

"He'll have Randolph's car with him or hidden away." Until the next victim, she thought, but didn't say the words aloud.

Nate looked at Cass. "Where are we on that stolen plate report for a 2005 burgundy Chrysler and Christiansen's 2010 Malibu?"

"Sixteen possibilities on the Malibu," she responded. "We've gotten in touch with all but three of the owners. Eliminated four of the reports because the theft happened out of state. Twenty-seven for the Chrysler. Started a map of the areas where the owners first noticed they were gone, leaving out those who weren't sure when it happened. Also have a list of the plates and associated VINs in case either car surfaces with a new ID."

"Still don't understand how it took so long for Parker's car to register with impound," Shroot grumbled.

"The VIN switch was expertly done," Nate said. "Whoever this guy is, he either has the skills or access to someone who does. The plates and VIN matched up to a vehicle belonging to an elderly woman who had been hospitalized recently, so there was no reply to messages regarding the tow. Since she doesn't use her vehicle often, she didn't even realize her plates were missing. At any rate, I think Parker's car may have been used to abduct Sherman Tull, as well. So we're going back to the traffic cameras—" There was a collective groan from a few of the detectives. Nate gave a wry smile. "I know. But now that we have a vehicle to look for, let's go back and check in increasing circles around the man's house. See if that car showed up somewhere before it was dumped in the lot the night of Christiansen's murder. Hoy and Mendall?"

"Yeah, yeah. Check the cameras," Mendall said without enthusiasm.

Nate called on the rest of the teams, who submitted verbal and written reports on their assignments. "Brandau and Recker, canvass Christiansen's neighbors again. See if anything has jogged their memories now that the shock has worn off."

"Shroot," he looked at the tall angular man. "The UNSUB had to have gotten to Randolph's some way. Get a copy of the list for possible new plates on the Malibu and check streets around Randolph's. I'm guessing he abandoned it nearby."

"Alberts and Finnegan, we've got the victims' financials." Nate could feel the sudden tension emanating from his silent captain in the corner. He knew exactly what the man was thinking and chose his words carefully. "We're checking on whether the men held outside jobs in their free time. Parker and Christiansen's widows indicated their husbands did, although neither had a clear idea of what the job entailed. Maybe there's a connection there. See if you can find anything that would help us figure out who or what they were working for."

Next would come the more delicate job of approaching banks to ask whether the victims held lockboxes there. Tull at least had had a key in his desk drawer at home that looked like it would fit one. If the men were involved in something illegal, something that made them enough money to enable Nora Parker to pay a cool million for a house, they had to keep records of it somewhere. Even if they were savvy enough to stash it overseas, there had to be bankbooks like Parker's widow had found. Statements. Records of some type.

And those were exactly the type of questions he'd be asking Mark Randolph's estranged wife.

Cheryl Randolph was dry-eyed and full of questions when Nate and Risa walked into the interview room. She was dressed in a pale pink summer suit that might have been considered appropriate office wear if it hadn't been for the plunging neckline on the white blouse beneath it, which showed her impressive cleavage off to advantage. Her artful blond curls looked like they'd been aided by a bottle, and there wasn't a flicker of sorrow on her face for the man she was not yet divorced from.

"So I heard Mark was burned to death." She looked queasy at the prospect. "Like those other cops. Is that true?"

"We believe he was a victim of the same killer, yes." Risa tried to keep the irony from her next words. "We're sorry for your loss."

The woman blinked. "Oh. Thank you. Mark and I . . . Our divorce is almost final."

And you moved on long ago, Risa thought. That was clear enough. She remained silent as Nate asked the woman questions about her relationship with her husband, her last communication with him, and the nature of that communication. For the first time, Cheryl Randolph showed a flicker of emotion.

"Actually we argued on the phone just last week. This divorce is dragging out because Mark won't agree to the financial split. He could be an as— He could be stubborn," she amended. "And he was as cheap as the day was long. I had to explain every nickel I ever spent, even though I brought home a paycheck, too. I think that's what got to me in the end. I just got tired of fighting about money all the time."

"Was your husband having financial problems?" Risa put in.

The other woman grimaced. "The only problem Mark had with money is when he couldn't hang on to his pennies long enough. He hated spending on anything. Unless it was something he wanted, of course."

"Do you know if he worked a second job?"

She looked puzzled at Nate's question. "A second job? How would he have managed that with the crazy hours you guys work?"

"So he didn't mention putting in some time working security or protection or helping out a friend with their second job?"

Cheryl screwed up her brow, looked from Nate to Risa and back again. "He didn't say a word about any of that. He wasn't home a lot. He pulled overtime whenever he could, so we usually met each other coming and going. Once in a while he'd meet up with some friends for drinks or something. But to tell you the truth, I was busy with my own work, and we weren't getting along for a while before we split. I just can't be sure what he'd been up to recently. Can I ask you a question?" The words were addressed to Nate. Risa assumed when the woman leaned in confidingly, the gape in her blouse was for his benefit, as well.

"Of course."

"I don't want to be indelicate, but I don't know when I'll be able to talk to someone about this." She moistened her lips and then curved them slowly. "Since we weren't divorced yet . . . do you know if that means I'll get Mark's pension?"

———

"Ni-ice," Risa drawled as they headed back to Nate's office. "Seems doubly a shame that he was murdered. Being married to her should have qualified as suffering enough."

"Hell of it is, unless he changed his will and the beneficiary on his pension, she'll probably get everything. I'll have Alberts and Finnegan search his house again, this time concentrating on any financial information he might have around. One thing is certain, he wasn't regularly working overtime for extra money. The city pulled out all the stops for this task force, but we're usually in a budget crunch. They discourage overtime, and she made it sound like he worked extra shifts, which is impossible."

"So we have four victims who were doing 'something' in their spare time. We know that something equaled a big payoff for at least Parker." She and Nate reached out for the doorknob for his office in tandem. Her jacket gaped open. When she saw his gaze fix on her weapon, she let her hand drop to her side. Just the act of loading and strapping on her weapon had had her shaking the entire ride to work this morning. Probably would have had her jittery all day if she hadn't had far worse to concentrate on.

The memory of the blackened form in the crumbling cellar spilled across her mind like a dark stain. There was nothing quite as torturous as "knowing" something and still being unable to prevent it. Because it was knowledge she shouldn't have and couldn't explain.

And in Mark Randolph's case, it had come much too late.

"It's been a long day after staying late last night."

She sat down at her computer as Nate was talking. When he didn't finish, she turned to look at him inquiringly.

He looked oddly ill at ease. "I'm just saying, if you want to call it a day, I don't expect you to keep pace with the hours I'm putting in here."

"Trying to get rid of me?"

He gave a purely masculine shrug and rounded his desk. "Just offering you an out. You seemed . . . on edge today."

She stilled. Of course he would notice. Which meant that she wasn't nearly as good at hiding her nerves as she would like to believe. She wasn't sure which of them was more surprised when she offered him a shred of truth. "Raiker insists on his investigators being armed at all times." Just talking about it had her palms dampening. "He cleared it with the commissioner when he offered him my services. I haven't touched my weapon since my last case. In Minneapolis."

His dark gaze met hers. She thought she couldn't bear the question in his eyes. Found the understanding there somehow worse. "The one where you were wounded?"

"It ended badly," she said bleakly. Badly. An innocuous word for a scene that had ended with several SWAT operatives wounded, two of them fatally. A five-year-old boy dead. And left Risa doubting she'd ever be able to bring herself to face another case again.

"Yet here you are," he murmured.

"Here I am." Because she needed to look away, needed something, anything else to focus on, she powered up her computer. "I won't take you up on your offer to cut out early, but I wouldn't say no to a pizza. Meat lovers with extra cheese."

"A woman after my own heart."

The pizza had been devoured, and despite Nate's convenient memory, it was he who'd eaten two-thirds of it. He'd been in and out of the office, on the phone and then poring over reports at his desk. She'd overheard the tail end of one phone conversation that had sounded as if it was personal. His low tones had made it impossible to make out all of the words, but it had sounded like an argument. She wondered if he was talking to the sister he'd mentioned having problems with.

She clicked out of a site for old archived newspapers and clicked on another. Of course, she thought wryly, it was just as likely that he was talking to a woman he was involved with. Maybe one who wasn't happy about the hours he kept and was feeling neglected. It went without saying that a man who looked like Nate McGuire wouldn't want for female attention.

Risa narrowed her search to Philadelphia newspapers and then typed in her search command. She was half surprised to find a handful of stories that looked promising. Jotting down notes, she switched from one story to the next. And then moved on to another site and started over. Finally she looked up, barely concealed excitement in her voice. "It says here that the fire at Tory's back in '86 was suspected arson."

Nate looked up. "What made them think that?"

Risa read from her notes. "The investigators could find no electrical reason for the fire. It also mentions the owner didn't carry insurance. According to Baltes, her boyfriend was asleep upstairs while she was waiting on customers in the bar. A fire broke out when she was cleaning up and she tried to get it under control herself. When that failed, she ran outside to a neighbor's and had them call the fire department."

She looked up to meet his gaze. "The article intimates that the fire department's response time was slower than usual because of the neighborhood the call came from. By the time they arrived, it was too late to do much for the building. And efforts to save the man in the upstairs apartment were in vain." She couldn't suppress the excitement from her voice any longer. "And get this . . . the victim named in the article is a Lamont Frederickson. Has a lot of immediate surviving family listed, including a younger brother by the name of Javon Emmons."

Nate looked as stunned as she'd felt upon reading the article. "What are the chances he's the same Javon Emmons . . . Juicy?"

"I'm guessing damn near one hundred percent."

A door pushed open on the passenger side of the gleaming black town car idling at Risa's curb. She'd barely parked before Adam Raiker emerged from it and waited impatiently for her to join him.

"Adam."

His tone was wry. "Please. Rein in your excitement. The constant adulation gets wearing."

Her mouth quirked. "I'll take your word for it." She let him lead the way up to the front door before she stepped in to unlock it and allow him entry. When he ensconced himself once more on the sagging flowered couch, she had a flash of déjà vu.

"I didn't expect to see you so soon. Any news on the assassin?"

His hand tightened on the polished knob of his cane. "As a matter of fact. Got the call today. The FBI has him under surveillance. They were supposed to move on him tonight. I've been invited to sit in on some of the interviews once he's in custody."

She smiled at his disgruntled tone. It wouldn't suit her boss to allow another organization to lead when it had been his life at risk. "I'm glad. Hopefully you'll get some answers about who hired him."

"We will if I'm doing the interview." He stared at her long enough then to make her uncomfortable. Then, in his usual abrupt manner, he said, "Paulie thinks I misjudged you. That I pushed too hard."

Oddly touched, she found it difficult to speak for a moment. If Adam Raiker harbored self-doubts, she'd never seen evidence of them. And the thought that Paulie's words would have had him second-guessing himself on her behalf meant more than it should have. In answer, she opened her jacket a bit.

His face creased into a self-satisfied smile. "You're wearing your weapon."

She was suddenly glad he would never know how long it had taken her just to force herself to touch it. How she'd shaken like a leaf in a hurricane loading it this morning. The effort it'd taken to bring herself to strap it on.

"It's just geography. It's not in the drawer anymore, but what good is it if it's only window dressing? I don't know that I can draw it. Fire it."

"Do you know how many surgeries I had after I escaped and killed LeCroix?"

She could only shake her head in bemusement. Adam rarely spoke of anything remotely personal. And she couldn't remember him ever offering information about the most intensely traumatic event of his life.

"Thirteen. I was in and out of hospitals for months. Completely helpless part of the time. Dependent on others for my care and feeding." The fierceness of his tone told her better than words just how much he'd despised that. "There's no way I could have gotten through it if I'd thought about it in terms of how long it was going to take. Worried about the end result. I just took it one surgery at a time. It's a process, Marisa. Healing doesn't happen all at once."

She hoped he couldn't tell how desperately she wanted to believe him. Needed to. "We had another victim today." Her throat dried out. It took a moment to manage the rest of the words. "I knew who it would be. Dreamt the whole thing last night. And there wasn't a damned thing I could do to stop it."

His gaze went watchful. "Did you see the killer's face?"

"No."

"Did you check on the potential victim?"

She knew exactly where this was going. It didn't lessen the guilt. "I couldn't reach him."

"It was already too late."

Risa looked away, sick at the knowledge that the dream probably occurred at the same time Mark Randolph was burning to death.

Adam remained silent for several moments. There was nothing to say. Both of them knew it. Finally he spoke. "You know from experience there will be more. And when there are, you'll use every detail at your disposal to help progress this case. But it's you and the rest of the task force who will solve it. With or without help from your psychic subconscious. Now." He used the cane to help him rise. "Walk me to the car. You can fill me in on the details."

They went out the front door and down the steps, the security light providing a soft pool of illumination as they crossed the front yard. His driver turned on the car headlights as they approached. Adam listened intently as she reported the events of the day. She'd forgotten how satisfying it was to get his view on a case she was working. Risa was by no means alone in believing there was no finer criminal mind in the country.

A car started and moved slowly up the street. "Whatever the detectives were involved in, it was highly illegal; hence, the profits you're talking about," Raiker was saying. "My guess would be drugs, unless you have reason to believe they could have been . . ."

Several things happened simultaneously then. The car screeched to a stop. Caution reared even before comprehension filtered in. Raiker's driver opened his car door. Adam lurched in front of Risa, his hand going for his weapon.

Three loud reports filled the air. Risa hit the ground hard.

A weight pinning her. There were several more gunshots. The sound of a car accelerating. A crash.

The weight on top of her didn't move.

"Adam!" She grasped him and gave a huge shove. Turned him over and leaned above him. "Adam, are you . . ." It was only then that she saw the blood soaking the white shirt he wore beneath his suit.

She ripped open his shirt to find the source of the wound. Nearly wept when she saw three bullet holes. "Hold on." Risa pulled off her jacket and wadded it up into a makeshift compress and pressed it against the wounds, maintaining constant pressure.

"Adam, stay with me." She checked his pulse. Found it irregular. "Hang on until we can get you help."

"Risa, what the hell's going on? Are you hurt?"

She jerked in the direction of the familiar voice. Jerry Muller was tearing across her lawn toward them. "Call nine-one-one."

He stopped, peered at her uncertainly. "Who's there with you?"

"Jerry, get an ambulance now!" She watched until he turned to hurry back to his house before turning back to Adam, her heart in her throat.

His eye was narrowed in fierce concentration. "So much . . . for . . . fed . . . surveil . . . lance."

A sob shuddered out of her. "You'll have some major ass-kicking to do when this is over."

His breathing altered. "Adam?" Panic flooded through her. "Adam, look at me. Dammit, don't you die!"

But his eye closed. And no matter how many times she called his name as she applied first aid, he didn't respond again.

Chapter 15

Risa sat in a darkened corner of the surgical waiting room staring blindly at the floor. The first hour after the shooting had been a frenetic blur of activity. After the EMS ambulance crew had taken over, her first call had been to Morales, who'd promised to alert the commissioner. A second ambulance had to be summoned for Adam's driver, who'd been wounded when he'd exchanged fire with the occupant in the other vehicle.

The shooter had been killed. Raiker's driver was in stable condition.

Adam hadn't regained consciousness.

She was too weary to stem the bleak tide of dread at the thought. Glancing at the clock, she saw that two hours had passed since they'd wheeled him into surgery. No one had been out with an update. But no one had come to tell her he was dead either, and Risa was clinging to that fact with all the optimism she could muster.

It hadn't taken long for the local FBI field agents to make an appearance. Had taken even less time for her to demand how they could have so thoroughly screwed up. The ensuing conversation hadn't been pleasant, hence the three agents' stance across the room, all studiously ignoring her.

The commissioner and his deputy had come and gone after conferring with both her and the federal agents. Impossible to believe that in all the activity, time still insisted on dragging.

Someone approached to stand next to her. She heaved a mental sigh. She really couldn't summon the energy to contemplate another go round with one of the federal agents. But when something was placed around her shoulders, she did look up. Found Nate.

"You looked cold." He nodded toward the suit jacket he'd draped around her.

Risa stood, unwilling to admit to the thread of relief filtering through her. "They keep these places freezing." Noticing the direction of his gaze, she looked down. Saw her blood-stained tank. "It's not mine."

"Gave me a bad start at first. But Morales said you were uninjured."

"Raiker survived four attacks on his life. The only reason he was here was because the bureau claimed to have the guy responsible. He was under surveillance, they said." She aimed another resentful look toward the three agents talking in low tones on the other side of the room. "I've yet to hear an explanation for how someone under surveillance managed to put three bullets into my boss."

Her voice cracked on the last words and Nate reached out. Hauled her into his arms. "He's going to be okay." The assurance was whispered in her ear.

Risa closed her eyes and swallowed hard, willing it to be true. "You can't possibly know that."

"As a matter of fact I do. Me and the big guy," he jabbed a finger skyward. "We're really tight. He called me a just a minute ago and gave me the news."

She let out a helpless laugh that a moment ago she would have sworn was beyond her. "I'm pretty sure that's considered sacrilegious in almost every religion."

"Only if it's not true."

Letting out a long sigh, she rested against him for just a moment. "It's been a helluva day."

She could feel his lips in her hair. And his arms remained tight around her. "That it has."

Somehow the next hour passed more quickly than the previous three. And that had everything to do with the man at her side, who kept her hand clasped tightly in his the entire time.

"Risa." She looked up to see Paulie Samuels and Kellan Burke hurrying toward her. Disentangling her fingers from Nate's, she immediately missed the warmth of his touch.

Caught in a bear hug by the effusive Samuels, she clung for a moment, before he was shoved aside so Burke could take his place. "Glad to see you in one piece."

"I'm not the one they've spent the last few hours putting back together." She stepped back, gave the men a wan smile. "No news yet. Nothing since they took him in for surgery."

"I can't believe they haven't sent anyone out to update you." Paulie's tone was irate, but his eyes were worried.

Belatedly, she remembered a semblance of manners. "Lieutenant Detective Nate McGuire, PPD." She gestured to Nate, who'd risen. "Paulie Samuels, Adam's right arm, and Kellan Burke, a fellow investigator for Raiker Forensics." She caught Kellan's sidelong glance and realized what she'd said. Of course he would have gotten wind of her resignation. Probably had heard of Raiker's refusal to accept it. Burke knew Adam better than most of them, second only to Paulie. There was some sort of history between the two men that had never been fully explained.

"Had a heck of a time getting away without Macy, but she flies to LA for a big trial tomorrow." Kellan's fiancée was a forensic linguist who also worked for Raiker Forensics. "If I know her, she'll find a way to swing by here on her way home." None of them mentioned the obvious. That if Adam didn't make it, there'd be no reason for the trip.

"Did they give you any idea how they could have screwed up with Jennings so badly?" Paulie inclined his head toward the federal agents.

"Our conversation didn't exactly end on good terms. They were a lot more interested in asking questions than answering them. Commissioner Lawton didn't mention anything either." She sent a quizzical look at Nate, which he interpreted correctly.

"Morales only told me about the shooting and that you were here."

There was something indiscernible in his tone. Something that had Kellan looking at Nate more carefully, and then at Risa.

"They'll damn well tell me something." Paulie strode across the waiting room. Risa silently wished him luck. It wouldn't be wise for the FBI agents to underestimate the man, even if he was wearing a tie sporting decks of cards and poker chips. Samuels still had a lot of contacts in the bureau. If he didn't get the answers he was seeking from the field agents, he'd be on the phone demanding them from someone much higher on the bureau's food chain.

It was nearly fifteen minutes later before Nate's low voice alerted her.

"Risa."

Turning, she saw one of the surgeons she'd seen earlier coming out of one of the interior doorways, looking about the room.

"Adam Raiker?"

She and Kellan nearly tripped over each other as they lunged across the room. "How is he?" they asked simultaneously. Holding her breath, she examined the woman's expression. It was grave, which told her absolutely nothing.

"He's made it through surgery." Her next words stemmed the relief flowing through Risa. "We lost him once but were able to stabilize him and continue." Finally, she offered a small smile. "He's made of strong stuff."

"You have no idea," Kellan said feelingly.

"His condition is critical." The doctor's look encompassed Paulie, who had hurried up to them. "We were able to remove the bullet fragments. Unfortunately, one of them nicked his heart, and the repair gave us a few bad moments in there. He's stable at the moment. If he makes it through the next twenty-four hours, his chances will improve dramatically."

Kellan's pale green eyes beneath the trendy-framed glasses were unusually sober. "So you're telling us after waiting for the last several hours . . . we need to wait."

The doctor nodded, not without sympathy. "Praying might be a good way to pass the time."

An hour later, Risa, Paulie, Kellan, and Nate were huddled over coffee. They'd moved to the ICU waiting room, but the only change was the location. Same décor. Same endless passage of time. Adam was still in recovery and hadn't been brought to a room yet. When he was, he'd be allowed only one visitor for fifteen minutes every hour.

"Jennings beat the feds at their own game," Paulie was telling them with barely reined fury in his voice. "Raiker and I had been holed up in a hotel while some lookalike stood in for Adam trying to lure Jennings out. The op was a total bust. Jennings never took the bait. So we flew back to DC. Barely got there before we got a call from the bureau saying they'd closed in on him. Their intelligence was solid. They'd trailed him to a known acquaintance's of his, and he didn't leave again."

"Someone didn't leave again," Risa put in. "But it must not have been Jennings they had surrounded at that house."

"No, he was found dead in the vehicle in front of your place. I don't know the identity of the man they arrested, and he isn't talking yet. But they share a better than passing resemblance. Jennings must have paid him off to distract the feds by heading to a place he knew they'd be watching while he made one last attempt on Adam's life."

"With his death, our chance of learning who he was working for dramatically decreases," Kellan said with disgust.

Paulie was surprisingly calm at the possibility. "The feds will get warrants for his homes and financials. We still may get a lead, although I doubt even Jennings knew the identity of his employer. It was probably all handled anonymously."

"Is there going to be a guard around the clock on him?" Nate voiced the worry that had been preying on Risa. When they all looked at him, he shrugged. "I'm just saying. Now that Jennings isn't around anymore, there's a chance that whoever hired him will line up someone else. Or else try to finish the job himself."

———

Johnny had been up all night thinking about it. With the help of Jim Beam, the answers had become increasingly clear.

Someone from the John Squad was responsible for the recent deaths.

He tipped another finger of bourbon into his glass and tossed it back. Welcomed the scorching path it took down his throat. The motivation wasn't important. Greed or guilt, he figured, but the why never mattered worth a damn to the dead. It was the living who mattered. And Johnny had no doubt which of the surviving members was behind this.

Juan didn't have the guts. He'd probably already loaded up and hauled ass out of the city, given his behavior earlier today. Hans . . . Johnny surveyed the bottle consideringly. Hans had the guts. He had the brains. But Johnny would stake his life that the other man was solid. This job relied as much on instincts as it did police work, and he'd trust Hans with his life. The man had handpicked him. Brought him into the group. Been a mentor of sorts to him all those years ago.

No, it wasn't Hans. Not just because he didn't want it to be but because it didn't make sense. The older man wasn't the one acting crazier than a mental patient off his meds.

That description only fit Jonas.

He wouldn't have thought Jonas had it in him either, but all his talk earlier of atonement had convinced Johnny otherwise. Maybe he was having some sort of mental breakdown. Maybe he'd already gone whack-job loony. But Johnny thought it was past time to discover which, once and for all.

Glancing at the clock, he took one more swig from the bottle before getting up to collect a few items. He knew where Jonas lived, although he'd never been inside. He'd hit a pay phone on the way and tell him to expect him and Hans.

The lie would be exposed when Johnny showed up alone. But it would have Jonas opening up the door, which he may not have otherwise.

Which would mean, of course, that the man wasn't totally crazy.

———

Jonas swung open the door and turned to walk back into the darkened room, leaving Johnny to follow. He pushed the door shut with the sole of his shoe. He didn't have a plan.

Not really. But there was no sense being careless and leaving fingerprints.

The other man was still dressed from work, although it was the middle of the night. He looked like shit, though. Worse, if it were possible, than he had at the meet. And he'd looked bad then.

Johnny had practiced his story on the way over and launched into it without delay. "Hans should be here any minute. He was going to meet me."

No answer. Apparently Jonas didn't give a shit. "Beer?"

"No thanks."

The man pulled one from a twelve pack at the foot of the chair he'd been sitting in and popped the tab. Swayed slightly as he drank. Johnny didn't need the empty cans on the floor to attest that the guy was well on his way to smashed.

Which might make the upcoming conversation easier.

"Listen, Hans and I got to talking after you guys left and the thing is, we think maybe Juan might be behind this whole thing." He waited for Jonas's exclamation of surprise. It didn't come. He watched the other man more carefully. "Makes sense if you think about it. Whoever is doing this has to know all of us. And Juan has always bitched that his associate brought in lower earnings than the rest of ours. Remember that? He hasn't been happy with his share since he started."

"Juan is running for his life right now." Jonas gave him a grin that had Johnny's flesh crawling. "Just like you should be. And Hans."

He didn't think it was the bourbon that had him reacting to Jonas's words. They were a threat. "But not you?"

"I'm not afraid. Not anymore." He drank a long swallow. Wiped his mouth on his sleeve. Not like the perfect gentleman he always acted like before. "Things become very clear when you know what has to be done. When you know you're doing God's will. Finally. Seems like I've been scared for years." He peered closely at Johnny in the semidarkness. "That'll seem pussy to you. Never frightened of anything, are you, Johnny? Bet you're afraid now, though. If you have any brains, you're scared out of your fucking mind."

Thoughts racing, he played along. "Hell yeah, I'm scared.

Think I'm stupid? But you and me and Hans, we're going to put an end to this. We need to take Juan down before he gets to another one of us."

A little smile was playing around Jonas's mouth. "Juan's hundreds of miles away by now. I know it. So do you." He reached down for another beer. Brought up a gun he'd laid down behind it. "You should have gone, too."

"Hey, buddy!" Johnny held up his hands with a half laugh. Scanned the area to get the layout. "You've had one too many beers tonight. Better put the weapon down." Or he'd pull his throw gun from his ankle holster and do what he'd come here prepared to do.

Get rid of the crazy prick once and for all.

That smile was back. The one chock full of loony. "I don't think so. It's taken a lot of courage to get me this far. More than you can know. Sort of sorry it's going to end this way, though. Was kind of hoping you'd be the next to burn." He raised the weapon.

Johnny threw himself to the floor, rolled, frantically pulling at the gun in his ankle holster. The first shot sounded before he'd cleared the holster. But he managed to return fire. Before he realized he'd misjudged the situation. About as badly as anyone could.

Gray matter was spattered on the nearby wall. On the carpet. And blood was pooling beneath what was left of Jonas's head. Johnny's bullet must have caught the man in the chest as he was falling. But only after he'd swallowed his own gun.

"Jesus." He wiped one damp palm on his pants. Switched the weapon to his other hand and wiped the free one. "Jesus." Belatedly, he crossed to the window, looked out. The house next door remained dark. But as he watched, an upstairs light snapped on in the house across the street. He had to get the hell out of here. Fast.

Dammit. He needed to think but his mind was a jumble. He reholstered the weapon and took a quick walk through the place, being careful to skirt the unmoving body. He'd known the guy was unraveling. Just hadn't correctly guessed the reason for it.

He pulled latex gloves out of his jacket pocket, put them on. A quick glance through the man's dresser drawers showed nothing important. Similarly the desk tucked into the corner of the bedroom. But the next bedroom had him stopping in his tracks.

The place was a fucking shrine. Crosses all over the wall and a big-ass picture of Jesus. A statue with candles beside it. And at the statue's feet was a sheaf of papers.

Dammit, was that a siren in the distance? Without waiting to listen more carefully, he grabbed up the papers and retraced his steps, this time heading toward the back door he could see through the open kitchen doorway.

He folded the papers and shoved them in his pocket, then fumbled for the lock on the door. Resecuring it, he pushed open the screen door and shut both doors quietly behind him.

The sound *had* been a siren. And it was getting closer. Johnny lost no time jumping off the back stoop and heading across the dark yard, staying close to the shadows, head down. He'd taken the precaution of parking on the other side of the block. He'd known the night was going to end badly.

He just hadn't thought it'd go down quite like this.

It took longer than it should have to reach his car. He had to avoid the houses with lights on. But the ones closest to where he'd parked were dark. Maybe he'd finally gotten lucky.

He got in the vehicle, lost no time pulling away from the curb. He caught the strobe of lights between houses as he drove by. At the corner, he turned away from Jonas's block. And kept driving. It took him well over an hour before he stopped for the first time. After ejecting the magazine from his weapon, he tossed it down the sewer. Got back in the car and drove toward the river. The gun would be thrown in it. And on the way home, he'd get rid of his shoes in a Dumpster. He could expect that to get raided by a homeless person before the night was over.

He'd bet money he hadn't picked up any trace evidence, but he'd caught more than his share of smart guys who would have sworn the same. So he'd burn the rest of the clothes he was wearing before the evening was out. Starting with his jacket.

His jacket. Johnny shoved his free hand into the pocket and pulled out the papers he'd snatched at Jonas's place. Probably a bunch of prayers, given the looks of that room.

He'd known the man was a do-gooder but there was a thin gray line between religious and nuts in his book, and Jonas had obviously taken a giant leap across it.

Unfolding the papers, he took his eyes off the road long enough to glance down at them. It was too dark to make out much. But a single word at the top seemed to scream out at him. *Confession.* He swerved involuntarily. A horn blared in response as an oncoming car passed, missing his by inches.

But that's not what had a vise squeezing in his chest. He looked for the nearest place to pull over. Didn't give a shit when he had to double-park to do so. Punching on the overhead light, he held the papers up and read, disbelief battling panic.

My last confession . . .

He skimmed rapidly, growing more frantic by the second.

. . . since 1985 I have been a member of . . .

. . . we called ourselves the John Squad, as each member had a nickname . . .

. . . shared profits with local drug lords, in turn providing protection . . .

Sonofabitch, sonofabitch, sonofabitch! He pounded the steering wheel in disbelief. And fear. Jesus Christ, if the Cop Killer stood over him at this moment with a lit match, he couldn't be more shit-faced scared.

Hell, he'd half convinced himself that Jonas was the Cop Killer. Had *wanted* to believe it. But no. Johnny drew a deep breath and forced himself to read the two pages in his hand carefully. The bastard had ratted them all out. Given details dating back nearly three decades. Johnny gave a grim smile when he saw the son of a bitch had spent two paragraphs on Johnny and the fire that had destroyed Tory's. He'd always known the bastard had hated him as much as Johnny did him.

Balling the papers in his fist, he forced himself to think logically. And when he did, the blood congealed in his veins. He had a bit more to worry about than destroying any evidence that he'd been at Jonas's tonight.

Like whether the man had left any other letters of confession around the house.

Letters that would send Johnny to the gas chamber.

———

Nate pulled into his drive, weariness weighing on him. He wondered if Risa had turned in for the night yet. Or if she did, whether she'd sleep.

His mind lingered on the shock and worry in her eyes when he'd held her. And he couldn't help recalling that first fist-in-the-gut reaction when he'd seen her shirt soaked with blood. Even knowing that it wasn't hers, couldn't be hers, his immediate flare of fear had been telling.

There was more there, much more than he should be feeling for a colleague. More than the unheeded protectiveness he experienced with Cass. Unease spiked. Risa didn't even live around here. Not permanently. And he knew nothing about her.

Except that she had an unexpected wit. Was hot shit on a basketball court. Despite his exhaustion, a corner of his mouth kicked up. She had great instincts when it came to an investigation that had apparently deserted her when it came to taste in husbands.

And after tonight he knew what it felt like to have that long, lithe body against his, even briefly. A flicker of guilt warred against hormones. Was wrestled away. He'd used the portable strobe on his dash to get to the hospital as quickly as possible because he'd wanted—needed—to see for himself that she was all right. That first look at her covered in blood had shaved a good year off his life before logic kicked in.

He waited for the garage door to open and eased the car inside. When he did, all thoughts of Risa Chandler were shoved aside by the frustration that licked up his spine. Kristin's car was missing.

She wouldn't have pulled the same shit as a few days ago. He wanted to believe that as he unlocked the door from the garage and entered the house. After their go-round he expected to see a babysitter sitting in the family room. From habit, he toed off his shoes before going to check. Tucker was a light sleeper. And Nate wasn't up to a battle with him tonight.

His gut tightened when he stepped into the kitchen. Found it empty. Moving swiftly through the house, he discovered no one watching TV. Or stretched out on the couch asleep.

His eyes squeezed shut for a moment and his fists clenched.

As hard as it was to believe Kristin would leave Tucker home alone at night—again—he was going to have to face that she had.

And then he was going to have to call the lawyer tomorrow and put plans in motion that he'd hoped for far too long that he could avoid.

Nate went to Tucker's room, listened outside it before easing open the door. What he saw had ice chasing over his skin. Panic sprinting up his spine.

Tucker's bed was neatly made. And empty.

In disbelief, he strode in, yanked open the closet door. Back when Tucker had been fascinated by Batman, he'd snuck out of bed to sleep in his closet a couple times. Had insisted stubbornly that it was his bat cave.

But the closet was empty, too.

A curse on his lips, he strode out of the room and down the hall. Soundlessly entered his sister's bedroom and flipped on the light.

Dresser drawers had been hastily opened and not quite closed. A quick look in her closet showed an empty space where her duffel bag should be.

Nate was compelled to recheck Tucker's room, like the boy might have materialized in the last minute.

He realized then that the bed had never been slept in. Which meant the two of them had left before Tucker's bedtime.

Ah shit. A wave of bleak disappointment swamped him then. He sagged against the doorjamb. Scrubbed his face with his hands. At eight o'clock, he and Risa had still been at the station. Something Kristin would have counted on, since he hadn't been home much the last several days.

He wheeled around and headed to the kitchen in the forlorn hope that she'd left a note. Was unsurprised to discover none. If Kristin had wanted to tell him where she was going, she could have called him at any time.

She hadn't. Because she didn't want him to know. Just the opposite.

A surge of anger had him slamming his fist against the counter. Nate forced himself to think logically. Many of their things had been left in their rooms but that meant nothing.

Kristin tended to think in terms of packing light and moving swiftly. It didn't necessarily mean she planned on coming back.

And at the moment, there wasn't a damn thing he could do about it.

He pulled the phone out of his pocket and without much hope punched in her number. It went immediately to voice mail.

He considered his options. Found them depressingly limited. They weren't considered missing persons. Kristin had a legal right to take her son wherever she wanted. She just had damn little money and seemingly less sense, not to mention a smoldering resentment of her brother that had its roots in their childhood. She still had full custody over Tucker, because Nate had wanted to believe that her months-long sobriety meant that she'd finally changed. He'd thought having them live with him would give him a chance to make sure while keeping Tuck safe. Hell, maybe he'd just wanted to believe it.

And if he'd dragged her through a custody hearing months ago, that wouldn't have changed a damn thing. She'd still be gone right now. And so would Tucker.

So he did the only thing he could do. Crossing to the desk in the kitchen, he rooted around in a drawer until he found the list of contacts he kept. Kristin's contacts. Her friends. Their numbers and addresses. He'd shamelessly culled them from her phone the first week she'd moved in with him and Tucker. Because despite their relationship—or because of it—he was a cop first. And maybe he'd known he was going to need every tool he could get his hands on.

Pulling out a chair from the kitchen table, he sank into it and dialed the first number on the list. He didn't care whom he woke up. One of them would know something about where she had headed with his nephew. And they'd damn well share that information with him.

It was hardly surprising that Risa would dream that night. But the subconscious images were a jumble of faces and events from the last several days and made little sense. A burning man standing in the window above Tory's became an adult Juicy, who in turn morphed back twenty years, racing down a darkened street with a blond boy at his side. Morales frowned at her with unspoken disapproval before growing wavy at the edges and disappearing. Nate was by her side, whispering in her ear. *Did you draw your weapon?*

I couldn't find it, the dream Risa responded. *Your jacket was so big.*

Juicy's young friend looked up at her with pleading in his eyes. But when he spoke, it was another boy's words she heard. *Risa, don't leave me.*

And through it all the shots echoed over and over. Her brain told her hand to move. To draw her weapon. But it remained frozen at her side. Adam fell against her. Knocked her to the ground. His blood soaked her shirt before she turned him over.

Jerry Muller bounced the basketball in the driveway without looking their way. Just kept his head down and dribbled. Dribbled. Dribbled. *Call an ambulance,* dream Risa called.

You killed him. Jerry dribbled again. *He'll burn up before it gets here.*

And when Risa looked again, Adam was in flames. The smoke billowed and plumed, making her cough and turn away. The blond boy morphed into Darrell, holding a full carafe. *It's just Flo's coffee.* He laughed. *She always burns the coffee.*

But the smell grew stronger and Adam melted away. Risa looked down and saw the flames shooting up her arm. There wasn't pain but the smoke made her choke and her lungs heaved for oxygen . . .

Her coughing woke her. Disoriented, she sat up, waited for the sleep-induced haze to clear from her mind. But the haze didn't clear. It filled her nose and settled in her lungs and made it difficult to breathe.

It took a moment to realize that it wasn't part of the dream. Another to identify it as smoke.

Risa bounded from her bed, went to her closed bedroom door. The heat emanating from the doorknob had her snatching her hand away again. She grabbed the comforter from the bed and folded it, wedging it tightly at the bottom of her door. Then she flipped on the light switch. Found it not working.

"Mom!" Her mother would be home by now. Light was edging along the shade on the window. She'd be home and soundly asleep after working all night. Risa crawled across the bed and slapped a searching hand on the bedside table. Found nothing. With a stab of frustration she remembered that her cell was in her purse. Which was setting on a table right inside the front door.

She lunged up from the bed and crossed the room to pound on the adjoining wall. "Mom! Wake up!"

But though she pounded until her fist ached, her mother didn't respond. And it wasn't getting any easier to breathe in the room.

Rounding the bed, she went to the window. Unlocked it and struggled to shove it open. The house was outfitted with double-hung windows, which meant only the bottom would move. It would be enough space to wiggle through. But first she had to remove the combination storm.

Which proved more difficult than she'd imagined. The house was over fifty years old. The outside windows may not have been removed in that time. And the smoke was making it difficult for her to see. To breathe.

Racked with coughing spasms, she ran back to the bed and pulled on the table. Then shoved it over near the window. Climbing on top of it, she kicked out one foot against the storm. Once. Twice. Again.

It held tight. Her throat and lungs were burning. She leaned down and opened the drawer of the table. Took out the holstered weapon she'd placed there. She hadn't unloaded it when she'd come home. Had been so exhausted it was all she could do not to fall into bed fully clothed.

She drew the weapon with hands that shook. Nearly dropped it because of the sudden dampness on her palms.

Then fired two shots at the base of the outside storm. And this time when she aimed a kick at the window, it flew open. Hung loosely.

Risa lost no time replacing the safety on the weapon and

squeezing through the window to drop to the ground.

The shots fired had her neighbor tumbling from the house next door, security light blazing. "Did he come back? I'm ready this time, Risa!"

Ordinarily the sight of the barefooted, short, burly Jerry Muller in a satin robe swinging a baseball bat would have given her pause. But she was on her knees, weapon beside her, gasping for air. "Fire!" Weakly, she pointed toward her mother's window. "Hannah."

She wanted to tell him to call the fire department. Would just as soon as she could croak the words out of her smoke-damaged throat. But he was already running for the house. Came back much too soon.

In the next moment, comprehension bloomed. The folding step stool he carried was set beneath Hannah's window. He climbed it with a surprising agility and cocked the bat like a baseball player waiting for a fast pitch. Then swung with all his might and shattered the window. Knocked out the jagged shards surrounding the sash and did the same to the inside window. And then, to her horror, he dropped the bat and hoisted himself up and attempted to squeeze through it.

The fear that he'd get stuck had her staggering to her feet. Stumbling over. She could hear him grunting and swearing. Then he disappeared inside the room.

Time slowed to a stop. An eternity passed. Compelled to move, Risa scrambled up the stepladder, intent on checking on Jerry's progress. He met her at the window. Holding a limp Hannah Blanchette.

"Help me get her through there!"

Risa grasped her mother's shoulders and helped thread her through the window's opening. It was more difficult than it should have been. She was dead weight. Unresponsive. And Risa couldn't help remembering just a few hours earlier when Adam had been the same.

Panic fueled adrenaline. Powered strength. She hauled her mother out of Jerry's arms and balanced her awkwardly over her shoulder as she backed down the stepladder. Hannah was nearly as tall as Risa although spare as a rod. Her height meant that her legs tangled with Risa's as she staggered toward Jerry's drive. Tripped. They both went sprawling.

On her knees now, Risa rolled her mother over. Checked for a pulse. Sagged in relief when she found it thready and weak. Glancing over her shoulder she noted Jerry was squeezing through the window, his robe agape and showing much too much hair-covered skin.

For the second time that evening she told him, "Call an ambulance."

Chapter 16

"You should be in bed, too."

Risa winced at her mother's smoke-roughened voice. Knew that hers sounded much the same. "Don't talk," she admonished her gently, and stroked Hannah's gray hair away from her face. "That'll just make your throat hurt worse."

"What happened?"

Risa shook her head in mock impatience. But she answered honestly, "I don't know yet. It'll be a while before the investigators will have answers. Don't worry about that now, Mom. It could have been anything. Faulty wiring. An appliance that shorted out." She paused to sip from the water glass on the nearby table. Then made sure her mother took another drink from her own cup before continuing. "We won't know the extent of the damage until I talk to the firemen." The fire truck had arrived shortly before the ambulance had, and at the time, the house had been the last thing on Risa's mind.

Tears filled Hannah's eyes. The sight squeezed Risa's heart. "Silly." The older woman managed. "It's just a house. Filled with things that can be replaced."

"And everything will be replaced." Risa picked up her mother's hand to squeeze it reassuringly. Although silently she wondered how long a process that would be. There were things she'd have to see to immediately, for her mother and for herself. She could maybe have coworkers Abbie or Ramsey ship her some more clothes from her place near Manassas. But she'd need some things now. And so would her mother.

"Look at the bright side." She tried for a teasing tone. It still sounded raspy. "You wanted to get rid of those sketches of mine. Chances are, wherever you stashed the drawing pad, it's destroyed, too."

But her mother just looked puzzled. "I didn't have your drawing pad, dear. You keep it on your bedside table. I never understood . . ." A fit of coughing seized her then and Risa helped her sit up straighter until it passed. Then forced more water on her in its aftermath.

"It doesn't matter." And it didn't. It had been a poorly constructed attempt to get her mother's mind off her troubles. And it had apparently worked too well because Hannah returned to the topic even after she sank back against her pillows.

"The last time I saw it, it was on your table." A hint of color flushed her cheeks. "I'll admit I looked through it. We talked about that. But I know you need your privacy. Even when you were little, you insisted on it."

Risa remembered. Privacy had been hard to come by in her childhood, which had consisted of a long line of Hannah's boyfriends in a series of houses. The men and the houses had seemed to deteriorate over time. And once she'd hit puberty, there'd been one man in particular that she hadn't felt safe around. That was when she'd insisted on a lock on her bedroom door.

But the pad hadn't been in her room. She'd looked the next morning again before work. Frowning, Risa recalled her frustration at the time. It hadn't fallen beneath the bed, although she'd found the pencil there. Wasn't tossed in the closet or stuffed in a drawer. It'd been *gone*.

The only other answer would be that someone had taken it. She reached for her water again. Drank. And if it hadn't been Hannah, she was out of answers. The house had a good security system. She'd insisted on having it installed when she'd bought the place for her mother.

But the home was also equipped with smoke detectors.

The memory had her hand jerking in the act of replacing the water glass on the table. She'd replaced the batteries herself just last month. In truth, there hadn't been a lot to keep her occupied as she'd healed. Risa had checked the alarms to be sure they were in working order.

And they had been. One might have malfunctioned. But all of them?

A cold wash of dread spread over her. Her gaze flew guiltily to her mother's face. Because she was suddenly certain who had started that fire.

And why.

———

Eduardo Morales gave a perfunctory knuckle rap on Nate's door before pushing it open. "I've got news."

Stomach tightening with adrenaline, Nate glanced away from the computer screen. "Could use some good news for a change." One look at his captain's face had him doubting he was going to get it.

"Risa's mother's house burned down last night." Morales walked farther into the room and sank into a chair.

Shock had Nate speechless for a moment. "Last night? Hell, she couldn't have gotten home much before three. We left the hospital together."

Morales cocked a brow at that, but said only, "The call went out at about five forty-five this morning. Jett Brandau can tell you more. Apparently he contacted the fire department after he heard. He's got a relationship with a lot of those guys. Might have some details."

Sometime Nate had come to his feet. He didn't remember rising. His gut felt like it was twisted into pretzels. "Was she hurt?"

Morales looked surprised. "What? God, no, I'm sorry. Risa's okay. They treated and released her. Her mother is staying overnight. Apparently her smoke inhalation was worse. Or maybe because of her age. Anyway, don't be surprised if you don't see Risa today. Or hell." He ran a hand through his dark hair. For the first time Nate noticed that he looked like he'd aged years in the last week. "Don't be surprised if she shows up either. She's the toughest woman I know."

Nate believed it. The only sign of vulnerability he'd ever seen in the woman was last night when she'd allowed herself to lean against him. Just a little. And her hand had remained in his, her fingers grasping tightly, until they'd been joined by the others.

First her boss. Now her mother. She had to be going nuts. And he knew her well enough to know she wouldn't be thinking about herself and her needs. She'd be checking on everybody else. He glanced at the clock. Nine thirty. There wasn't a damn thing he could do for her now. Or for the rest of the day.

Because he saw Morales looking increasingly speculative, he sank down in his chair again. Felt like a tightly coiled spring readying for release. "She didn't need this on top of the shooting last night."

"Any reason to think the two things are related?" Poleaxed, Nate could only stare at the captain, who then went on. "FBI is on Raiker's shooting. Then the house burns hours later. They're looking at every angle."

"From what Risa said last night, they're just in full cover-your-ass mode. Sounds like a massive federal screwup led to Raiker even being there last night. The assassin was shot and killed. I don't know how burning the house down later would change anything."

The captain nodded, as if not expecting any differently. "Told the commissioner as much, but he directed me to ask anyway. My mind was heading in a completely different direction. Any chance this is related to the cop killings?"

Nate blinked. The thought had never even occurred to him. "I don't see how. Or why." He shook his head. "It's not widely known that Risa is helping on the investigation. Even the task force members aren't sure of her role. She'd have to be seen as a threat of some sort in order for her to be targeted by the offender, and where would that perception come from?"

"Maybe from within the department." Eduardo held up a hand to stem anything Nate might have said next. "I realize you didn't know her then, but Marisa Chandler was making quite a name for herself with the PPD before Raiker snatched her away. Others might have been familiar with her reputation."

Dryly, he responded, "Does that mean I need to install a

few more smoke detectors, or am I to believe that my own reputation for ineptitude will be enough to save me from a similar fate?"

The man had the grace to flush. But his voice, his expression was serious when he said, "It means be damn careful. At least until we get an idea on how that house fire started. You're the face of the investigation." Nate supposed that was true, if standing next to the commissioner while he gave a few sound bites to the press counted. "Someone starts watching you, they see Risa. You've been paired for the investigation. It's a stretch, but given our guy's liking for matches, what happened last night makes me uneasy enough to warn you to watch your back."

Nate rolled his shoulders. His house hadn't burned down last night, but things had gone up in flames, regardless. If any of his sister's friends knew where she was, they weren't talking. At least not to him. He'd called the school and the babysitter this morning to let them know Tucker wouldn't be there today. Given that he'd already pissed off Kristin's boss and a coworker with his calls in the middle of the night, her work already had a heads-up she wouldn't be in until further notice.

Whether his sister still had a job left when she returned was the least of his worries. *If* she returned.

Shoving the thought aside, he concentrated on the captain's words. He needed to see Risa to assure himself that she was okay. The same way he had last night in the hospital, but this time he wasn't going to be given that chance. And maybe that'd be okay. Especially if it allowed her to grab some sleep at her mother's bedside. Or at Adam's.

"There's more." There was a gleam in Morales's eye that should have warned him. The man took an envelope out of his jacket pocket. "You have the still photos IT was able to enlarge from the man in the video you found at the scene. Of the man they called Johnny." He barely waited for Nate to nod before going on. "For the last couple days we've been working on trying to match those pictures to department IDs."

It took effort to keep his voice even. When he spoke, he realized he hadn't quite managed it. "You've been working on that a couple of days?" Because this sure as hell was the first he'd been told about it.

"You have to understand the delicacy of the situation." There was no apology in the captain's tone. "You identified a man in the video as a cop. Not just a cop, but one of the victims."

"I've since paired Johnny with another of the victims. He was found in a picture with Christiansen." Because his fist had clenched, he consciously relaxed it. "There's a damn good chance Johnny is a cop, too."

"Which made it all the more imperative that it be kept as quiet as possible while we made sure. Hell, can you imagine the outcry from our ranks if word got out we were looking at one of our own being involved with this?"

He met Morales's gaze. Held it. "I can more easily imagine the outcry in the public if the media ran with the rumor."

The man lifted a shoulder. "Politics play a part in our job, and it'd be useless denying it. Whether you want to believe it or not, me taking the front on this meant I served as shit deflector if it got out we were trolling our own personnel photos to ID someone who might be involved with this case."

Being kept in the dark still stung, but Nate had to grudgingly accept that the explanation made sense. At any rate, there was nothing to be done about it now. "And did you find a match?"

In answer, Morales opened the envelope and withdrew several photos, arrayed them in a row. The first one Nate recognized as Johnny from the video. The next several were obviously department ID pictures. The captain tapped the final picture. "Walter Eggers. Been on the force over three decades. This is his most recent. And here's an added note of interest—he's the subject of an Internal Affairs investigation."

Nate's interest sharpened. "Corruption?"

"Excessive use of force." He pushed away from the desk. "Proving corruption will be on you. You can start by getting him in here." He stood, making no move toward the door, and Nate's chest tightened.

"There's more?"

"Cass Recker has been removed from the task force."

"What?" Anger flared, mingled with dread.

The captain looked sober. "Internal Affairs doesn't like the company she keeps. And a few days ago Donald Larson was questioned in conjunction with a burglary ring. They found a department cell phone on his person that had been issued to Recker."

Nate wanted to drop his head to the desktop and start banging it. His jaw tightened. "Is she implicated?"

Morales hesitated. Then, sharing more than he probably wanted to, he said in a low voice, "Calls to another suspect in the ring came from her phone. Larson isn't doing her any favors. Claims she must have made them. She's been suspended with pay while the investigation is ongoing."

Sick at heart, Nate looked away. He'd never claim to have all the answers, but people like Kristin and Cass just never seemed to learn. You could tell them a million times they were in the path of an oncoming train, and each time they'd let it run over them and then wonder what the hell had happened.

Morales moved to the door. "I don't have to tell you that this is confidential."

"No," Nate said bleakly. "You don't have to tell me." The captain went out the door after casting him one last look that was not without sympathy. When the door closed behind him, Nate scrubbed both hands over his face and then regarded the ceiling blindly. What the hell could happen next?

Since no answers were forthcoming, he reached for the most recent picture of Eggers and turned it over. Morales had obligingly written the man's contact information on the back. Withdrawing his cell phone, he punched in the number. His mood had taken a turn for the vicious. He figured there was no better time to question the man who might hold the key to this entire case.

———

"Slumming?"

Turning around at the familiar voice, a smile spread over Risa's face. "Ramsey!" She hugged the other woman, real delight filling her. Although they were colleagues, caseloads kept Raiker's employees scattered across the country. Their paths didn't cross often enough.

They parted, and Risa took a quick visual assessment. The woman's light brown hair was still streaked with highlights that owed nothing to a bottle, but it was longer than her usual shaggy short style. Those shrewd green gold eyes were the same, though, and they regarded her now with a bit of trepidation in them.

"Where's the new husband?"

She jerked a thumb toward the hallway behind them. "Dev's getting coffee for everyone. Even the feds like him. He's good at keeping people at ease."

He was, Risa recalled. She'd met him only the one time at the couple's wedding several months ago, but his charm had been readily apparent. As was his devotion to his wife.

"Marriage agrees with you." She said it lightly, was prepared for the slight grimace she got in response. Ramsey was a self-acknowledged commitment-phobe, so everyone had been shocked when she'd announced her engagement.

"Having Dev agrees with me. He's a traditional guy, so marriage it is." Her expression went wry. "He's also sneaky as hell. Had me in a white dress standing in front of a church before I knew what hit me."

Risa laughed. Followed her friend's gaze to Adam's CCU room across the hall. After returning a glower with the agent stationed outside it, she ignored him. The curtains were closed over the sliding glass door. "Is the doctor in with him?"

Shaking her head, Ramsey lowered her voice. "No, I'm supposed to be in there. I strong-armed Burke into giving me his next turn since we just got here. Then in waltzes some broad I've never seen before, and Paulie jumps up like his pants are on fire. They go into a big hug-hug-kiss-best-buddy reunion before he hustles her away. Next thing I know, I can't get in to see Adam because *she's* in there."

Mystified, Risa asked, "Who is she?"

"That's just it; none of us know. Well, Paulie obviously does, but you know what it's like getting information about Adam from him, under any circumstances. He's in full mamabear mode. And he's not saying a word."

A sudden thought struck her. "Adam hasn't taken a turn for the worse, has he?" Anxiety reared. She'd been splitting her time between here and her mom's room. Logically she knew someone would have contacted her if he had. But emotions weren't logical.

"His condition remains unchanged. That's a quote from the doctor, and she was just by about fifteen minutes ago." Seamlessly she shifted subjects. "How's your mom? And what's this I hear about you shooting a window last night?"

Risa gave a helpless laugh. "She's fine. And the other's a long story."

"You had a narrow escape, I hear." Ramsey looked across the hall again. There was no activity so she returned her speculative gaze to her friend. "Glad to hear it. Gladder yet to hear that you used your weapon."

They exchanged a look. Ramsey was the one who'd turned in Risa's weapon and resignation. The only one that Risa would have trusted to face their intimidating boss with that kind of unwelcome news.

Her gaze slid away. "My palms sweat every time I touch it," she admitted softly. "And I didn't even think of drawing it last night when Raiker was shot. What's that say about me? That I can only put the fear behind me when it's my neck on the line?"

"Maybe it says you're healing." Ramsey had a way of making things sound clear-cut when they seemed anything but. "And it was your mother's life on the line, too, the way I heard it. As for Adam, why the hell would you have gone after the shooter when his driver was so much closer? Maybe it's me, but I'm thinking when he wakes up he might be a bit more grateful that you kept him alive rather than chase down Jennings."

The words made Risa feel a modicum better, even while she still doubted their truth. "Knowing Adam, I wouldn't be so sure. He was pretty pissed about that bomb destroying his townhouse."

There was activity across the hall then, and the two of them went silent at the same time Dev Stryker ambled up carefully carrying a tray of coffees. "Risa, you're lookin' lovely as ever. No ill effects from last night?"

Ramsey shushed him and his brows shot up. Risa took a coffee from the tray and nodded toward the couple coming out of Adam's room. Paulie had his arm around a woman with shoulder-length mink-colored hair, and they were speaking in hushed tones as they walked by the trio watching them.

Although she looked closely, Risa could see little of the woman's features. Even so, when Ramsey gave her a quizzical look, she shook her head. She didn't recognize her either.

A tall blond man who looked like he could have wandered in on his way to a casting call greeted the duo at the end of the hallway. The three stopped and talked, and it looked like they all knew each other.

"Who *is* she?" Ramsey muttered as she took a coffee from the tray Dev balanced.

"Who, the woman?" Dev took a sip from the last cup while shoving the empty tray in a nearby trash container. "Her name's Jaid Marlowe."

Risa and Ramsey's attention snapped to him. "How do you know that?" his wife demanded.

"Saw her in the cafeteria earlier. She actually ran into me and made me dump the first tray of coffees I'd bought. Real nice lady. I bought her one to calm her nerves, and we introduced ourselves. Don't think she drank much of it, though. She seemed pretty upset."

"Upset." Ramsey had returned her gaze to the trio down the hallway. "So wonder what Pretty Boy's story is."

"Unless you're talkin' about me—and as a newlywed you really should be—he's probably an FBI agent. That's how Jaid knew Adam. They were in the bureau together." This time he took their open-mouthed reactions as his due. "It's the southern charm, ladies. People open up to me."

Ramsey eyed him coolly over the top of her cup as she drank. "I may mold you into an investigator yet, Stryker."

"I'm putty in your hands, sugar." His tone was droll. "Do with me what you will."

Paulie and the blond stranger were walking their way. During the short exchange with Dev, the woman—Jaid Marlowe—had vanished. When the pair reached them, Risa revised her original estimation. The stranger was older than she'd first thought, mid-forties maybe. Old enough, perhaps, for him to have been a colleague of Adam's in the bureau.

"Special Agent Tom Shepherd." Paulie made the introduction in an uncharacteristically brusque manner. "DC sent him out to figure how the field agents screwed up so badly."

"I wanted to come." The man gave them a sober look.

"Raiker . . . he's still a legend at the bureau. He dropped in to see me just a few months ago. I was still doing penance in Bismark." Paulie nodded, as if he'd known about the visit. Probably he had. There was little about Raiker that he wasn't apprised of.

"He hadn't realized I'd been banished after he came in and solved that first Mulder kidnapping I worked a few years back. But six weeks after he stopped by, I received word that I was being transferred back to DC." His eyes strayed to the CCU room across the hall. "He'd never admit it, but I know he put in a word. The man's still got pull in the agency, even being gone as long as he has."

He excused himself then and moved toward the agent stationed outside Adam's door. Since it was the same one Risa had had a go-round with earlier, she was half hoping to listen in on the conversation. But when Paulie caught her eye and gave a slight jerk of his head, she gave an inner sigh and followed him back into the waiting room, with Ramsey and Dev trailing her.

It didn't escape her that with Adam out of commission Paulie had lost a great deal of his normal effusiveness and taken over some of their boss's no-nonsense mannerisms. It wasn't the same. Wouldn't be until Adam was better and snapping orders at them all again.

———

Jett Brandau stuck his head in the door. "You got time?"

Nate looked up from the questions he was jotting down. He hoped to have Javon Emmons and Walter Eggers back in for interviews before the day's end. With outside investigations embroiling both men, he had to be careful in the information he elicited and the manner in which he did it.

But Jett might have details on Risa's house fire. "Sure." He put his pen down and nodded to a chair.

The man looked drawn as he slouched in a seat. "Been a helluva day already."

"Tell me about it," Nate responded feelingly.

"Thought you'd like to know . . . I've been in contact with the battalion chief from the fire station that responded to the call at Risa's house. Lloyd Bennett. Good guy."

"And?"

Jett lifted a shoulder. "And . . . not much. Yet. Place is still smoldering. They had to do a surround and drown—hose down the houses on either side of it to keep the fire from spreading. It was burning pretty hot. He'll keep me posted when they have more details."

"Would they be able to determine by now whether there was a forced entry?"

Brows shooting upward, Jett said, "You mean there's a question of arson? Really? Because if there is, they need to request a fire inspector to look at it."

"Morales asked because of the investigation," Nate affirmed. "It should be checked out. I think it's a stretch to believe the offender targeted Risa, but we need to take every precaution."

"I hope to God he doesn't have her in his sights." Jett tapped his fingers nervously on the arm of the chair.

"You and me both. Like I say, it's a stretch." But he damn sure didn't want to take any chances with Risa's safety.

"I'll bug Bennett throughout the day and report back. He owes me a favor."

Jett seemed to think the city was abounding with people who "owed him." Nate hoped that for once the man was right.

The conversation lagged. When Brandau didn't rise, Nate knew the man had something else on his mind. And he was pretty certain what it was.

"You heard about Cass."

The familiar weight settled in his gut. He nodded, said nothing.

"She knows she screwed up, Nate." A smile flickered. Disappeared. "Guess she doesn't need anyone telling her that."

"It's too late to tell her anything." Not that he hadn't tried, unsuccessfully, time and again. Too often it seemed like he was a helpless bystander watching people he cared about make one destructive decision after another. Cass wasn't Kristin. At least she hadn't dragged a kid down with her.

"She wants to talk to you but didn't want to jam you up. She had to turn in her department-issued cell."

Nate nodded. It was more likely that IA was holding it for

evidence. Additionally she'd have been asked to turn in her access cards, ID, radio, and weapon, along with her shield.

"But she'd like to talk to you, if you think you can meet her and not have it come back on you some way."

Interest sharpening, Nate asked, "Where is she?"

"Around the corner at Barney's. That little diner? Shouldn't be anyone from here at this time in the morning. But if you want me to let her know it should be somewhere else—"

Glancing at the clock, Nate rose. Grabbed his jacket. "I'll meet her now." Morales might not be thrilled with the decision, but he'd leave the politics to the brass. There were times when friendship superseded the job.

This was one of those times.

———

Cass Recker huddled over a coffee at Barney's cracked laminate counter, the picture of dejection. Nate slid onto the stool next to her, caught the waitress's eye, and she ambled over. "Coffee."

Trying for a smile that didn't quite come off, Cass said, "I wasn't sure you'd come. That you could." Then her eyes filled with nerves. "This isn't going to get you in trouble, is it?"

"Don't worry about me. How are you doing?" He accepted a steaming mug from the woman in the pink uniform and hoped it was at least as good as Darrell's.

She lifted a shoulder. "Wishing I'd listened to you. I just can't believe Donny would do this to me." Cass lifted her cup to her lips. Drank. "I know what you're thinking. I've taken a lot of shit from him. But this . . . he's telling them he didn't make those calls on my cell. That I did it. Can you believe that? He's implicating me in a burglary ring."

"Look at me." He waited until she did. Hoped that she was paying attention with her head as well as with her ears. "You have to cut him loose. Here." He tapped her chest above her heart. "This is about survival. He's thrown you to the wolves. You don't owe him a thing. And if you try to help him, you're going down with him." Fear flared in her eyes. Good. Nate hoped to hell she was scared. He was scared for her.

"I know it. I do," she insisted, when Nate opened his

mouth again. "My rep says no contact, and believe me, if he came near me right now, I'd be tempted to put a bullet in him." Her smile was bitter. "If I hadn't had to hand in my weapon."

"Hopefully IA has enough on the burglary ring that ties him to it, and it'll end up being his word against yours. Cop. Known felon. Balances out in your favor."

"Cop who's been colluding with known felon." Her tone and her eyes were bleak. "Believe me, I know the score here. I might lose my shield over this."

He didn't give her false platitudes. They both knew she was right. Whatever the outcome, she wouldn't be returning to work with him. If she was reinstated, this was a stain that would remain on her record for years to come. Nate leaned in to bump her shoulder companionably. "This'll give you a chance to catch up on those soap operas you've been missing out on."

"Jesus." She gave a short laugh, swiped at her eyes. "Shoot me now."

"You can always go visit your mom and sisters."

"Two hours in a room with them and I want to jump out a window. Three hours, and they're lining up to give me a push."

A thought struck. He hesitated, then said slowly, "Or if you're really desperate for something to do . . . Kristin has disappeared. Took Tucker with her. They were gone when I got home last night."

Clearly glad to have something other than her own misery to concentrate on, Cass touched his arm. "Shit. I'm sorry, Nate. Any ideas where she went?"

He shrugged. "No note. Her friends aren't talking. At least not to me."

"But they don't know me. I might get something out of them." Her expression lightened. "I wouldn't mind looking into it. It'll give me something to concentrate on. And I need to take my mind off this mess, or I'm going to jump off a bridge, I swear."

She sounded only half kidding. He felt a little better about the idea. He had absolutely no idea where to start looking for his sister. Was pissed enough that he probably wouldn't look right now if it were just Kristin involved. But it wasn't. It was also Tucker. If Cass was able to get one of Kristin's friends to open up and give her a general location to look, he could maybe ask for a favor from the police department in that city. Blue to blue. Put them on the lookout for her car. Something.

As it was, she still wasn't answering her phone. He still didn't know if Tuck was being taken care of. He wanted to think Kristin had changed. The last week made that hard to believe.

He looked at his friend. "I'd appreciate it, Cass. But think of yourself first, okay? They'd have told you not to leave the area, so don't. Just get done what you can here. If I get an idea of Kristin's destination, I can do the rest."

"Sure." She seemed buoyed at the prospect. And Nate knew then just how much she'd been dreading the long, empty days ahead of her.

"Here." He dug out his keys and took his house key off the ring. "In the kitchen desk drawer, I have a list of her contacts and their numbers. Feel free to look around in their rooms if you think that will help. Lock up and leave the key on the counter. Unlock the house entrance to the garage. I'll get back in tonight that way."

Contemplating the key for a moment, she looked like she would cry. Nate felt a familiar tug of panic at the prospect of a female's tears. But she didn't. Cass was made of tougher stuff than that. Even if her decision making in her personal life left something to be desired. "You're a good friend."

Trying to lighten the mood, he said, "Because I just laid my messy personal baggage at your doorstep? Yeah, I'm a prince."

Slipping the house key into her pocket, she picked up her coffee mug again. "I wouldn't go as far as royalty. But you're a good guy to have on my side."

"Preliminary autopsy results indicate that Randolph was killed in a manner similar to the other three victims." Nate was addressing the task force. "The only difference was that she had to cut the remnants of something off his face and head. We think it was some sort of mask or fitted hood. That's been turned over to the lab for analyzing. Hopefully they can identify it."

"The change in location was also a difference," Finnegan drawled. "Does this mean he's branching farther abroad?"

"It means he went to a lot of trouble to scout locations for the crimes before he ever began carrying them out."

Nate jerked around when Risa's voice sounded behind him. He hadn't heard her come in. Hadn't expected to see her at all today. The quick once-over he gave her was as involuntary as it was instinctive. She'd been to hell and back in the last several hours. Her voice was far raspier than normal, probably from the smoke she'd inhaled. Those incredible eyes had dark shadows beneath them, and there were some scrapes and bruises on her face. But she was alive and standing. He'd been assured she was fine. But seeing for himself had relief swamping him.

It took effort to return his attention to the front of the room and continue his report. "Parker's car hasn't turned up much in the way of trace evidence. His blood was identified in the trunk. We eliminated the prints for him and his wife. There are plenty of others, but nothing that popped on the Automated Fingerprint Identification System. Forensics isn't done with it but it's not looking hopeful."

"Why'd it take so long for impound to make the connection?" Shroot wanted to know. There was a murmur of agreement in the room.

"The plates that were on it had only recently been reported as stolen. And the Vehicle Identification Number had been changed. Professional job, too. That's the best lead we're probably going to get from the car. It's possible our offender has a record for auto theft. Maybe he's affiliated with a local chop shop. In any case, Alberts and Finnegan, take a look at parolees in the area released in the last three years with something similar on their sheet."

"Brandau and Shroot." His gaze encompassed the two men. "We're trying to trace the former owner of Tory's, which was the building shown in the video left at the third crime scene. Full name Tory Marie Baltes. She had a son." He waited for their nods before continuing. "See if you can track them down."

"I can save you a bit of trouble there," Risa spoke again. "I slipped away from the hospital long enough today to replace my phone." She held one up, and Nate recalled that her old one, along with her computer and most of her personal belongings, would be toast after last night. The way she'd very nearly ended up herself. "Had some time on my hands so I did some searching online. I found an obituary for Baltes less than two years after the fire. Have already started tracking her family."

Nate nodded. "So you two can take another task. I have a key found at Sherman Tull's home that might fit a lockbox. You'll check with the banks to see if it belongs to any of them. Tomey and Edwards, I've got a packet of photos up here. I want you to watch the footage we shot of the victims' memorial services, see if you can pick out any of the people from these pictures." He'd included photos of Sam Crowley, Javon Emmons, and Walter Eggers, as well as of Tull, Christiansen, and Randolph. A visit from one of the men who would later be victims might help prove a relationship between the men. "Mendall and Hoy, keep combing through the victim's personal lives. With Randolph as the latest victim, there's another intersection to look for." He was very aware of Morales standing silently against the wall behind him. There would be no mention made at this time of the ID of PPD Sergeant Eggers as the man in the video. That he'd handle personally.

After he dismissed the team, he gave the packet to Edwards and turned to find Brandau and Morales speaking to Risa. When he joined them, Jett looked up. "I was just telling Risa I spoke to Bennett, the battalion chief of the fire station an hour ago. They've got a fire inspector coming in to work with them tomorrow. There was no sign of forced entry at the house."

"There were three smoke alarms installed there." Nate almost winced at the scratchy sound of her voice. It sounded as though it were painful to speak. "I never heard any of them."

Jett hesitated. "Bennett said none had batteries in them."

"They did." Risa's tone was emphatic. "I replaced them

myself in the last month or so. It's a small house. Even if one malfunctioned we should have been able to hear the other two."

"Maybe your mom disconnected them," Nate suggested, leaning against the wall facing her. "People do sometimes. Run out of batteries for something and take them out of the detectors, resolving to put them back later. And then they forget. It happens."

She shook her head, unconvinced. Looked at Jett. "How does an arson investigation work? What will they look for?"

The man scratched his jaw. "The investigator will interview everyone. You. Your mom. The firefighters. He'll want to know what you heard and saw. Appliances and wiring will be checked to see if there was a short or malfunction. The department will have taken pictures, and he'll want to look at the burn patterns. Most accelerants will leave traces behind. Those can sometimes be picked up with a VTA machine."

"So if someone started it, there'll be trace evidence left behind."

His pause had everyone looking at him. "Presumably," he said finally. "But if an arsonist doesn't want to leave a trace, he'll use rubbing alcohol for the accelerant. The water used to fight the fire will wash it away." With a quick look at Risa's face, he hastened to add, "But burn patterns can still tell them quite a bit. You might want to check with your mom to see if and when she opened the windows. There were two opened on either side of the picture window in the front room, and one in the kitchen."

When no one responded, he added, "Fires need oxygen. The open windows provided plenty of it."

Chapter 17

Morales followed Risa and Nate back to Nate's office. He waited until the door was closed behind them to ask, "Did you notice whether the windows were open last night?"

She made a beeline for her desk chair. It would be bad form to collapse on the job, but exhaustion from the night before was crowding in. Sinking into it, she tried to recall. "Mom is pretty security conscious. She's lived in Philly all her life, and some of the neighborhoods I grew up in weren't the best. I'll ask her, but I don't think she would have left the windows open all night. Ordinarily I'd notice something like that but . . ."

"You'd had a helluva night already."

She nodded at Nate's words. "I'm almost certain they weren't open, but again, I can't be positive. The thing is, I didn't get in until close to three. A CSU team was just finishing up after the shooting." She looked at both the men. "If someone did set it, there was very limited opportunity to do so." Unless, of course, she thought with a chill, he'd been inside the house all along. Waiting. Watching. Her skin prickled. Hannah didn't get off work until two A.M. She'd probably barely gotten home before Risa had herself. Someone would have to know their habits.

And been intent on killing them both, not just destroying the house.

"I'll find out who was assigned to the crime scene," Morales said. "See if anyone saw any activity around your place."

There'd been plenty of activity around it that evening, she thought with a pang. If someone had entered and lain in wait, he'd have had to be in the basement. Just a couple hours had passed between nightfall and her return from work. And then once the ambulance and police had been on scene, how likely was it that someone could have crept into the house unnoticed?

Doubt reared. She was tired. Maybe more than a little paranoid. After the events of the day, she was entitled. It would be all too easy to second-guess her conclusions.

Except that the drawing pad had disappeared. She believed her mother when she insisted she hadn't removed it.

And there was one person who might find the sketches in them a threat.

Belatedly, she realized the two men were waiting for her to respond. "I'll talk to Hannah tonight about it."

Eduardo shoved his hands in his jacket pockets. "You two have a place to stay?" His expression went wry. "Not saying my place is the Ritz, but we can juggle the kids, free up a bedroom. It's yours for as long as you need it."

Touched, she smiled at him. "Thanks, Eddie. I'd like to come by sometime to see Renee and the family, but I don't want to disrupt your home. The hospital released Hannah this afternoon and I've already got her situated." And the argument she'd lost in that regard still rankled. "The next-door neighbor is the son of my mom's best friend. She's gone now. But he offered to let her stay there." Hannah was jittery enough to be attracted by that familiarity, Risa realized now. She couldn't go home, but she was as comfortable in Eleanor's house as she would be in her own. Surrounded by a neighborhood that represented the longest time she'd spent in one place in . . . well, maybe in forever.

Some of the earlier ire she'd felt when they'd had this discussion faded. Although Risa would prefer having her mother with her, it might be safer for the older woman if she wasn't.

Because *if* the offender had targeted Risa on account of those sketches, he just might try again since she'd survived the fire. She'd like Hannah far away from her if that happened.

"That still leaves you," Eddie pointed out.

She waved a hand. "I'll get a hotel." Not one close to work or the hospital, as she'd already found out when she'd spent an hour on the phone that afternoon. It was Saturday, after all, and a sell-out concert, coupled with a home game for the Phillies, was making the search challenging. Risa had no doubt she'd have better luck looking farther out. The thought held little appeal. Which is why she decided more calling could wait a few hours. If nothing else, she could stretch out in the CCU waiting room that evening.

Apparently satisfied, Morales switched the subject. "Doubtful this has anything to do with us, but I did get word of another police slaying last night."

Risa practically bolted upward in her chair. "What? Where?"

"Nothing like our case. The victim's name was Joseph Mauro. It would have been ruled a suicide. The victim definitely ate his gun. Gray matter all over the place. Residue on his hand. But he had a different caliber bullet in his chest and that weapon wasn't found. Had to have been a second party in the room." He shook his head. "Why someone would shoot him when he was committing suicide anyway is anyone's guess. But because of the suspicious manner in which it happened, we got tipped off, in case it ties in with ours somehow."

"Do you have a photo of Mauro?" Nate rolled his shoulders when the captain looked at him. "I'll add it to the ones I gave Tomey and Edwards."

"I can get it to you." Morales stepped forward to pat Risa's shoulder. "Glad you and your mom are okay. And what's the update on Raiker?"

"His condition has been upgraded to serious. He isn't conscious for long periods of time, but he did speak this afternoon when I was in with him." Her mouth quirked. "He said, 'Get me the hell out of here.'"

The two men smiled. "A man after my own heart," Eduardo said. He crossed to the door. "I'll track down the picture of Mauro for you," he told Nate. And then to Risa, he said, "Darrell's still on duty. I'll have him look into getting a hotel room for you."

"That's not necessary . . ."

"Let's see what he can do." Eddie winked. "The guy's a magician sometimes."

When the door had closed behind him, she looked at Nate. Couldn't identify the expression he was regarding her with. "Listen," she said, a bit unsteadily. "About last night . . ." She needed to tell him that she'd appreciated his presence. His strength. Even while panic still flickered at how natural it had seemed to lean on him. To accept support when she was much more used to relying only on herself.

She didn't get any of it out. Because Nate was on his feet and rounding the desk. He had her hauled out of her chair and into his arms with a sneaky ease that she might have suspected came with long practice. If she'd been thinking.

When his mouth settled over hers, surprise held her still for the first few seconds. But then a familiar weakness stole to her knees. Her arms went around his hard waist, and she returned the pressure of his mouth with her own. His kiss was demanding. Edged with desperation. It fired an immediate answering response as heat rocketed through her system. When he tore his lips away a moment later, it was all she could do not to haul them back to hers.

His voice, when it came, sounded as raspy as her own. "Twice in twenty-four hours is a bit much to take."

His arms loosened and she tilted her head back, comprehension filtering slowly through the haze of desire. "First seeing you covered in Adam's blood. Then hearing you'd barely escaped a fire with your life."

Awkwardly, she stepped away, uncomfortable with both the gesture and the sentiment. And her emotional responses to each. "I'm sure it was a shock."

"Not as big a shock as recognizing how hard it hit me, thinking you'd been hurt." His words were blunt. The look in his narrowed midnight gaze intent. "I didn't expect this. Don't want it. But lots of things are jumping up to knock me on my ass recently, so why should you be any different?"

She wasn't following his meaning. She didn't *want* to follow his meaning. The conversation was skating much too close to the personal, and she was usually careful to avoid that. Notwithstanding the last couple minutes. Carefully, she responded, "I haven't knocked you on your ass, McGuire. Although if you ever agree to a little one-on-one, you'd probably end up there. Just saying."

The gibe brought a quirk to his mouth, but his gaze remained fixed on her. "I've got female friends. I know how I'm supposed to feel when one of them gets hurt or catches a bad break. I damn well know that it shouldn't be like taking a brick to the chest. I don't want to feel this."

Panic was starting to steal in. One sneaky inch at a time. "Then don't."

"That's all you've got? Just order the emotions aside and ignore them?"

She felt hunted. "It could work."

"It doesn't work for me," he said flatly. "Timing hasn't always exactly gone in my favor. But this? Between us?" He waggled his index from one of them to the other. "There's something here that can't be ignored. I won't let you ignore it. Just fair warning."

She watched him move back to his desk, wanting to get her hands on that brick he'd mentioned earlier so she could heave it at his arrogant head. "You won't *let* me?"

"Poor choice of words. Blame it on the late night. The worry about you. Oh, and throw in the fact that my sister took off, my nephew in tow, for parts unknown last night, and yeah, I'm probably lacking a bit of my usual finesse. Give me twelve hours of sleep and this case solved, and I'll do better."

Her temper dissipated as quickly as it had flared. "You don't know where they went?"

He gave her a tight smile. "The workings of my sister's mind have long been a mystery. She resents me, has since we were kids, really." He rolled his shoulders, looked away. "Can't say I blame her. I was the football star, the one the parents were always bragging on. She was five years younger and had to fight just to get noticed. It . . . shaped her, I guess. By the time she was a teen, she was searching for more and more outrageous ways to get their attention. And she got it, all negative." His expression turned guilty. "I was in college by then, but my folks still attended the games. It was a vicious cycle for her."

She contemplated him, glad for not the first time that she'd never had siblings. "She wouldn't have gone to see your parents?"

He shook his head, picked up a pen from his desk, and clicked it. "They died within a few months of each other about seven years ago. They never knew Tucker." An unwilling smile tugged at his lips. "They would have loved Tuck. He's a great kid. Anyway." He set the pen down again. It began a slow roll to the edge of his desk. "I've got someone working to track her down. Kristin still has custody; there's not much to do about her leaving. I just want to make sure they're okay."

"I hope you find them," she said softly. Seemed like both of them had been through an emotional wringer in the last eighteen hours or so. And likely that's what had elicited his unexpected declaration. The thought should have made her feel better. Somehow it didn't.

He reached out to nab the pen before it fell to the floor as a knock sounded at the door. It pushed open a ways and Darrell appeared. He held a piece of paper out toward Risa. "I haven't found anything yet for tonight, but here's a couple hotels not too far from here that would have a room starting tomorrow."

"Wow. You work fast." She got up to take it from him.

"I know a gal who's a travel agent. I'll keep you posted if something else turns up. Also . . ." His gaze encompassed her and Nate. "They just showed someone to interview two. A Sergeant Walter Eggers. I was told you wanted to see him."

"Thanks, Darrell."

When he'd withdrawn, Risa sent a frown to Nate. "Why do we want to see him?"

"Because we've got an ID on 'Johnny' from the video." Nate rose, picking up a notebook that was sitting on the corner of his desk from this morning. "And he just happens to be a Philadelphia police detective."

Adrenaline kicked through her veins. Had her beating Nate to the door. "Then Darrell was right. We definitely want to see him."

Walt Eggers sat motionless in the chair, his hands on his lap. Alarm was doing a fast skitter up his spine, but he'd be damned if he'd show it. He knew how these things worked. He'd been on the other side of the table more times than he could recall. There might be someone behind the mirrored glass on the far side of the room. Somebody else monitoring the video recording from that camera secured above the door. And McGuire himself would be watching for nervous tics. Telltale body language. Convince the cops you had nothing to hide and you were halfway home.

Except that he hadn't expected to end up in a formal interview. He swallowed convulsively. Best-case scenario, he'd hoped to maybe waltz in here, talk to McGuire cop-to-cop. Answer any questions he had as truthfully as possible while still lying his ass off on pertinent details. Get a slap on the back for his cooperation.

His palms were damp. He resisted the urge to wipe them on the front of his pants. Anyone reviewing the tape would take that as a sign of nerves for sure. So he wouldn't offer to shake hands. Problem solved.

Every problem could be solved if a person had the brains.

Minutes ticked by. He might have gotten away with feigning impatience, glancing at his watch, but he was keeping it cool for now. It gave him time to think through the scene logically. Plan out the best strategy.

He'd about shit himself when his captain had passed along the "request" to see McGuire today. The captain had been none too pleased either. Bastard still was pissed about the IA bullshit. Once the panic had receded though, he'd been able to think more clearly. And he was almost certain there was no fucking way this was tied to him being there when Jonas offed himself last night.

The task force wouldn't care about Jonas unless they'd tied him to the Cop Killer. And even if they had, nothing tied Walt to Jonas. It was too early for any forensic evidence to have come back from that scene, so that wasn't it. And it'd been too damn dark for anyone to ID him. So this wasn't about last night.

Unless the son of a bitch had written more than one letter.

Walt could feel perspiration pop out on his forehead. What

if he'd sent one to the task force? Then planned to eat his gun and let the rest of them take the heat for it the next day? Walt figured the odds of that were about twenty-eighty. Which didn't exactly calm his nerves.

A sweating interviewee put a cop's instincts on full alert. He made a production of taking out a handkerchief. Wiping his nose and doing a quick swipe of his forehead while he was at it. Then went to work on his nose again. Better to be thought a nose picker than someone sweating out the thought of answering a few questions.

He wadded up the handkerchief in his right palm, sopping up the dampness there before putting it back in his pocket. Sleight of hand. A measure of his normal confidence returned. Fuck McGuire. Walt Eggers had been around long enough to outwit some hotshot cowboy. Probably thought he was the shit because he'd gotten himself named to lead the task force. The pricks with big egos were always the easiest to fool.

The door pushed open. He forced himself to breathe evenly. Maybe let a little impatience show in his expression. Bullshit power play when you're interviewing another cop, but mostly he was all cooperation. With a little puzzled thrown in for good measure.

A woman entered first. A looker, too, with legs long enough to strap around a man while he pounded it to her. McGuire was right behind her. Walt had caught him on the televised press releases a time or two, looking like a gutless monkey standing silently next to the commissioner while he used valuable air time to say exactly nothing.

"McGuire?" He rose. Held out his hand. Better to take the initiative in these things. "Walt Eggers. Got a message you wanted to see me. Came right after my shift."

"We appreciate that." McGuire shook his hand briefly. "This is Risa Chandler, a special consultant on the task force."

The consultant. Walt shook her hand, too, was distracted for a moment when she looked at him. Damned if he'd ever seen eyes like that before on a woman. Almost gold, like a cat's, with hair a couple shades darker hanging down to her shoulders. On the fuckable scale, she topped the charts.

He sat back down and the two settled across from him.

Adrenaline flared. He waited for one of them to speak. No nervous talking from him.

"You're familiar with the cases we're working on."

Chandler's words weren't a question but he answered anyway. "There's not a cop on the force who's not aware of it."

She gave a nod. "Did you know any of the victims?"

He'd known this question would be asked and was ready for it. "Yeah, I knew Patrick Christiansen. Great guy. The best. Damned shame what happened to him. No one deserves to die that way." Which wasn't a lie. It'd taken a few hours for him to realize he'd have to own up to knowing Giovanni if he was asked. That damned fishing trip they'd gone on all those years ago. Everyone and their fucking sister had had a camera. He couldn't be sure a picture wouldn't surface with him in it.

"How well did you know him?"

He lifted a shoulder like it was no big deal. And it wasn't. These two were strictly amateurs. He didn't have to feign nonchalance. "I dunno. Long time. We fished together sometimes."

"You went on trips together?"

"Went to the lake with him a couple times. Just on one overnight trip. Eight years or so, I guess it was. There were five of us."

"Do you remember their names?"

He did, because he'd spent the afternoon tracking down the information. It didn't matter if they had the names. None of them but he and Giovanni had been from the John Squad. "Paul Schwartz. Carmine Knowles. Ted Andersen. Frank Paulus." He stopped, as if trying to remember. It'd seem rehearsed if he could rattle them off without any trouble. "Shit, what was that guy's name?" He rubbed his jaw. "Big guy. Used to play hockey. Always had the jokes." He shook his head, gave them a rueful smile. "It'll come to me. When I'm not thinking about it."

Chandler smiled back. "That's how it goes, isn't it?"

Oh yeah. Definitely fuckable.

"How'd you meet Christiansen?"

"At the gym. Probably fifteen years ago." Which was a lie, but since they couldn't check it out, it didn't matter.

"Which gym?" McGuire wasn't smiling. Maybe that was their playbook. Let the bitch act all warm and friendly, with that raspy voice of hers causing a man's thoughts to stray far off path. Then the other cop digs for the details. The prick.

"Hell, I don't know. I've belonged to several over the years and it was a long time ago."

McGuire shoved a blank yellow tablet at him. "Would you mind writing down the names of the gyms you've belonged to? And the people you recall being on that trip with you and Christiansen."

Walt wrote slowly as if trying to recall. Which he was, because the gym answer had been bullshit. He'd belonged to the same gym for nearly eighteen years. But he wrote down the names of a few others anyway. It's not like they'd have records going that far back.

"Did you work with Detective Christiansen after shift?"

The blood in his veins turned icy. Sneaky bitch. The only other job Giovanni had had—that any of them had had—had been the work they'd done in the John Squad. "Huh?" If in doubt, play dumb.

"Christiansen and you. Did you work the same second job?"

He shrugged. "I don't know about Pat, but I've never moonlighted. The department is more likely to sanction it these days, but frankly, I like my free time."

"So he never said anything about a second job." This from McGuire.

"Not to me."

"But the two of you were close." Chandler looked puzzled. "You were fishing buddies."

"That's right. But we're not women." His look invited McGuire to share in the joke. "We went fishing; we talked about fish. Not our life stories."

"Maybe you did other things together, then," she suggested. "What about sports? Poker?"

"Naw." He relaxed a bit in his chair. "Just fishing."

"When's the last time you saw him?"

As if he didn't have a ready answer for McGuire's question, Walt rubbed his chin and looked at the ceiling. "Man, I don't know. Last year? Yeah, maybe last summer sometime. He called and asked if I wanted to go to Raystown with him."

"So you say you were friends." His attention switched to Chandler. She was smiling again but it was different this time. Cool. Not at all friendly. "Fishing buddies. Known him for years, you said."

Definitely a bitch that needed to be shown her place. A different time, under different circumstances, Walt would have been glad to show it to her. "That's right."

"Then we'll see you in the footage taken at his funeral? His memorial service?"

He stared at her, his mind racing. Hell no, he wouldn't be on the footage. He hadn't gone to any of the services because none of the John Squad were supposed to attend. That had been Hans's idea. Dumbest thing in the world to get tied to the victims by showing up and having someone be able to place you there later, he'd said. Walt had pointed out that plenty of cops would go who didn't know the victims. A show of support. But Hans had won that argument, at least Walt had thought so at the time. But who the hell knew if the others had followed the man's orders?

He looked at the table. Let his jaw work, as if the question got him emotional. "I'm not good at that stuff." A moment later he met her gaze head-on. "It just pisses me off, you know? Thinking of him dead, and like that? And the asshole is still out there. I wanted to go, but . . . I couldn't handle it." He let the words trail off. Suck on that, bitch.

"So Christiansen is the only victim you knew? Never met any of the others?"

Growing bored, Walt looked at Nate. Jesus, no wonder the killer was still out there. If this was all the department had to throw at the case, they were royally screwed. "That's what I said."

"Then maybe you can explain this." The detective took a photo from his jacket pocket. Laid it on the table and nudged it toward him.

And his bowels went to water. Because it was the John Squad. Although only him, Johann and Sean were shown. And the shot of Sean was a blurry profile. But he and Johann were plainly depicted, if much younger. Walt no longer had to wonder how he'd come to their attention. First they must have identified Johann as Roland Parker. Dug around in the department ID photos and matched his to the picture.

Perspiration snaked down his back. He didn't remember the date specifically, but he recalled the location. It'd been snapped at Tory's. The summer of '86.

About three weeks before he'd torched the place and let it burn with Lamont Fredericks locked in the apartment upstairs.

————

"He's lying."

Risa paced the length of the office and back, her movements jerky with frustration. "He knows it. He knows we know it. And there's not a damn thing we can do it about it right now."

Nate's voice was grim. "I'll talk to Morales, see if he can get us more. But we don't have enough for warrants. Not yet. And you can bet the cocky little bastard realizes that, too."

"He's sweating, though." The thought was the only thing that gave her a measure of satisfaction. That had been evident in the flush on that smug face. The tension in his squared-off body. "He was scrambling at the end, trying to backpedal."

"Yeah, he was feeding us a line. None of the gyms he wrote down match the ones on file for Christiansen. But it's within the realm of possibility that it's like he says. A photo of him in a bar. That long ago, who remembers? Maybe you go with a friend, they have friends there, who also invite a friend." Nate shrugged. "Bullshit, but plausible enough to prevent us from getting a warrant."

She shot him a look, still fuming. "You're taking this remarkably well."

"We knew he wasn't going to break down and confess." His tone was practical. "We wanted to get an impression of him and we got it. He claims he never played poker with Christiansen, but his widow names him as one that her husband said he was playing cards with. We can figure they weren't playing cards, and it's not much of a stretch to guess what they were doing."

"Running interference for local drug lords while taking a cut of their profits."

He stopped then, narrowed his eyes at her. "You're guessing."

"An educated guess," she corrected him. Risa propped a hip on his desk. "Not much else to do sitting in the hospital so I used my new phone to search the web. Found some articles on Lamont Fredericks. One of them said he was suspected of being involved in drug dealing in the neighborhood where he died."

"He actually did time for it." There were a pile of file folders on his desk. Unerringly he reached for one in the middle of the stack and flipped it open and then turned it around for her to look at. "Eight years for possession with intent. He'd been out ten years and was charged a couple times, but the charges ended up getting dropped."

She folded her arms and studied the page in the folder. "So Fredericks was involved with dealing drugs and lived above Tory's. Eggers, Parker, and unidentified friends hung out in Tory's. Christiansen told his wife he was spending time with Eggers—who he referred to as Johnny—as well as others. Playing cards. We know Christiansen and Parker tucked away a tidy amount from a second job Eggers claims he knows nothing about."

"From there on we've got assumptions." Nate leaned back in his desk chair, hands hooked behind his neck. Risa was female enough to appreciate the way the pose showed off his muscled chest. Cop enough to resent noticing. "The victims—Parker, Tull, Christiansen, and Randolph—had something in common. Likely it was what they did off hours and equally likely it was illegal."

"Drugs, Raiker guessed." He'd been about to lodge another opinion when the shooting had started, she recalled sickly. "Fredericks got a couple drug charges dropped. How did he do that? Lose evidence? Get to the DA? With a cop shielding him, he might be able to manage either one. But this city is full of territory that has been carved out by dealers. If each member of the group took a cut from a different one . . . well, after a couple decades your wife has enough to buy beachfront property."

"Okay." Nate leaned forward to rest his forearms on the desk. "So was the tape in that video reused by the killer or were we meant to find it?"

"No one was ever seen in the vicinity returning for it, right?" She glanced questioningly at Nate and he shook his head. "And it occurs to me that our best leads in the case stem directly from the scene that hadn't been taped over. Almost like the offender was sending us a message of exactly what was motivating these deaths." *Justice had been a long time coming.* The snippet from the dream echoed in her mind. It had never left any doubt these were revenge killings. "Which brings us back to who would have filmed that original scene in the bar."

"The cops had no reason to. The last thing they'd want is evidence of their relationship with one another." He drummed his fingers for an instant. "It was most likely Tory Baltes or Lamont Fredericks."

"And with both of them dead, who's going to have possession of it? Either Juicy or Tory's son."

"Which is why we need to find and talk to them both." Nate took out his cell phone and punched in a number. "But if you ask me, given his relationship to Lamont, Juicy has the best reason to hate these guys' guts."

———————

The knowledge continued to burn through him, searing like a white flame.

Chandler had made it out alive.

He tapped his fingertips against the steering wheel, waited for a break in the incessant traffic. The shock at the discovery had long since passed. He'd had the fire rolling hot before he'd slipped out the back. He'd have thought she and the old lady would be toasty by dawn. Overcome by the smoke as they slept and burned to a crisp. All in all not a bad way to go. The smoke would kill them before they ever felt the kiss of the flames. There were a few dead police detectives who would agree they'd be getting off easy.

But he'd never imagined they could escape altogether.

He inched forward a few feet before cars ahead jammed again. Maybe Chandler had known he was there. Maybe she'd felt his presence in that damp cellar, just waiting for a chance to start the fire and then slip out again. Instead, nothing had gone according to plan.

Nerves skittered down his spine. Chandler didn't know shit. She couldn't, or he wouldn't still be free. Maybe he'd overreacted. Those sketches had spooked him.

They continued to spook him every time he looked at them.

The pictures hadn't depicted what they'd found at the crime scene. She'd drawn the events of that night, the exact time that Patrick Christiansen had finally gotten what was coming to him. The picture had captured the plumes of smoke, the twisted graceful dance of a man meeting his fate.

And his own pose silhouetted against the flames.

A chill worked under his skin. He'd spent far too many years of his life being afraid. As usual, fear made him angry.

And anger so easily turned to rage.

Chandler might have thought she'd outsmarted him. She'd discover that once he made up his mind, no one escaped. Not for long.

She was just as dead as the next three cops.

Chapter 18

Risa stopped short when Nate halted at the butt-ugly tan car. Her eyes met his. "Your requisition came through."

Her lack of enthusiasm was echoed in his tone. "Another example of being careful what you wish for. I'm holding on to their promise of getting the other one back with a new paint job."

"They'll probably only paint the one door." She rounded the hood and waited for him to unlock the passenger side.

"And even that will be will be an improvement over this one." He immediately corrected himself. "If they use a matching-color paint."

She buckled herself in and he lost no time nosing the car out of the lot. Reaching for the overhead visor, he slid her a quick glance as he withdrew his sunglasses. "How'd you get a cell phone so quickly?"

"My one-hour marathon shopping spree while Mom was napping. Bought both of us some necessities and went to Best Buy for a replacement phone, computer, and software." She'd contacted Gavin Pounds, Raiker's cyber wizard back in the Manassas headquarters, to tell him that her agency-issued laptop was toast. He'd promised to equip her new one with all the necessary access codes to databases and other sensitive information as soon as she returned. Then he'd demanded an update on Adam's condition, and the rest of their conversation had centered on their boss.

It wasn't until she'd hung up that she realized the man had assumed she'd be returning to the agency.

And that she hadn't disabused him of the notion.

Resolutely, she pushed the thought aside. She wasn't making life decisions right now. She had more than enough to keep her occupied.

"Are you sure you have time for this?" He stopped for the red light at the corner. "I know you'll want to check on your mom tonight yet. And Adam."

"We can make a couple stops first." Nate's phone call to the officers tasked with bringing in Juicy for questioning again had been fruitless. If the man had been seen around his old neighborhood lately, no one was talking about it. "Maybe we'll get lucky and trip over Emmons."

"Lots of rat holes in that area," he muttered. The light turned green and he turned right. Another of his shortcuts, undoubtedly. "And I'll bet he knows every one to disappear in."

"Vice won't be too happy if he goes underground."

"Vice can get in line." They drove for a time in silence, with Nate taking side streets and alleys that had her doubting her direction sense. But when the neighborhoods started their visual decline she assumed he was heading the right way.

She used the time to call the hospital. Talked to Burke about Adam's condition. It remained unchanged since she'd been there earlier. The only way to contact Hannah was by contacting Jerry Muller's number, which she'd programmed into her new phone when she'd taken her mom there this afternoon. But his line was busy so she gave up and dropped the cell back into her new purse.

Nate was on his own phone, but was doing more listening than speaking. She reached forward, fiddled with the radio. Was mildly amused to discover it didn't work. Risa was half looking forward to Nate's reaction when he made the same discovery. Things hadn't changed much since the days when she was on the force here.

He hung up, silent for a few minutes. His jaw was tight. "That was Cass," he said abruptly. "She claims that one of Kristin's coworkers told her my sister talked about going to Atlantic City."

She eyed him carefully. It was difficult to tell from his expression what he was thinking. "That's not far. What? An hour by car?"

"She quit her job." His mouth was set in a flat straight line. But she thought if she could see his eyes, hurt might flicker in them. "That tells me she doesn't plan on coming back."

"Where did she work?"

"A fast-food place." He took the next corner a bit sharper than usual.

"So it's not like she couldn't get another one like it without much trouble. She may have just intended to go for a few days and couldn't get time off so she quit. People do."

"Maybe." Clearly, he wasn't convinced. "But she could have told me that. Hell, she'd have to explain once she got home anyway."

"What would your reaction have been if she had told you?"

He was silent for a long moment. "I'd have made her leave Tucker with me."

Risa didn't respond. She didn't figure she needed to. Whatever problems Nate and his sister were having, it seemed clear to her that Kristin didn't mind letting her brother suffer a little. Risa had never missed having siblings. Now was no different. But she couldn't help sympathizing with his obvious concern.

He slowed on a familiar street. On the next block, she recalled, would be Juicy's apartment building. "I'm not convinced that's really where she headed, but Cass will check with hotels there and see if she can find anything out." One corner of his mouth pulled up slightly. "She's showing some real aptitude for pretext calls."

"How does Recker have time to be doing all this?"

His sideways look was sharp. "I forgot. You missed out this morning." She listened with growing disbelief as he filled her in, with short succinct sentences about Recker's removal from the task force. He finished with, "It's a case of her decisions coming back to bite her in the ass. Something she has in common with my sister, unfortunately. I just don't want Kristin's decisions to end up hurting Tucker, too."

He parked behind a rusted-up small pickup and opened the door. She joined him on the street, but both of them paused before heading toward the apartment building. "Looks a little different from last time," she murmured.

The street was nearly deserted. Across the way there was someone hurrying up a cracked concrete porch and into a building. But there was no one on the sidewalk up ahead. And as they approached, Risa saw that the porch to Juicy's apartment building—the one that had been jammed with young men when they'd been here two days ago—was empty.

They walked up the stoop, pushed open the unlocked front door. Retraced their steps to the apartment upstairs. But this time when Nate pounded on the door, no one answered it. They knocked at every single door on that floor and not at one did anyone acknowledge their presence.

Babies still cried. Music still played too loudly. People were inside. They just weren't interested in talking to Nate and Risa. They headed back downstairs. Nate rapped at the building super's apartment door. "Philadelphia PD. Open the door now or you'll have a whole lot of unwanted company on this street. In this building. And then you can come downtown and explain your shyness there."

A chain rattled. The door was pulled open the length of it. A visual slice of a short, stocky African American man clad in a tank-style undershirt and shorts could be seen through it. "Don't have nothing to say to you." The door began to close. Was halted by Nate's foot.

"Where's Jasmine? The woman in apartment two eighteen?"

"Moved out. Yesterday. Don't know where she went and didn't ask questions. Rent's paid up and it's none of my business anyways. It don't pay to ask too many questions."

"What about the guys who hang out on your stoop?"

"Don't know what you're talking about. Let me shut the door." The one brown eye that was visible in the wedge of opening had worry flickering in it.

"Where's Javon Emmons? Juicy?"

"Don't know him. Don't know where he is."

Nate and Risa exchanged a look, and Nate stepped back. The door was shut firmly.

"I think he found a different place to live," she observed as they headed back down the empty steps.

"And made damn sure no one around here talked about him after he was gone."

Spying an ancient stooped man sweeping the porch a couple doors down, she hurried toward him. "Excuse me." She saw his lips moving. Couldn't hear what he was saying until she drew much closer.

"Don't know nuthin'. Don't see *nuthin'*."

"Yeah." She blew out a disgusted breath as she turned back to rejoin Nate. "There's a lot of that going around."

"He's not far," Nate said after they'd gotten back into the car. "He can't be and still be able to run his business."

"Think Randolph was working the protection profit angle with Emmons?"

"He was his arresting officer," Nate pointed out, turning the key in the ignition. "On the other hand, as such, he was in a perfect position to make sure evidence disappeared before the appeal. Maybe that's how he worked out the deal with him." He pulled away from the curb. "At any rate, even if we get to talk to Juicy again, I'm not going to be able to ask any questions like that. But I'd sure like to ask a few regarding Lamont."

"He'll have to come up for air sometime." It took effort to tamp down her impatience. "A man like him doesn't trust his business dealings to underlings for long."

"Earlier you said you had time for a couple stops. Did you have somewhere else in mind?"

She turned toward him in the seat, as much as the belt would allow. "When I found Tory Baltes's obituary earlier today, it listed a surviving sister, a Carly Williams. I've got her address. We could always stop by and see if she's more forthcoming about her sister than Juicy's neighbors are about him."

As it turned out, Carly Williams had plenty to say in answer to their questions. And all of it was delivered in a self-righteous half sneer that did little to endear her to Risa.

"I don't like speaking ill of the dead." The bone-thin woman spoke the words with the relish reserved for people who thrived on doing just that. "Tory and I took different paths all our lives. She followed a path of self-indulgence and it eventually destroyed her. Tragic, but I used her as an example with my kids and now with my grandkids. Straying from the path of the Lord leaves us stumbling in darkness." She turned away from the screen door then to check on the welfare of the three children sitting in a row on the couch, eyes all glued in the same direction. The sound of cartoons could be heard.

"Do you remember what she did after her business burned down? How'd she make a living?"

The woman patted her graying bun and gave a slight sniff. "Not sure the bar was ever her business to begin with. I think that man she took up with gave her the cash for it. Had her put it in her name, and I told her at the time, there's no good reason a man does that, unless he's trying to hide something. Did she listen?"

Obviously the question was meant to be rhetorical. Carly didn't wait for an answer. "He was bad news from the start, and I told her that, too. He'd been in prison and he didn't make his living any way that I could see, so where'd that money come from? She was doomed to come to a bad end from the day she met him. And she should have known better, with a kid to take care of and all."

"So the boy didn't belong to Fredericks?"

The woman shook her head hard enough that it should have set her hairdo to unraveling. Not a strand moved. Risa was beginning to believe it was shellacked in place. "Can't tell you where the kid came from, but he appeared long before she took up with that Fredericks. I will say," and the words were uttered so grudgingly they appeared painful for her, "he was good enough to the boy. Sammy idolized him. Was real broken up when he died. I always figured it was drugs brought Fredericks and Tory together. She'd had her own problems with that stuff before, but after his death, she just spiraled further and further downward." For the first time a hint of true emotion flickered over her face. "Maybe I didn't try hard enough with her. Might have been a bit too strong in my opinions back then. But she sort of pulled away. When I heard she'd overdosed, I hadn't seen her in almost a year."

"What happened to her son?"

A pious expression crossed the woman's face. "Well, it was my Christian duty to raise my sister's boy, so I did my best. No matter that we didn't get a dime to take him in, either. Tory certainly didn't leave anything behind when she died. But things didn't work out. My husband hurt his back and was on disability. He and Sammy never did get on together. And he was just all the time causing problems with my own two kids. Things got tight and we had to give him over to Social Services. They treated him right," she hastened to say. "They got families who take kids like that, with nowhere else to go."

It was impossible not to feel a tug of sympathy for a long ago young boy who lost everything in a few short years. The man who'd taken an interest in him. His mother. And the only other living relatives he had.

"Do you have an address for Sammy now? Know where we can find him?"

"He's in Bethany Alliance Cemetery, buried right next to his mother. We didn't have the money for a proper stone, but there's a marker on his grave. We did right by the boy in death, even though he never had much use for us after he was grown."

Risa's heart dropped to the vicinity of her stomach. "Sammy Baltes is dead?"

The woman nodded, and if she felt a shred of sorrow over the thought, it didn't show in her expression. "Car crash three years ago. And I don't like to speak ill of the dead, but that boy was headed for a bad end, in any case. There was a slyness about that one. You ask me, he didn't care a bit about anyone but himself."

"So you identified the body?" Nate asked.

She lifted one bony shoulder. "I identified the car. It was registered to him. Wasn't much I could do with the body. The car rolled several times before bursting into flames. What was left of Sammy was burnt to a crisp."

———————

Johnny waited for Hans to speak. And the longer the silence stretched, the uneasier he got. "You don't have to worry," he repeated as the older man stared at the untouched beer sitting in front of him. "I could tell from the questions that the task force is running in circles. They don't have anything solid to tie me to the others. And, of course, they know nothing about you and Juan." He thought that was worth mentioning. Johnny wasn't the type to rat out the other members of the group. Hans should trust him on that.

But when the other man shifted his gaze from the bottle to him, trust wasn't exactly the emotion Johnny read on his face. "You leavin' anything out of the story, Johnny?"

"I told you every question they asked. Couple amateurs, which means we're going to have to nail this cocksucker ourselves. McGuire couldn't lead a bunch of Girl Scouts in a pissing contest, much less a task force."

"He led the task force to *you*." Deliberately the man picked up his beer. Drank.

Irate now, Johnny growled, "That was Giovanni's fault. I just read the best way to deal with the situation and did damage control. I'm in front of this thing. I expected a little more support."

"I'm sure you did." There wasn't a hint of friendliness in the other man's gaze. "I'll bet Jonas did, too."

Shock kept him silent. Hans smiled. A chilling stretch of the lips. "I've been around long enough to have friends in lots of different districts. I hear things. Blew himself away with his own gun, but maybe you were there, too, huh? Convinced him to do it? What was the bullet in his chest for, insurance? You were afraid they might be able to pack his brains back together again?"

"That's not the way it happened." He couldn't believe this. Hans never looked at him that way. Talked to him that way. He'd brought Johnny into the group. Groomed him for the position. "I just went over there to talk to him. Iron things out between us. He pulled out a gun and what was I supposed to do? I thought the motherfucker was going to kill me, so of course I drew on him. I didn't figure he was going to blow his own brains out." He pulled the folded-up sheets that he'd taken from Jonas's home out of his pocket. Smoothed them out for Hans to read. "Look at this, he was going to fucking rat us all out. Take the easy way out for himself and leave us holding the bag. I didn't go over there planning any of this, but I damned sure took care of it. The way I've always taken care of problems."

"Yes." For a moment Johnny thought finally Hans was seeing sense. Until he went on. "Exactly the way you've always taken care of problems. Use an elephant gun to kill a mosquito, that's your fuckin' motto."

Johnny snatched up the papers, crumpled them in his fist. "Fuck you. Fuck you." He was nearly trembling with rage. "Don't you think the motherfucking Cop Killer would love this? To see us turning on each other? You gonna let that cocksucker win?"

Picking up the bottle, Hans took a long drink. Set it down and looked at it contemplatively. "No," he finally said. "That's not what I'm gonna do. But right now we have to be smart. There's too much attention so we have to stop our outside business practices. As of now."

Johnny's jaw dropped. But he wasn't given a chance to object. "How do you know you weren't followed here? McGuire could have put a tail on you. That pulls me into things, you get that, right?" Hans shook his head. "It's over. For all of us. We pull away from our associates. Cut all ties. With each other, too. The three of us." He looked at Johnny and added, not unkindly, "They're looking at you so you're poison for me and Juan. Maybe it's not fair, but that's the hand we're dealt. Don't contact me again. Don't contact either of us."

He slid out of the bench seat of the booth. Turned and shuffled toward the back door. Johnny watched him in disbelief. Hans would come back. He never left a partial beer behind. He'd never leave Johnny behind.

But as the door closed after the man, and five minutes stretched into ten, Johnny was forced to admit Hans had done just that.

And for the first time, he felt totally alone.

"You don't have to do this."

"You're beginning to sound like a broken record." Nate pulled into Jerry Muller's driveway and tried to avoid looking at the charred structure on the other side of it. "I didn't mind taking you to the hospital. It was closer to Williams's place than it would have been for you to return to the station house for your car."

"And this place is across the city from the hospital, and even farther from my vehicle."

He aimed a level stare at her. "The last time I watched you drive away, you barely managed to make it out of a burning house alive. Consider me extra security."

Because he was fairly certain he didn't want to hear any response she would make to that, he got out of the car and headed for the side door of the house.

But it was impossible for him to wait for her there and not sneak a look at the home that could have been her coffin.

He'd have to walk all around the structure to get a clearer picture of the damage, but what he could see from here was enough to have his chest hollowing out.

The side facing them would have held the bedrooms. And the fire had gutted the area. The outside wall was all but destroyed. Parts of the roof had caved in. And the thought that Risa could have been caught in that . . . unaware of what lay in wait until the smoke had already ensured that she'd never regain consciousness . . . A muscle clenched in his jaw as his mind skirted the thought.

She joined him on the step and followed the direction of his gaze. And he thought he saw a hint of nerves in her expression when she looked at him. "Sometimes you don't question luck. You just accept it."

"And sometimes," he said grimly, as he reached out to rap

at the door, "luck runs out. Which is why you're not by your-self tonight."

The door was opened then and Nate blinked, his attention diverted by the guy in the doorway.

Stocky, about five-eight, the man's receding hairline was in no danger of being duplicated anywhere else on his body. His tropical print shirt was open to his navel, and the gold chains he wore were half hidden in the thicket of fur that covered his chest. He bore the slightest resemblance to an ewok of Star Wars fame. Nate slid a sideways glance to Risa. She'd let her mother stay *here*?

"Risa! Come in, your mom is just watching TV. I hope you changed your mind about staying here, too. You can have my room and I'll take the couch. I wouldn't mind a bit."

Nate smiled grimly as he stepped through the doorway after her. Yeah, he'd bet this Muller guy would be all over that idea. Which was just another reason he was glad he'd come along.

The house was small and hadn't been updated in half a century. From what he'd seen through the open doorway the first day he'd been sent to collect Risa, the layout was very similar to her mother's home. Or former home.

Hannah Blanchette was ensconced in an easy chair watch-ing what appeared to be a Christian broadcast of some sort. She smiled in their direction but didn't get up. Nate tried, and failed, to find any resemblance to Risa in her face.

"I'm fine," the woman was saying in response to her daughter's query. "Can't seem to stop myself from dozing off every hour or so, but other than that, I feel all right." Her voice sounded raw, even worse than Risa's raspy tones today. "You should be resting, too, not running off to do heaven knows what."

Risa bent down to brush a kiss over her mother's cheek. "I'm fine, too. This is Nate McGuire, a PPD detective I'm working with."

Hannah offered her hand and Nate crossed the room to take it. "Ms. Blanchette. I'm glad to see you doing so well after your ordeal."

The older woman seemed flustered. "Well, I owe that all to Jerry, here. He saved my life. He's a genuine hero."

The man beamed a smile, but Nate noted it was aimed as much at Risa as toward the other woman. "I even got an idea for a future film from the rescue. It's all material, right?"

"Risa, Jerry mentioned having you appear in it." Hannah appeared to be tiring. "I told him that wouldn't be your cup of tea. You never did like being in the limelight."

An odd observation, Nate thought, given the fact that Risa must have garnered a lot of attention from her college basketball days. But he was distracted by the information on Muller. Slanting him a glance, he said, "You're in the film industry?"

The other man shrugged modestly. "Most is straight to video, but I do okay." He nodded toward a shelving unit next to the TV. "I sent Mom a couple of my awards to keep for me. She got a kick out of them."

"I had no idea you were so accomplished," Risa was saying as Nate moved closer to examine the awards. Cut glass atop a brass footing, the name of the award was etched, along with Muller's name and the title of the film. He stopped. Squinted harder. Then turned and pinned the other man with a look.

"A Peavy?"

"Actually I've won four. In recognition of cutting-edge industry excellence."

"Uh-huh." He was joined by Risa then. He slanted a glance at her. "You should get more detail from Jerry about possibly starring in one of his films. It could be the beginning of a promising new career for you." She made a deprecating sound in response, before the cell in his pocket vibrated. Excusing himself, he stepped into the kitchen to take it. And the ensuing brief conversation with Morales had his earlier humor vanishing abruptly.

He reentered the living room to hear Risa saying, "I talked to the insurance company after I dropped you off. There's a stipend available for temporary housing so you don't have to rely on Jerry's hospitality indefinitely."

"I don't mind a bit . . ." the man started.

"Jerry and I have already talked about it. He'll be flying back to California in the next couple weeks." The older woman stopped for a drink from the water glass on the table next to her. "He'll rent Eleanor's place to me for as long as I need it." She aimed a hopeful look at her daughter. "He's going to list it for sale. Maybe we could buy it with the insurance money. I feel as at home here in Eleanor's house as I did in my own."

"The policy only pays if you rebuild on the same property," Risa began, before catching sight of Nate in the doorway. Something must have shown on his face because she crossed the room to her mother's chair. "But I'll call the agent again, see if there's any wiggle room." She bent to kiss her mother's cheek. "Get some sleep. I'll check in again tomorrow."

"My offer's still open." Jerry followed them out into the kitchen. "Just give me a call if you want to stay, Risa."

"Thanks, Jerry. But I'll find something."

She waited until they were in the car before looking at him. "What happened? One minute you're making obnoxious cracks about me starting a new career as a porn star and the next you're radiating impatience to get out of there. Who was on the phone?"

But as he backed out of the drive, Nate was momentarily distracted by her earlier words. "Wait a minute. You knew Muller was involved with porn videos?"

"You think I'd let my mother stay with someone I hadn't completely checked out? I had some of my colleagues run a complete background on him before agreeing to let her stay there."

"Because a director of porn videos is so trustworthy." It was going to take a bit of time to wrap his mind around the logic of that one. He headed the car back in the direction of the station house.

"Sometime I'd be intrigued to hear how you happened to know the Peavy award was given for porn flicks"—he winced a little at that—"but, yeah. Other than his interesting choice of occupations, Muller checks out okay. And Hannah is comfortable with him. She's met him before, when he came to visit his mother. Of course she'd be appalled if she knew what he did for a living, but her friend never did, I'm guessing. There's no reason to tell her."

He could feel her regard as he drove. "Was the call about

the case or something personal? If you had plans for this evening, you should have taken me to my car. I could have gone to the hospital and to Jerry's alone."

Grim humor filled him. He knew what she was asking. Wondered why the hell she'd even think it. He'd already made it pretty clear earlier today that she was the only woman who held any personal interest for him. It occurred to him then that she wasn't exactly trusting when it came to men. With what he knew of her ex, it wasn't hard to see why.

"The call was from Morales. There's still been no sighting of Juicy but maybe he's been occupied elsewhere. He just got a call from Vice. Someone dropped Sam Crowley off a ten-story building last night."

Chapter 19

"Got some more details after I called you." Eduardo Morales looked like he'd already been home before returning to work. He was dressed in jeans and a T-shirt rather than the suit and tie he normally wore. Nate and Risa were seated in his office. He faced them, hips propped against his desk. "Apparently Vice had contacted Crowley about setting up a sting. The plan was to wait until Emmons called him next time about meeting to exchange the books. Crowley convinced them that if he reached out sooner than their regularly scheduled meets, Emmons would suspect something. So they were resigned to wait another week or more for their first chance at getting their hands on his financials."

"They didn't have someone on Crowley at all times?"

Morales's face was grim as he answered Nate's question. "They were planning to get that set up in the next few days. He hadn't actually done anything for them yet, so they figured they had time. But somehow Emmons must have been tipped off that Crowley was going to flip on him."

"Chances are it was Crowley himself." He rolled his shoulders to loosen some of the knots that seemed to have taken up residence there. "Crowley seemed to trust Juicy more than he did cops when we talked to him. Might have decided to curry some favor by alerting him about what was coming. The way he'd figure it, that would get him a free walk from us for cooperating and insulates him from retribution from Emmons, too. Maybe they'd figure out a way to double-cross the PPD, feed them false info. Crowley would have liked that idea."

"And he seemed much more scared of Emmons than he was of the police," Risa added.

"With good reason, as it turns out." Nate filled Morales in on their lack of success finding the man earlier that day. "I think it's time to put a citywide BOLO out on him. He's got a lot of answers to give."

"And departments will be standing in line to ask the questions." But Morales nodded. "I'll see to it. In the meantime, Vice wants a copy of your interview with him."

"He didn't learn of the upcoming sting from us."

"I know that. So we'll give them the copy and they'll realize it, too." Morales looked at his watch. "Now get out of here so I can send out the alert and get back before the kids' bedtime. Renee is never too happy when she has to wrestle all three of them down for the night."

They exited his office. Risa knew she wasn't going to be able to remain upright for much longer, but as long as they were here, she tugged at Nate's sleeve. "Let's do a quick run on that fatal car accident involving Baltes."

He didn't argue, and soon he was ensconced behind his computer with Risa leaning close to look at the screen. "A fiery accident," she murmured, reading from the article he found. "Seems like a lot of that going around in this case."

"Maybe not coincidental. Too many people involved in this investigation are ending up the same way."

"But why Baltes? Did he see something, overhear something when he was a kid? If so, why wait until he was"—she stopped a moment to check the screen again—"twenty-six before getting rid of him?"

Nate couldn't answer. After he exhausted the online archived articles on Baltes's death, he ran a quick DMV check. The results had him sitting back in his chair, a grim sense of purpose filling him. "One more question for Emmons."

The DMV report listed Sam Baltes as owner of the car that crashed and burned three years ago. But it also listed the transfers of ownership.

And it just so happened that one Javon Emmons had previously owned Baltes's car.

Risa turned to him. She swayed slightly, balanced herself with one hand to his desk. "Maybe we could . . ."

"Wait until tomorrow for anything more on this? Great idea." He shut down the computer and pushed his chair back. She was exhausted. Risa pushed herself so hard that it was easy to forget for periods of time what she'd been through the night before.

"I was going to say we could request a copy of the accident report. Maybe talk to the responding officer."

He nodded as he rose and took her by the elbow. Steered her toward the door. "And we'll do that. Tomorrow. But right now you need to get some rest. And Darrell's lack of success notwithstanding, I just remembered a place you can get a room. They always keep one in reserve."

Her face brightened a little. "Really? Do you have the number? I'll give them a call."

"I'll do even better than that." He opened his office door. Guided her through it. "It's right on my way. You can follow me there."

———

Risa left her car in the driveway and aimed a hard stare at Nate, who was exiting the open garage door toward her, his computer case in hand. "Let me guess. The Hotel Chez McGuire."

"I didn't lie. I have a couple rooms open and you don't have to call ahead." Jamming his free hand in his jacket pockets, he arched a brow. "C'mon, it won't be that bad. It beats a couch in the CCU waiting room and damned if I'm going to let you go back to Muller's."

"Let me?"

Something in her tone must have warned him because he held up one palm placating. "You don't want to stay there either. You turned his offer down three times that I heard."

True enough. But even with depressingly limited options,

something had her hesitating. This couldn't be a good idea. She'd have been better off at Morales's than to stay with Nate, especially after being in his arms this morning.

Especially after her *reaction* to being in his arms this morning.

As if reading her mind, he said, "From the looks of you, you'll be unconscious within an hour. Give me a few minutes to throw a frozen pizza in the oven, change the sheets . . . you get something in your stomach and go to bed." The smile he gave her was crooked and much too appealing. "You won't even have to see me until the morning. At which time you can show your eternal gratitude by cooking me breakfast. Tucker's usual choice is frozen pancakes, and it'd be a treat to eat something that doesn't have to be thawed in a toaster."

Something inside her relaxed a fraction. He was making this simple. And if the niggling thought occurred that it could be just that easy between them, if she let it, Risa would refuse to allow the thought to put down roots.

"I do make a mean eggs Benedict."

"Change the English muffin to a bagel, a poached egg to over easy, and switch the sauce for cheese and you've got a deal." When he started back toward the garage, she fell in step beside him.

"I believe you can get that off the breakfast menu of most drive-throughs."

"Ah, but then it wouldn't be made by an ex-college basketball standout, soon to be porn star." The elbow jab she aimed at his gut for that crack didn't seem to faze him. "Think of my thrill of being able to say, I knew you when." He pushed open the door to the house and then hit the switch to lower the garage door.

Risa preceded him into the home. "You never did say how you happened to recognize what a Peavy was."

"I'm not a perv, if that's what you're implying. But I've attended my share of bachelor parties. Even hosted a few. Been to college. Take your pick. Haven't watched one of those things in years." He set his computer case down. Without a shred of embarrassment on his face, he grinned at her. "But if you're really considering a career change, I could be persuaded to change my viewing habits."

She fixed him with a jaundiced look. "You might want to consider the fact that I'm armed." He didn't need to know that the thought of drawing her gun and aiming it at another person still made her knees weak. Maybe if she pictured him as a window.

"Armed. But that's not what makes you dangerous." The teasing light had disappeared from his eyes to be replaced with something much harder to resist. "If it makes you feel any better, I've always preferred a private one-on-one to watching a couple strangers. For future reference."

She should have made a witty retort. Said something, anything, to defuse the suddenly charged silence. Exhaustion could only be blamed for so much. The temptation the man represented had her senses reeling.

And that's exactly what made him so lethal. This wouldn't be a man to enjoy and then leave without regrets. Without memories haunting her. And knowing that was just one more reason to maintain her distance.

Until she had her own life in order, she certainly didn't need to complicate someone else's. Especially someone who came with his own set of complications.

"Ah . . . let me change those sheets."

Relieved that he'd managed to break the awkward silence, she turned into the kitchen. "I'll find the pizza." She rummaged in the freezer and found one before preheating the oven. Then she headed out the front door to her car to retrieve her purse and the sack containing the personal items she'd bought that day. Locking her car, she headed back into the house. Nate still hadn't reappeared so she unwrapped the pizza and put it in the oven. Then gave in to the urge to look around.

There was more here that gave away the personality of the people living in it the house than her own apartment would, Risa mused. The mandatory big screen would be Nate's choice, of course, as was the leather furniture. But the gaming system and pile of kids' game cartridges would belong to his nephew. Tucker.

She stepped closer to examine the photos on shelves that lined one corner of the room. There were many of a dark-haired boy. Swinging. Riding a bike. Singing into a mike. A few featured the boy with Nate. A couple with a woman with long dark hair and a strong resemblance to Nate who had to be his sister. And some older photos of a much younger Nate and Kristin posing with a couple that were probably their parents.

But despite the photos, there was little in the house that stamped it with Kristin's personality. Or any woman's.

"Okay, maid service performed." Nate appeared in the hallway behind her. "If you want to follow me, I'll show you where you can put your things." She trailed behind him. "Here we go." He reached into a room to flip on the light. "Bathroom is next door."

There was a bit more here to mark it as a female's room. The half-open closet door showed a few hangers that hadn't been vacated. There was an eight by ten of Kristin with Tucker. Another of her parents at some sort of formal function. A vase of dried flowers.

But none of the items had been important enough for her to take along with her.

"Tuck's room is down the hall. Next to mine. He doesn't sleep well some nights. It helps to have someone right next door."

She set her bag and purse on the bed. Studied his expression. "You miss him."

He ran his hand through his dark hair. And didn't try to hide the worry in his expression. "I had him for nearly two years, from the time he was three. Kristin dropped him off one night for a round of babysitting and forgot to come back." His mouth twisted. "It was an eye-opening experience for me. But eventually things worked out. I shopped around for a good pediatrician. The doctor was the one who first suspected Tuck was autistic. And after the diagnosis was confirmed I saw that he got special education services. Read up on the disorder." His expression was bleak. "It was a steep learning curve, I'll admit that, but we had started to get a routine going."

"And then Kristin came back."

He inclined his head. "She'd spent her last few months away getting sober. And I couldn't undercut that by taking her to court. Getting full custody. But I didn't totally trust her sobriety either." His smile lacked humor. "Kristin's been on the wagon before. She doesn't so much fall off it as leap. I'm afraid . . . I'm afraid this disappearance means a repeat of old patterns. Only this time she's involving Tuck."

There was a tug in her chest. And more than a little admiration. She knew she wouldn't have handled it nearly as well if she'd found herself the unexpected guardian of a small boy.

She'd failed one boy who had relied on her in the most hellish way imaginable.

"Maybe Cass has found out more," Risa said shakily, beating back the old memory before it could lodge and sink its fangs deep into her chest.

"I'll check with her again tonight. If she has solid information placing them in Atlantic City, maybe I'll call another buddy of mine who went private. Have him track down their hotel." He stepped back into the hallway. "Guess we'd better check on that pizza."

She stayed where she was. "I think I'm going to skip it and turn in now." Stemming the protest she saw on his lips, she added, "The bed is looking pretty tempting. When it comes to a choice between sleep and food, this is one time·sleep wins, hands down."

She must have looked worse than she thought because he gave her one searching gaze before nodding. "All right. I'll see you in the morning, then."

"See you in the morning," she echoed. And gave an inner sigh of relief when he disappeared.

She hadn't been lying. She was in desperate need of sleep.

But she was more desperate to avoid giving in to temptation and making a decision that both of them might come to regret.

———

Risa fell asleep almost immediately. But it wasn't restful. Images fast-forwarded through her mind, too many to be individually identified. Myriad snippets that made a visual collage that melded and reformed into a constantly changing kaleidoscope of images.

Kristin figured in them, although not the one-dimensional

image from the photos. *"Just give me a chance,"* she told the unsmiling man with a shaven head. *"Let me show you."* Smoke filled the room and the two of them began to cough. And Risa felt her lungs heave and gasp for oxygen again.

Jerry Muller peered through her window but did nothing to help. *"Hannah,"* dream Risa cried. *"I have to shoot the window but my weapon doesn't work."*

"That's because it's wet," Jett Brandau told her. *"Rubbing alcohol all over it."* She watched as Jett faded to be replaced by a young blond boy racing down the street outside Tory's. The boy shimmered at the edges, transformed into Darrell. *"You can't get good coffee at Tory's,"* the dream Darrell informed her. *"It always burns. Burns right down."*

A car hurtled through the air, somersaulting over and over before bursting into flames. Juicy emerged from it, carrying a gas can. *"Dead is dead,"* the man pronounced. *"Unless it isn't."*

Scenery flashing by a car window backdropped against a night sky. Slowing at the Route 104 sign. Turning left. Then bumping over the rutted road, branches scratching at the car top. On the windows. The branches started on fire, flames licking along them, allowing them to reach into the car and wrap the figure inside in a smothering embrace.

Then the branches separated to show a man, eyes wide with terror. He was tied to a chair with flames shooting up all around him, smoke rolling through the air.

Walter Eggers.

"I'd do it again," he shouted, rage and panic battling in his voice. *"I'd do it all again."*

And then she was back in her mother's home, eyes glued to the damaged roof, the flames gnawing merrily at the edges of her bed. And no matter how hard she tried, dream Risa couldn't get off that bed. Not even when the fire hissed and crackled next to her ear, turning her hair into a halo of flames. Melting the skin from her face like wax dripping down a candle . . .

The sound of panic was torn from her. She sat straight up in bed, her heart hammering like a Thoroughbred's just under the wire. She was cold, frigid straight through, but her flesh was hot to the touch. As if the fire from the dream had licked along it as the flames consumed her bed.

But it was the victim in the dream that she was most concerned about. It had been too late to save Mark Randolph. She couldn't be too late to save Eggers, too.

On weak knees she went to the dresser where she'd left her purse. Took out her cell and then tiptoed to the bedroom door. Eased it open. Nate's door was closed. And the relief that filled her at the thought made her limbs go even weaker.

Quietly, she moved down the hallway. Turned unerringly toward the garage door. But didn't find the computer case he'd left there. Undeterred, she padded barefoot into the kitchen. Then checked the family room.

Nate had left his laptop on the leather couch, as if he'd worked while he watched TV before turning in. It was off, but she'd watched him boot it up earlier that day. When she did so, she typed in the username and password he'd used to access it at the station. And then she opened the investigation case file and scrolled through it until she found the number she was looking for.

Her fingers were shaking so much she twice had to start over. And found herself holding her breath. Expected the phone to ring and ring endlessly. Or go straight to voice mail.

It did neither. After several rings, a groggy and very pissed-off voice answered. "Who the hell is this?"

Walter Eggers wasn't dead. Not even close.

Risa clicked off the phone without saying a word. Checked the time. Two thirty A.M. If the Cop Killer were coming for Eggers, it wouldn't be tonight. It would be dawn in a few hours.

But he was coming. And this time, Risa was going to stop him.

Shutting off the computer, she set it aside. Went to the kitchen and feverishly rifled through drawers. Found what she was looking for when her search elicited a yellow legal pad and pencil in the desk. Flipping the light on, she carried the pad to the kitchen table, sat down, and began to sketch. Slowly at first. Then with growing desperation. Page after page. Images from the dream, in sequence, as much as she could recall.

She didn't know how long she sat there. Long enough to have her fingers grow cramped and sore. But she didn't stop, didn't look up until a small noise startled her. Her gaze flew upward. Found Nate with a shoulder propped against the side of the refrigerator. Watching her with enigmatic eyes.

Everything inside her froze. Deliberately, she set the pencil down. Turned the pad over. "How long have you been standing there?"

"Awhile."

Which told her absolutely nothing. She slanted a look at the clock. Was shocked that nearly an hour and a half had passed. "I . . . woke up and couldn't get back to sleep. Decided to work until I was tired again."

"Is that what you were doing?"

Her heart started hammering a frantic beat. "I'm a good artist. I try to capture my dreams sometimes. They're usually about the case I'm involved in."

"I hear you. It's hard to turn off our minds, even when we sleep."

His easy acceptance of her explanation calmed her pulse a bit. Driven to move, she pushed back the chair. Rose. "Which cupboard do you keep your water glasses in?"

In answer, he moved past her to a cupboard next to the sink. Went to the ice water spigot on the fridge and filled the glass. Handed it to her. She took it gratefully, leaning against the counter facing him as she drank.

He had a pair of loose-fitting athletic shorts on. Noticing what he was wearing, and what he wasn't had her pulse doing a quick stutter. His chest was bare and impressively solid. His arms roped with muscle. The shorts covered him decently, just as the loose fitting T-shirt she'd bought to sleep in covered her. There was no reason to feel like the scene was imbued with a sense of intimacy. It was the hour that lent that feeling. She'd apologize for waking him. They'd return to their rooms. And tomorrow making breakfast would seem routine enough that the memory of this moment would be dispelled.

And then he spoke. "Was it this case you were dreaming about? Or your last one?"

Her heart took one desperate leap and then slowed. Unnaturally so. Her lungs stopped drawing air. The blood halted in her veins. And her voice, when she managed to form words, sounded cracked and harsh. "Been doing a little research, McGuire?"

There was a hint of guilty flush over his cheekbones. But his dark gaze never strayed from hers. "You said it ended badly. The articles I found didn't give much detail. Enough to figure that the operation to rescue those boys went awry."

Awry. An anguished laugh almost escaped her. What an innocuous word for the indescribable horror that had been that night. "Yes." The word was rasped out. "It went *awry*."

"And you blame yourself." The softness of his voice offered understanding where none could be had. None was deserved.

"Because it was my fault." She set the glass on the counter without drinking from it. She was afraid it would slip from her nerveless fingers. "I led them there. I told them where they could find Tyler Temple. We already had our sights on Martin Volk, the pedophile who'd kidnapped him. The team had his house surrounded. Big piece of property. Shanties and decrepit structures all over it, surrounded by a twelve-foot wooden fence. I suspected Tyler would be in one of those structures."

But she'd been wrong about that, too. It wouldn't be the first mistake she'd make that night.

"There was a two-pronged assault. The tactical unit planned to breach the house. I went with the hostage recovery team. Led them right to the structure where I thought he was held."

"But he wasn't there?"

She shook her head blindly. The only thing she saw now was the scene replaying itself in her mind. "He was beneath it. We discovered a rabbit warren of tunnels under that shack. Connecting all the structures. The house."

"Jesus." There was comprehension in his tone. And something else, something that would have touched her if she'd identified it. But she heard neither. Nothing but the echoes of voices that haunted her memory.

"It was primitive. The tunnels were earthen packed, with an occasional kerosene lantern in the center of the walkway to light it. Cells were dug out along the way, fixed with rough wooden doors and padlocks. That's where he'd keep them. It was in one of them that we found Tyler Temple."

They'd sent her in, thinking the boy would respond best to a woman. And he had. When she'd given her name and told him they were taking him home, he'd launched himself at her and clung for all he was worth. *Risa, don't leave me!* She hitched a shuddering breath at the memory of the boy's voice. Each time she tried to hand him off to one of the other members, his wailing would get louder. It was easier, they'd thought, to leave him be.

"The radios didn't work for shit down there. We had the boy so we turned around, headed out the way we'd come. We never would have gotten out otherwise. But as we started back, we realized that the team wasn't all there. We'd started with four. There was only one detective and me left. So we thought we'd take our chances backtracking. But it was dark. The lanterns had gone out. And when I heard a sound behind me and looked, the remaining detective was gone, too. I didn't know how yet. Not then."

She could almost feel the dampness of the walls. Smell the rich moist aroma of earth. And something else. The stench of decay.

"I made my way through the tunnels as quickly as I could, my hand over the boy's mouth." Tyler had been sobbing, a soft, hopeless weeping. The walls had been close and claustrophobic. And with every step, they'd seemed to crowd in nearer. As if trying to crush them alive.

"I heard a sound in back of me and whirled. Saw that one of the lamps had been lit." The torch had been dropped on the earthen floor to burn itself out. "Someone had dodged into one of the cells." And she still held the boy. Had tried to put him down, peel him off her so she would have an unobstructed shot. He'd clung like a leech. He'd been screeching by then, shouting her name over and over.

Risa don't leave me.
Risa don't leave me.

"When the cell door opened again, Martin Volk stepped out holding a second child in front of him. Ryder Kremer. Held him like a human shield, with a butcher knife at his throat."

"You don't have to tell me the rest."

She barely heard his quiet voice. Couldn't have heeded it if she tried. The memory was as impossible to halt as lava flow. "I couldn't get a good shot. The lighting . . . There were mostly just shadows. I thought about going for Volk's knee. Shatter his kneecap and he might drop the knife. But it wouldn't incapacitate him. He could still slice the boy." The decision hadn't taken more than a few seconds. But her hesitation had been enough. "I squeezed off a shot, but the boy was already falling. And the knife was hurling through the air. I shoved Tyler down, shot again . . ."

"You killed him. Martin Volk was dead, the article said."

"So was Ryder Kremer. So were two detectives." The other two had survived their attack, barely. "I never even knew he had another boy down there."

"No one did, apparently." Nate looked like he wanted to take a step toward her. Didn't. His hands clenched involuntarily. "You can't blame that on yourself. You all had the same intelligence."

Feeling suddenly ancient, she leaned more heavily against the counter. She didn't trust her legs to hold her. Because she should have known. The same way she'd known to zero in on Volk. The same way she'd known where to find him and Tyler Temple.

But the dreams, the damned dreams, hadn't held a clue of Ryder Kremer.

"My hesitation probably cost him his life," she said flatly. Knowing that—accepting it—had made it almost impossible to touch her weapon since.

"You can't know that." There was a thread of anger in Nate's voice. "It's like you said, he'd probably have been dead either way. The knee shot didn't necessarily mean Volk would just give up."

"We'll never know." Her voice was bleak.

"When things go that wrong . . ." His tone softened. Turned gentle. "We're harder on ourselves than anyone else would think of being. The press made you out as a hero. The whole team. We have to celebrate the good stuff because all too often in our work there are no happy endings. One boy went home to his parents. Hold on to that."

"And one boy didn't. Somehow that's easier to recall."

As if galvanized into action, he closed the distance between them. Placed his hands on the counter on either side of her. And leaned in.

His kiss was whisper soft. Meant to comfort rather than to arouse. She stood stock still, shocked at the contact. Shocked even further at its effect on her.

She released a long, shuddering sigh that she hadn't realized had been trapped in her chest. His lips parted, as if to inhale it. Their breath mingled. And he was careful, very careful not to touch her anywhere else.

The press of his mouth became a bit harder and the firmness was as welcome as his earlier gentleness had been. She wasn't a woman to need a man for comfort. To depend on one in any way. And maybe that, too, had led to the failure of her marriage. It was hard to grow closer to someone when one was determined to stay a little distant.

Risa indulged herself by returning the kiss, sinking into it in a way that had nothing to do with dependence and everything to do with need. She'd learned a few things about the man over the course of the time they'd known each other. But she didn't know the important things. Didn't know his taste, his flavor. The feel of his muscled chest against her curves or the hard angles where sinew met bone. It seemed imperative to learn those things now. In the dead of night, when it seemed no one else in the world was awake but the two of them. In a time when two people could banish ghosts and make memories that had to be easier to bear than the ones that haunted her.

Her tongue touched his lips and his body jerked, grazing hers for an instant before he eased back. He would have ended the contact there. She knew that instinctively. Which was why she closed the space between them and slipped her arms around his waist.

He was motionless against her. In another time, with another man, she might have been mortified, thinking she'd misjudged the situation. Mistaken his interest or intent. But she recognized what his inaction cost him. Felt the tremble of his body against hers and heard the sharply indrawn breath against her lips.

"This isn't why I brought you . . ." His words trailed off when she scored his bottom lip with her teeth. And thought it sweet that he felt the need to assure her of something she already knew.

"I don't need protecting," she whispered against his mouth before cruising her lips along his jawline. "Not from the past. Or the present. But I do appreciate the sentiment." She nipped lightly, right where the muscle would clench in his jaw sometimes and was rewarded when it jumped. "I know what I want. The question is, do you?"

He tilted his head back far enough to look at her through slitted eyes. "I want it all. Whatever you'll give me. And then more."

Panic flared briefly. The demand had been made boldly. Leaving no room for denial. But his hands came up to cradle her face and his lips met hers again. His tongue swept into her mouth, a frankly carnal invasion. And she knew intuitively that he wouldn't offer her another chance to retreat.

She didn't want one. Risa welcomed the hot hunger in the kiss. Returned it. Palms itching to explore, she saw no reason to deny herself the feel of him. Smooth skin covered the ridges along his sides. And when she moved one hand to skate across his belly, the muscles beneath her fingers jumped.

It would be easy to get used to determining the pace. The speed. The depth. But she'd known intuitively she'd battle him for control. He wouldn't be a man to give it up easily. They were well matched.

Because neither would she.

Her resolve suffered a jolt when his hand slid up her thigh, branding her with heat. The edge of her T-shirt didn't stop him. He halted only at the elastic and lace panties that she wore beneath it. And she knew his hesitation wouldn't last for long.

His mouth found a spot beneath her ear that she hadn't known was sensitive. And when he teased it with tongue and teeth, the floor rocked a bit beneath her feet. A strange sort of lethargy was creeping into her limbs. Weighting her down while reaction skipped along nerve endings, firing an answering response.

In sensual retribution, she hooked a finger in the elastic

waistband of his shorts. Traced the boundary where fabric met flesh across his abdomen. Then abruptly lost her concentration when she felt his hand slip inside her panties to cup her butt.

Tearing her mouth away from his, she pressed it blindly to his chest. To trace with lips and teeth every hard angle and hollow found there. Nate smoothed his palm over one cheek and squeezed lightly, before his palm reversed its path, moving to the front to trap the moist heat between her legs.

A slight moan escaped her as his fingers stroked her damp flesh. And suddenly it was important to wrest control of the pace. Because she didn't want slow and wouldn't last through languorous. Which meant she needed to drive him a little bit crazy as well.

She drew her leg up to rub against his, losing herself for a moment in the sensation of hair-roughened skin against her flesh. She traced a finger over the straining length of him, once. Again. Was rewarded by the sound he made, something between a curse and a groan. And reveled for an instant in his response.

Without warning, he swept her T-shirt over her head and paused to enjoy the sight of her breasts, peaked and waiting. Leaning forward, he caught a nipple between his lips and sucked strongly from her. And her senses began to fragment.

Distantly his words echoed across her mind. *I want it all. Whatever you'll give me. And then more.* She knew the demand should frighten her. It would have, if she didn't reciprocate it fully.

Risa wanted everything he had to give. Everything he'd seek to hold back. And somehow, she'd managed to still those inner alarms that he might just manage to elicit the same unbridled response from her.

With more haste than finesse, she pushed the shorts over his hips. Freed him from their confines and shoved the fabric down his thighs. With short, swift movements, he divested himself of them before scooping her up in his arms and walking with her back toward the darkened hallway. And into his bedroom.

She would have liked a chance to look at the area, to see what she could learn of the man from the space he slept in.

But desire was twisting through her, clawing for release. He dropped to the bed without releasing her and rolled to stretch out atop her. And this time when his mouth found hers, there was an edge of desperation in his kiss.

Recognizing it would have been more satisfying if it didn't whip up an answering frenzy of need. She clutched his hard biceps. Tested the shoulders layered with muscles. The sleek expanse of his back. The tight, curved butt. And every nerve inside her stretched as taut as a bow.

There was a ferocious hunger in the sweep of his hands over her breasts. Raw unvarnished passion in his touch, just shy of rough. He left her for a moment, and her eyelids dragged open uncomprehendingly before his weight settled again and his mouth went between her thighs.

It took only the first stabbing movement of his tongue against the hypersensitive cluster of nerves to have the orgasm slamming into her. Eddies spiraled endlessly. She struggled for breath. Twisted away from that demanding mouth.

But he held her legs in place, knees bent and splayed outward, leaving her vulnerable. Sensitive. And lavished stroke after sensual stroke with lips and tongue until need—so recently satiated—began climbing again.

Risa withstood the sensual assault as long as she could. But the next time she pushed at his shoulders, he relented. Raised his head. And she sat up, pressed him back on the bed and straddled his thighs.

There was a purely masculine smile of satisfaction on his lips. One that would have bothered her if she weren't so certain he'd be losing it within moments. His hand reached out, pulled open the drawer of the bedside table, and fumbled for something. Handed it to her.

Taking her time, she tore open the foil packet and took inordinate care in sheathing him. A fraction of an inch at a time. Stripping off her panties she straddled him again, taking his hardness in her hand and guiding him inside her.

His hands went to her hips and he gave a quick upward lunge to seat himself fully. And for a moment, for one dizzying instant, she doubted her ability to carry out her vow. To control the pace until he was aware of nothing else. Until his senses were steeped in her.

When he would have moved again, taken over the tempo and set a pace that would drive them both to madness, she pushed his hands away from her hips. Laced their fingers instead. And watched him in the darkness as she finally moved. Keeping her movements slow and shallow. Saw the moment the smile faded from his lips and his jaw clenched.

She could feel his urgency in the taut muscles beneath her palms. The way they quivered beneath her touch. His hands, when they rose to cup her breasts, trembled slightly.

But he didn't take control of the speed or the act. Not even when his thighs went tense beneath her hips. His breathing sounded harsh and ragged. And she wanted, needed, to see that control unleashed.

Quickening the pace, she rode him faster. Harder. Deeper. Reached between them to touch his heavy masculinity and felt his restraint snap. Nate's hands went to her hips as he surged inside her. She met him stroke for stroke, the edge of her vision graying. This was what she wanted. The primal unharnessed need given full rein. She'd known it would be starkly satisfying to watch him lose control.

She hadn't realized his loss would fuel her own. Heat, quick stabbing spears of it, arrowed up her spine. The shadows enveloped them in a tight black cocoon of sensuality. There were only the two of them racing each other to climax. The sound of flesh against flesh. The rasp of their breathing. The creak of the bed.

Her blood beat a rapid tattoo in her veins. In her ears. Their hips pounded together in a frantic tempo. Nate gave one last violent surge and colors shattered behind her eyelids. Sanity fractured.

But as they both hurtled over the edge of passion, his name was on her lips.

Chapter 20

Risa opened her eyes, disoriented in the unfamiliar surroundings. It took a moment to remember she was in Nate's
house. Another to recall that she was in his bed.

And another to set aside a bit of pique to find herself
alone in it.

Shoving aside the emotion, she rolled to the side of the
mattress, stood. Her muscles felt pleasantly lax. It was hard
to set aside the sense of well-being, she acknowledged as she
searched for her T-shirt, after a night of good sex.

And impossible to set it aside after a night of *superb* sex.

She found her shirt neatly folded at the base of the bed,
which saved her having to do a nude search for it. Not that
she would have managed that with aplomb, but she wasn't
quite up to parading in front of the man naked.

Pulling the tee over her head, she finger combed her hair
and headed to the bathroom to brush her teeth. She'd promised him breakfast. And since it was difficult to recall the last
time she'd eaten, she might just match him, appetite for appetite. Much as she had a few hours earlier.

Strolling in a languid manner to the kitchen, it took only

the sight of him to have tension shooting into her limbs. Ice filtering through her veins.

With a slight frown on his face, Nate was studying the sketches she'd made last night. The drawings she should have taken back to her room. Tucked in her bag, away from prying eyes.

But she hadn't gone back to her room, she recalled sickly. And her mind definitely hadn't been on the drawings.

He looked up then, saw her standing there, and raked her figure with his heated midnight gaze. "You look good all sleepy and rumpled." Satisfied memory sounded in his voice. And something else. Something that promised to make them both late to work if she gave him half a chance.

She found it exceedingly difficult to match his even tone. Heading toward the fridge, she swung the door open, anxious for an excuse to avoid watching his attention shift back to the sketches.

"I didn't know you were artistic."

Making a production of gathering up eggs, cheese, and milk to set on the counter, she didn't answer.

"These are good. A bit . . . macabre."

"I have dreams sometimes. It helps to sketch out the images. Where do you keep the bagels?" She hoped to distract him. "And the frying pan?"

He crossed to find both for her and set them on the stove. Again clad in the shorts from last night, he appeared in no particular hurry to get ready for work. When she snuck a glance at the clock, she realized it wasn't even six thirty.

"More like nightmares, I'd say." Her spine stiffened as he wandered over to look at the sketches again. "Weird, the way dreams are, with everyone and anyone you've encountered in the last few days all jumbled together. Emmons. Muller." He paused. "Geez, that's a good likeness of Jett. Darrell." He laughed a little. "Should I be hurt that I didn't appear in your dreams?" She heard the sound of another page turning. Then silence.

Risa forced herself to turn around. And saw the exact moment he flipped to the page of Walter Eggers. He stilled. Stared at it fiercely. And when he didn't speak . . . when one long minute stretched into the next, she made a tentative stab at an explanation. More of one then she'd ever offered anyone else, outside of Raiker.

"He'll be next. Not last night. I called and he was still home in bed. But soon." He stared at the sketch a moment longer. Then finally raised his gaze to meet hers. What she saw in it nearly made her weep.

"Risa . . . it was just a dream. A horrible one, I'm sure. But packed with visuals from our day, from our worries . . . hell, I don't know." He raked his hand through his short dark hair. "It's our subconscious playing mind games on us. I used to have this recurring dream of being captured by a clown who insisted on painting a big-ass goofy grin and tear drops on me. It was terrifying. I hate clowns."

His attempt at humor fell flat. "Dreams are the way I zeroed in on Martin Volk. Tyler Temple. And dozens of others before that. Hundreds."

There was a guarded expression on his face that stabbed deeper than Volk's knife had. Caused more damage. "You're confusing instincts with something else." Something, given his careful choosing of his words, that he didn't want to identify.

"You need to put an around-the-clock guard on Eggers." She hated the note of pleading in her tone.

"Because he's going to be next."

"Yes."

The silence was interminable. Then he gave a short nod. "Okay."

Stunned, she could only stare at him. Nate cocked a brow. "Even without . . . this"—he tapped the page with the drawing of the man—"we can be certain he has knowledge of the background leading up to this thing. With the IA investigation on him and his connection to our case, I can make a solid argument to Morales that he's crucial to our investigation. He can go up the line and get the strings pulled to keep him on a desk job." He paused questioningly and she nodded. That would take care of the man's work hours.

"And you'll keep him under surveillance after that?"

"I can keep an officer on him."

Something inside her eased. A tendril of hope unfurled.

"If the Cop Killer comes for him, we might be able to catch him in the act."

Nate rifled through the pictures again. "Anyone else here you want us to keep an eye on? Although Juicy is a given . . . Hey, you even have a sketch of . . ." He looked at her. "Is that Kristin?"

She busied herself cracking eggs into a bowl she'd found in the cupboard. "Not everything in the dreams is relevant. A lot is open to interpretation." Like the melding of one image into the next. Random snippets of conversation that made little sense.

"That's what I'm saying, Risa." Something in his tone alerted her. "They're just dreams. Open to interpretation."

Strength leeched out of her body. Her shoulders sagged. She felt as if she were folding in upon herself. Because it was clear by that statement that he still didn't believe her. Like her mother hadn't. Like she'd always known her ex wouldn't.

She'd been stupid to think that Nate McGuire would be any different.

Jett Brandau was hovering outside Nate's office when they arrived. Taking in the sight of Risa coming in behind him, he said, "Boy, you guys timed your arrival perfectly." He stopped then, looked more carefully from one to the other.

Nate busied himself unlocking the door. "Is there a reason you're haunting my office?"

Still watching them both, Jett said slowly, "Yeah, I got news. I told you I'd keep you both updated." He followed them into the office, shot Nate a what-the-hell look.

Nate kept his expression carefully impassive. The man could draw his own conclusions about Risa's and his simultaneous arrivals. But there was no way he could fail to pick up on the charged current between them. It'd been present all through the breakfast she'd cooked, then barely eaten. Had continued when she'd joined him in the station house lot. Walked with him inside.

Nate had the sinking feeling that he'd been given an opportunity and had failed miserably at it. The hell of it was, he wasn't quite sure what his failure had been.

That he hadn't, what, accepted her dreams as fact? As some sort of psychic road map outlining the future of this case? Just the idea summoned incredulity again. He was a man mired in logic. In reason. And dammit, Risa should be, too. She dealt with the same sort of facts and detail that he did himself. Their job required it.

He'd handled things badly back at the house. He could admit that now. Setting his computer case on his desk, he sat down. But for the life of him, he couldn't see what he could have done differently.

The watch on Eggers had made sense. He'd accepted that readily enough. And she hadn't mentioned anything else, so why the hell did he feel like he'd just bombed a test?

"You two are balls of joy in the morning." Jett dropped into a free chair. "Should I have Darrell bring in coffee?"

"He doesn't work weekends," Nate responded automatically. Risa still hadn't said a word. "I heard Morales tell him he wasn't to let anyone talk him into trading hours either. They all take advantage of him."

Jett looked crestfallen. "If I'd known that I'd have stopped somewhere for coffee before coming in this morning." Then shaking off his disappointment, he got to the point. "I spoke to Lloyd Bennett again this morning. The battalion chief at the fire station that responded to Risa's fire?" At Nate's impatient nod, he went on. "Apparently the arson investigator isn't coming up until today, but he started the interviews by phone yesterday afternoon and reviewed the photos last night. He told Bennett this morning that right now he'd qualify the fire as suspicious."

"When I asked yesterday, Hannah was unsure whether she'd closed the windows that night," Risa said quietly. "She did seem fairly certain that she hadn't opened all you reported that were found open. And she flatly denied taking the batteries out of the smoke detectors."

Nate hadn't heard that conversation. It must have taken place when he'd been on the phone. But although Risa had seemed to accept what that meant, there still was doubt in his mind.

Or hell. More like hope. He was already distracted by Kristin and Tucker's disappearance. How the hell was he supposed to concentrate on the case knowing the Cop Killer had Risa in his sights? His nape prickled. That he'd already made one attempt on her life?

Jett was talking again. "You and your mom have a place to stay? Because I know this gal who runs this sweet little bed-and-breakfast just over the line in Montgomery County." He grinned. "If I send her some business, she just might start talking to me again."

"Risa's staying with me." The brusque pronouncement had both of the others looking at Nate. Jett with surprise, Risa with something a bit more dangerous. He directed his explanation to her. "We're not going to let this guy get another shot at you."

"Meaning that a woman on her own is fair game, but one with a big strong man around will scare him off?"

He didn't trust the sweetness of her tone. Knew her well enough to be certain sarcasm lurked beneath it.

Help arrived from an unexpected quarter. "He's right," Jett told her. "Hell, there's safety in numbers." To Nate, he said, "But it wouldn't hurt to double-check your security system. Your smoke detectors." His expression was sober. "If Risa's a target, so are you. Hell, maybe anyone affiliated with the investigation is."

The rap on the door sounded a mere instant before it was pushed open. Captain Morales stood in the doorway, taking in its occupants with one sweeping gaze. "Good, you're here," he said, looking at Nate. "Javon Emmons was scooped up in the BOLO last night. The commissioner says we get first shot at him."

Emmons was slouched in his chair, a hat pulled low over his eyes. He was more dressed up than the last time they'd seen him. Black-striped jeans and a collared shirt were topped with a butter-soft leather jacket the color of olives. His expression was the same, though. Cocky, with a hint of underlying slyness.

"McGuire. I hear you're looking at my old apartment. Want to rent it, I hear." His teeth flashed. "Man, I'll let you in on a secret. Place has cockroaches the size of rats. Matter of fact, I seen a death match between a cockroach and a rat in the building. Crowned that roach champ."

"Good to know." Nate sat back in his chair and surveyed him. "You're a hard man to find."

"I'm a rolling stone. Got people to see. Can't be sitting around waiting for the po-po to come calling every time you gets a notion."

"Tell us about your brother," Risa put in.

He sent a lazy glance her way. "Which one? I got lots of brothers. I got stepbrothers, half brothers, full brothers . . . got sisters, too. Want to hear about them?"

"No. Just Lamont Fredericks."

Something flashed in his eyes, there and gone too quickly to identify. "What about him? Lamont, he was a half brother and a lot older than me. Hardly knew him. He died when I was just a kid."

"He died in that fire at Tory's."

"That's right." He slipped a little farther down in his chair. "He wasn't wearin' his asbestos pjs. Never made it out of the fire alive."

"Who do you think is to blame for that?"

"Well, I guess it'd be whoever created fire."

"The police report indicated the origin was undetermined. Do you know what that means?"

"Shit means they don't know if someone started it or not."

"That's right." Risa nodded. "If someone started it, who do you think would want to burn Tory's down?"

He shrugged. "My brother was a businessman, just like me. Had a lot of enemies."

"Did those enemies have names?" Nate asked.

Javon spread his hands expansively. "Now, this is nice. Warms my heart to see y'all so worried about how Lamont died. More than twenty years late, but hey, that's the rate you guys get things done, ain't it? Better late than never."

"That doesn't answer the question."

He looked at Risa. "Naw, I don't know. How would I? I was just a little kid at the time."

"But you're in the same kind of business he was in. Even the same territory, from what I can figure."

Juicy wagged a finger at Nate. "Now that sort of talk is

what they call entrapment. Trying to make me say something that ain't true. I sell . . . what you call it? Mary Kay products." He laughed.

"Tell us more about Tory Baltes's son." She folded her arms across her chest. "The one you used to run with sometimes when you were kids."

Humor faded to be replaced by boredom. "What about him?"

"Do you remember his name?"

"Should I? He was some kid. Kids came and went in that neighborhood all the time. Still do."

"The name Samuel Baltes ring a bell?" Nate watched the man closely.

"Sammy. Yeah, maybe it was Sammy. Never saw him again after that fire. His old lady grabbed him and moved away."

"That's interesting." Risa took a sheet out of the file folder in front of her and pushed it over for him to look at. "Because you sold him a car a few years back." She paused a beat. "So you must have seen him at least once more after he moved."

He heaved a long breath. "I meant I didn't see him any more when we was kids. Saw him once or twice after that. When we were grown."

"And one of those times you sold him a car."

"That's right." Nate's words didn't seem to faze him. "Dumb shit got himself killed in it, too." His shrug said it didn't matter to him one way or another. "It's a dangerous world out there."

"Is that what you told Sammy Baltes?"

He grinned, leaned forward to slap his hand on the table. "Can't tell Sammy a thing, can I? Dead is dead."

"Unless it isn't." To Nate's surprise, Risa said the next words in unison with the man. Juicy looked gleeful. "See? She knows what I'm talkin' about. Baltes is dead. His old lady is dead. Lamont is dead. There's just no way of bringing 'em back."

"We could have argued the Crowley murder falls within the realm of our investigation," Risa mused on the way back to Nate's office.

"And I would have if I thought it would shed any light on whoever is torching up these cops. But what we got from Crowley led us to Juicy, and he's the one of interest here." Nate was still trying to figure just how involved he was in this case. "It wasn't worth waging turf wars over it. Let someone else sift through the scores of phony witnesses Juicy will have willing to swear he was somewhere else when Crowley took the dive off that building."

Detectives Tomey and Edwards turned a corner, nearly ran into them. "Good," the older Tomey grunted. "We were just looking for you."

Interest quickened inside him. "You get a match on those photos I gave you?"

"We didn't see any signs of the others, but this guy?" Tomey tapped the picture Nate had added to the packet before giving it to them this morning. "He's front and center at two of the services."

The picture was of Joseph Mauro. The suicide that had somehow ended up with a bullet in his chest.

"Good work," he told the pair of detectives. "Any chance the other men in the pictures could have been there and not shown up on the camera?"

"Camera placement was pretty solid," the more laconic Edwards put in. "But there are definitely areas on the video that can be looked at more closely. The services were huge. I heard officers from all over the state, even some outside the state, were there to pay their respects."

"Which makes it," Risa murmured when they continued on their way to Nate's office, "even more interesting that Randolph didn't show. Or Eggers."

"I didn't go to the last memorial," Nate pointed out, as he headed back to his desk. "I went to the visitations for each victim, but once the investigation was up and running, I felt my time was better spent trying to solve the thing."

He could tell he hadn't convinced her when she settled into a contemplative silence. When his cell rang, he took it out and checked the caller ID. His pulse quickened. He lost no time answering it. "Kristin."

"Call off the dogs, Nate." His sister's tone was caustic. No surprise there. "Who do you have sniffing around? Cass?

Some other female cop? I know you have someone hounding all my friends. Tell them to back off."

"Where are you?"

"If I'd wanted you to know that, I would have told you before leaving, wouldn't I?" He knew his sister well enough to recognize the false bravado in her voice. "Just for once give me a little space. A little credit. I'm just trying to find a better job."

"In Atlantic City?"

Silence was his only answer. He barely noticed when Risa walked by, dropping a slip of paper on his desk before heading out the door. "I can get a PI buddy of mine to verify where you are. To locate your hotel."

"And then what? Come to haul me kicking and screaming back home?"

The visual image wasn't a pretty one. Mostly because it mirrored pretty closely what he'd had in mind. "Tuck needs to be in school. And he does best with consistency. With familiar surroundings."

"Tucker's fine. School will be out in a couple weeks anyway. Sometimes I think you wish he were your son and not mine. But he is mine, Nate. And I have to have a way to provide for him. We can't depend on you forever."

"And what will you find in Atlantic City that you can't find here?" Even he recognized the note of resignation in his voice.

Her tone was cautious, as if not trusting in his too easy capitulation. "A job. I got a tip the night I went downtown with some friends last week that they were looking for dealers. But if that doesn't work out, I might be able to get hired on as a bartender. I've already got a line on a college student who could watch Tucker at night, while he's sleeping. That'd be easier on him than leaving him with a stranger during the day, Nate. You know it would."

He could have pointed out that Tuck's current babysitter wasn't a stranger. But the battle was lost, and he knew it. Unless he wanted to engage in a long, ugly custody battle, one that would take months to resolve, he had to let Kristin go. If she wasn't currently drinking, his grounds would be shaky, at best.

"You didn't have to leave like that, Kristin," he said bleakly. "How long would you have gone without a word if Cass hadn't picked up your trail?"

"I'm sorry." The words sounded choked. "But you would have tried to talk me out of it and I thought . . . I'd planned to call once I had a job lined up."

His throat clogged. Staring blindly at the wall of his office, he cleared it. "Daily phone calls from now on. And I'm going to want to be able to speak to Tucker."

"I can do that. It's just until I earn enough money for school. A couple years maybe. And Atlantic City is only about an hour from Philadelphia."

"You've got it all figured out." His attempt at lightness fell flat.

"I'm trying to anyway." Kristin's laugh was shaky. "About time, don't you think?"

After another minute in which the conversation seemed to grow more strained, Nate made his excuses and hung up. Then stared at the phone in his hand, his chest tight. He'd never minded stepping in to offer a helping hand when his sister needed it. And although taking on the raising of Tucker for a couple years had meant a major life and attitude adjustment for him, it had become his new normal. And it hadn't hurt that Tucker, despite the challenges presented by his disability, was so great to be around.

Now apparently it was time to see how he was at stepping aside when that helping hand was no longer needed. Or wanted.

Drawing a deep breath, he dialed Cass's landline number to tell her thanks. And that she could stop looking for Kristin.

Because Risa felt a measure of guilt for lying to Nate about where she was going, she assuaged it by making a point of swinging by both the hospital and Jerry's first. And then, a couple hours later, she headed to her intended destination.

Carly Williams answered the door and looked at her without enthusiasm. "You again."

"I'm sorry to bother you." Risa flashed a smile that wasn't

returned. "I wondered if you'd remembered anything else about your sister, Tory, that might be helpful."

"Look, I told you two everything I knew yesterday. Now I've got grandkids to lay down for naps and a house to clean, so if there's nothing else . . ." She made to close the door.

"Actually, there is," Risa said quickly. "Would you happen to have any pictures of your nephew? Sam Baltes."

The woman screwed up her brow. "You mean when he lived here?"

"No, after he was grown. You'd indicated you saw him some after he got out of foster care."

But Williams was shaking her head. "No, I don't have anything like that. He was like a stranger when he came round after he got older. Didn't have any reason to be snapping photos of him."

"Would you mind looking at these sketches?" She handed her a sheet taken from the legal pad she'd drawn on last night. "Does either of these two men look familiar?"

Impatiently, the woman snatched it from her, glanced at it. Then she stared harder at the sketches of Jett Brandau and Darrell Cooper. "Who's the artist? You? That's a fine likeness there. Other than the hair color, you caught Sam darn near perfectly."

"Darrell Cooper is Sam Baltes?" Stunned surprise sounded in Nate's words.

"That's what his aunt claims." Risa lowered her cell phone for an instant as she slowed to make room for the moron in the next lane intent on cutting in front of her. A moment later she resumed the conversation. "Which means he's donned another identity for some purpose. Probably that of the guy found burnt to death in his car."

"Slow down," he cautioned. "It might have been a case of his aunt making the wrong identification at that time."

"And he decided to leave the Sam Baltes ID behind because the opportunity arose?" A mental fragment from the last two dreams flashed across her mind. Of the young blond boy racing down the street with Juicy. Of the image of the boy melding, transforming, into Darrell. There wasn't a doubt in her mind. But she knew without his saying a word that Nate would take much more convincing.

"I need Darrell's address." She checked her rearview mirror and took the next exit.

"I'll call him. Have him come in."

"Let me go by there first." Risa waited for a break in the traffic to pull onto the interstate. "I want to get an idea of where he lives." How he lives. And if there were anything in the vicinity of his home that would point to his involvement.

"Absolutely not." His tone was emphatic.

"He doesn't have to know that I'm around. Although as long as I'm there, it would make sense for me to drive him in for questioning."

He was silent for a moment. Then, "You can locate the residence. Then call me. You stay put, keep an eye on the house."

Since it was as good a deal as she was likely to get, she agreed with alacrity.

"I'm serious, Risa." His tone brooked no argument. "I'm trusting you not to be stupid enough to try and accost him yourself. Promise me."

"I can promise I won't do anything stupid." She held the line while he located the address. When he began speaking again, she snatched a pen from the visor and wrote on the back of the sketches. "Got it."

"I'm trusting you." The note in his voice gave her pause. "I want a call back in an hour or the next BOLO will be for you."

"Give me an hour and a half." She glanced at the notation she'd made once more before returning her gaze to the highway. "Traffic is murder today."

There was no vehicle in front of the address save for the 1980 Impala parked in the drive, its paint gleaming in the afternoon sun. And although Risa watched for over twenty minutes, she saw no one but the octogenarian slowly clipping the manicured hedge with a large pair of trimmers.

The name on the mailbox read A. HASTINGS. And after surveying the scene for a few more minutes, Risa knew the lead was a dead end.

She got out of the car, the sheet with the address on it clutched in her hand. As she approached, the lady in the wide-brimmed hat straightened, shielding her eyes to watch her.

"Hello. Isn't it a lovely day?"

Risa smiled in return, but her gaze was scanning the area. There was only a carport, no garage. And the house could most aptly be described as a bungalow. "It is," she agreed with an enthusiasm she was far from feeling. "Unfortunately, I think I'm lost." She read the address off the pages she held.

"Well, you certainly aren't lost, dear." The woman's smile was sweet. "That's this address."

"Oh." Risa didn't have to feign her confusion. "But I'm looking for Darrell Cooper's residence."

"You found that, too," the woman said cheerfully. "Well, not his home, you understand. Just his mailing address. I'm Aurelia Hastings. This is my house."

"How do you know Cousin Darrell?" Risa figured the pretext of being a relative was as good as any.

"Well, it's just the sweetest story." Aurelia set the clippers carefully down on the lawn as if they'd grown heavy. "He carried my groceries out to my car one day. And the next week when I went back to the store, darned if he wasn't there and did it for me again. We got to talking, and he told me about not having a permanent address on account of that messy divorce." Her voice lowered conspiratorially.

"It was an ugly one." She played along. "I never did like his wife. Told him that when he was dating her."

Aurelia smiled. "Well, live and learn. Not everyone can have fifty years together like me and my dear Horace. He was in manufacturing, you see. The first time I met him . . ."

Shifting the conversation back to the topic she was most interested in, Risa said, "Do you have any way of knowing how I can reach him? I don't have his phone number and I'm only going to be in town one more day."

The older woman looked distressed. "I don't, I'm sorry. I don't have his number either. Darrell comes by once a week and picks up any mail. There's rarely anything here for him. And he insists on giving me fifty dollars a month for my trouble. No trouble at all, I try to tell him. But he's quite insistent and . . . well, I am on a fixed income. I always say I should be paying him. He's so good about fixing little things around here. He's just the sweetest thing."

Walt Eggers stomped out of the station house and strode across the parking lot, his rage growing stronger with every step. Confined to a desk. The captain's words still rang in his ears. Sure he was just passing along orders from higher up, but the prick didn't have to act so smug about it. He was still pissed off about that IA investigation, even though Walt had assured him again and again that the charge was bullshit. The dirt bag he'd arrested would never be believed over Walt. He was a decorated police sergeant, detective second class. The whole thing was a crock of shit. No one had witnessed the scene. Walt had made sure of that.

And no matter what the captain had told him, Walt knew the reason he was given had been bullshit, too. If IA were going to get him confined to a desk for the duration of the investigation, they'd have done it when they first started looking into the charges.

Which meant this had something to do with the interview with McGuire yesterday. He unlocked his car door and yanked it open with all the fury he was feeling. When this was over, somewhere down the line McGuire was going to get his. No one pulled this shit on Walt Eggers and got away with it.

He turned the key in the ignition. And while he was at it, he'd plan a little payback for that bitch, Chandler, too. Something a little more personal that the ass kicking he'd give McGuire. Something he'd get a helluva lot more pleasure out of.

He peeled out of the lot and shot into the street. After a horseshit day like this, ordinarily he'd call Hans to go out for a brew. Maybe even Giovanni.

But Giovanni was dead and Hans . . . Walt never thought he'd see the day, but Hans was running scared. He'd come around. Eventually. But right now he needed some space. Which meant the bottle of Jim Beam he normally picked up after work would be drunk alone tonight.

He turned at the corner, headed toward his favorite liquor store. No one bitched there when he occasionally picked up a twelve pack on his way out the door, after he'd paid for the liquor. They didn't dare. That's the way it'd been early in his career, when people on the street and the storekeepers respected cops. Didn't give them no lip.

Those had been the days.

———

Plainclothes officer John Huxley, ensconced in a navy Camry straight from police impound came to attention when Detective Eggers headed for his car. Starting his own vehicle, he put down the newspaper he'd had in front of his face and watched for his chance in traffic. He'd follow the guy from four cars back. It was doubtful Eggers would notice him, but if he did, a second officer would pick up the tail in a black Monte Carlo.

Likely the detective would go directly home, but Huxley almost wished he didn't. There was nothing more boring than stakeout work. Running a tail at least took some talent. It damn sure broke up the monotony.

He timed the next light, made sure he got through the yellow because Eggers had. But they missed the next one, and he stopped, waited. The loud jacked-up older model Cutlass in the lane next to him seemed crammed with people, most of them jiving to the rap music blaring from the speakers.

Exchanging a look with the unshaven guy in the passenger seat, he returned his eyes to the road. The city had noise ordinances, but he had a job to do. Let some traffic cop bust them for the tinted windows and the noise.

Ought to be a ticket they could write for bad taste in music.

From the corner of his eye Huxley saw movement from the car. He glanced its way again. He had only a fraction of an instant to recognize the barrel of a sawed-off shotgun pointing at him.

In the next instant he was dead.

———

Eggers came out of the liquor store with a bottle and a twelve-pack, feeling a modicum better. The feeling lasted about as long as it took him to notice the man hanging around his car, trying to seem inconspicuous by looking at a city map. Failing big time.

Paranoia mingled with logic. It was still light outside, for chrissakes. No one was going to make a move on him in the daylight. He drew a bit closer, and recognition hit him. Although he couldn't quite place the guy, he'd seen him before.

"Walter Eggers?"

"Who wants to know?"

"I have a message for you from Jim Gorenson."

Bullshit he did. "Oh, yeah?"

The guy looked around and lowered his voice. "He asked me to deliver something to you."

Walt hesitated. Maybe he'd been too quick to jump to conclusions. This Cop Killer thing was making him jittery. Could be this was some sort of entrapment trick from that wiseass McGuire. Because he suddenly remembered where he'd seen this dumbass redhead before. He was a PA at the seventh district. He'd checked in with him before talking to the task force dickhead.

"I don't know any Jim Gorenson." He had to get the booze in the car so his hand would be free to draw his weapon if he needed to. Nonchalantly he set down both purchases while he used the remote to unlock his vehicle. McGuire was pathetic if he was behind this. Although a part of him wondered how the task force had gotten Gorenson's name.

"Maybe you know him better as Hans. Listen." The guy sounded like he was getting impatient. "I'm parked in the alley out back because Gorenson said you might have a tail on you. He doesn't want to call because your phone might be tapped. I don't know what's going on and frankly I don't care. You want what he sent with me for you, fine. If not, I'll take it back to him."

Hans. There was no one outside the John Squad who knew about their names. No way that could have been figured out, was there? Walt wasn't taking any chances. He set the booze in the backseat, making damn sure he never had his back to the man. The whole thing was probably bogus but there was only one way to find out.

"Okay, let's see what you got."

"Not here." The little weasel actually looked nervous. "He said you might have someone watching you. I'm going to walk into the liquor store and out the back door. You follow me in a few minutes."

The hair on the back of Walt's neck prickled. Yeah, he'd follow him all right. He'd follow him and ram his nine-millimeter up the guy's ass. "Whatever."

He jammed a finger at the guy's map and said in a loud voice, "You're way the hell on the wrong side of town. If you want to get to Center City, you need to follow this road and then hang a right here." He traced the path on the map and got in his car. The guy folded the map and headed into the liquor store.

Then Walt reached inside his jacket and removed his weapon. Tucked it into his waistband at the small of his back. Whatever the jackass out back was trying to pull, he was about to get a very big surprise.

Walt dawdled inside the store for a few minutes, drawing an anxious look from the clerk before he headed for the back door. Sure enough, there was the dickwad with the map, fidgeting anxiously next to a burgundy Chrysler.

"Oh good," he said, with relief evident in his voice. "Here. I've got what Hans sent in my trunk."

Walt smiled grimly. He waited for the man to turn to open it then closed the distance between them, shoving the guy's head down hard against the trunk lid, yanking his weapon out to press it against his temple. "What the hell you pulling here, limp dick? Huh? Who the hell do you think you're dealing with?" He almost hoped McGuire had sent the little weasel. Yeah, he wouldn't mind humiliating that asswipe.

"Jesus, Jesus, what are you doing?" The guy was practically sniveling. And there was a satisfying amount of blood running down his face. "Did you break my nose? I think you broke my fucking nose!"

"And that's not the last thing I'm going to break. Now let's open that trunk nice and easy, and you can tell me all about this bullshit story you dreamed up."

"Fuck. Fuck." The guy's voice was muffled. "This is the last time I'm doing Jim a favor."

Walt kept the weapon ready while the trunk lid opened. Saw a large brown envelope and a box of black notebooks in a cardboard box. "What the hell is all this?"

The guy was shaking like a leaf. Probably going to piss himself at any minute. "The envelope is from him. It should have some kind of explanation in it. He said the books were old records. He wants you to get rid of them."

A flare of bitterness spurted. Yeah, let good ol' Johnny get caught with the records. Which should have been destroyed fifteen years ago when they'd gone to computer spreadsheets. He was good enough to take care of all the dirty work, but not good enough to be seen with anymore.

"Take out the envelope." He cast a careful eye up and down the alley, but there was nothing back here but an overflowing Dumpster and a mangy cat. "Take out what's inside it."

The guy obeyed, but his hands were shaking so badly he dropped the letter he withdrew onto the ground. "Oh shit, my nose hurts," he whined.

What a fucking pantywaist. Walt bent down to get the letter and suddenly the guy wasn't there anymore. Something was shoved in his face, and he fought to turn around, to aim his weapon.

But he couldn't see to point it. The world around him was spinning. Until consciousness receded completely and the gun dropped from his hand.

Chapter 21

"The address is fake," Risa reported glumly as she pulled away from the curb in front of Hastings's house. "And I called Cooper's number a couple times. He isn't answering."

"If he's the one behind these killings, he's been busy," Nate responded tersely. "The tail I had on Eggers was just taken out in a drive-by shooting."

Ice water splashed through her system. "And Eggers?"

"Your guess is as good as mine. He hasn't returned home. I dispatched officers there as soon as I heard about Huxley."

"Cooper got to him." She'd seen this, she recalled sickly. Had known it would happen. And yet again, had failed to prevent it. "Eggers is the next victim. I told you that this morning."

"Eggers could just be running scared. We don't know anything, other than the fact that we need to bring him in. We put a BOLO out on his car, and it was found within fifteen minutes in front of a liquor store near the station house. I'm on my way over to question the clerk."

Meaning he'd follow procedure. And in the meantime, Eggers's chances of surviving would decrease by the minute.

He was a putrid little man. Not the sweet innocent that

Ryder Kremer had been. But the courts should mete out justice for his actions. Not Darrell Cooper.

Or Sam Baltes.

She looked down at the seat where she had the drawings from last night. Balanced the steering wheel with her knee as she shook one after the other open. A blaring horn behind her had her grabbing the wheel again and returning her attention to the road.

"What's that?" Nate demanded.

"Bad driver." No need to mention that the bad driver was she. Risa turned onto a residential street and eased to the curb. Put the car in park and picked up the sketches to study them.

"Listen I don't have time to wait for you. I'm heading out now. But here's the address." He rattled off the location of the liquor store. She didn't bother to write it down. "You can meet me there."

"I'm going to check something else out first."

The sketch of the road sign swam on the page in front of her. Left off 104. A deeply rutted road. Overgrown, with branches scraping the vehicle as it bumped by.

"Risa." Nate's voice held a tone of warning. He was on the move. She could hear the change in the background noise as he moved through the station house. "Get back here. I can't afford to be worrying about you with all hell breaking loose."

"You don't have to. Because I'm not going to take any chances." She didn't dare, did she, when she couldn't even trust herself to draw her weapon. To fire it.

But she'd never forgive herself if she didn't check this out. Especially if they discovered tomorrow, or the next day, that Eggers had been burned to death just like the other victims. And that this time the scene was right off 104.

She wasn't sure she could bear another failure.

"Keep me posted on your progress, and I'll do the same."

"Risa!" She clicked the phone off on the urgent word. She knew he was worried. Knew he wouldn't believe her when she told him that he didn't have to be. She wasn't about to run headlong into danger.

But she needed to check out the road sign from her dream. She owed the next victim that much.

Dusk was fast approaching when she slowed on route 104. She looked instinctively to her left. There was nothing to set the road apart from any of the others that she'd passed. Nothing but a chill working down her spine. And a flash of memory from the dream the night before.

Bumping over the rutted road, branches scratching at the car top. On the windows.

Sometimes the dreams were a depiction of what had happened. What might happen. And sometimes they were a jumble of past, present, and future. Dreams were open for interpretation, just like Nate had said. The pieces in them couldn't be fit together like a puzzle. Some of the elements in them made no sense.

The prickling along her spine told her that this piece fit. But Nate would require proof.

She pulled over on the opposite side of the road, ahead of where the turnoff was. It'd be better to walk in. She could stay inside the underbrush that way. Even if the thought of pushing aside those branches—the ones that had been licked with flame in her dreams—turned her skin to ice. Swallowing hard, she hesitated for a moment. Then forced herself to plunge inside the wooded area.

It was darker without the setting sun overhead to illuminate the way. Easier to stumble over fallen limbs hidden beneath a layer of decaying leaves. After several minutes she began thinking she had miscalculated by not taking a more direct route. A half hour later she was certain of it.

Until she saw something through the trees that had all other thought fleeing from her head.

Fumbling for the cell in her pocket, she pulled it out. Punched in a familiar number. Was rewarded a few moments later with a growled, "McGuire."

"You need to come out here."

"Risa? Wait." The din in the background made it almost impossible to hear him. A few moments later when he came back on the line again the noise had lessened. "Where are you?"

"Twenty miles west of interstate one on route one oh four. My car is on the side of the road. The path you'll want to take is on the left. It's overgrown and on foot it's a thirty-minute walk in."

"Listen, all hell is breaking loose here. We've got a good lead on the car of suspects who fired at Huxley. If we can track them down and discover their identities . . . or who hired them . . ."

"Best guess is Juicy. I think he and Darrell are working together somehow. But listen." Her voice was low but no less urgent. "What kind of car did Randolph drive? The one that disappeared when he did?"

"A burgundy Chrysler, why?"

She peered out between the branches at the vehicle parked on the rutted road another quarter mile ahead. "Because I think I'm looking at it right now."

There was dead silence on the other end of the phone. Then, "Give me the directions again." She did so. "Risa, I want you to go back to your car and wait for me."

"I'm not going to do that, Nate." She squinted into the distance. But beyond the car she could see nothing. "It'll be dark soon. I have to track them while I can still see where I'm going. But I don't have any intention of making a move unless Eggers is in immediate danger."

His curses were fluid and creative. "Dammit, I mean it. Don't take another step until I get there."

"I'll call you back when I have more information." She cut off the call and set the phone to vibrate. Then she visually measured the distance between her location and where the car was parked. Using the underbrush for cover, she crept closer.

Ten minutes later she was at the empty vehicle. There was nothing to see through the windows in the car. The trees grew thicker up ahead. The overgrown road became impassable, which was likely why the vehicle had been abandoned here. Staying low, she crept along the rutted path, the branches of the low-hanging trees clutching at her as she passed with greedy grasping fingers.

The sun had disappeared over the horizon. And soon . . . much too soon, the area would be shrouded in darkness.

As she moved farther past the car, she heard the sound of voices. She couldn't make out the words at first. But the closer she pressed, the clearer they became.

"Fuck you. Think I'm going to say I'm sorry? If I had it to do over, I'd burn the fucker again. And again."

Risa drew in a shaky breath. Eggers. She stopped at the ring of trees and squinted through the leafy branches. What she saw had her catching her breath.

Eggers was secured to a straight-backed chair in the center of a clearing. His tone taunting, Cooper was standing in front of him.

But not Darrell Cooper, she reminded herself. Sam Baltes.

"We'll see what you have to say once I drop a match. That was a mixture of diesel fuel and gasoline I sprayed you with. It burns nice and hot when it gets going. You should have seen what it did to your friends. There really wasn't a whole lot left of them to bury."

Risa froze. There was no way to get closer without leaving the shelter of the trees. But she began to doubt that she was going to have the luxury of waiting for Nate before being forced into action.

"I did you a favor by burning that motherfucker," Eggers screamed at him. "If Lamont had lived, you'd have ended up hooked on the same poison he had your mother shooting in her veins. You should be thanking me."

"You're right. And I've arranged a very special thank you. I wanted you to be last. I hated you the most. But flexibility is the key. I can come for the other two later. When Juarez and Gorenson least expect it." There was blood on Baltes's face. His voice sounded strange. Risa's best guess was that Eggers had put up a fight.

Her hand crept to her weapon. Hovered above the holster. Damn, she *could* touch it. Could use it. She'd proved that the other night, hadn't she?

"I've dreamed of this moment since I was eight years old. Today is justice day. But you're not going to die quickly." The hatred in Baltes's voice was apparent. "It'll be slow. Agonizing. And I want you to remember when you start begging and pleading what it was like for me to hear Lamont die. Remember you started this whole thing."

"He was a lying sack of shit and a cheat." There was a thud when Baltes's fist planted in Eggers's face. But it didn't stop the man. He spit blood at Baltes and continued. "Tried to cut us out of his operation and, when that failed, threatened blackmail. Burning him was an example, and an effective one for over twenty years. No one dared try to screw with us after that."

"You're going to scream." Baltes's voice held an element she'd never heard in it when he'd pretended to be Darrell. "You're going to beg. I won't be able to watch your death dance with this setup." There was no mistaking the regret in his voice. "But I think you'll agree that this is a little extra special. Think about that for the next few minutes."

With supreme effort, Risa forced herself to grasp her gun. Draw it out. And then nearly dropped it, her hand shook so violently. Baltes was on the move. She may be given no better opportunity to release Eggers. If only she knew how far the other man was going. Back to the vehicle? To a stash inside the brush? There was no way of being certain. But he had already faded into the darkness. Which meant she had to move.

She approached Eggers in a swift crouch. Her weapon hand was steadier now. But holding the gun was a far cry from pulling the trigger. Just like shooting a window bore no resemblance to shooting a man.

Martin Volk swam across her mind, holding a terrified Ryder Kremer. Should she have taken a chance with the man's kneecap? The cost of her moment's hesitation had been devastating.

Risa shook the image from her mind. There would be no reason for indecisiveness if she had the opportunity to wound Baltes.

Unless she froze in the act of pulling the trigger.

There was brush on two sides of Eggers. But a huge clearing was in the center of it. There was no protection as she hurried toward the victim, even as she took care to stay down. Whichever way Baltes approached from, she and the detective would be plainly visible.

She was coming up on Eggers from behind when she

slowed. There was a huge trench dug around the man. Two feet wide. A foot deep. And it was lined, she noted sickly, with brush and branches. It was all too easy to imagine what Baltes had in mind.

He planned to surround Eggers with a ring of fire.

For a moment, horror at the thought held her motionless. Then she straightened enough to leap over the trench. Piles of discarded dirt were piled inside the circle. She stumbled over an abandoned shovel as she raced across the twelve-foot expanse of grass to where the solitary victim sat waiting for death.

"What the . . . Keep away from me!"

"Quiet," she hissed at Eggers. "Stay still." He was twisting in his chair, trying to see behind him. Risa had to set her weapon down to fumble with his bonds. She didn't want to admit to the slight relief she felt when she no longer had to hold the gun.

"Hurry up! That fucker will be back any minute. Where are the others? Where's McGuire?"

"Don't worry," she muttered. He was secured with duct tape, she realized with a sinking heart. And the most effective way to release him was with a knife to cut through it.

She didn't have a knife. By touch alone she discovered that the tape trussed the man's entire body to the chair. Even if she were able to free his hands, she couldn't afford to expend the time necessary to loosen all of it.

Which meant she wouldn't try. She reached out and tipped the chair toward her. Pulled.

"What the hell are you doing?" His whisper was harsh. Terrified. "Cut me loose!"

Risa bent to retrieve her weapon, but she had to holster it. She couldn't drag Eggers to safety without both hands free. "Unless you happen to have a knife on you . . ." She pulled the chair with all her strength. Dragged it several feet before having to stop and rest for a moment. The man had to weigh one eighty. She pulled again. Moved him several more feet.

Then a shot rang out, kicking up dirt several yards away. She tipped the chair over in an attempt to make Eggers a less visible target and dropped to the ground, drawing her weapon with unconscious fluidity.

"Whoever is there, I'm giving you one chance to walk away. Leave him and save yourself."

Risa strained to place the origin of the voice. It was coming from the brush on the opposite side of the clearing from the way she'd approached. "Baltes?" she called. "Philadelphia PD. You're surrounded. Put your weapon down and come out with your arms raised."

There was a moment of silence. Then, "Chandler?" The incredulous joy in that single word filled her with dread. "You're not with the force anymore. But no one will ever know about that lie you just told. You'll be dead by morning." Another shot. This one closer. She rolled, her wet palms making her grip on her weapon slippery.

"We know about Lamont Fredericks," she called, scanning the cover of brush and trees opposite her. "Eggers burned down Tory's with Lamont in it. We know about your mother's death. The foster homes. But you've left a string of bodies behind you. Darrell Cooper had nothing to do with this case. He was innocent. Killing him makes you as bad as Eggers."

"Fuck that," the detective screamed from his position on the ground. "Fredericks got what he deserved."

"Cooper was a means to an end," Baltes called out. His voice seemed to be coming several yards farther away from where it had last time. "No one was going to miss one more former foster kid after the system spit him out. This is your last chance, Chandler. I never wanted you to die."

She saw a flash of movement. Aimed. One second stretched into another. It took every ounce of determination she had to finally squeeze the trigger.

Too late. She knew it even as the shot sounded. A quick little stab of fear arrowed through her. How much time had passed since she'd talked to Nate?

Not enough, she realized immediately. Her heart sank to the vicinity of her stomach. The only chance they had was for her to get beyond the fear. Beyond the past.

But if determination alone could accomplish that, Raiker wouldn't have had to force her weapon on her again.

Belatedly, she answered the man. "You made a damn good attempt for someone not wanting me to die. You were scared, weren't you? Scared of the sketches you saw on that pad you stole from my bedroom."

"If you knew as much as you thought you did, I'd be in jail right now."

She sited on the area the voice seemed to be coming from. Squeezed the trigger again. A moment passed. Had she hit him? The thought had the weapon trembling a bit in her hand.

"And you're right. I want you dead almost as much as I do Eggers. McGuire I gave a pass to. Just pushed his sister to run to arrange a little distraction for him. But you . . . I don't know what you are. How you drew those pictures. But you'll die with Eggers. I've never had a twofer. I'm going to enjoy this one."

A light blazed in the darkness. Came sailing through the air. Fell short of the trench Baltes was aiming for. And Risa recognized with sick fear that he meant to trap them both in the circle by surrounding them in fire.

"Shoot him! Shoot the little fucker now! Give me the gun. I'll put a bullet between his eyes!" Eggers was screaming in fury and panic.

Risa tuned him out. Waited with bated breath for Baltes to try again. He'd have to get closer with the next try. And when he did, she was going to put a bullet in him. She chanted the mental vow over and over in her mind. Visualize it. Overcome the hesitation and the ghosts from the past. Make it happen.

Her heart was thundering inside her chest. Sounding in her ears. She didn't have long to wait. The light was the first visual cue. The blaze cut through the darkness. Risa took a deep calming breath. Squeezed the trigger. Baltes's cry brought no sense of triumph. Instead, she scrambled backward to reholster her weapon. Grabbed the back of the chair and start pulling again. She needed to get Eggers beyond the trench.

"Wait, wait!"

But Risa had already seen it. Baltes's last torch had found

its mark, landing in the trench. The wood inside had to have been treated with something. The fire leapt wildly, licking around the circle with a harrowing speed.

"I can't cross that!" Eggers was screaming. "He sprayed me with that shit. My clothing is flammable."

Risa wished that were the only danger here. But plumes of smoke were already rising from the fire. Clouding their vision. Breathing it in for too long would kill them before the flames had a chance to.

Swiftly she shrugged out of her jacket and used the sleeves to tie it around her nose and mouth like a mask. The fire was only halfway around the circle. They still had time to cross the unaffected area if she headed in a different direction.

Sound filled the air. A noise she couldn't place. She started for the chair again, and saw coming through the smoke and haze a sight that filled her chest with ice. Baltes.

He was staggering crazily toward them, another lit torch in his hand. Her weapon was drawn before she had the conscious thought to do so. And shook only slightly when she brought it up. Fired.

He swayed like a piñata in a windstorm. Toppled in slow motion. His gun dropped to the ground.

And so did the torch.

He fell inside the trench, the lighted torch landing beside him. And even as she raced back to Eggers, the speeding flames cut off their escape route. The ring of fire was complete.

Baltes's screams were hideous. They drowned out the deafening noise overhead. The shouts in the distance. Frantically, Risa raced to where she'd tripped over the shovel. The haze of smoke in the air made it difficult to see. It burned her eyes, and despite the makeshift mask, her lungs were raw. Scrambling on her hands and knees now, she searched wildly, relief sparking inside her when she found it.

The cries of the damned filled her ears. Baltes's screeches had reached a high-pitched, animal-like sound. Eggers was shouting and cursing by turn, coughing spasmodically. Risa staggered to a pile of dirt. Used the shovel to throw it back on the fire. Smother it. Without fuel, it'd cease to burn. At least in theory. Logic receded, instinct took over. Dig and throw. Dig and throw.

She blinked. Squinted. Her efforts were paying off slowly. Much too slowly. But a small portion of the flames were suffocated. She dropped the shovel. Staggered. If she could get to Eggers. Drag him across that flame-free expanse . . .

An alien-looking creature loomed in front of her, spit from the fire. Followed by a second one. Another dream, she thought foggily. Nothing made sense.

And then thought ceased as her knees buckled. Her senses receded rapidly as the ground came up to meet her.

Chapter 22

"You look like hell."

Risa's hand went to her hair self-consciously. Trust Raiker to offer the plain, unvarnished truth. She hadn't caught a glimpse of herself in a mirror, but she'd seen the towels after the nurse had cleaned her face and hands. The ends of her hair felt crispy, as if it'd break off at her touch.

"She *looks*," Nate said grimly, with a dark glance in her direction, "like someone who needs to be in a hospital bed."

"Trust me. They're not all they're cracked up to be."

A nurse hovered outside the door of Adam's room. Risa assumed it was because he had two visitors at once. But her boss's condition had been upgraded to stable, and he was ready to be moved out of CCU. Paulie had told her, once he'd released her from a bone-crushing hug, that he was transferring Adam to George Washington University Hospital, where he had a nationally renowned specialist on hand to treat Adam.

"Give me a rundown."

Before she could open her mouth, Nate interrupted. "I'll talk. Save your voice."

She wasn't totally sorry. Her throat felt like she had razor blades lodged in it.

"Approximately twenty-five years ago a group of Philadelphia police officers formed a group they called the John Squad. Each member was known by a variation of 'John' and all culled a midlevel drug dealer from the mix. They offered protection in exchange for a slice of the profits. Refusal wasn't an option. Since their group included a high-profile assistant DA at the time, they had a lot to offer."

Risa raised her brows at him questioningly. "Eggers?" she rasped out the word.

Nate shook his head. "Eggers is still denying everything, much like when we hauled him in for that interview. But after the drive-by last night, we got a visit from a Detective Jim Gorenson. He's seeking immunity. Didn't get it but likely he's hoping his cooperation will count with the jury. He gave us names. Dates. And a history. Tory's was a hangout for the police group when they met. Apparently Lamont Fredericks was giving them some trouble. Threatened blackmail. Gorenson claims it was Eggers who set fire to the place, after making sure Fredericks was locked in the bedroom upstairs. The idea was to set an example for any of their other associates who might get similar ideas."

And yet Eggers had been spared a similar death. There was a twisted irony in that, Risa thought.

"A couple others of the original group had retired and moved away, including the assistant DA. Once the members of the group started being victimized, Eggers reached out to the other two. Discovered each of them had been killed months earlier. A house fire and a fiery car accident."

"Baltes was good at that." He narrowed her a look and she subsided. Brought the bottled water that he'd bought her to her lips and drank.

For Raiker's sake he explained, "The owner of the bar that burnt was Tory Baltes. She died a couple years later but her son ended up in foster care. Fredericks had been good to him, and the kid watched the man die from the sidewalk outside the place."

"And so an obsession was born," Raiker murmured.

Nate nodded. "Three years ago Baltes must have put his plan in motion. It's looking like he faked his own death, switching identities with that victim. We're tracking down the real Darrell Cooper."

"They were in foster care together," she managed. Just those few words had her throat raw.

"That would make sense. There was one more kid who saw the fire. Javon Emmons, Lamont's younger half brother. He and Baltes were close as kids. Now we're reaching into supposition, but I'm guessing Baltes showed up again, ran his idea for revenge by Emmons, who was only too happy to assist any way he could. It was he who got the car used for Cooper's accident. And Gorenson claims Emmons also has connections to a chop shop. Big operation. We know from finding the victims' former vehicles that someone was fairly adept at changing VIN numbers."

Raiker sent Nate a pointed look. "You should have had someone on Eggers."

"We did." His retort was mild. "Maybe Baltes heard somehow what we planned. More likely he just expected it and was ready. The officer was killed in a drive-by shortly before Baltes snatched Eggers. We've already got the shooter and the occupants of the car. Chances are one of them will talk and implicate Emmons." He paused for a moment before adding, almost as an afterthought, "I asked Christiansen about the symbolism of the badges left at the scene. He wasn't sure, but he did recall the station houses having boxes of them back in the eighties. Officers kept them in their cars or pockets and handed them out to kids they came across while on the job." He shrugged. "Maybe a member of the John Squad had given one to Baltes when he was a kid."

Likely he was right. There had to be some personal connection for the offender to have included one at each scene. But Risa had moved on to a more pressing question. "How did you get to me so quickly?" She'd lost track of time after talking to him on the phone the night before. And he'd been in no mood for answering questions at the crime scene.

And with the medical personnel efficiently bustling around her, there hadn't been much opportunity to ask then.

"Police helicopters," he said tersely. "I'll give him credit, when I called Morales, he had the commissioner on the line in minutes. And from there things moved fairly quickly."

She recalled now the noise that had filled the air. The shouts she'd heard. But her vision had been hampered by the smoke. Her focus on keeping Eggers and her alive.

"Jett rounded up some fire blankets and gear and sent that with the first two teams. Fire trucks were dispatched." And it would have been hard to miss the flicker of lingering fear in his eyes.

Raiker was silent for a few moments. His dark hair and eye patch contrasted starkly with the white sheets beneath his head. His condition didn't detract from the fierce intelligence blazing from his single bright blue eye. But he was tiring rapidly. Risa caught Nate's attention. Jerked her head slightly toward the door.

But before either of them could move, Raiker said abruptly, "I want to talk to Risa alone."

She recognized the stubborn expression on Nate's face. So she gave him a slight shove to get him moving toward the hallway. He'd been hovering like a guardian angel since she'd regained consciousness.

Catching a glimpse of a determined-looking nurse through the door before it closed, she looked at her boss and advised, "Better talk fast. The cavalry is getting restless."

"How did you follow Baltes with his last victim?"

Adam needed no urging to get quickly to the point. "I saw it."

He nodded, accepting what she didn't say. The way he'd always accepted the dreams as the source of her instincts. Always, at least, since she'd apparently passed the battery of tests he'd thrown her way during the prehiring phase.

"Didn't see the helicopters in the dreams, did you? Or the rescue. Probably not your own danger there."

"They don't work that way, you know that. I get snippets, not the whole. I have to make sense of the pieces."

"I do know that." He nodded. "Just wanted to make sure you finally recalled it yourself. Dreams, instincts . . . whatever the hell it is that drives your knowledge, are tempered by what you know. What you can deduce. The dreams mean nothing without the innate ability to connect the pieces." His gaze dropped to her hand. Traveled upward again. "You shot Baltes."

Surprised, she met his gaze. He smiled wryly. "Think I don't have outside sources? You drew your weapon. Fired it. Hit your target."

"Do you need to pronounce it when you're right?"

"No. I need to pronounce you cured. Now get out of here. Tell Paulie to put you back on the active list." His voice was growing weaker. Which just seemed to make him more irritable.

Her throat grew full. But there was no objection on her lips. Not anymore. "Thank you, Adam."

Giving up what appeared to be a losing battle, his eye closed. "For what?" he muttered. "Not accepting your resignation? There's a little matter of you saving my life. Call it even."

She gave a laugh that was dangerously close to a sob. And eased out of the room before he could call her on it.

Nate sprang away from his stance against the wall at her appearance. She noted with some pleasure that a number of her colleagues were gathered in the waiting room. But when she would have headed to join them, he guided her past the waiting-room door.

She had a moment to recognize Shepherd, the fed sent from DC to evaluate the failed operation resulting in Adam's shooting. Then they were past the windows in a more isolated area of the hallway. "I want to get a chance to talk to Special Agent Shepherd."

"I can tell you everything Dev repeated." He held up a cup of coffee. "He's as good with information as he is at dispensing caffeine. He said Ramsey told him that Shepherd had been all through Jennings's financials. Had found his bankbook for the overseas account, where I guess the payment for potential hits would go. There were no deposits over the last six months. He's guessing at this point that Jennings was working for himself."

Risa shook her head. "There was no connection. Adam had never arrested Jennings. He'd never been involved in one of Adam's cases."

"But Jennings once had a girlfriend whose father was put

away for life by your boss." Nate brought the cup to his lips. Drank. "That's all the details Shepherd shared, but it's looking more and more like that personal connection will have to be explored further."

She considered the possibility. "Personal connections can get sticky." Her voice was sounding more hoarse from the effort of talking. But there was still something she hadn't told Nate. "Baltes is the one who gave your sister the idea to take off. I don't know how or why they met up. A distraction, he called it."

He looked shocked. And more than a little anxious. "Last week she didn't come home one night. I assumed she'd gone clubbing with friends. Maybe he arranged to run into her there." He shook his head, as if bemused.

But when he looked at her again, his eyes were intent. "I do know how complicated personal connections can be. When I was running across that clearing and saw you trapped in that ring of fire . . ." His voice cracked, just a little on the last word. "I don't pretend to understand it, whatever it is you dream. What causes it. But that will be the last damn time I ever discount it."

It was, she thought sappily, more touching than the most fervent declaration of love. And something that had never been offered to her before, by anyone other than her boss. "I can't tell you what that means to me."

The muscle in his jaw clenched. "I promised myself after our last phone conversation that I'd still have the chance to tell you exactly what *you* mean to *me*. I'm in love with you, Risa." As if to stem any protest she would make, had she been able to summon the power of speech to do so, he went on. "Yeah, I can guess what you're going to say. I know exactly how many days we've known each other. It's too soon. But it's still there. And if there's one thing I've learned in the last few hours, it's that time doesn't mean a thing. It's the now that matters. And you're my now. My future."

One hand came up to cup her jaw. Her senses swam. Shakily she managed, "Psychological studies indicate that situations of high stress cause heightened emotion in the involved parties."

His faced lowered to hers. "Exactly why I'm going to

make sure we have plenty of boring years together to prove the psychologists are full of shit."

She shook her head. Paused to savor the kiss he pressed against her lips. A moment later she murmured, "You don't have to prove anything to me. I don't need psychologists to tell me what I feel. I love you, Nate. But I wouldn't say no to some uneventful times, regardless." A thought struck, and for the first time worry pierced the fog of happiness. "Adam proclaimed me ready to return to work."

He caught her bottom lip in his teeth. Tested it lightly. "Two and half hours by car in good traffic. Less by train. C'mon, after the last few days, we've overcome far more important things than distance."

She tilted her head back to regard him soberly. He was more right than he could know. She'd confronted her fears. All of them. And although she knew she had further to go in that regard, she was overcoming the self-doubt that had crippled her for the last several months.

"We have," she agreed. "I'd say we make a damn good team." His arm went around her waist to pull her closer. She slipped her hand around his neck and sank into his kiss.

Long moments went by before she opened her eyes again. Another two or three before the fog in her brain lifted enough to realize they had an audience.

"Risa." Ryne Robel, another of Adam's investigators raised his coffee in salute. "Good to see you again. You're looking . . . well." He managed, barely, to dodge the punch his diminutive wife, Abbie, aimed at his arm.

Embarrassment filtered in. But not enough to have her stepping out of Nate's arms. "Privacy?"

"If you want privacy, you shouldn't be making out in a hospital corridor," Kellan Burke observed laconically. "They've got rooms here, you know."

"Everyone out." Ramsey and Macy Reid, Kellan's fiancée, shooed the group back to the waiting room.

Zach Sharper threw an arm over the shoulders of Cait Fleming, the willowy former model turned forensic anthropologist. As they trailed after the rest of her colleagues, Cait raised her hand over her shoulder, waggled her fingers for Risa's perusal. The large emerald engagement ring was hard to miss. "Congratulations, Cait. Zach," she called. The man sent them a self-satisfied grin before they turned into the doorway of the waiting room.

Risa looked at Nate. "You realize they're all going in there to talk about us."

He didn't look upset at the prospect. "Then I say"—his face lowered to hers—"let's give them plenty of material."

————

He lowered the binoculars as the gleaming private jet, loaded with medical personnel and equipment, taxied down the runway. Raiker was heading back to the East Coast. Alive, unfortunately.

The frustrated rage that surged would serve no useful purpose. Jennings had been the best. And to give the man credit, he hadn't given up. Each attempt on Raiker's life had been more daring than the last.

For the money he'd been paid, such effort had been expected.

Failure was not.

He slipped back into the crowd. Moved with it toward the airport corridor. His father, abusive old bastard that he was, had been fond of a particular saying: If you want something done right, do it yourself.

It was abundantly clear that the only way to assure Raiker's death would be to take the man out himself.

A plan already forming, he settled his sunglasses on his face and strolled toward the airport's exit.

Turn the page for a preview of
the sixth book in Kylie Brant's
exciting Mindhunters series

DEADLY SINS

Available August 2011
from Berkley Sensation!

Chapter 1

Death was rarely the result of divine intervention. Often nature could be blamed. More frequently another person was the cause. On that drizzly gray evening in early November, nature had an alibi.

If Supreme Court Justice Byron Reinbeck had known what fate had in store for him that day, he'd have spent less time writing the scathing dissenting opinion on Clayborne vs. Leland. Which, in turn, would have had him leaving his chambers at a decent hour. That would have negated the need to stop at his favorite sidewalk vendor for flowers to take to Mary Jo, his wife of twenty-five years. She was having a dinner party that evening and he was running unforgivably late.

But not being blessed with psychic powers, he pulled over at the sidewalk in question. Danny was there, rain or shine. Seven days a week, as far as Byron knew. And he never folded up shop until he'd sold his entire inventory.

"Mr. Reinbeck, good to see you." A smile put another crease in Danny's grizzled, well-worn face. A three-sided awning protected him and his wares. "I gots just the thing. Just the thing." He sprang up from his battered lawn chair with a surprising spryness.

Byron turned up the collar of his overcoat, belatedly remembered the umbrella in the backseat. Hunching his shoulders a bit, he pretended to contemplate the bouquet of yellow roses thrust out for his approval. He suspected Jimmy stocked them daily, on the off chance that he'd stop.

Yellow roses were Mary Jo's favorite.

He reached for his wallet. "You're a lifesaver, Danny."

The older man's cackle sounded over the crinkle of the wrapping paper he was fixing around the bundle. "You has to be in big trouble for these flowers not to do the trick."

A quick glance at his watch told Byron that he was only a handful of minutes away from "big trouble." He withdrew a couple bills, intending to leave without waiting for change.

He didn't have a chance to turn around when the sharp "crack" of the rifle sounded behind him. But he saw the splash of crimson on the front of Danny's stained brown hoodie. Had a split second to feel pain and shock before pitching forward, his lifeless body crushing the fragrant long-stemmed beauties against the plywood table.

Adam Raiker rapped softly at the door of the library. Although there were three occupants in the room, only one voice bade him to enter.

Because it was the only one that counted, he eased the door open, his gaze going immediately to Mary Jo Waverly-Reinbeck. "Everyone's gone."

Even grief stricken as she was, there was no mistaking the command of the woman. The red sheathe she wore accentuated her pale blond hair and ice blue eyes. She was brilliant and witty and had been known to dismantle a seasoned defense attorney with a few well-chosen lines.

But it was her devotion to one of Adam's closest friends that had endeared her to him.

Tears still running freely down her face, she held out a hand to him. "Thank you, Adam." He crossed the room to her, aware of the impatience emanating from the other two in the room. He took her hand in his and, at her urging, sank into the seat beside her.

FBI deputy director Garrett Schulte leaned back in his chair and offered Adam a polite smile. But there was no pretense of civility from the other man. Curtis Morgan served in Homeland Security in some capacity, Adam recalled. Given his presence here, it was a position of some import. Regardless, it was Byron Reinbeck's widow who held his focus.

"Gentlemen." She took a moment to wipe at her face with a tissue. "I'm sure you both know Adam Raiker, by reputation if not personally. Adam is a dear family friend." When her voice broke, she paused to compose it. "I'd like a few moments with him now. We can resume our discussion in fifteen minutes. If you'd excuse us?"

Schulte and Morgan exchanged a startled glance but the assistant director recovered first. "Of course." When he rose, the other man followed suit. "Is there anything we can get for you?"

"I'd like a copy of the investigative report updated daily and delivered to me." Even under the circumstances it was difficult for Adam to suppress a smile at the men's reactions to Jo's crisply worded request. "Perhaps you can discuss the details involved for making that happen."

Without another word, the men moved to the open door. Through it. And when it shut behind them, Adam knew the woman had successfully distracted the two from his presence here. They were going to be kept busy employing a duck-and-dodge strategy that would allow the investigation to continue in confidence while still placating the widow of one of the most powerful men in the country. The focus on her connection to Byron Reinbeck also meant they'd underestimate the fact that Jo Waverly-Reinbeck was a brilliant assistant U.S. attorney in her own right.

If the situation were different, he might feel a bit sorry for them.

"Thank you." She squeezed his hand and sent him a watery smile. "For making the necessary calls. For getting the people out of here . . . God. I just couldn't deal with that."

"What about the kids?" he asked quietly. The couple had two sons, both blond like Jo, both in their teens. So far they were being shielded from the breaking news of their father's death.

"They're with my parents. They'll keep the boys away

from the TV until I can go and tell them in person." Her chin quavered once, before she firmed it. "We discussed this. Byron and me. Given our professions, I always thought I'd be the likelier target. God knows I've had plenty of threats. Remember that Calentro drug cartel trial last year? Somehow the USMS managed to keep me safe through that, but Byron hasn't had a serious threat in years. And still . . ."

Because there were no words, Adam released her hand to slip an arm around her shoulders. The passing minutes were filled with her soft weeping. Causing a growing desolation inside him. Helplessness. There was nothing he hated worse.

Moments later, she drew away, mopped her face. And he recognized the determined expression she wore. "You've told us often enough over the last couple months, but are you truly okay? Completely recovered?"

The non sequitur had him blinking. "The bullets caught me in the one area of the chest that wasn't already scarred. I'm still a bit miffed about that, but otherwise I'm fine."

Her gaze was intent. "Who will have jurisdiction on this? The bureau?"

"DCPD will have been first to the scene. Marshals will have sent backup. Then you have the FBI and Homeland Security, just for starters. It'll depend on what's discovered at the crime scene. At the location of . . ."

"Of the shooter," she continued for him. Her tears had disappeared, as if she'd successfully willed them away. "With Byron a sitting justice, we're likely to have every alphabet agency coming out of the woodwork trying to get a piece of this." Her smile was fierce. "I've read the justice reports. Regardless of 9/11, the agencies still haven't learned to share intelligence. I don't want Bryon getting lost in a bureaucratic pissing match."

He couldn't refute her logic. Although he'd left the FBI years ago, Adam had been an agent long enough to recognize the potential pitfalls of the upcoming investigation. "What are you proposing?"

"They won't keep me in the loop of the investigation." She waved away anything he would have said. "I know they can't. That's not my forte anyway." Her pause then was laden with expectancy. "But it is yours. And that of your agency."

With certain regret he answered, "As good as we are at Raiker Forensics, there's zero chance that the feds would invite us to consult on a case of this magnitude. They'd see it as a duplication of services, for one. And my relationship to Byron would be considered a conflict of interest." Although given the man's far-reaching career thus far, he was likely personally acquainted with several top officials in both the FBI and DHS.

"Perhaps under ordinary circumstances." A small sound was heard in the hallway. Jo lowered her voice as she reached out to grip his hand. "I have a few hours to trade on the expressions of sympathy that will be coming my way. Having the sitting U.S. attorney general as a former boss is about to come in handy. And I fully expect the White House to call soon. President Jolson is responsible for Byron's seat on the Supreme Court. I think he'll grant his widow this one favor."

Shock flickered. "Jo, if you accomplish that, I'd be working with the task force put together for this case. And given its sensitivity, I couldn't—"

"—report directly to me? I know." She leaned forward, her expression urgent. "But I trust you. Byron trusted you. And if you're on this case, I won't worry because I know you'll cut through all the bureaucratic bullshit to get the answers." Her voice grew thick with tears again, although there were none in her eyes. They gleamed with purpose. "I want my husband's killer. And if things get messy, I want the real facts, not the sanitized version or whatever the feds deem publicly palatable." Her grasp on his hand tightened. "Before I beg my former employer and the president for a favor, Adam, I'm requesting one from you."

I've never asked you for anything, Adam. I'm asking now.

There was no reason for Jo's words to have memory ambushing him. To evoke the image of another time years earlier, from another woman with similar entreaty in her eyes. In her voice. Turning away from that woman had been the right thing to do. He still believed it.

And still lived with the searing regret that lingered.

He looked down at their clasped hands. Her pale, smooth

skin contrasted sharply with the furrowed scars crisscrossing the back of his palm. Some decisions, made for the best of reasons, left haunting remorse in their wake. This one didn't even require a second thought.

"I'll do everything I can."

"The prudent thing to do—for all concerned—is to bow out gracefully." FBI Executive Assistant Director Cleve Hedgelin looked at a point beyond Adam's shoulder as he parroted the suggestion, which had no doubt stemmed from a loftier position in the agency's hierarchy. But it was equally likely that Cleve shared the sentiment. He might have been Adam's partner eight years ago, but he'd stayed on at the bureau. Had risen in its ranks to head of the Criminal Investigation Division. An agent didn't do that without learning to toe the political line.

And after the spectacular ending of the last case they'd worked together, Cleve likely harbored his own reasons for keeping his distance from Adam. "There's nothing that you can add to the case, and your involvement is a needless distraction."

The office was outfitted more grandly than the cubicle Adam had been assigned when he'd worked in the J. Edgar Hoover Building. He settled more comfortably into the plush armchair and sent the man a bland smile. "Stop wasting time. Attorney General Gibbons has already approved my full inclusion on this investigation. The president himself assured Jo Reinbeck that her wishes in this matter would be heeded. The agency's objections to my presence are expected and duly noted. Let's move on, shall we?"

An unwilling smile pulled at the corners of Hedgelin's mouth. "Same ol' Adam. You never were much for small talk."

"Is that what that was?" When his thigh began to cramp, he shifted position to stretch his leg out. "And here I thought it was the usual bureaucratic BS. Agency's been painted into a corner with Gibbons and Jolson weighing in but still thought it was worth a shot to appeal to my more tender sensibilities."

"You never had many."

"And I haven't developed any in the time since I left. Tell your superiors you gave it the college try and I'm not budging. So." His hands clenched and unclenched on the knob of his cane, an outward sign of his flagging patience. "Catch me up."

Cleve smoothed a hand over his short hair. It was more gray than brown now, but his pale brown eyes were covered by the same style gold wire-framed glasses he'd favored eight years ago. His build was still slim, but the intervening years had left their stamp on the man's face. Adam didn't want to consider what showed on his own.

"We've got more agencies than we can handle jockeying for position in this investigation."

"I imagine that kind of juggling comes with the job."

The assistant director grimaced. "You have no idea. But in this case it means doling out pieces of the case to teams comprised of agents, and members from DHS, USMS, the DC police department . . . and now you."

"Nice to know I'm not crowding the field." Adam wasn't without sympathy for the man's position. But the emotion didn't run deeply enough to have him bowing out and making it easier for Hedgelin or the agency. He'd made a promise to Jo. She'd done her part. She'd gotten him placed on the investigation. He had no illusions; it would have been her connections—and Byron's—that had landed him here. Despite his past in the agency—or perhaps because of it—his presence would make them uneasy. His last case for the FBI had nearly killed him. Although he didn't care about such things, to some it had made him a hero. But because he'd chosen to cut his ties with his former job, the bureau might regard him much differently.

That part didn't matter. The investigation did.

"You'll be partnered with two of our seasoned agents. I believe you know both from your time here. And Lieutenant Frank Griega will be your liaison from the DCPD." Hedgelin dropped into his high-backed leather desk chair and shot Adam a small smile. "Given that our best guys in the Behavioral Analysis Unit were actually instructed by you, we'd be interested in any profile of the offender you put together."

Adam inclined his head. Since he hadn't made a point to keep up with many from the bureau once he'd left it, he had no idea who was still left in the BAU. But Cleve was right. Profiling had been a specialty of his while he'd been an agent. Now it was his employees at Raiker Forensics who received his tutelage. "Of course." His pause was laden with meaning. "But it'd help to get some background on the case first."

The agent leaned forward and stabbed at a button on his desk phone with the stump that remained of his right index finger. Adam wasn't the only one who bore old injuries from the last case they'd worked. He rarely considered his own. When it came to human nature, it was only the scars on the inside that were worth noting.

Moments later the door to the office opened and a man and woman entered. With a glance, Adam determined that Cleve was right. He did know the agents. His gut clenched tightly once before he shoved the response aside with sheer force of will. He'd had recent dealings with Special Agent Tom Shepherd, as well as knowing him slightly when they'd both been with the bureau.

But his reaction had nothing to do with Shepherd.

"You recall Special Agents Shepherd and Marlowe?"

"Of course." He gave them a curt nod.

Shepherd's broad smile complemented his aging Hollywood golden-boy looks. "You're looking a sight better than you did a few months ago in the Philly CCU. I've been hearing the doctors took to calling you the miracle man."

Her voice and face devoid of expression, Jaid Marlowe raised a brow at him. "Just a word of advice—you aren't actually bulletproof. Next time you have an assassin after you, try Kevlar."

"Now that I've discovered bullets don't bounce off me, I may have to." His tone was as mild as her own. No one would suspect that only a few short months ago Jaid had sat at his bedside clutching his hand, silent and pale, her wide brown eyes drenched in tears. In a medicated fog at the time, he might have thought she was an image produced by his subconscious. She'd taken up permanent residence there eight years ago, like a determined ghost refusing to be banished.

Cleve stood, taking three oversized brown folders from a pile on his desk and leaning across the desk to pass them out. Flipping his open, Adam saw it contained copies of the case file. Regardless of the minutes wasted trying to convince him to bow out, a file had already been prepared for him just in case. Which made him wonder if his response to Hedgelin's persuasive tactics had been predicted from the start, or whether the extra file had been prepared for the absent DCPD lieutenant.

The thought vanished when he focused on the pictures contained in the first manila folder inside. There was a clutch in his chest when he recognized his friend crumpled on top of the stained, broken plywood, bright yellow roses crushed beneath him. The depth of emotion blindsided him. He took a moment to acknowledge the feeling before tucking it away. Subjectivity crippled an investigator. Turning those feelings into purpose was the only way to help Byron Reinbeck.

With that intent in mind he riffled through the pictures, plucking out a few to arrange on his lap atop the open folder, side by side. After studying them for a moment he looked up. "The shooter was on a rooftop across the street?" His gaze lowered again. "The building was at least five stories. Rooftop most likely. Or top floor, although being inside the building would increase his risk of being identified."

"The roof," Cleve affirmed. "Seven-story building. The second folder has the scenes shot there."

There was a note in the man's voice that alerted Adam. He went to the next folder and shuffled through the photos there. There was little to see in the images. No evidence of a rifle or scope. No tripod. No shell casings. The shooter had coolly taken the time to pick up before fleeing the scene. There was nothing except . . . He squinted his one good eye at a photo of what looked like an ordinary five-by-eight white index card encased in a plastic Ziploc. On it was scrawled one word in what looked to be red marker.

Wrath.

As if reading his thoughts, Jaid said, "Wrath? The shooter was angry at the victim?"

Riffling through the rest of the photos in that file, he stopped at one that showed the card before it'd been disturbed. "Oh, he wanted this to be found, didn't he?" Adam murmured. He'd first thought the bag protecting the card was one used by the crime scene technicians, but now he realized the shooter had left it that way. Encased in plastic, with a fist-sized piece of broken concrete holding it in place on the pebbled flat roof of the building. "Wrath. One of the seven deadly sins." Feeling the others' eyes on him, he looked up. "Not that I'm all that well versed in the tenets of Catholicism, but I had some exposure in my youth."

"A passing exposure, obviously." Jaid's wry remark had the corner of Adam's mouth quirking.

"It didn't take, no. Much to the Jesuits' despair."

"Funny you should mention it, though." Hedgelin took a large manila envelope off his desk and opened it to shake out a single photo. Bracing himself with one fist planted on the desk, he leaned forward, holding the image up for them to see.

"That's not Reinbeck," Shepherd noted, shifting to better view what was obviously a crime scene photo.

"This victim's name was Oliver Samson." The deputy director paused but when no one commented he went on. "He had a global investment and securities firm. Samson Capital."

"One of the too-big-to-fail companies that plundered unfettered until the financial collapse a few years ago." Recognition was filtering now, of the victim's name and his company. Both had been on the receiving end of some unbelievably bad press after the upheaval, worsened further when its obscene bonuses paid to top executives came to light. Adam assumed Samson had ridden out the rocky times with help from the government-issued bailout funds. He recalled the media surrounding the man's death had been lacking in details. "When was he killed? Last month?"

"Five weeks ago in the parking garage of his building on I Street NW. Stabbed. You can't tell in this picture but there was an identical card left at the scene." Cleve's expression turned grim. "It was impaled on the knife left in his heart."

Intrigue spiking, Adam guessed, "Avarice."

The deputy director nodded. "Close enough. The word

'greed' was written on the card, in red marker, much like the one found at the site of Reinbeck's shooter. If I'm not mistaken, that's yet another biggie according to church dogma. The DCPD is compiling copies of the complete report on that ongoing investigation. Griega will get it to us when it's ready."

"You think these two are serial killings?"

Hedgelin raised his hand as if to halt Jaid's line of thought. "Let's not get ahead of ourselves. I don't want the media even considering that idea. It's going to be all I can do to control what they get regarding the facts surrounding Reinbeck's death. The manner of deaths was completely different. We're a long way from tying the two homicides together at this point."

"But the religious connotation of the notes give us a link worth following up on."

The deputy director didn't reply to Shepherd's observation. Instead, he took off his glasses to polish them with his handkerchief, a habit Adam recalled from their time partnered together. "We're in the midst of having all the evidence gathered for the Samson homicide transferred from the state crime lab to Quantico, where it will be given top priority. If there's a link to be found in the evidence, we'll soon know about it. In the meantime, another team is looking into connections between the two men. We still have a large group of DCPD officers canvassing the area surrounding last night's shooting. Once we have ballistics back, agents will be assigned to trace those leads."

Despite his cautionary note regarding a serial killer being responsible, it was obvious the bureau was looking closely into a link between the cases. "What about the threats the justice received? Depending on how many clients took a bath on the financial collapse, Samson probably had more than his share of enemies, too."

Adam's comment elicited a nod from Hedgelin. "Since it's the USMS Judicial Security Division's duty to anticipate and deter threats to the judiciary"—his voice was heavy with irony—"they'll have a thorough file on any targeting Reinbeck. It'll take some time to compare them to those received by Samson. You won't be involved in that end of things.

Right now you're headed over to the Supreme Court building to help with the interviews there. It's the JSD's turf, so play nice. With over three hundred permanent staff members alone, it's going to be a daunting task, made worse because it's a Saturday and they're all being summoned in to work. You'll be part of the contingent focusing on the staff who worked most closely with the justices. There are close to forty clerks, four fellows, administrative assistants, and God knows who else in there with direct access to the judiciary. Your first focus will be on Reinbeck's clerks and his admin."

His attention shifted to Shepherd. "Take Raiker to security and pick up a temporary ID badge for him." His smile was thin as he included Adam in his glance. "They'll need to take a picture for it. Shouldn't take longer than fifteen minutes or so."

Barely restraining a grimace, Adam rose. Photos were a necessary evil at times, but one he avoided at all costs whenever possible. It clearly wasn't going to be possible this time around. And the realization already had him feeling surly.

When the agents rose as well, Hedgelin looked at Jaid. "Agent Marlowe, if you'd stay for a minute?"

The order couched in the request had Adam's instincts rising, but he didn't look at her as he and Shepherd headed to the door. He'd been given a reprieve. He had the next ten or fifteen minutes to figure the best way of handling the constant proximity of the woman who represented the biggest regret in his life.

———

Since she wasn't invited to sit again Jaid remained standing, her eyes fixed on the executive assistant director. The pseudocivility that had permeated his voice for the earlier briefing had vanished. The gaze he regarded her with was hard. "I had an opportunity to speak to Shepherd earlier. I'm going to tell you the same thing I told him. I want Raiker supervised at all times. He doesn't conduct interviews alone. He doesn't follow up on any leads without one of you accompanying him. The bureau may have had its arm twisted into including him on this case, but damned if we're going to sit still and allow him to turn this thing into another chapter for his sensationalized memoirs."

There was absolutely no reason for his tone, his words, to have her hackles rising. Feigning puzzlement, she asked, "He's writing his memoirs?"

Hedgelin sent her a sharp look but she knew her expression was blank. She didn't wear her emotions on her face anymore. Adam Raiker had begun that lesson, all those years ago. Life had completed it.

"I'm certain you know what I mean. You're to keep him firmly contained within the investigative parameters you're given. In addition to the report you or Shepherd file online nightly, I want details on Raiker's behavior. His thoughts about the case. Who he talks to. Anything he says of interest."

In short, she was to spy on him. Just the thought filled her with distaste. She'd run her share of surveillance ops in her career, but reporting on another member of her team was especially abhorrent. Especially since she suspected his most grievous crime was his mere presence in this investigation. The petty politics involved in the agency was her least favorite aspect of the job.

But she knew how to play the game. Or at least how to appear to. "Understood."

He stared hard at her, long enough to have her flesh prickling. "I understand you knew him when he was with the agency."

"I took a class he taught for the BAU." The words were delivered in a bland voice. And didn't reflect the sudden weakness in her knees. "Worked a couple cases with him after that."

Hedgelin gave a nod, as if satisfied. "It's to our advantage that you and Shepherd are on a friendly footing with him. That should keep him off guard. Just be sure you don't let that friendship interfere with your duties regarding him."

"It was a long time ago."

He picked up a folder on his desk and opened it, clearly dismissing her. "Join them in security."

Without another word Jaid turned for the door. She'd seen Adam twice in the last eight years. Each of those times he'd been in CCU, clinging to life. It had taken a wealth of strength to accept this assignment, realizing it would place her at his side for days, possibly weeks on end. She'd convinced herself that she could handle it. Could handle *him*.

But it had never occurred to her that she might be called on to betray him.